OXFORD ENGLISH NOVELS

General Editor: JAMES KINSLEY

RATTLIN THE REEFER

EDWARD HOWARD

RATTLIN THE REEFER

Edited with an Introduction by

ARTHUR HOWSE

LONDON
OXFORD UNIVERSITY PRESS
NEW YORK   TORONTO
1971

Oxford University Press, Ely House, London W. 1

GLASGOW NEW YORK TORONTO MELBOURNE WELLINGTON
CAPE TOWN SALISBURY IBADAN NAIROBI DAR ES SALAAM LUSAKA ADDIS ABABA
BOMBAY CALCUTTA MADRAS KARACHI LAHORE DACCA
KUALA LUMPUR SINGAPORE HONG KONG TOYKO

ISBN 0 19 255333 X

ت

PRINTED IN GREAT BRITAIN

CONTENTS

―――

INTRODUCTION

———

Rattlin is a novel of adventure, presenting a lively picture of English life in the Napoleonic period. Notwithstanding its catchpenny nautical title, its major preoccupation is with youthful experience acutely felt and feelingly expressed. From the very start, the author's emotional engagement with his young self is undisguised and foreshadows the pathetic treatment of childhood familiar to us in the later novel. Pathos and subjective analysis are curiously (and in the light of Dickens's development, perhaps significantly) embedded in the jocular, ironical style of the Augustan novelists, a style still flourishing in the essay and light fiction of the time and soon to be revivified in *Pickwick* and *Oliver Twist*. Baker found the style of *Rattlin* 'as forcible and mordant as Smollett's' and the hero's introspection 'suggestive of Melville and Conrad'.[1]

Howard published the first version of the novel while working for Marryat on the *Metropolitan Magazine*. As *The Life of a Sub-editor* it ran from September 1834 onwards. The *New Monthly*'s memoir of Howard in 1838 declared authoritatively that 'he learned the romantic story of his birth and infancy from his nurse and we may be sure that so far as he knew the facts himself they are faithfully recorded. [His schooldays and] the earlier adventures of Rattlin on board the *Eos* are again undoubtedly the true experiences of Edward Howard.' This factual basis, corroborated by his daughters,[2] is indicated in the notes to this edition.

By February 1836, however, he had, according to Marryat,[3] reached the point where 'he could not proceed without involving living characters in his details [and] at the instigation of his publisher, [he] finished in fiction what he began in fact'. The dates were altered apparently to make identification more difficult, and

[1] E. A. Baker, *History of the English Novel*, vii. 109.
[2] Preface to W. L. Courtney's edition of *Rattlin* (1896).
[3] His notice of *Rattlin* in the *Metropolitan*, Aug. 1836.

his hero (previously Edward Percy) was renamed after Smollett's Jack Rattlin. The melodramatic denouement (which Baker deplores) interprets the birth mystery in terms of a disputed inheritance modelled on that of *Peter Simple*, which had just ceased serialization in the magazine. This version Bentley bought for £400 and published anonymously as a three-volume novel, *Rattlin the Reefer; edited by the author of Peter Simple*, having induced Marryat to lend his valuable name in order to gain his friend a hearing. In fact he contrived—with 'low cunning', Marryat complained —to identify Marryat more closely with the novel by cutting part of the Advertisement, and reviewers were disgruntled at finding this old magazine material masquerading as a new novel by Marryat. As a result of its continued anonymity,[1] *Rattlin* was absorbed into the Marryat canon[2] and judged in this context as a tale of nautical adventure.

In veiling in anonymity the story of his life, it was almost certainly the feelings of the Norfolk family Howard was sparing. The lady, who in chapter 1 totters from her carriage to give birth to the hero in a wayside inn at Reading, was most probably Lady Elizabeth Howard,[3] Lady Melbourne's niece, who in 1789 had been forced into a repugnant marriage with Bernard Edward Howard, third cousin and acknowledged heir (there being a rival claimant) of the 11th Duke ('Jockey') of Norfolk. Familiarity did not reconcile her to Howard and whether her second child was in fact his son was a matter of some doubt, since in July 1793, a few months before our hero's birth, she had eloped with her childhood sweetheart, the gay but impecunious Richard Bingham, heir of the first Lord Lucan. She was known to be pregnant at that time and had a clear motive for concealing the birth late in 1793 of a son who would be capable 'in certain circumstances of laying claim to the premier dukedom of the realm'[4] and staining, as that notorious

---

[1] The astute Colburn ascribed all Howard's later novels correctly but misleadingly to 'the author of Rattlin the Reefer'.

[2] Hannay, Marryat's biographer, provoked demur when in 1889 he stated that *Rattlin* was not from the hand of the master and George Bentley, son of Howard's publisher, found it necessary to state categorically in 1892 that '*Rattlin* was no novel of Marryat's . . . Howard took it to Marryat who lent his name as editor . . . but otherwise had no hand in it', *N. & Q.*, ser. viii. 2 (1892), 403.

[3] Supporting evidence for this and the facts of Howard's biography in general is given in the editor's unpublished thesis on Howard (Univ. of London, 1956).

[4] *Trial of the Hon. Richard Bingham* (1794), pp. 9–10.

womanizer Jockey of Norfolk bitterly complained, the purity of
his line. Had the birth been known, the damages secured by
Howard in the *crim. con.* case which he brought in 1794 would
have been materially greater and the return of Elizabeth's £12,000
marriage portion, which lay in the power of the House of Lords,
would have been jeopardized.

Elizabeth, however, as the history of her first marriage showed,
was a woman of a most tenacious affection. It would be entirely
natural for her to wish to keep alive and watch surreptitiously over
this unacknowledgeable, ailing child of hers. As the seldom seen,
beautiful visitor who becomes idealized and confused in the child's
imagination with the stained-glass mother of God, she had him
fostered and nursed, sent to Flower's school at Islington, then
rescued and taken under her own care at Sydenham, and finally
found a midshipman's berth. His eventful two and a half years'
naval service in the West Indies, which forms a good half of the
whole novel, ended in October 1810. He was discontented with his
superiors and afflicted, as the result of the physical strains he had
undergone, with deafness and a recurrent haemorrhage, which
eventually proved fatal. Accordingly, when his ship docked he
decided to quit the Navy and go, like Marryat's Japhet 'in search of
a father'.[1] In return apparently for renouncing any claim to the
dukedom, Howard was handsomely provided for and in 1814 or
1815, when he came of age, 'embarked his very considerable
fortune' in an enterprise for the sale of gunpowder, a venture
which, not surprisingly, failed speedily after Waterloo. Howard
was unfortunate also in his partners, and emerged from the bank-
ruptcy with his honour intact but his fortune gone. He seems there-
after to have earned a modest living as hack writer while his wife
kept school, until 1832 when he renewed acquaintanceship with
Marryat and became his sub-editor. The two men were tempera-
mentally ill suited.[2] Marryat would chide Howard for diffidence
in business matters and for being 'too good-natured to the Whigs'[3]

[1] Marryat treated this father-quest theme twice: once, in *Japhet*, soon after
renewing Howard's acquaintance, humorously; then, just after Howard's death,
dramatically, in *Percival Keene*, the aggressive hero who extorts the recognition of
which Howard dreamt and wrote.

[2] See Howard's prologue to *The Life of a Sub-editor* in the *Metropolitan*, Sept.
1834, reproduced in the Textual Notes, page 401.

[3] Letters from Marryat to Howard (transcribed by Sadleir) of July 1833 and
11 May 1835.

and so half-hearted a champion of his employer in the latter's numerous and violent literary quarrels. Marryat was the complete autocrat, with assured social status. Finding his early realistic portrayal of naval discipline was being used by the radicals, he quickly veered round to the complacent official line. Howard, however, the classless liberal, used his harsh naval experience to dramatize in his novels and stories the conflict of authority and humanity.

Marryat could claim with justice, however, that he had introduced Howard to the literary world and suggested the autobiographical work which came to fruition as *Rattlin*. The novel was a marked success, going into three editions between July 1836 and June 1837 with a single volume edition in 1838. It gained for Howard *entrée* to the exclusive annuals; and when Saunders and Otley bought the *Metropolitan* from Marryat in 1836 Howard became editor. Before he died in 1841, from the bursting of a blood vessel after dining well with friends at Christmas, he had written four more works,[1] helped by his second wife, a girl of twenty-two devoted to her 'clever husband'.[2]

Howard paints his self-portrait in chapter 10 of *Rattlin* as a boy tall for his years with wavy hair, fair complexion, and a countenance of a deceptively feminine cast, who was characterized by an 'imagination worked upon even from my earliest childhood and the great nervous excitability of my temperament' (page 73). He was prone to violent anger which would quickly yield to sentimental reconciliation, the readiest avenue to his sympathy being through an appeal to his filial instincts. The tall youth grew into the 'man on a large scale and very deaf so that the conversation had to be repeated for his benefit' whom George Bentley remembered[3] and whose adult likeness by Osgood accompanied the *New Monthly* memoir. The curls still cluster round the soft contours of an oval face: the nose is long and straight and the full curving lips end with an upward twist suggestive of persistent optimism. The eyes, the dominant feature, are kind and the preoccupations of his

---

[1] *The Old Commodore* (1837), a bitter little book of tyrannical family pride; *Outward Bound* (1838), an immature Byronic work revised; *Jack Ashore* (1840), a Whiggish reply to the ultra-conservative Samuel Warren's view of society in *Ten Thousand a Year*; and a life of Henry Morgan which was published posthumously.

[2] *N. & Q.*, ser. viii. 3 (1893), 73.

[3] *N. & Q.*, ser. viii. 2 (1892), 403-4.

literary work are faithfully reflected in a countenance which 'was always the seat of some sentiment or passion'.[1]

His sentimentality appealed in his own day; but the ill-regulated, subjective intensity, the florid rhetoric with which he bares his soul alienates the modern reader more, perhaps, than the conventional plot machinery. The confessional habit of the Methodists, indelibly impressed upon his infant spirit, mars the easy, ironical conduct of the tale. Romantic literary influences may have reinforced this tendency. In Rousseau's *Confessions* he would have recognized the portrait of a kindred spirit and found in the first book of *Emile* support for his instinctive and pathetically reiterated plea that 'the child's real home is in his mother's arms'. More recently and nearer home, the childhood chapters of two autobiographical novels may have encouraged Howard's introspection and lyricism—Trelawny's analysis of the childhood roots of Byronism in his *Adventures of a Younger Son* and the lyrical subjectivism of C. R. Pemberton's childhood reminiscence in *Pel Verjuice* which was, as Howard wrote, being serialized in W. J. Fox's *Monthly Repository*. In carrying their work further and dwelling as frequently and as lyrically as he does upon the renovating function of childhood memories, he is introducing a poetic theme which was to flourish abundantly in the novel and carries us forward twenty years to George Eliot's famous celebration of the potency of childhood impressions in the fifth chapter of *The Mill on the Floss*.

In extending the story of his childhood and youth from the two or three initial chapters devoted to it by Trelawny and Pemberton, to engross all but the final sixth of the book, Howard made *Rattlin* the exception which is the best proof of Kathleen Tillotson's dictum[2] that 'to put a child at the centre of a novel for adults was virtually unknown when Dickens wrote *Oliver Twist* and *The Old Curiosity Shop*'. This novel with a child-hero published on the eve of Dickens's agreement to write the novel which became *Oliver Twist* must interest the Dickensian reader. Root's resemblance to Squeers and Creakle may be thought merely to emphasize the reality of the models from which Dickens drew: nevertheless, Howard's close observation of the hypocritical, sycophantic, sadistic schoolmaster is of a kind and intensity to be found again in the 1830s only in Dickens. To the monstrous Root and the

---

[1] p. 38.
[2] *Novels of the Eighteen-Forties* (1954), p. 50.

canting Methodist Cate, who had frightened him into fits as an infant, Howard opposes the tender-hearted woman of the working classes—to whom (abandoned by his kin) he owed all that he knew of motherly love—and her husband, the illiterate, intemperate top-sawyer, with whom he had lived intimately enough to see his better side. They are set up as symbols of the natural domestic affections and simple pleasures which he, like Dickens, is concerned to champion against the unnatural kill-joy respectability and intolerance of their betters. At a time when the conception of class relations in the novel was still largely feudal, Howard and Dickens were exceptional in having been thrown into close contact with the common people at the most impressionable age; and the effect is evident as much in the social connotation of Ralph's adoption by the Brandons as in the companion piece, the selection of a wet-nurse for Paul Dombey. Jo Brandon, Ralph's foster-father, plays Weller senior to the hypocritical Cate and gives his 'shepherd' a good drubbing,[1] and again in the last glimpse we have of him—his 'hard-featured, grinning physiognomy'[2] beaming triumphant from the top of the school wall, successful at last in the quest for his 'poor Ralph'—his allegorical force is clearly implicit. His visit, with the gift of food to the lonely love-starved boy from his loving foster-mother, lightens the boy's gloom for a time, but is never to be repeated. Brandon 'is threatened with the constable'. Howard's indignation at the high-handed archbishops who destroyed poor people's walks or sought to deprive them of their hot Sunday dinner anticipated Dickens's sarcasms in *Sunday under Three Heads*.

One passage in *Rattlin* raises inevitably the question of a direct debt by Dickens to Howard's book—Daunton's death, so like that of Sikes, by a self-made noose in an effort to escape from the constables and clamouring populace.[3] And it is entirely natural that Dickens should be drawn to Howard's account of his childhood and even identify himself emotionally with it. Here was a boy's story, a self-portrait, giving form to Dickens's own

[1] p. 29.

[2] p. 53.

[3] Chandler (*Literature of Roguery*, ii. 404) noting the resemblance, and mistakenly ascribing *Rattlin* to 1838, spoke of *Oliver Twist*'s influence on it, at the same time noting that Daunton's role in *Rattlin* is that of Monks, Oliver's half-brother, to whom the hero is bound by a strange attraction and who seeks to ruin his reputation as a step to depriving him of his patrimony.

desolating sense of abandonment, suffering and parental neglect, the deprivation of birthright, home, and a mother's love. The passage in chapter 8 of *Rattlin* beginning 'Home, what solace is there in its very sound . . .' anticipates the intensely emotional conception of domestic cosiness familiar to us in Dickens.

When those two sickly infants Ralph Rattlin and Oliver Twist made their appearance, the rights of men and the wrongs of women had been canvassed, but those of children were being asserted for the first time; practically by philanthropists, imaginatively by the novelists who strove to create a new mental and emotional attitude to the child, counteracting Calvinist fanaticism by picturing the child's pathetic loneliness and defencelessness. In Howard's many passages of intensely emotional presentation of childhood feeling, pathos, already entrenched in the minor verse of the period, can be seen starting its notable invasion of the novel. Howard seems to have been the first to strike that particular pathetic chord which reverberated at the deaths of Little Nell and Paul Dombey, reducing readers to tears. Most powerful for his readers[1] was Ralph's forlorn isolation in a haunted bedchamber, lulling himself into 'the repose of innocence'. To counteract the baleful glance of the carved Medusa, leering from the roof, he would summon in imagination the painted Madonna on the altar piece of the Islington church whom he equated with the beatific memory of his briefly encountered mother. Her 'glory' 'much assisted my imagination' in fulfilling his yearning for mother love. This set of symbols, drawn from his own experience, seems to have become a sort of emotional shorthand ready for use in the portrayal of the forlorn and ill-treated waifs of Victorian literature. Little Nell, Florence Dombey, and Jane Eyre, to take familiar examples, are all isolated in similar grand but horrific and hypnotic surroundings. David Copperfield associates the 'tranquil brightness' of a stained glass church window seen in childhood with Agnes Wickfield 'ever afterwards'.[2] Part of the ambiguity of young Harry Esmond's feeling for Lady Castlewood arises from the initial confusion of divine love with human in the imagination of a love-starved orphan. She first appears to him as a *Dea certe*, 'the sun making a golden halo

---

[1] See the metrical paraphrase of this subject in the *New Monthly* memoir of Howard (1838), probably by Mrs. Abdy, one of the female versifiers whom Howard gathered about him on the *Metropolitan*.

[2] *David Copperfield*, ch. 15.

round her hair':[1] little Beatrix gathers up the suggestive similes—
'he is saying his prayers to mama'—and Lord Castlewood echoes
the theme when he speaks of his wife 'when she used to look with
her child more beautiful by George than the Madonna in the
Queen's chapel'.[2]

Rattlin, in Baker's judgement, presented 'gloomy strength and
penetration into a concentrated, gloomy mind . . . which at this
time of day seems suggestive of Melville and Conrad'.[3] Ralph
indeed carries with him to sea his highly developed sensibilities
and the naval incidents are tinged with the hero's emotion to a far
greater extent than in any other nautical fiction before Melville.
Nothing as sensitive as the parable of Reuben Gubbins, the land-
lubber in the grip of the relentless naval machine, had previously
been achieved in the genre. Here Howard comes near to sub-
limating into tragedy the theme of the conflict of natural human
feeling with the unnatural and often inhuman discipline afloat, as
Melville was to do in *Billy Budd*. It is presented within the frame-
work of the hero's emotional reactions. The symbolism—at once
personal and universal—is well expressed in a style appropriately
simple, but rich in emotional overtones. The old man's 'loving
pursuit' was for the author the aptest symbol of all that fate
had cheated him of. The constable's reduction to impotence by
losing his staff as he boards the ship points, in Melvillean style,
to the fact that the law of the land had little or no validity at
sea. The pragmatical clerk's uneasiness emphasizes the fearful
strangeness of the nautical world for even the most self-assured
landsman.

The affinity of the two writers is perhaps clearest in the resemblance of *Rattlin* in conception, form, narrative method, and—
above all—in the character of the protagonist, to *Redburn* (1849),
Melville's imaginative, retrospective portrait of his raw youth at
sea. Both present subjectively the sentimental reactions to ship-
board life of a friendless youth, modelled upon his creator, sensitive, introspective, and abnormal. They provide not, like Marryat,
the universal comedy of adolescence, but an analysis of their own
chronic disillusionment in youth. The reader may compare, for
example, the comedy of Redburn's social visit to Captain Riga
(ch. 14) with the less urbane and exaggeratedly comic account of

---

[1]   Bk. I, ch. 1.   [2]   Bk. I, ch. 14.
[3]   Op. cit., p. 109.

Rattlin's discomfiture in an attempt to shake hands with his captain (ch. 27).

In *Rattlin* Howard was bridging the gap between the primitive fun and simple values of the earlier nautical tradition and the Melvillean sophistication. Daunton's macabre behaviour and villainous contrivances are handled with an imaginative suggestiveness which prompts the question whether this Gothic villain in a nautical setting contributed anything directly to the embodiment in the later romantic novel—from Melville's Jackson, Bartleby, and Babo to Conrad's Nigger—of the dramatic paradox of the inexplicable domination of the strong by the weak, of the many by the one. Paradox is strong also in the character of Captain Reud, Ralph's psychopathic commander, unstable, unheroic, tyrannical, and sentimental by turns, a figure of fun but for his evil potentiality, himself in part the victim of the pernicious system which worked upon his defects. His final pathetic interview with Ralph, the childless man with the fatherless child, rounds off dramatically a character built up by a succession of pedestrian scenes in the naval novel manner.

By following Coleridge's prescription for an interesting book,[1] Howard, that disinherited sprig of the nobility, contrived for a brief moment to gain the ear of the world and present his first-hand testimony against fanaticism and tyranny. He was early in the field in which Dickens and Melville were to become such redoubtable champions.

---

[1] 'I could inform the dullest author how he might write an interesting book. Let him relate the events of his own life with honesty, not disguising the feelings that accompanied them' (*Biographia Epistolaris*, ed. Turnbull, i. 5).

NOTE ON THE TEXT

THE text has been set up from the British Museum copy of the August 1836 reissue of the first edition published in the previous month. It is described on the title-page as 'second edition'; and in the imprint Richard Bentley no longer styles himself 'successor to Henry Colburn' as in the first edition.

Both issues were in three duodecimo volumes, each volume having a frontispiece and two plates by Auguste Hervieu. In the first edition the list of illustrations was inset, but in the second it is on the verso of the Advertisement. The set of three volumes sold for 31s. 6d.

The original version of the first fifty-eight chapters was serialized in the *Metropolitan Magazine* from 1834 to 1836. The changes and omissions from this version which were made in the July 1836 and later editions are noted in the Textual Notes (p. 401).

BIBLIOGRAPHY

RICHARD BENTLEY published *Rattlin the Reefer; edited by the author of Peter Simple* in three volumes on 23 July, 5 August 1836, and 16 June 1837. A one-volume, shortened version appeared as number 69 of Bentley's Standard Novels in July 1838, reprinted in 1850, and again by Routledge *c.* 1871. Routledge issued various cheap editions: a yellow-back with a cover designed by Phiz sold at 1*s.* 6*d.* in 1856. An 1873 Routledge edition of the novel illustrated by E. Evans was reissued as part of the yellow-back 'Author's Copyright' edition of Marryat in 1875 and it appeared also in that firm's 'Handy volume Marryat' in 1880.

In March 1897 Dr. W. L. Courtney included it in his 'King's Own' edition of Marryat, illustrated by E. F. Wheeler, noting Howard's authorship in the preface and giving brief biographical details. This edition was issued also by Estes and Co. of Boston, and reissued by Routledge in smaller format in 1903. Howard's name appeared on the title-page for the first time in Guy Pocock's Everyman edition in 1930.

Two single-volume, pirated editions of *Rattlin* in English appeared in Paris in 1836, published by Galignani and Baudry respectively. Three separate French translations appeared in 1837, 1838, and 1854. Marryat's French publishers issued all Howard's novels as if they were Marryat's until a review of *Jack Ashore* in the *Revue Britannique* (1840) revealed Howard as the author. Throughout the last century and even in this, Howard's works were included in German editions of Marryat, sometimes to the exclusion of Marryat's authentic works.

The novel was dramatized by J. T. Haines in August 1836 (Duncombe's *New British Theatre*, vol. 24).

BIBLIOGRAPHY. Michael Sadleir, *XIX Century Fiction. A Bibliographical Record*, 2 vols. (1951).

CRITICISM. Brief mention of the novel occurs in F. W. Chandler, *Literature of Roguery* (1907), vol. ii, Oliver Elton, *Survey of English Literature, 1830-80* (1920), vol. ii, and M. Sadleir, *Excursions in Victorian Bibliography* (1922). The longest published appreciation of Howard's work is in E. A. Baker, *History of the English Novel*, vol. vii (1936). His life and work are fully treated in the present editor's unpublished thesis (London, 1956).

B

BIOGRAPHY. The primary sources are the *New Monthly Magazine* Memoir of Howard (vol. liv (1838), 560-1), the obituaries in the *Annual Register* (1842, p. 241), the *Athenaeum* (8 Jan. 1842) and the *Gentleman's Magazine* (N.S. vol. xviii (1842), 436), Goodwin's article (1891) in the *Dictionary of National Biography*, George Bentley's recollections in *Notes and Queries* (1889 and 1892-3) and Dr. Courtney's preface to *Rattlin* in his 1897 edition.

Some of Howard's letters to Richard Bentley are at the University of Illinois. Some of Marryat's letters to Howard (present location unknown) were copied by Sadleir and used in the preface of his edition of *Peter Simple*, others have been quoted in part in Maggs's auction catalogues.

A CHRONOLOGY OF
EDWARD HOWARD

———

RATTLIN
THE REEFER

EDITED BY

THE AUTHOR OF 'PETER SIMPLE'

'All hands REEF topsails—Away, aloft!'

ADVERTISEMENT

———

A portion of the following work has appeared in the pages of the Metropolitan Magazine. It has now been re-arranged, and fiction, in the latter part, blended with fact. In consenting to be the literary sponsor to these volumes, in the shape that they now assume, I am actuated but by one motive; that of enabling the author to appear before the public, and thus to give him an opportunity of being tried by an ordeal by which alone he must either stand or fall.

F. M.

LONDON, *May*, 1836.

VOLUME I

CHAPTER I

I begin a life without similitude with a simile—Start off with four horses—and finally I make my first appearance on any stage under the protection of the 'Crown.'

IN the volumes I am going to write, it is my intention to adhere rigidly to the truth—this will be *bonâ fide* an auto-biography—and, as the public like novelty, an auto-biography without an iota of fiction in the whole of it, will be the greatest novelty yet offered to its fastidiousness. As many of the events which it will be my province to record, are singular and even startling, I may be permitted to sport a little moral philosophy, drawn from the kennel in Lower Thames Street, which may teach my readers to hesitate ere they condemn as invention mere matters of absolute, though uncommon fact.

Let us stand with that old gentleman under the porch of St. Magnus's church, for the rain is thrashing the streets till they actually look white, and the kennel before us is swelled into a formidable, and hardly fordable brook. That kennel is the stream of life—and a dirty and a weary one it is, if we may judge by the old gentleman's looks. All is hurried into that common sewer, the grave! What bubbles float down it! Every thing that is fairly in the middle of the stream seems to sail with it, steadily and triumphantly —and many a filthy fragment enters the sewer with a pomp and dignity not unlike the funereal obsequies of a great lord. But my business is with that little chip; by some means it has been thrust out of the principal current, and now it is out, see what pranks it is playing. How erratic are its motions!—into what strange holes and corners it is thrust! The same phenomenon will happen in life. Once start a being out of the usual course of existence, and many and strange will be his adventures ere he once more be allowed to regain the common stream, and be permitted to float down, in silent tranquillity, to the grave common to all.

About seven o'clock in the evening of the 20th of February, 17—,[1] a postchaise with four horses drove with fiery haste up to the door of the Crown Inn, at Reading. The evening had closed in bitterly. A continuous storm of mingled sleet and rain had driven every being who had a home, to the shelter it afforded. As the vehicle stopped, with a most consequential jerk, and the steps were flung down with that clatter post-boys will make when they can get four horses before their leathern boxes, the solitary inmate seemed to shrink farther into its dark corner, instead of coming forward eagerly to exchange the comforts of the blazing hearth for the damp confinement of a hired chaise. Thrice had the obsequious landlord bowed his well-powdered head, and, at each inclination wiped off, with the palm of his hand, the raindrops that had settled on the central baldness of his occiput, ere the traveller seemed to be aware that such a man existed as the landlord of the Crown, or that that landlord was standing at the chaise-door. At length, a female, closely veiled, and buried in shawls like a sultana, tremblingly took the proffered arm, and tottered into the hotel. Shortly after, mine host returned, attended by porter, waiter, and stable-boy—and giving, by the lady's orders, a handsome gratuity to each of the post-boys, asked for the traveller's luggage. There was none! At this announcement the landlord, as he afterwards expressed himself, was 'struck all of a heap,' though what he meant by it was never clearly comprehended, as any alteration in his curiously squat figure must have been an improvement. While he remained in perplexity and in the rain, the latter of which might easily have been avoided, another message arrived from the lady, ordering fresh horses to be procured, and those, with the chaise, to be kept in readiness to start at a moment's warning. More mystery and more perplexity! In fact, if these combined causes had been allowed to remain much longer in operation, the worthy land-lord, instead of carrying on his business profitably, would have been carried off peremptorily, by a catarrh, his wife's nursing, and a doctor; but, fortunately, it struck one of the post-boys that rain was not necessary to a conversation, and sleet but a bad solvent of a mystery; so the posse adjourned into the tap, in order that the subject might be discussed more at the ease of the gentlemen who fancied themselves concerned in it.

'And you have not seen her face?' said mine host of the Crown.

'Shouldn't know her from Adam's grandmother,' said the post-boy, who had ridden the wheel-horses. 'Howsomedever I yeerd her sob and moan like a wheel as vants grease.'

'You may say that,' said the other post-boy, a little shrivelled old man, a good deal past sixty; 'we lads see strange soights. I couldn't a-bear to see her siffer in that ere manner—I did feel for her almost as much as if she'd been an oss.'

The landlord gave the two charioteers *force de complimens* for the tenderness of their feelings, the intensity of which he fully comprehended, as he changed for each his guinea, the bounty of the lady. When he found them in proper cue, that is to say, in the middle of their second glass of brandy-and-water, he proceeded in his cross-examination, and he learned from them, that they had been engaged to wait at a certain spot, on an extensive heath, some twelve miles distant; that they had hardly waited there an hour when a private carriage, containing the lady in question and a gentleman, arrived; that the lady, closely veiled, had been transferred from the one conveyance to the other, and that the post-boys had been ordered to drive with the utmost speed to the destination where they now found themselves.

This account seemed to satisfy the scruples of the landlord, which, of course, were by no means pecuniary, but merely moral, when in bounced the fiery visaged landlady. He was forced to stand the small shot of his wife. Poor man! he had only powder to reply to it, and that, just now, was wofully damp.

'You lazy, loitering, do-little, much-hindering, prate-apace sot! here's the lady taken alarmingly ill. The physician has been sent for, and his carriage will be at the door before you blow that ill-looking nose of yours, that my blessed ten commandments are itching to score down—you paltry——ah!'

With a very little voice, and a very great submission, mine host squeaked out, 'Have you seen the lady's face?'

'Face! is it face you want? and ladies' faces too—hav'n't I got face enough for you—you apology, you!'

What the good woman said was indubitably true. She had face enough for any two moderately-visaged wives, and enough over and above to have supplied any-one who might have lost a portion of theirs. However, I will be more polite than the landlady, and acquaint the reader, that no one yet of the establishment had seen the lady's face, nor was it intended that any one should.

As this squabble was growing into a quarrel the physician arrived; he had not been long alone with the unknown, before he sent for a surgeon, and the surgeon for a nurse. There was so much bustle, alarm, and secrecy above-stairs, that the landlord began to consider which of the two undertakers, his friends, he should favour with the anticipated job, and rubbed his hands as he dwelt on the idea of the coroner's inquest, and the attendant dinner. The landlady was nearly raving mad at being excluded from what she supposed was the bed of death. Hot flannels and warm water were now eagerly called for—and these demands were looked upon as a sure sign that dissolution approached.

The stairs approaching the lady's chamber were lined with master, mistress, man-servant, and maid-servants, all eagerly listening to the awful bustle within. At length, there is a dead silence of some minutes. The listeners shuddered.

'It is all over with her!' ejaculates one tender-hearted manœuverer of the warming-pan, with her apron in the corner of her eye; 'Poor lady! it is all over with her!'

It was exactly two in the morning of the 21st that a shrill cry was heard. Shortly after, the door was flung open by the nurse, and a new edition of an embryo reefer appeared in her arms, and very manfully did the play of his lungs make every one present aware that *somebody* had made his appearance. The supposed bed of death turned out to be a bed of life, and another being was born to wail, to sin, and to die, as myriads have wailed, and sinned, and died before him.

CHAPTER II

I am decidedly an incumbrance—Begin life with half a dozen
fruitless journeys—Find a home and a foster-father—and talk
learnedly of triangles and Archbishops.

WHAT is to be done with the child? It is a fearful question, and
has been often asked under every degree of suffering. Of all possible
articles, a child is the most difficult to dispose of; a wife may be
dispensed with without much heart-breaking—even a friend and
rubbish may be shot out of the way, and the bosom remain tranquil;
but a helpless, new-born infant!—O there is a pleading eloquence
in its feeble wail that goes to the heart and ear of the stranger—
and must act like living fire in the bowels of the mother.

The whole household were immediately sent in quest of a wet-
nurse. At length, one was found in the very pretty wife of a
reprobate sawyer, of the name of Brandon. He had seen many
vicissitudes of life—had been a soldier, a gentleman's servant, had
been to sea, and was a shrewd, vicious, and hard man, with a most
unquenchable passion for strong beer, and a steady addiction to
skittles. His wife was a little gentle being, of an extremely compact
and prepossessing figure; her face was ruddy with health, and, as
I said before, extremely pretty, and, had it not been for an air of
what I fear I must call vulgarity, for want of a more gentle term,
she would have merited the term of beautiful. Brandon was a top-
sawyer, but, as three out of the six working days of the week he was
to be found with a pot of porter by his side, pipe in mouth, and the
skittle-ball in his hand, it is not surprising that there was much
misery in his home, which he often heightened by his brutality.
Yet was he a very pleasant fellow when he had money to spend,
and actually a witty as well as a jovial dog when spending it. His
wife had not long given birth to a fine girl, and the mother's
bosom bled over the destitution with which her husband's recklessness had now made her so long familiar.

All this time your humble servant was squalling, and none were
found who, under all the strange circumstances, would take upon
them the charge of an infant, about to be forsaken immediately by
its mother. At length one of the maid-servants at the inn remembered
to have heard Mrs. Brandon say, that rather than live on among

all her squalidness and penury, she would endeavour to suckle another child besides her own; and, as she was then in redundant health, and had two fine breasts of milk,—for *a* fine breast of milk would not then have served my turn, or rather, Mary and I must have taken it by turns,—she was accordingly sent for. Yet, when she understood that I was to be placed immediately under her care, that no references could be given, and no address left in the case of accident, all her wishes to better herself and babe were not sufficiently strong to make her run the risk. A guinea and a-half a-week was offered, and the first quarter tendered in advance, but in vain; at length, an additional ten pound note gave her sufficient courage, and much flannel being in request, I was thus fitted out before I was three hours old, to leave the roof that I cannot call maternal, and be launched to struggle with the world. The frantic kiss of the distracted mother was impressed on my moaning lips, the agonized blessing was called down upon me from the God that she then thought not of interceding with for herself, and the solemn objurgation given to my foster-mother, to have a religious and motherly care of me, by the love she bore her own child; and then, lest the distress of this scene should become fatal to her who bore me, I and my nurse were hurried away before the day of my birth had fully dawned.

This day happened to be one in which the top-sawyer had been graciously pleased to toss his arms up and down over the pit— not of destruction but of preservation. He had started early, and, whilst he was setting the teeth on edge of all within hearing, by setting an edge to his saw, some very officious friend ran to him to tell him, how that his wife was increasing his family, without even his permission having been asked. Instead, therefore, of making a dust in his own pit, he flung down his file, took up his lanthorn, and hurried along to kick up a dust at home. The brute! may he have to sharpen saws with bad files for half an eternity! He swore —how awfully the fellow swore!—that I should be turned from his inhospitable roof immediately—and my gentle nurse, adding her tears to my squalls, through that dismal sleety morning, that was then breaking mistily upon so much wretchedness, was compelled to carry me back to my mother.

The most impassioned intreaties, and an additional five pounds, at length prevailed on Mrs. Brandon to nestle me again in her bosom, and try to excite the sympathy of her husband. She returned to him, but the fellow had now taken to himself two counsellors, a drunken mate that served under him in the pit, and his own avarice. I am stating mere facts: I may not be believed —I cannot help it—but three times was I carried backwards and forwards, and every transit producing to the sawyer five extra pounds, when, at length, my little head found a resting-place. All these events I have had over and over again from my nurse, and they are most faithfully recorded.

Before noon on that memorable morning, the chaise-and-four were again at the door, and the veiled and shawl-enveloped lady was lifted in, and the vehicle dashed rapidly through the streets of Reading, in a northerly direction.[1] I pretend not to relate facts of which I have never had an assured knowledge; I cannot state to where that chaise and its desolate occupant proceeded, nor can I give a moving description of feelings that I did not witness. When I afterwards knew that that lady was my mother, I never dared question her upon these points, but, from the strength, the intensity of every good and affectionate feeling that marked her character, I can only conceive, that if that journey was made in the stupor of weakness and exhaustion, or even in the wanderings of delirium, it must have been, to her, a dispensation of infinite mercy.

She deserted her new-born infant—she flung forth her child from the warmth of her own bosom to the cold, hireling kindness of the stranger. I think I hear some puritanical, world-observing, starched piece of female rigidity exclaim, 'And therein she did a great wickedness.' The fact I admit, but the wickedness I deny utterly. Proudly do I range myself by the side of my much-injured parent, and tell the strait-laced that there was more courage, more love, more piety, in that heroic act, than in the feeling and *respectable* fondness of a thousand mothers, whose sole recommendation is a correctness of conduct, correct because untried, and whose utmost pleasure is sneering at sacrifices that they never could have made, and mocking at a heroism they cannot comprehend.

That there were misery and much suffering inflicted, I do not deny; but of all guilt, even of all blame, I eagerly acquit one, whose principles of action were as pure, and the whole tenor of whose life was as upright, as even Virtue herself could have dictated. Let the guilt and the misery attendant upon this desertion of myself be attached to the real sinners; may they lie as a burthen on their bosoms, when they would rise to plead at the last tribunal; and may their deeds cover their faces with the burning blush of shame, at that hour when the world's worshipper shall not dare to coun-tenance the meanness and the villanies of the worldly great, and when man's actions shall be weighed in the balance of an Omniscient justice.

I have before said that Brandon was a *top* sawyer. We must now call him Mr. Brandon—he has purchased a pair of *top* boots, a swell *top* coat, and though now frequently *top* heavy, thinks him-self altogether a *top*ping gentleman. He is now to be seen more frequently in the skittle-ground, grasping a half-gallon, instead of a quart of beer. He decides authoritatively upon foul and fair play, and his voice is potential on almost all matters in debate at the Two Jolly Sawyers, near Lambeth Walk, just at the top of Cut-throat Lane.

All this is now altered. We look in vain for the Two Jolly Sawyers. We may ask, where are they? and not Echo, but the Archbishop of Canterbury, must answer where—for he has most sacerdotally put down all the jollity there, by pulling down the house, and has built up a large wharf, where once stood a very pretty tree-besprinkled walk, leading to the said Jolly Sawyers. Cut-throat Lane is no more; yet, though it bore a villainous name, it was very pretty to walk through; and its many turnstiles were as so many godsends to the little boys, as they enjoyed on them, gratis, some blithe rides that they would have had to pay for at any fair in the kingdom. We can very well understand why the turnstiles were so offensive to the dignitary; in fact, all this building, and leasing of houses, and improvement of property,[1] and destroying of poor people's pleasant walks, is nothing more than an improved reading of the words, '*benefit of clergy*.' Still, we cannot help regretting the turnstiles: and sorry are we for their sakes, and for ours, that their versatility should be looked upon as an ever-revolving libel, which thus caused their untimely destruction.

CHAPTER III

My foster-father forsakes the right line of conduct chalked *out
for him—I grow ill—Find Pot-luck and Baptism—Go to Bath,
and take my first lessons in the arts of Persuasion.*

WHEN I was placed with the Brandons, it was stipulated that they
should remove immediately from Reading; and, whilst I was in
their family, they should return there no more. For this purpose
the necessary expenses were forwarded to them by an unknown
hand. To Lambeth they therefore removed, because it abounded
in saw-pits; but this advantage was more than destroyed by its
abundance of skittle-grounds. Mr. Joseph Brandon had satisfied
his conscience by coming into the neighbourhood of the said sawpits: it showed a direction towards the paths of industry; but,
whilst he had, through his wife for nursing me, 81*l.* 18*s.* per annum,
he always preferred knocking down, or seeing knocked down, the
nine pins, to the being placed upon a narrow plank, toeing a chalked
line. This was not a line of conduct that he actually chalked out for
himself; only it so happened, that, when he was settled at Lambeth,
on the third day he went out to look after work, and going down
Stangate-street, he turned up Cut-throat Lane, and, after passing
all the turnstiles, he arrived at the Two Jolly Sawyers, himself
making a third. In his search for employment he found it impossible, for the space of a whole month, to get any farther.

But he was not long permitted to be the ascendant spirit among
the top and bottom men. Whether it be that Mrs. Brandon over-
rated her powers of affording sustenance, or that I had suffered
through the inclemency of the weather in my three journeys on my
natal day, or whether that I was naturally delicate, or perhaps all
these cases contributing to it, I fell into a very sickly state, and
before a third month had elapsed, I was forced to another migration.

Though no one appeared, both myself and Mrs. Brandon were
continually watched, and a very superior sort of surgeon in the
neighbourhood of Lambeth, from the second day of my arrival
there, found some pretence or another to get introduced to my
nurse, and took a violent liking to the little, puny, wailing piece of
mortality, myself. I was about this time so exceedingly small, that
at the risk of being puerile, I cannot help recording, that Joseph

C

Brandon immersed me, all excepting my head, in a quart pot. No one but a Joe Brandon, or a top sawyer, could have had so filthy an idea. I have never been told whether the pot contained any drainings, but I must attribute to this ill-advised act, a most plebeian fondness that I have for strong beer, and which seems to be, even in these days of French manners and French wines, unconquerable.

My health now became so precarious, that a letter arrived, signed simply, E. R., ordering that I should be immediately baptized, and five pounds were enclosed for the expenses. The letter stated that two decent persons should be found by Mrs. Brandon to be my sponsors, and that a female would appear on such a day, at such an hour, at Lambeth Church, to act as my godmother. That I was to be christened Ralph Rattlin, and, if I survived, I was to pass for their own child till further orders, and Ralph Rattlin Brandon were to be my usual appellations. Two decent persons being required, Joe Brandon, not having done any work for a couple of months, thought, by virtue of idleness, he might surely call himself one, to say nothing of his top-boots. The other godfather was a decayed fishmonger, of the name of Ford, a pensioner in the Fishmongers' Company, in whose alms-houses at Newington, he afterwards died. A sad reprobate was old Ford— he was wicked from nature, drunken from habit, and full of repentance from methodism. Thus his time was very equally divided between sin, drink, and contrition. His sleep was all sin, for he would keep the house awake all night blaspheming, in his unhealthy slumbers. As I was taken to church in a hackney-coach, my very honoured godfather, Ford, remarked, that 'it would be a very pleasant thing to get me into hell before him, as he was sure that I was born to sin, a child of wrath and an inheritor of the kingdom of the devil.' This bitter remark roused the passions even of my gentle nurse, and she actually scored down both sides of his face with her nails, in such a manner as to leave deep scars in his ugliness, that nine years after he carried to his grave. All this happened in the coach in our way to church. Ford had already prepared himself for the performance of his sponsorial duties, by getting half drunk upon his favourite beverage, gin, and it was now necessary to make him wholly intoxicated to induce him to go through the ceremony. As yet, my nurse had never properly seen my mother's face; at the interview, on my birth, the agitation of both parties, and the darkened room, though there was no attempt at concealment, prevented Mrs. Brandon from noticing her sufficiently to know her again; when, therefore, as our party alighted at the gate of the churchyard, and a lady deeply veiled, got out of a carriage at some distance, Mrs. Brandon knew not if she had ever seen her before.

I have been very unfortunate in religious ceremonies. Old Ford was a horrid spectacle, his face streaming with blood, violently drunk, and led by Brandon, who certainly was, on that occasion, both decent in appearance and behaviour. The strange lady hurried up to the font before us. When the clergyman saw the state in which Ford was, he refused to proceed in the ceremony. The sexton then answered for him, whilst he was led out of the church. The office went on, and the lady seemed studiously to avoid looking upon her intended godson; I was christened simply, Ralph Rattlin. The lady wrote her name in the book the last, and it was instantly removed by the clerk. She thrust a guinea into his hand, and then, for the first time, bent her veiled face over me. I must have been a miserable looking object, for no sooner had she seen me, than she gave a bitter shriek, and laying hold of the woodwork of the pews, she slowly assisted herself out of the church. Two or three persons who happened to be present, as well as Mr. and Mrs. Brandon, stepped forward to support her, but the clergyman, who seemed to have had a previous conversation with her, signed them to desist. It was altogether a most melancholy affair. Old Ford, when we left the church, was helped into the coach again, and Joe Brandon, being either justly irritated at his conduct, or angry that he could not see my unknown godmother's face, when we were all fairly on our way home, gave the old sot such a tremendous beating, that Mrs. Brandon nearly went into fits with alarm, and Ford himself was confined to his bed for a week after. When I reflect upon the manner in which I was christened, though I cannot exactly call it 'a maimed rite,' I have a great mind to have it done over again, only I am deterred by the expense.

All now was bustle in removing from Felix Street, Lambeth, to Bath, where it was ordered that I should be dipped every morning in some spring that, at that time, had much celebrity. Old Ford was left behind. At Bath I remained three years, Joe Brandon doing no work, and persuading himself now, that he actually was a gentleman. In my third year, my foster-sister, little robust, ruddy Mary, died, and the weakly, stunted, and drooping sapling lived on. This death endeared me more and more to my nurse, and Joe himself was, by self-interest, taught an affection for me. He knew that if I went to the grave, he must go to work; and he now used to perform the office himself of the dry-nurse to me, taking me to the spring, and allowing no one to dip me but himself. When I grew older, he had many stories to tell me about my pantings, and my implorings, and my offers of unnumbered kisses, and of all my playthings, if he would not put me in that cold water—only this one, one morning. And about a certain Dr. Buck, who had taken a wonderful liking to me, after the manner of the Lambeth surgeon, and had prescribed for me, and sent me physic, and port wine, all out of pure philanthropy; and how much I hated this same Dr. Buck, and his horrible 'give him t'other dip, Brandon.' But all these are as things that had long died from my own recollection.

CHAPTER IV

My proximity to the clergy impels me to preach—advocate the vulgar; and prove that neither the humble nor the low are necessarily the debased—consequently, this chapter need not be read.

WHAT with dipping, port wine, bark, and Dr. Buck, at the age of four years my limbs began to expand properly, and my countenance to assume the hue of health. I have recorded the death of my foster-sister Mary; but about this time, the top-sawyer, wishing to per-petuate the dynasty of the Brandons, began to enact *pater familias* in a most reckless manner. He was wrong; but this must be said in extenuation of his impiously acting upon the divine command, 'to increase and multiply,' that at that time, Mr. Malthus had not corrected the mistake of the Omniscient,[1] nor had Miss Harriet Martineau begun her pilgrimage after 'the preventive check.'[2] There was no longer any pretence for my remaining at Bath, or for my worthy foster-father abstaining from work; so we again removed, with a small family, in our search after sawpits and happiness, to one of the best houses in Felix Street, somewhere near Lambeth Marsh. This place, after the experience of some time, proving not to be sufficiently blissful, we removed to Paradise Row, some furlongs nearer the Father in God His Grace the

Archbishop of Canterbury. I have a laudable pride in showing that I had a *respectable*—I beg pardon, the word is inapplicable—I mean a grand neighbour. 'I am not the rose,' said the flower in the Persian poem, 'but I have lived near the rose.' I did not bloom in the archbishop's garden, but I flourished under the wall, though on the outside. The wall is now down, and rows of houses up in its place. I had a great inclination to be discursive on the mutability of human affairs, when I had finished the last sentence; but I have changed my mind, which is a practical commentary upon them, and will save me the trouble of writing one.

In our location in Paradise Row, the house being larger than we required for our accommodation, we again received old Ford, the only paradise, I am rather afraid, that will ever own him as an inmate. An awful man was old Ford, my godfather. His mingled prayers and blasphemies, hymns and horrid songs, defiance and remorse, groans and laughter, made every one hate and avoid him. Hell-fire, as he continually asserted, was ever roaring before his eyes; and as there is a text in the New Testament that says, there is no salvation for him who curses the Holy Ghost, he would, in the frenzy of his despair, swear at that mysterious portion of the Trinity by the hour, and then employ the next in beating his breast in the agony of repentance. Many may think all this sheer madness; but he was not more mad than most of the hot-headed Methodists, whose preachers, at that time, held uncontrolled sway over the great mass of people that toiled in the humbler walks of life. Two nights in the week we used to have prayer-meetings at our house;[1] and, though I could not have been five years old at the time, vividly do I remember that our front room used, on those occasions, to be filled to overflow with kneeling fanatics, old Ford in the centre of the room, and a couple of lank-haired hypocrites, one on each side of the reprobate, praying till the perspiration streamed down their foreheads, to pray the devil out of him. The ohs! and the groanings of the audience were terrible; and the whole scene, though very edifying to the elect, was disgraceful to any set who lived within the pale of civilization.

I must now draw upon my own memory. I must describe my own sensations. If I reckon by the toil and the turmoil of the mind, I am already an old man. I have lived for ages. I am far, very far on my voyage. Let me cast my eyes back on the vast sea that I have traversed; there is a mist settled over it, almost as impenetrable as

that which glooms before me. Let me pause. Methinks that I see
it gradually break, and partial sunbeams struggle through it. Now
the distant waves rise, and wanton, and play, pure and lucid. 'Tis
the day-spring of innocency. How near to the sanctified heavens
do those remote waves appear! They meet, and are as one with the
far horizon. Those sparkling waves were the hours of my childhood—the blissful feelings of my infancy. As the sea of life rolls
on, the waves swell and are turbid; and, as I recede from the
horizon of my early recollections, so heaven recedes from me. The
thunder-cloud is high above my head, the treacherous waters roar
beneath me, before me is the darkness and the night of an unknown
futurity. Where can I now turn my eyes for solace, but over the
vast space that I have passed? Whilst my bark glides heedlessly
forward, I will not anticipate dangers that I cannot see, or tremble
at rocks that are benevolently hidden from my view. It is sufficient for me to know that I must be wrecked at last: that my mortal
frame must be like a shattered bark upon the beach ere the purer
elements that it contains can be wafted through the immensity of
immortality. I will commune with my boyish days—I will live in
the past only. Memory shall perform the Medean process, shall
renovate me to youth. I will again return to marbles and an un-
troubled breast—to hoop and high spirits—at least, in imagination.

I shall henceforward trust to my own recollections. Should this
part of my story seem more like a chronicle of sensations than
a series of events, the reader must bear in mind that these sensations are in early youth real events, the parents of actions and the
directors of destiny. The circle in which, in boyhood, one may be
compelled to move, may be esteemed low; the accidents all around
him may be homely, the persons with whom he may be obliged to
come in contact may be mean in apparel, and sordid in nature; but
his mind, if it remain to him pure as he received it from his Maker,
is an unsullied gem of inestimable price, too seldom found, and
too little appreciated when found, among the great, or the fortuit-
ously rich. Nothing that is abstractedly mental is low. The mind
that well describes low scenery is not low, nor is the description
itself necessarily so. Pride, and a contempt for our fellow creatures,
evince a low tone of moral feeling, and is the innate vulgarity of the
soul: it is this which but too often makes those who rustle in silks,
and roll in carriages, lower than the lowest.

I have said this much, because the early, very early part of my life was passed among what are reproachfully termed 'low people.' If I describe them faithfully, they must still appear low to those who arrogate to themselves the epithet of 'high.' For myself, I hold that there is nothing low under the sun, except meanness. Where there is utility, there ought to be honour. The utility of the humble artisan has never been denied, though too often despised, and too rarely honoured; but I have found among the 'vulgar' a horror of meanness, a self-devotion, an unshrinking patience under privation, and the moral courage, that constitute the hero of high life. I can also tell the admirers of the great, that the evil passions of the vulgar are as gigantic, their wickedness upon as grand a scale, and their notions of vice as refined, and as extensive, as those of any fashionable *roué* that is courted among the first circles, or even as those of the crowned despot. Then, as to the strength of vulgar intellect. True, that intellect is rarely cultivated by the learning which consists of words. The view it takes of science is but a partial glance—that intellect is contracted, but it is strong. It is a dwarf, with the muscle and sinews of a giant; and its grasp, whenever it can lay hold of any thing within its circumscribed reach, is tremendous. The general who has conquered armies and sub-jugated countries, the minister who has ruined them, and the jurist who has justified both, never at the crisis of their labours have displayed a tithe of the ingenuity and the resources of mind that many an artisan is forced to exert to provide daily bread for himself and family; or many a shopkeeper to keep his connexion together, and himself out of the workhouse. Why should the exertions of intellect be termed low, in the case of the mechanic, and vast, profound, and glorious, in that of the minister? It is the same precious gift of a beneficent power to all his creatures. As well may the sun be voted as excessively vulgar, because it, like intellect, assists all equally to perform their functions. I repeat, that nothing that has mind is, of necessity, low, and nothing is vulgar but meanness.

CHAPTER V

I receive my first lessons in pugnacity—and imbibe the evil spirit— Learn to read by intuition, and to fight by practice—Go to school to a soldier—Am a good boy, and get whipped.

AT six years of age my health had become firmly established, but this establishment caused dismay in that of Joe Brandon. As I was no longer the sickly infant that called for incessant attention and the most careful nurture, it was intimated to my foster-parents, that a considerable reduction would be made in the quarterly allowance paid on my account. The indignation of Brandon was excessive. He looked upon himself as one grievously wronged. No sinecurist, with his pension recently reduced, could have been more vehement on the subject of the sanctity of vested rights. But his ire was not to be vented in idle declamation only. He was not a man to rest content with mere words: he declaimed for a full hour upon his wife's folly in procuring him the means of well-fed idleness so long, threatened to take the brat—meaning no less a personage than myself—to the workhouse: and then he wound up affairs, in doors, by beating his wife, and himself, out of doors, by getting royally drunk.

This was the first scene that made a deep impression upon me. Young as I was, I comprehended that I was the cause of the ill-treatment of my nurse, whom I fondly loved. I interfered—I placed my little body between her and her brutal oppressor. I scratched, I kicked, I screamed—I grew mad with passion. At that hour, the spirit of evil and of hate blew the dark coal in my heart into a flame; and the demon of violent anger has ever since found it too easy to erect there his altar, of which the fire, though at the time all-consuming, is never durable. From that moment I commenced my intellectual existence. I looked on the sobbing mother, and knew what it was to love, and my love found its expression in an agony of tears. I looked on the tyrant, I felt what it was to hate, and endeavoured to relieve the burning desire to punish with frantic actions and wild outcries. Old Ford, who had been present and enjoyed the *fracas*, immediately took me into his especial favour; he declared that I was after his own heart, for I had the devil in me—said that I had the right spirit to bring me to the gallows, and

he hoped, old as he was, to live to see it: he then entreated of the
Lord that my precious soul might be saved as a burning brand out
of the fire—took me by the hand and led me to the next gin-shop
—made me taste the nauseating poison—told me I was a little man,
and it was glorious to fight—doubled up for me my puny fists, and
asserted that cowards only suffered a blow without returning it.
A lesson like this never can be forgotten. I ground my teeth whilst
I was receiving it—I clenched my hands, and looked wildly round
for something to destroy. I was in training to become a little tiger.
From what I then experienced, I can easily conceive the feelings
that actuate, and can half forgive the crowned monsters who have
revelled in blood, and relished the inflicting of torture; as pander-
ing to their worst passions in infancy resolves them into a terrible
instrument of cruelty, the control of which rests not with themselves. But this lesson in tiger ferocity had its emollient, though
not its antidote, in the tenderness of the love which I bore my
nurse, when, on my return, I flung myself into her arms. Ever
since that day I have been subject to terrific fits of passion; but
very happily for me, they have long ceased to be but of very rare
occurrence.

The next morning, Master Joseph came home ill, and if not
humbled, at least almost helpless. He had now three children of
his own, and the necessity of eschewing skittles, and presiding over
the sawpit, became urgent. With all his vices and his roughness,
he was surprisingly fond of me. He, too, applauded my spirit in
attacking himself. He now rejoiced to take me to the sawpit, to
allow me to play about the timber-yards, and share with him his
al fresco mid-day meal and pot of porter. I always passed for his
eldest son, my name being told to the neighbours as Ralph Rattlin
Brandon. I knew no otherwise, and my foster-parents kept the
secret religiously. At seven I began to fight with dirty little urchins
in the street, who felt much scandalized at the goodness of my
clothes. It is hard work fighting up-hill at seven years of age. Old
Ford would wipe the blood from my nose, and clap the vinegar
and brown paper on my bruises with words of sweet encouragement; though he always ended by predicting that his hopeful
godson would be hung, and that he should live to see it. I have
certainly not been drowned yet, though I have had my escapes,
and old Ford has been dead these thirty years. As one part of
the prophecy will certainly never be fulfilled, I have some

faint hopes of avoiding the exaltation hinted at in the other.

About this time, I began to notice that a lady, at long intervals, came to see me. She seemed exceedingly happy in my caresses, though she showed no weakness. She passed for my godmother, and so she certainly was. She was minute in her examination in ascertaining that I was perfectly clean; and always brought me a number of delicacies, which were invariably devoured immediately after her departure, by me and those little cormorants my loving foster-brothers and sister. Moreover, my nurse always received a present, which she very carefully and dutifully concealed from her liege lord of the pits. However, I cannot call to my mind more than four of these 'angelic visits' altogether. 'Angelic visits,' indeed, they might be termed, if the transcendent beauty of the visitor be regarded. At that time, her form and her countenance furnished me with the idea I had of the blessed inhabitants of heaven before man was created, and I have never been able to replace it since by anything more beautiful. The reader shall soon know how, at that very early age, I became so well acquainted with angelic lore.

At eight years of age I was sent to school. I could read before I went there. How I picked up this knowledge I never could discover. Both my foster-parents were grossly illiterate. Perhaps old Ford taught me—but this is one of the mysteries I could never solve, and it is strange that I should have so totally forgotten all about an affair so important, as not to remember a single lesson, and yet to hold so clear a recollection of many minor events. But so it is. To school I went: my master was a cadaverous, wooden-legged man, a disbanded soldier, and a disciplinarian, as well as an a-b-c-darian.

I well remember old Isaacs, and his tall, handsome, crane-necked daughter. The hussy was as straight as an arrow, yet, for the sake of coquetry, or singularity, she would sit in the methodist chapel, with her dimpled chin resting upon an iron hoop, and her finely formed shoulders braced back with straps so tightly, as to thrust out in a remarkable manner her swan-like chest, and her almost too exuberant bust. This instrument for the distorted, with its bright crimson leather, thus pressed into the service of the beautiful, had a most singular and exciting effect upon the beholder. I have often thought of this girl in my maturer years, and confess that no dress that I ever beheld gave a more piquant interest to the wearer, than those straps and irons. The jade never wore them at home. Perhaps the fancy was her father's, he being an old soldier, and his motto 'eyes right! dress!' Whosoever fancy it was, his daughter rejoiced in it. 'Eyes right! dress!' is as good a motto for the ladies as the army—and well do they act up to it.

The most important facts that my mind has preserved concerning this scholastic establishment are—that one evening, for a task, I learned perfectly by heart the two first chapters of the Gospel according to St. John; that there was an unbaked gooseberry pie put prominently on the shelf in the school-room, a fortnight before the vacation at Midsummer, to be partaken of on the happy day of breaking up, each boy paying four-pence for his share of the mighty feast. There were between forty and fifty of us. I had almost forgotten to mention, that I was to be duly punished whenever I deserved it, but the master was, on no account, to hurt me, or make me cry. I deserved it regularly three or four times a-day, and was as regularly horsed once. Oh! those floggings, how deceptive they were, and how much I regretted them when I came to understand the thing fundamentally. Old Isaacs could not have performed the operation more delicately, if he were only brushing a fly off the down of a lady's cheek. *He* never made me cry.

CHAPTER VI

This chapter showeth, in a methodical manner, how to find a faith and lose all religion; also, to procure a Call for persons of all manner of callings.

I HAD, as I have related, been encouraged in fits of passion, and had been taught to be pugnacious; my mind was now to be opened to loftier speculations; and religious dread, with all the phantoms of superstition in its train, came like a band of bravoes, and first chaining down my soul in the awe of stupefaction, ultimately loosened its bonds, and sent it to wander in all its childish wildness in the direful realms of horrible dreams, and of waking visions hardly less so. I was fashioning for a poet.

My nurse was always a little devotional. She went to the nearest chapel or church, and, satisfied that she heard the word of God, without troubling herself with the niceties of any peculiar dogma, which she could not have understood if she had, and finding herself on the threshold of divine grace, she knelt down in all humility, prayed, and was comforted. Old Ford was a furious Methodist; he owned that he never could reform; and, as he daily drained the cup of sin to the very dregs, he tried, as an antidote, long prayer, and superabounding faith. The unction with which he struck his breast, and exclaimed, 'Miserable sinner that I am!' could only be exceeded by the veracity of the assertion. Mrs. Brandon only joined in the prayer-meetings that he held at our house, when Ford himself was perfectly sober—thus she did not often attend—Brandon never. Whilst he wore the top-boots, he was an optimist, and perfectly epicurean in his philosophy—I use the term in the modern sense. When he had eighty pounds odd a-year, with no family of his own, no man was more jovial or happier. He had the most perfect reliance on Providence. He boasted, that he belonged to the Established Church, because it was so respectable—and he loved the organ. However, he never went in the forenoon because he was never shaved in time; in the afternoon he never went, because he could not dispense with his nap after dinner; and, in the evening, none but the serving classes were to be seen there. He ridiculed the humble piety of his wife, and the fanatical fervour of his lodger. He was a high churchman, and satisfied. But when he was obliged, with an increasing family and a decreased income, to work from morning till night, he grew morose, and very unsettled in his faith.

The French revolution was then at its wildest excess. Equality was universally advocated in religious, as well as political establishments. The excitement of the times reached even to the sawpit. Brandon got tipsy one Saturday with a parcel of demagogues, and when he awoke early next Sunday morning—it was a beautiful summer day—he made the sudden discovery that he had still his faith to seek for. Then began his dominical pilgrimages. With his son Ralph in his hand, he roved from one congregation to another over the vast metropolis, and through its extensive environs. I do not think that we left a single place, dedicated to devotion, unvisited. I well remember that he was much struck with the Roman Catholic worship. We repeated our visits three or four times to the Catholic chapel, a deference we paid to no other. The result of this may be easily imagined. When an excited mind searches for food, it will be satisfied with the veriest trash, provided only that it intoxicates. We at length stumbled upon a small set of mad Methodists, more dismal and more excluding than even Ford's sect: the congregation were all of the very lowest class, with about twelve or thirteen exceptions, and those were decidedly mad. The pastor was an arch rogue, that fattened upon the delusion of his communicants. They held the doctrine of visible election, which election was made by having a call—that is, a direct visitation of the Holy Ghost, which was testified by falling down in a fit—the testification being the more authentic, if it happened in full congregation. The elected could never again fall:[1] the sins that were afterwards committed in their persons were not theirs—it was the evil spirit within them, that they could cast out when they would, and be equally as pure as before. All the rest of the world, who had not had their call, were in a state of reprobation, and on the high-road to damnation.

All this, of course, I did not understand till long afterwards, but I too unhappily understood, or at least fancied I did, the dreadful images of eternal torments, and the certainty that they would soon be mine. First of all, either from inattention, or from want of comprehension, these denunciations made but a faint impression upon me. But the frightful descriptions took, gradually, a more visible and sterner shape, till they produced effects that proved all but fatal.

The doctrines of these Caterians just suited the intellect and the strong passions of Brandon. The sect was called Caterians, after the Rev. Mr. Cate, their minister. My foster-father went home, after the second Sunday, and put his house in order. As far as regarded the household, the regulations would have pleased Sir Andrew Agnew:[2] the hot joint was dismissed—the country walk discontinued—at meeting four times a day. Even Ford did not like it. Brandon was labouring hard for his call. He strove vehemently for the privilege of sinning with impunity. He was told by Mr. Cate that he was in a desperate way. Brandon did all he could, but the call would not come for the calling. Mrs. Brandon got it very soon, though she strenuously denied the honour. My good nurse was in the family way, and Mr. Cate had frightened her into fits, with a vivid delineation of the agonies of a new-born infant, under the torture of eternal fire, because it had died unelected. However,

Brandon began a little to weary of waiting and long prayer, and perhaps of the now too frequent visits of Mr. Cate. He commenced to have his fits of alternate intemperate recklessness, and religious despondency. One Sunday morning, well do I recollect it, he called me up early, before seven, and I supposed, as usual, that we were going to early meeting. We walked towards the large room that was used as a chapel. We had nearly reached it, when the half-open door of an adjacent ale-house let out its vile compound of disgusting odours upon the balmy sabbath air. My conductor hesitated—he moved towards the meeting-house, but his head was turned the other way—he stopped.

'Ralph,' said he, 'did you not see Mr. Ford go into the public-house?'

'No, father,' said I, 'don't think he's up.'

'At all bounds, we had better go and see; for I must not allow him to shame a decent house by tippling, on a Sunday morning, in a dram-shop.'

We entered. He found there some of his mates. Pint after pint of purl was called for; at length, a gallon of strong ale was placed upon the table, a quart of gin was dashed into it, and the whole warmed with a red-hot poker. I was now instructed to lie. I promised to tell mother that we had gone into a strange chapel; but I made my conditions, that mother should not be any more beaten. It was almost church-time when the landlord put us all out by the back way. The drunken fellows sneaked home—whilst Brandon, taking me by the hand, made violent, and nearly successful, efforts to appear sober.

After a hasty breakfast we went to meeting. My foster-father looked excessively wild. Mr. Cate was raving in the midst of an extempore prayer, when a heavy fall was heard in the chapel. The minister descended from his desk, and came and prayed over the prostrate victim of intoxication, and, perhaps, of epilepsy, and he pronounced that brother Brandon had got his call, and was now indisputably one of the elect. He did not revive so soon as was expected—his groans were looked upon as indications of the work-ings of the Spirit, and when, at length, he was so far recovered as to be led home by two of the congregation, the conversion of the sawyer was dwelt upon by the preacher, from a text preached upon the chapter that relates to the conversion of Saul, and the cases were cited as parallel. Let the opponents of the Established Church rail at it as they will, scenes of such wickedness and impiety could never have happened within its time-honoured walls.

When we returned to dinner, we found that Brandon had so far recovered, as to become very hungry, very proud, and very pharisaically pious. Mr. Cate dined with us. He was full of holy congratulations on the miraculous event. The sawyer received all this with a humble self-consequence, as the infallible dicta of truth, and, apparently, with the utter oblivion of any such things existing as purl and red-hot pokers. Was he a deep hypocrite, or only a self-deceiver? Who can know the heart of man? However, 'this call' had the effect of making the 'called one' a finished sinner, and of filling up the measure of wretchedness to his wife.

CHAPTER VII

I too have my call—to death's door—A great rise in life—Brandon allows neither slugs nor sluggards in his sawpit—Is ruined, and beats the reverend Mr. Cate.

ALL this was preparatory to an event, to me of the utmost importance, which is, perhaps, at this very moment, influencing imperceptibly my mind, and directing my character. Brandon's call, in our humble circle, made a great deal of noise. He had taken care that I should know what drunkenness meant. I thought he ought to have been drunk on the afternoon of his election, yet he so well disguised his intoxication that he appeared not to be so. I listened attentively to the sermon of the preacher that followed. I no longer doubted. I could not believe that a grave man in a pulpit could speak anything but truth, when he spoke so loudly, and spoke for two hours. My mind was a chaos of confusion. I began to be very miserable. The next, or one or two Sundays after, produced the crisis. My dress was always much superior to what could have been expected in the son of a mere operative. I was, at that time, a fair and mild-featured child, and altogether remarkable among the set who frequented the meeting-house. Mr. Cate had been very powerful indeed in his description of the infernal regions—of the abiding agonies—the level lake that burneth—the tossing of the waves that glow, and, when he had thrown two or three old women into hysterics, and two or three young ones into fainting fits, amidst the torrent of his oratory, and the groaning, and the 'Lord have mercy upon me's,' of his audience, he made a sudden pause. There was a dead silence for half a minute, then suddenly lifting his voice, he pointed to me, and exclaimed, 'Behold that beautiful child—observe the pure blood mantling in his delicate countenance—but what is he after all but a mouthful for the devil? All those torments, all those tortures, that I have told you of, will be his; there, look at him, he will burn and writhe in pain, and consume for ever, and ever, and ever, and never be destroyed, unless the original sin be washed out from him by the "call," lest he be made hereafter one of the "elect."'

At this direct address to myself, I neither fainted, shuddered, nor cried—I felt, at the time, a little stupefied: and it was some hours after (the hideous man's words all the time ringing in my ears) before I fully comprehended my hopeless state of perdition. I looked at the fire as I sat by it, and trembled. I went to bed, but not to sleep. No child ever haunted by a ghost-story was more terrified than myself, as I lay panting on my tear-steeped pillow. At length, imagination began its dreadful charms—the room enlarged itself in its gloom to vast space—I began to hear cries from under my bed. Some dark bodies first of all flitted across the gloaming. My bed began to rock. I tried to sing a hymn. I thought that the words came out of my mouth in flames of bright fire. I then called to mind the offerings from the altars of Cain and Abel. I watched to see if my hymns turned into fire, and ascended up to heaven. I felt a cold horror when I discovered them scattered from my mouth exactly in the same manner that I had seen the flames in the engraving in our large Bible on the altar of Cain. Then there came a huge block of wood, and stationed itself in the air above me, about six inches from my eyes. I remember no more—I was in a raging fever.

I was ill for some weeks, and a helpless invalid for many more. When again I enjoyed perception of the things around me, I found myself in a new house in Red Cross Street, near St. Luke's. My foster-parents had opened a shop—it had the appearance of a most respectable fruiterer's. Mr. Brandon had become a small timber merchant—had sawpits in the premises behind the house, and men of his own actually sawing in them. But the most surprising change of all was, that the reverend Mr. Cate was domesticated with us. Brandon, as a master, worked harder than ever he did as a man. My nurse became anxious and careworn, and never seemed happy—for my part, I was so debilitated, that I then took but little notice of anything. However, the beautiful lady never called. I used to spend my time thinking upon angels and cherubs, and in learning hymns by heart. I suppose that I, like my foster-father, had had my call, but I am sure that after it, I was as much weaker in mind as I was in body. When I became strong enough to be again able to run about, I was once more sent to a day-school, and all that I remember about the matter was, that every day about eleven o'clock I was told to run home and get a wigful of potatoes from Brandon's, the venerable pedagogue coolly taking off his wig, and exchanging it for a red night-cap, until my return with the provender.

Things now wore a dismal aspect at home. At length, one day, the broker sent his men into the shop, who threw all the green-grocery about like peelings of onions. They carted away Mr. Brandon's deals, and planks, and timber, and, not content with all this, they also took away the best of the household furniture. My nurse called Mr. Cate a devil in a white sheet—her husband acted as he always would do when he was offended and found himself strong enough: he gave the reverend gentleman, most irreverently, a tremendous beating. The sheep sadly gored the shepherd. After-wards, when he had nearly killed his pastor, he seceded from his flock, and gave him, under his own hand, a solemn abjuration of the Caterian tenets. How Brandon came to launch out into this expensive and ill-advised undertaking of green-groceries and sawpits, how he afterwards became involved, and how much the preacher had been guilty in deceiving him, I never clearly under-stood. However, my nurse never, for a long time after, spoke of the reverend gentleman without applying the corner of her apron to her eyes, or her husband without a hearty malediction. We removed to our old neighbourhood, but, instead of taking a respect-able house, we were forced to burrow in mean lodgings.

D

CHAPTER VIII

*Another migration—from the ruralities of Cut-throat Lane to the
groves of Academus—I am forced into good clothes and the paths
of learning in spite of my teeth, though I use them spitefully.*

MISFORTUNES never come single. I don't know why they
should. They are but scarecrow, lean-visaged, miserable associates, and so they arrive in a body to keep each other in countenance. I had been but a few weeks in our present miserable abode,
and had fully recovered my health, though I think that I was
a little crazed with the prints, and the subjects of them, over which
I daily pored in the large Bible, when the greatest misfortune of
all came upon the poor Brandons—and that was, to add to their
other losses, the loss of my invaluable self.

The misery was unexpected—it was sudden—it was over-
whelming. Brandon was toeing a chalked line on a heavy log of
mahogany, unconscious of the mischief that was working at home.
He afterwards told me, and I believe him, that he would have
opposed the proceeding by force, if force had been requisite.
A plain, private, or hired carriage, drove up to the door, and, after
ascertaining that the Brandons lived at the house, a business-like
looking, elderly gentleman stepped out, paid every demand immediately, and ordered my best clothes on. When I was thus equipped,
my nurse was told that she was perfectly welcome to the remainder
of my effects, and that I must get into the carriage.

The good woman was thunderstruck. There was a scene. She
raved, and I cried, and the four little Brandons, at least three of
them, joined in the chorus of lamentation, because the naughty
man was going to take brother Ralph away. I had been too well
taught by old Ford, not to visit my indignation upon the shins and
hands of the carrier away of captives, in well-applied kicks, and
almost rabid bites. There was a great disturbance. The neighbours
thought it very odd that the mother should allow her eldest son
to be carried off by force, by a stranger, before her eyes, in the
middle of the day; but then it was suggested, that 'nothing could
be well termed odd that concerned little Ned Brandon, for hadn't
he been bit last year by a mad dog, and, when so and so had all
died raving, he had never nothing at all happen to him.' When the

stranger heard this story of the mad dog, (which, by-the-bye, was fact, and I have the scars to this day,) he shook me off, pale with consternation, and was, no doubt, extremely happy to find that my little teeth had not penetrated the skin. I believe that he heartily repented him of his office. At length he lost all patience. 'Woman,' said he, 'send these people out of the room.' When they had departed, marvelling, he resumed: 'I cannot lose my time in altercation. I am commissioned to tell you, that if you keep the boy in one sense, you'll have to keep him in all. You may be sure that I would not trouble myself about such a little ill-bred wretch for a moment, if I did not act with authority, and by orders. Give up the child directly,' (I was now sobbing in her arms) 'take your last look at him, for you will never see him again. Come, hand the young gentleman into the carriage.'

'I won't go,' I screamed out.

'We shall soon see that, Master Rattlin,' said he, dragging me along, resisting. I bawled out, 'My name's not Master Rattlin—you're a liar—and when father comes from the pit he'll wop you.'

This threat seemed to have an effect the very reverse of what I had intended. Perhaps he thought that he had already enough to contend with, without the addition of the brawny arm of the sawyer. I was forcibly lifted up, placed in the coach, and, as it drove rapidly away, I heard, amidst the rattling of the wheels, the cries of her whom I loved as a mother, exclaiming, 'My Ralph—my dear Ralph!'

Behold me then, 'hot with the fray, and weeping from the fright,' confined in a locomotive prison with my sullen captor. I blubbered in one corner of the coach, and he surveyed me with stern indifference from another. I had now fairly commenced my journey through life, but this beginning was anything but auspicious. At length, the carriage stopped at a place I have since ascertained to be near Hatton Garden, on Holborn Hill. We alighted, and walked into a house, between two motionless pages, excessively well dressed. At first, they startled me, but I soon discovered they were immense waxen dolls. It was a ready-made clothes warehouse into which we had entered. We went up stairs, and I was soon equipped with three excellent suits. My grief had now settled down into a sullen resentment, agreeably relieved, at due intervals, by breath-catching sobs. The violence of the storm had passed, but its gloom still remained. Seeing the little gladness

that the possession of clothes, the finest I had yet had, com-
municated to me, my director could not avoid giving himself the
pleasureable relief of saying, 'Sulky little brute!' A trunk being
sent for, and my wardrobe placed in it, we then drove to three or
four other shops, not forgetting a hatter's, and in a very short space
of time, I had a very tolerable fit-out. During all this time not a word
did my silent companion address to me.

At length the coach no longer rattled over the stones. It now
proceeded on more smoothly, and here and there the cheerful
green foliage relieved the long lines of houses. After about a half-
hour's ride, we stopped at a large and very old-fashioned house,
built in strict conformity with the Elizabethan style of archi-
tecture, over the portals of which, upon a deep blue board, in very,
very bright gold letters, flashed forth that word so awful to little
boys, so big with associations of long tasks and wide-spreading
birch, the Greek-derived polysyllable, ACADEMY! Ignorant as I was,
I understood it all in a moment. I was struck cold as the dew-damp
grave-stone. I almost grew sick with terror. I was kidnapped,
entrapped, betrayed. I had before hated school, my horror now
was intense of 'Academy.' I looked piteously into the face of my
persecutor, but I found there no sympathy. 'I want to go home,'
I roared out, and then burst into a fresh torrent of tears.

Home! what solace is there in its very sound! Oh, how that
blessed asylum for the wounded spirit encloses within its sacred
circle all that is comforting, and sweet, and holy! 'Tis there that
the soul coils itself up and nestles like the dove in its own downi-
ness, conscious that everything around breathes of peace, security,
and love. Home! henceforward, I was to have none, until, through
many, many years of toil and misery, I should create one for myself. Henceforth, the word must bring to me only the bitterness of
regret—henceforth I was to associate with hundreds who had that
temple in which to consecrate their household affections—but was,
myself, doomed to be unowned, unloved, and homeless.

'I want to go home,' I blubbered forth with the pertinacity of
anguish, as I was constrained into the parlour of the truculent
rod-bearing, ferula-wielding Mr. Root. I must have been a strange
figure. I was taken from my nurse's in a hurry, and, though my
clothes were quite new, my face entitled me to rank among the
much vituperated unwashed. When a little boy has very dirty hands,
with which he rubs his dirty, tearful face, it must be confessed that

grief does not, in his person, appear under a very lovely form. The first impression that I made on him who was to hold almost everything that could constitute my happiness in his power, was the very reverse of favourable. My continued iteration of 'I want to go home,' was anything but pleasing to the pedagogue. The sentence itself is not music to a man keeping a boarding-school. With the intuitive perception of childhood, through my tears, my heart acknowledged an enemy. What my conductor said to him, did not tend to soften his feelings towards me. I did not understand the details of his communication, but I knew that I was as a captive, bound hand and foot, and delivered over to a foreign bondage. The interview between the contracting parties was short, and when over, my conductor departed without deigning to bestow the smallest notice upon the most important personage of this history. I was then rather twitched by the hand, than led, by Mr. Root, into the middle of his capacious school-room, and in the midst of more than two hundred and fifty boys: my name was merely mentioned to one of the junior ushers, and the master left me. Well might I then apply that blundering, Examiner-be-praised line of Keats to myself, for like Ruth,

'I stood all tears among the alien corn.'

A few boys came and stared at me, but I attracted the kindness of none. There can be no doubt but that I was somewhat vulgar in my manners, and my carriage was certainly quite unlike that of my companions. Some of them even jeered me, but I regarded them not. A real grief is armour-proof against ridicule. In a short time, it being six o'clock, the supper was served out, consisting of a round of bread, all the moisture of which had been allowed to evaporate, and an oblong, diaphanous, yellow substance, one inch and a half by three, that I afterwards learned might be known among the initiated as single Gloucester. There was also a pewter mug for each, three-parts filled with small beer. It certainly gave me, it was so small, a very desponding idea of the extent to which littleness might be carried; and it would have been too vapid for the toleration of any palate, had it not been so sour. As I sate regardless before this repast, in abstracted grief, I underwent the first of the thousand practical jokes that were hereafter to familiarize me with manual jocularity. My right-hand neighbour, jerking me by the elbow, exclaimed, 'Hollo, you sir, there's Jenkins, on the other side of you, cribbing your bread.' I turned towards the supposed culprit, and discovered that my informant had fibbed, but the informed against told me to look round and see where my cheese was. I did; it was between the mandibles of my kind neighbour on my right, and when I turned again to the left for an explanation, pedagogue there had stripped my round of bread of all the crust. I cared not then for this double robbery, but having put the liquid before me incautiously to my lips, sorrowful as I was, I cared for that. Joe Brandon never served me so. I drank that evening as little as I ate.

CHAPTER IX

I prove to be, not one in a thousand, but one in a quarter of that number, to whom no quarter was shown—In spite of my entreaties I am evil entreated, and am not only placed on the lowest form, but made excessively uncomfortable on my seat of honour.

HEROES, statesmen, philosophers, must bend to circumstances, and so must little boys at boarding-school. I went to bed with the rest, and, like the rest, had my bedfellow. Miserable and weary was that night to my infant heart. When I found I could do so unobserved, I buried my face in the pillow, and wept with a perfect passion of wretchedness. Never shall I forget that bitter night of tears. It is singular that I did not weep long for myself. The mournful images that arose before me, and demanded each, as it came, its tribute of grief, ceased soon to be connected with my own individual suffering. My own abandonment and isolation no longer affected me. But I fancied my nurse was ill—that my foster-brother was lost in the streets, and wandering, hungry and in rags—my fancy even imaged to me Brandon having met with some accident, and pitifully calling in vain for his little Ralph to run and fetch mother. It was these fond imaginings that gave me the intense agony that kept me wakeful till the morning dawned—and the first streak of light that appeared through the window, heralded me to peace and sleep.

I had a hard, a cruel life at that school. When I lived with my nurse, the boys in the street used to beat me because I was too much of the gentleman, and now the young gentlemen thrashed me for not coming up to their standard of gentility. I saw a tyrant in every urchin that was stronger than myself, and a derider in those that were weaker. The next morning after my arrival, a fellow a little bigger than myself, came up, and standing before me, gave me very deliberately as hard a slap in the face as his strength would permit. Half crying with the pain, and yet not wishing to be thought quarrelsome, I asked, with good-natured humility, whether that was done in jest or in earnest. The little insolent replied, in his school-boy wit, 'betwixt and between.' I couldn't stand that; my passion and my fist rose together, and hitting my oppressor midway between the eyes, 'There's my betwixt and between,' said I. His nose began to bleed, and when I went down into the school-room, the 'new boy' had his hands well warmed with the ruler for fighting.

Alas! the first year of my academic life was one of unqualified wretchedness. For the two or three initiatory months, uncouth in speech, and vulgar in mien, with no gilded toy, rich plum-cake, or mint-new shilling to conciliate, I was despised and ridiculed; and when it was ascertained by my own confession, that I was the son of a day-labourer, I was shunned by the aristocratic progeny of butchers, linen-drapers, and hatters. It took, at least, a half-dozen floggings to cure me of the belief that Joseph Brandon and his wife were my parents. It was the shortest road to conviction, and Mr. Root prided himself upon short *cuts* in imparting knowledge. I assure my readers they were severe ones.

Mr. Root, the pedagogue[1] of this immense school, which was situated in the vicinity of Islington, was a very stout and very handsome man, of about thirty. He had formerly been a subordinate where he now commanded, and his good looks had gained him the hand of the widow of his predecessor. He was very florid, with a cold dark eye; but his face was the most physical that I ever beheld. From the white, low forehead, to the well-formed chin, there was nothing on which the gazer could rest that spoke of intellectuality. There was 'speculation in his eye,'[2] but it was the calculation of farthings. There was a pure ruddiness in his cheek, but it was the glow of matter, not that of mind. His mouth was well formed, yet pursed up with an expression of mingled vanity and severity. He was very robust, and his arm exceedingly powerful. With all these personal advantages, he had a shrill, girlish voice, that made him, in the execution of his cruelties, actually hideous. I believe, and I make the assertion in all honesty, that he received a sensual enjoyment by the act of inflicting punishment. He attended to no department of the school but the flagellative. He walked in about twelve o'clock, had all on the list placed on a form, his man-servant was called in, the lads horsed, and he, in general, found ample amusement till one. He used to make it his boast that he never allowed any of his ushers to punish. The hypocrite! the epicure! he reserved all that luxury for himself. Add to this, that he was very ignorant out of the Tutor's Assistant, and that he wrote a most abominably good hand, (that usual sign of a poor and trifle-occupied mind,) and now you have a very fair picture of Mr. Root. I have said that he was a most cruel tyrant: yet Nero himself ought not to be blackened; and I must say this for my master's humanity, that I had been two days at school before I was flogged; and then it was for the enormity of not knowing my own name. 'Rattlin,' said the pedagogue. No reply. 'Master Rattlin,' in a shriller tone. Answer there was none. 'Master Ralph Rattlin.' Many started, but 'Ralph Brandon' thought it concerned not him. But it did indeed. I believe that I had been told my new name, but I had forgotten it in my grief, and now in grief and in pain I was again taught it. When, for the first time, in reality, I tasted that acrid and bitter fruit of the tree of knowledge, old Isaac's (my soldier-school-master) mock brushings were remembered with heartfelt regret.

At that time, the road to learning was strewed neither with flowers nor palm leaves, but with the instigating birch. The schoolmaster had not yet gone abroad, but he flogged most diligently at home, and verily I partook amply of that diligence. I was flogged full, and I was flogged fasting; when I deserved it, and when I did not; I was flogged for speaking too loudly, and for not speaking loudly enough, and for holding my tongue. Moreover, one morning I rode the horse without the saddle, because my face was dirty, and the next, because I pestered the maid-servant to wash it clean. I was flogged because my shoes were dirty, and again flogged because I attempted to wipe them clean with my pocket-handkerchief. I was flogged for playing, and for staying in the schoolroom and not going out to play. The bigger boys used to beat me, and I was then flogged for fighting. It is hard to say for what I was not flogged. Things, the most contradictory, all tended to one end, and that was my own. At length, he flogged me into serious ill-health, and then he staid his hand, and I found relief on a bed of sickness. Even now, I look back to those days of persecution with horror. Those were the times of large schools, rods steeped in brine (*actual fact*), intestine insurrections, the bumping of obnoxious ushers, and the 'barring out' of tyrannical masters. A school of this description was a complete place of torment for the orphan, the unfriended, and the deserted. Lads then staid at school till they were eighteen and even twenty, and fagging flourished in all its atrocious oppression.

Let no one deem these details to be puerile. As the reader proceeds, he will find facts like these afford him a psychological study. He will see how a perverse mind was formed, or a noble one ruined : how all the evil passions were implanted, and by what means their growth was encouraged. He will trace by what causes a poetical temperament was driven almost to insanity; he has already seen how the demon of sudden anger got an unrelinquishing hold of a corner of my heart; and he will now see by whom, and in what manner, the seeds of worse vices were sown in a bosom, that was perhaps made to entertain only the noblest feelings, or soften to the most tender sentiments. This is not vanity. I know what a wreck I am. Allow me the poor consolation of contemplating what I might have been. There is piety in the thought. There is in it a silent homage to the goodness of the Creator, in acknowledging that he gave me purity and high capabilities of virtue; and there is hope also; for perhaps, at some future time, if not here, hereafter, that soul may again adore him, in all the infant purity in which he bestowed it, ere I was, in a manner, compelled into sin. I am, after years of suffering, no more than a shell, once beautiful, but now corroded and shattered, that is cast upon the sands. At times I think, that not all the former bright tints are defaced, and that if the breath of kindness be breathed into it gently, it is still able to discourse, in return, some few notes of 'most excellent music.'

This may be real vanity. But why should I appear masked before the public? I am vain. I have been assured of it by hundreds who have more vanity than myself. Verily *they* ought to know.

CHAPTER X

I grow egotistical, and being pleased with myself, give good advice—
A visit; and a strange jumble of tirades, tears, tutors, tenderness,
and a tea-kettle.

LET me now describe the child of nine years and a half old, that
was forced to undergo this terrible ordeal. We will suppose that,
by the aid of the dancing-master and the drill-sergeant, I have
been cured of my vulgar gait, and that my cockney accent has disappeared. Children of the age above mentioned, soon assimilate
their tone and conversation with those around them. I was tall for
my years, with a very light and active frame, and a countenance,
the complexion of which was of the most unstained fairness. My
hair light, glossy, and naturally, but not universally, curling. To
make it appear in ringlets all over my head, would have been the
effect of art; yet, without art it was wavy, and at the temples, forehead, and the back of the head, always in full circlets. My face presented a perfect oval, and my features were classically regular.
I had a good natural colour, the intensity of which ebbed and
flowed with every passing emotion. I was one of those dangerous
subjects whom anger always makes pale. My eyes were decidedly
blue, everything else that may be said to the contrary notwithstanding. The whole expression of my countenance was very
feminine, but not soft. It was always the seat of some sentiment or passion, and in its womanly refinement gave to me
an appearance of constitutional delicacy and effeminacy, that
I certainly did not possess. I was decidedly a very beautiful
child, and a child that seemed formed to kindle and return a
mother's love, yet the maternal caress never blessed me; but
I was abandoned to the tender mercies of a number of he-beings,
by many of whom my vivacity was checked, my spirit humbled,
and my flesh cruelly lacerated. Mothers! do you know how
few are the years of happiness allotted to the longest and most
fortunate life? Do not embitter, then, so large a portion of it
as playful infancy, by abandoning your offspring to the hireling and the stranger. If your children must away from you,
let them know that they have still a home; not merely a retreat
composed of walls and a roof, and of man-servants and maid-

servants; all these make not a home. The child's real home is in his mother's arms.

I dwell thus particularly on my school-boy life, in order, in the first place, to prepare the reader for the singular events that follow; and, in the second, (and which forms by far the most important consideration, as I trust I am believed, and if *truth* deserves credence, believed I am) to caution parents from trusting to the specious representations of any schoolmaster, to induce them to examine carefully and patiently into every detail of the establishment, or they may become a party to a series of cruelties, that may break the spirit, and, perhaps, shorten the life of their children. Unfortunately, the most promising minds are those that soonest yield to the effect of harsh discipline. The phlegmatic, the dull, and the common-place vegetate easily through this state of probation. The blight that will destroy the rose, passes ever harmlessly over the tough and earth-embracing weed.

I staid at Mr. Root's school for very nearly three years, and I shall divide that memorable period into three distinct epochs— the desponding, the devotional, and the mendacious. After I had been flogged into uncertain health, I was confined, for at least six weeks, to my room, and, when I was convalescent, it was hinted by the surgeon, in not unintelligible terms, to Mr. Root, that if I did not experience the gentlest treatment, I might lose my life; which would have been very immaterial to Mr. Root, had it not been a mathematical certainty that he would lose a good scholar at the same time. By-the-by, the meaning that a schoolmaster attaches to the words 'good scholar,' is one for whom he is paid well. Thus I was emphatically a good scholar; no doubt his very best. I was taught everything—at least his bill said so. He provided everything for me, and I staid with him during the holidays. He, therefore, ceased to confer upon me his cruel attentions; and abandoned me to a neglect hardly less cruel. The boys were strictly enjoined to leave me alone, and they obeyed. I found a solitude in the midst of society.

A loneliness came over my young spirit. I was a-weary, and I drooped like the tired bird, that alights on the ship, 'far, far at sea.' As that poor bird folds its wings, and sinks into peaceful oblivion, I could have folded my arms, and have lain down to die with pleasure. My heart exhausted itself with an intense longing for a companion to love. It wasted away all its substance in flinging out fibres to catch hold of that with which it might beat in unison. As turn the tendrils of the vine hither and thither to clasp something to adorn, and to repay support by beauty, so I wore out my young energies in a fruitless search for sympathy. I had nothing to love me, though I would have loved many, if I had dared. There were many sweet faces among my school-fellows, to which I turned with a longing look, and a tearful eye. How menial I have been to procure a notice, a glance of kindness! I had nothing to give wherewith to bribe affection but services and labour, and those were either refused, or perhaps accepted with scorn. I was the only pariah among two hundred and fifty. There was a mystery and an obloquy attached to me, and the master had, by his interdiction, completely put me without the pale of society. I now said my lessons to the ushers with indifference—if I acquitted myself ill, I was unpunished—if well, unnoticed. My spirits began to give way fast, and I was beginning to feel the pernicious patronage of the servants. They would call me off the play-ground, on which I moped, send me on some message, or employ me in some light service. All this was winked at by the master, and as for the mistress, she never let me know that it occurred to her that I was in existence. It was evident that Mr. Root had no objection to all this, for, in consideration of the money paid to him for my education, he was graciously pleased to permit me to fill the office of his kitchen-boy. But, before I became utterly degraded into the menial of the menials, a fortunate occurrence happened, that put an end to my culinary servitude. To the utter surprise of Mr. and Mrs. Root, who expected nothing of the kind, a lady came to see me. What passed between the parties, before I was ushered into the parlour appropriated to visitors, I know not; it was some time before I was brought in, as preparatory ablutions were made, and my clothes changed. When I entered, I found that it was 'the lady.' I remember that she was very superbly dressed, and I thought, too, the most beautiful apparition that I had ever beheld. The scene that took place was a little singular, and I shall relate it at full.

As I have rigidly adhered to truth, I have been compelled to state what I have to say in a form almost entirely narrative; and have not imitated those great historians, who put long speeches into the mouths of their kings and generals, very much suited to the occasions undoubtedly, and deficient only in one point—that is, accuracy. I have told only of facts and impressions, and not given speeches that it would have been impossible for me to have remembered. Yet, in this interview there was something so striking to my young imagination, that my memory preserved many sentences, and all the substance, of what took place. There was wine and cake upon the table, and the lady looked a little fluttered. Mr. Root was trying with a forty Chesterfieldean power to look amiable.[1] Mrs. Root was very fidgetty. As I appeared at the door timorously, the lady said to me without rising, but extending her delicate white hand, 'Come here to me, Ralph; do you not know me?'

I could get no farther than the middle of the room, where I stood still, and burst out into a passion of tears. Those sweet tones of tenderness, the first I had heard for nine months, thrilled like fire through my whole frame. It was a feeling so intense, that, had it not been agony, it would have been bliss.

'Good God!' said she, deeply agitated; 'my poor boy, why do you cry?'

'Because—because you are so kind,' said I, rushing forward to her extended arms; and, falling on my knees at her feet, I buried my face in her lap, and felt all happiness amidst my sobbings. She bent over me, and her tears trickled upon my neck. This did not last long. She placed me upon my feet, and drawing me to her side, kissed my cheeks, and my eyes, and my forehead. Her countenance soon became serene, and turning to my master, she said quietly, 'This, sir, is very singular.'

'Yes, ma'am, Master Rattlin *is* very singular. All clever boys are. He knows already his five declensions, and the four conjugations, active and passive. Come, Master Rattlin, decline for the lady the adjective felix—come, begin, nominative hic et hæc et hoc felix.'

'I don't know anything about it,' said I, doggedly.

'I told you he was a *singular* child,' resumed the pedagogue, with a most awkward attempt at a smile.

'The singularity to which I allude,' said the lady, 'is his finding kindness so singular.'

'Kind! bless you, my dear madam,' said they both together; 'you can't conceive how much we love the little dear.'

'It was but yesterday,' said Mrs. Root, 'that I was telling the lady of Mr. Alderman Jenkins—we have the five Jenkinses, ma'am—that Master Rattlin was the sweetest, genteelest, and beautifullest boy in the whole school.'

'It was but yesterday,' said Mr. Root, 'that I was saying to Doctor Duncan, (our respected rector, madam,) that Master Rattlin had evinced such an uncommon talent, that we might, by-and-by, expect the greatest things from him. Not yet ten months with me, madam. Already in Phædrus—the rule of three —and his French master gives the best account of him. He certainly has not begun to speak it yet, though he has made a vast progress in the French language. But it is Monsieur le Gros' system to make his pupils thoroughly master of the language, before they attempt to converse in it. And his dancing, my dear madam—O, it would do your heart good to see him dance. Such grace, such elasticity, and such happiness in his manner!'

A pause—and then they exclaimed together with a long-drawn, sentimental sigh, 'And we both love him so.'

'I am glad to hear so good an account of him,' said the lady. 'I hope, Ralph, that you love Mr. and Mrs. Root, for they seem very kind to you.'

'No, I don't.'

Mr. and Mrs. Root lifted their hands imploringly to heaven.

'Not love me!' they both exclaimed together, with a tone of heartfelt surprise and wounded sensibility, that would have gone far to have made the fortune of a sentimental actor.

'Come here, sir, directly,' said Mr. Root. 'Look me full in the face, sir. You are a singular boy, yet I *did* think you loved me. Don't be frightened, Ralph, I would not give you *pain* on any account; and you know I never did. Now tell me, my dear boy,' gradually softening from the terrible to the tender, 'tell me, my dear boy, why you fancy you do not love me. You see, madam, that I encourage sincerity—and like, at all times, the truth to be spoken out. Why don't you love me, Ralph, dear?' pinching my ear with a spiteful violence, that was meant for gracious playfulness in the eyes of the lady, and an intelligible hint for myself. I was silent.

'Come, Ralph, speak your mind freely. No one will do you any harm for it, I am sure. Why don't you love Mr. Root?' said the lady.

I was ashamed to speak of my floggings, and I looked upon his late abandonment and neglect as kindness. I knew not what to say, yet I knew I hated him most cordially. I stammered, and at last I brought out this unfortunate sentence, 'Because he has got such an ugly, nasty voice.'

Mr. and Mrs. Root burst out into a long, and, for the time, apparently uncontrollable laughter. When it had somewhat subsided, the schoolmaster exclaimed, 'There, madam, didn't I tell you he was a singular lad? Come here, you little wag, I must give you a kiss for your drollery.' And the monster hauled me to him, and when his face was close to mine, I saw a wolfish glare in his eyes, that made me fear that he was going to bite my nose off. The lady did not at all participate in the joviality, and, as it is difficult to keep up mirth entirely upon one's own resources, we were beginning to be a gloomy party. What I had unconsciously said respecting my master's voice, was wormwood to him. He had long been the butt of all his acquaintance respecting it, and what followed was the making that unbearable which was before too bitter. Many questions were put by the visitor, and the answers appeared to grow more and more unsatisfactory as they were elicited. The lady was beginning to look unhappy, when a sudden brightness came over her lovely countenance, and with the most polished and kindly tone, she asked to see Mr. Root's own children. Mr. Root looked silly, and Mrs. Root distressed. The vapid and worn-out joke that their family was so large that it boasted of the number of two hundred and fifty, fell spiritless to the ground, and disappointment, and even a slight shade of despondence, came over the lady's features.

'Where were you, Ralph, when I came?' said she; 'I waited for you long.'

'I was being washed, and putting on my second best.'

'But why washed at this time of day—and why put on your second best?'

'Because I had dirtied my hands, and my other clothes, carrying up the tea-kettle to Mr. Matthews' room.'

Mr. and Mrs. Root again held up their hands in astonishment.

'And who is Mr. Matthews?' continued the lady.

'Second Latin master, and ill a-bed in the garret.'

'From whence did you take the tea-kettle?'

'From the kitchen.'

'And who gave it you?'

'Molly, one of the maids.'

At this disclosure Mr. Root fell into the greatest of all possible rages, and, as we like the figure of speech called a climax, we must say, that Mrs. Root fell into a much greater. They would turn the hussey out of the house that instant; they would do that, they would do this, and they would do the other. At length, the lady, with calm severity, requested them to do nothing at all.

'There has been,' said she, 'some mistake here. There is nothing very wrong, or disgraceful in Ralph attending to the wants of his sick master, though he does lie in the garret. I would rather see in his disposition a sympathy for suffering encouraged. God knows, there is in this world too much of the latter, and too little of the former. Yet I certainly think that there could have been a less degrading method pointed out to him of showing attention. But we will let this pass, as I know it will never happen again. You see, Mr. and Mrs. Root, that this poor child is rather delicate in appearance; he is much grown, certainly; much more than I expected, or wished—but he seems both shy and dejected. I was in hopes that you had been yourselves blessed with a family. A mother can trust to a mother. Though you are not parents, you have known a parent's love. I have no doubt that you are fond of children,—["Very," both in a breath]—from the profession you have chosen. I am the godmother of this boy. Alas! I am afraid no nearer relation will ever appear to claim him. He has no mother, Mrs. Root, without you will be to him as one; and I conjure you, sir, to let the fatherless find in the preceptor, a father. Let him only meet for a year or two with kindness, and I will cheerfully trust to Providence for the rest. Though I detest the quackery of getting up a scene, I wish to be as impressive as I can, as, I am sorry to say, more than a year will unavoidably pass, before I can see this poor youth again. Let me, at that time, I conjure you, see him in health and cheerfulness. Will you permit me now to say farewell? as I wish to say a few words of adieu to my godson, and should I cry over him for his mother's sake, you know that a lady does not like to be seen with red eyes.'

The delicacy of this sickly attempt at pleasantry was quite lost upon the scholastic pair. They understood her literally; and Mrs. Root began, 'My eye-water——' However, leave was taken, and I was left with the lady. She took me on her lap, and a hearty hug we had together. She then rang for Molly. She spoke to the girl kindly, asked no questions of her that might lead her to betray her

employers, but, giving her half-a-guinea not to lose sight of me in
the multitude, and, to prove her gratitude, never to suffer me again
to enter the kitchen, she promised to double the gratuity when she
again saw me, if she attended to her request. The girl, evidently
affected as much by her manner as her gift,[1] curtsied and withdrew.
While she stayed at the school she complied with my godmother's
request most punctually.

CHAPTER XI

*Containeth a lecture on love from a personification of loveliness—
and showeth that superstition has its sweets as well as its horrors—
and also how to avoid the infection of the evil eye.*

WHEN we were alone, she examined me carefully under my
clothes, to ascertain if I were perfectly clean. It would have,
perhaps, been for me a happy circumstance, if Mr. Root had
flogged me this day, or even a fortnight previously. The marks
that he left were not very ephemeral. I don't know whether a flogging a month old would not equally well have served my purpose.
He certainly wrote a strong, bold hand, in red ink, not easily
obliterated. However, as he had not noticed me since my illness,
I had no marks to show.

When she had re-adjusted my dress, she hugged me to her side,
and we looked, for a long while, in each other's eyes in silence.

'Ralph,' said she, at length, forgetting that the fault was mutual,
'do you know that it is very rude to look so hard into people's faces;
why do you do it, my boy?'

'Because you are so very, very, very pretty, and your voice is so
soft; and—because I do love you so.'

'But you must not love me too much, my sweet child: because
I can't be with you to return your love.'

'O dear, I'm so sorry; because—because—if you don't love me,
nobody will. Master don't love me nor the ushers—nor the boys;
and they keep calling me the ——'

'Hush, Ralph! hush, my poor boy,' said she, colouring to her
very forehead. 'Never tell me what they call you. Little boys who
call names are wicked boys, and very false boys too. Hear me,

E

Ralph! You are nearly ten years old. You must be a man, and not love any one too much—not even me—for it makes people very unhappy to love too much. Do you understand me, Ralph? You must be kind to all, and all will be kind to you: but it is best not to love anything violently—excepting, Ralph, Him who will love you when all hate you—who will care for you when all desert you—your God!'

'I don't know too much about that,' was my answer. 'Mr. Root tells us once every week to trust in God, and that God will protect the innocent, and all that: and then he flogs me for nothing at all, though I trust all I can; and I'm sure that I'm innocent.'

My good godmother was a little shocked at this, and endeavoured to convince me that such expressions were impious, by assuring me that everything was suffered for the best, and that, if Mr. Root flogged me unjustly and wickedly, I should be rewarded, and my master punished for it hereafter; which assurance did not much mend my moral feelings, as I silently resolved to put myself in the way of a few extra unjust chastisements, in order that my master might receive the full benefit of them in a future state.

Moral duties should be inculcated in the earliest youth; but the mysteries of religion should be left to a riper age. After many endearments, and much good advice, that I thought most beautiful, from the tenderness of tone in which it was given, I requested the lady, with all my powers of entreaty, and amidst a shower of kisses, to take me home to my mother.

'Alas! my dear boy,' was the reply, 'Mrs. Brandon is not your mother.'

'Well, I couldn't believe that before:—never mind—I love her just as well. But who is my mother? If you were not so pretty, and so fine, I would ask you to be my mother; all the other boys have got a mother, and a father too.'

The lady caught me to her bosom, and kissing me amidst her tears said, 'Ralph, I will be your mother, though you must only look upon me as your godmamma.'

'Oh, I'm so glad of that! and what shall I call you?'

'Mamma, my dear child.'

'Well, mamma, won't you take me home? I don't mean now, but at the holidays, when all the others go to their mammas? I'll be so good. Won't you, mamma?'

'Come here, Ralph. I was wrong. You must not call me mamma,

I can't bear it. I was never a mother to you, my poor boy. I cannot have you home. By-and-by, perhaps.[1] Do not think about me too much, and do not think that you are not loved. Oh! you are loved, very much indeed; but now you must make your schoolfellows love you. I have told Mr. Root to allow you sixpence a-week, and there are eight shillings for you, and a box of playthings in the hall, and a large cake in the box; lend the playthings and share the cake. Now, my dear boy, I must leave you. Do not think that I am your mother, but your very good friend. Now, may God bless you, and watch over you. Keep up your spirits, and remember that you are cared for, and loved—O, how fondly loved!'

With a fervent blessing, and an equally fervent embrace, she parted from me; and, when I looked round and found that she had gone from the room, I actually experienced the sensation as if the light of the sun had been suddenly withdrawn, and that I walked forth in twilight. Exceeding beautiful was that tall, fair lady, and she must have been a spirit of light in the house where she moved, even a ray of gladness, and an incarnate blessing must she have been in the loveliness of her presence.

When I went up melancholy to my bed, and crept sorrowfully under the clothes, I felt a protection round me in that haunted chamber, in the very fact of having again seen her. This house, that had been now converted into a large school, had formerly been one of the suburban palaces of Queen Elizabeth;[1] it was very spacious and rambling; some of the rooms had been modernized, and some remained as they had been for centuries. The room in which I slept was one of the smallest, and contained only two beds, one of which was occupied by the housekeeper, a very respectable old lady, and the other by myself. Sometimes I had a bedfellow, and sometimes not. This room had probably been a vestibule, or the antichamber to some larger apartment, and it now formed an abutment to the edifice, all on one side of it being ancient, and the other modern. It was lighted by one narrow, high, gothic window, the panes of which were very small, lozenged, and many of them still stained. The roof was groined and concave, and still gay with tarnished gold. The mouldings and traceries sprang up from the four corners, and all terminated in the centre, in which grinned a Medusa's head, with her circling snakes, in high preservation, and of great and ghastly beauty. There were other grotesque visages, sprinkled here and there over that elaborate roof; but look at that Medusa from what point you might, the painted wooden eyes were cast with a stolid sternness upon you. When I had a bed-fellow it was always some cast-away like myself—some poor wretch who could not go home and complain that he was put to sleep in 'the haunted chamber.' The boys told strange tales of that room, and they all believed that the floor was stained with blood. I often examined it, both by day and by candle-light; it was very old, and of oak, dark, and much discoloured. But even my excited fancy could discover nothing like blood-spots upon it. After all, when I was alone in that bed-chamber, for the housekeeper seldom entered before midnight, and the flickering and feeble oil lamp, that always burned upon her table, threw its uncertain rays upwards, and made the central face quiver as it were into life, I would shrink, horror-stricken, under the clothes, and silently pray for the morning. It was certainly a fearful room for a visionary child like myself, with whom the existence of ghosts made an article of faith, and who had been once before frightened, even unto the death, by supernatural terrors.

But of all this I never complained. I have not merit enough to boast that I am proud, for pride has always something ennobling about it; but I was vain, and vanity enabled me to put on the appearance of courage. When questioned by the few schoolfellows who would speak to me, I acknowledged no ghosts, and would own to no fear. All this, in the sequel, was remembered to my honour. Besides, I had found a singular antidote against the look of the evil eye in the ceiling. What I am going to relate may be startling, and for a child ten years old, appear incredible; but it is the bare, unembellished truth. The moment that I shall feel tempted to draw, in these memoirs, on my invention instead of my memory, that moment, distrusting myself, I shall lay down my pen. I feel conscious that I could relate something infinitely more striking and amusing, had I recourse to fiction: but the moral force of the actual and stern verity would be lost to my readers.

This was my antidote alluded to. In the church where we went, there was a strongly painted altar-piece.[1] The Virgin Mother bent, with ineffable sweetness, over the sleeping Jesus. The pew in which I sat was distant enough to give the full force of illusion to the power of the artist, and the glory round the Madonna much assisted my imagination. I certainly attended to that face, and to that beneficent attitude, more than to the service. When the terrors of my desolate situation used to begin to creep over me in my lonely bed, I could, without much effort of imagination, bring that sweet motherly face before me, and view it visibly in the gloom of the room, and thus defy the dead glance of the visage above me. I used to whisper to myself these words—'Lady with the glory, come and sit by me.' And I could then close my eyes, and fancy, nay almost feel assured of her presence, and sleep in peace.

But in the night that I had seen my godmother, when I crept under my clothes disconsolately, I no longer whispered for the lady with the glory; it was for my sweet mamma. And she, too, came and blessed my gentle slumbers. Surely that beautiful creature must have been my mother, for long did she come and play the seraph's part over her child, and watched by his pillow, till he sank in the repose of innocence.

Lately, at the age of forty, I visited that church. I looked earnestly at the altar-piece. I was astonished, hurt, disgusted. It was a coarse daub. The freshness of the painting had been long changed by the dark tarnish of years, and the blighting of a damp atmosphere. There were some remains of beauty in the expression, and elegance in the attitude; but, as a piece of art, it was but a second-rate performance. Age dispels many illusions, and suffers for it. Truly, youth and enthusiasm are the best painters.

CHAPTER XII

Ralph lectureth on divinity and little boys' nether garments— Despondeth exceedingly—and being the weakest goeth to the wall, and there findeth consolation—An old friend with an old face, and excellent provent.

THE next morning, I arose the possessor of eight shillings, a box of playthings, a plum-cake, and a heavy heart. It is most true, that which Wordsworth hath said or sung,[1] the 'Boy's the *father* of the man.' When I mingled with my schoolmates, and the unexpected possession of my various wealth had transpired, I found many of them very kind and *fatherly* indeed, for they borrowed my money, ate my cake, broke my playthings, and my heart they left just in the same state as it was before.

But I will no longer dwell upon the portraiture of that saddest of all created things, the despised of many. I was taught the hard lesson of looking upon cruelty as my daily bread, tears as my daily drink, and scorn as my natural portion. Had not my heart hardened, it must have broken. But, before I leave what I call the desponding epoch of my schoolboy-days, I must not omit to mention a species of impious barbarity, that had well nigh alienated my heart for ever from religion, and which made me, for the time, detest the very name of church. Christianity is most eminently a religion of kindness; and, through the paths of holy love only, should the young heart be conducted to the throne of grace, for we have it from the highest authority, that the worship of little children is an acceptable offering, and may well mingle with the sweetest symphonies that ascend from the lips of seraphs to the footstool of the Everlasting. Our God is not a God of terrors, and when he is so represented, or is made so by any flint-hearted pedagogue to the infant pupil, that man has to answer for the almost unpardonable sin of perilling a soul. Let parents and guardians look to it. Let them mark well the unwilling files that are paraded by boarding-school keepers, into the adjacent church or chapel, bringing a mercenary puff up to the very horns of the altar, and let them then inquire how many are flogged, or beaten, or otherwise evil-entreated, because they have flagged in an attention impossible in the days of childhood, and have not remembered a text perhaps indistinctly or inaudibly given:—let those parents and guardians, I say, inquire, and if but one poor youth has so suffered, let them be fully assured, that that master, whatever may be his diligence, whatever may be his attainments, however high his worldly character may stand, is not fit to be the modeller of the youthful mind, and only wants the opportunity to betray that bigotry which would gladly burn his dissenting neighbour at the stake, or lash a faith, with exquisite tortures, into the children of those whom, in his saintly pride, he may call heretical.

At church we occupied, at least, one third of the whole of one side of the gallery. Two hundred and fifty boys and young men, with their attending masters and ushers, could not but fill a large space, and of course, would form no unimportant feature in the audience. Mr. Root, and the little boys, were always placed in the lower and front seats. There we sat, poor dear little puppets, with our eyes strained on the prayer-books, always in the wrong places, during the offertory, and, after the sermon had begun, repeating the text over and over again, whilst the preaching continued, lest we should forget it; whilst all this time the bigger boys in the rear were studying novels, or playing at odd-and-even for nuts, marbles, or halfpence. I well know that the mathematical master used, invariably, to solve his hard problems on fly-leaves in his prayer-book during the service, for I have repeatedly seen there his laborious calculations in minutely small figures; and he never opened his prayer-book but at church—as perhaps he thought, with the old woman of Smollett, that it was a species of impiety to study such works anywhere else. Whilst all this was going on in the back rows, Mr. Root, in the full-blown glory of his Sunday paraphernalia, and well powdered, attended exclusively to the holiness and devout comportment of his little chapter of innocents. Tablet in hand, every wandering look was noted down; and, alas! the consequences to me were dreadfully painful.

The absolution absolved me not. The 'Te Deum laudamus' was to me more a source of tears than of praise,—and the 'O be joyful in the Lord' has repeatedly made me intensely sorrowful in the school-room. In all honesty, I don't think that, for a whole half-year, I once escaped my Sunday flogging. It came as regularly as the baked rice-puddings. I began to look upon the thing as a matter of course; and, if any person should doubt the credibility of this, or any other account of these my school-boy days, happily there are several now living who can vouch for its veracity, and if I am dared to the proof by any one, by whose conviction I should feel honoured, that proof most certainly will I give.

I have stated all this, from what I believe to be a true reverence for worship, to make the offices of religion a balm and a blessing, to prove that there is a cherishing warmth in the glory of light that surrounds the throne of Exhaustless Benevolence, and that the Deity cannot be worthily called upon, by young hearts stricken by degrading fears, and fainting under a Moloch-inspired dread. Notwithstanding my eccentric life, I have ever been the ardent, the unpretending, though the unworthy adorer of the Great Being, whose highest attribute is the 'Good.' I have had reason to be so.

The man who has acknowledged his Creator amidst his most stupendous works, who has recognised his voice in the ocean-storm, who has confessed his providence amidst the slaughter of battle, and witnessed the awful universality of that adoration that is wafted to Him, from all nations, under all forms, from the simple smiting of the breast of the penitent solitary one, to the sublime pealings of the choral hymn, buoyed upon the resounding notes of the thunder-tongued organ in the high and dim cathedral,—the man, who has witnessed and acutely felt all this, and has no feelings of piety, or deference to religion, must be endued with a heart hardened beyond the flintiness, as the Scriptures beautifully express it, 'of the nether millstone.'[1]

But my *forte* is not the serious. I am intent, and quiet, and thoughtful, only under the influence of great enjoyment. When I have the most cause to deem myself blessed, or to call myself triumphant, it is then that I am stricken with a feeling of undesert, that I am grave with humility, or sad with the thought of human instability. But on the eve of battle, on the yard-arm in the tempest, or amidst the dying in the pest-house, say, O ye companions of my youth! whose jest was the most constant, whose laugh the loudest? Yet the one feeling was not real despondence, nor the other real courage. In the first place, it is no more than the soul looking beyond this world for the real, in the second, she is trifling in this world with the ideal. However, as in these pages I intend to attempt to be tolerably gay, it may be fairly presumed that I am very considerably unhappy, and dull, perhaps, as the perusal of these memoirs may make my readers.

As such great pains were *taken*, at least by me, in my religious education, it is not to be wondered at that I should not feel at all sedentary on the Sunday afternoons after church-time. In fact, I affected any position rather than the sitting one. But all the Sundays were not joyless to me. One, in particular, though the former part of it had been passed in sickening fear, and the middle in torturing pain, its termination was marked with a heartfelt joyousness, the cause of which I must record as a tribute of gratitude due to one of the 'not unwashed,' but the muddy-minded multitude.

I was stealing along mournfully under the play-ground wall, with no hasty or striding step, not particularly wishing any rough or close contact of certain parts of my dress with my person, my passing schoolmates looking upon me in the manner that Shakspeare so beautifully describes the untouched deer regard the stricken hart.[2] My soul was very heavy, and full of dark wonder. The sun was setting, and, to all living, it is either a time of solemn

peace, or of instinctive melancholy when looked upon by the
solitary one. Of a sudden I was roused from my gloom by the well
known, yet long-missed shout of, 'Ralph! Ralph!' and looking up,
I discovered the hard-featured, grinning physiognomy of Joe
Brandon, actually beaming with pleasure, on the top of the wall.
How glad he was! How glad I was! He had found me! Instead of
seeking the Lord in his various conventicles on the Sunday, he had
employed that day, invariably, after I had been taken from his
house, in reconnoitering the different boarding-schools in the
vicinity, and at some distance from the metropolis. To this, no
doubt, he was greatly instigated by the affection of my nurse, but
I give his own heart the credit of its being a labour of love. The
wall being too high to permit us to shake hands, at my earnest
entreaty, he went round to the front; but after having made known
his desire—literally, 'a pampered menial drove him from the
door.'[1] Well, the wall, if not open to him, was still before and
above him, and he again mounted it. Our words were few, as the
boys began to cluster around me. He let drop to me fourpence
halfpenny, folded in a piece of brown paper, and disappeared. Oh
how I prize that pilgrim visit! Forget it, I never can! That meeting was to me a one bright light on my dark and dreary path. It
enabled me to go forward; there was not much gloom between me
and happier days—perhaps the light of joy that that occurrence
shed, enabled me to pass over the trial. It might have been, that,
at that period, I could have borne no more, and should have sunk
under my accumulated persecutions. I will not say that so it was,
for there is an elasticity in early youth that recovers itself against
much—yet I was at that time heavy indeed with exceeding hope-
lessness. All I can say to the sneerer is, I wish, that at the next
conclave of personages who may be assembled to discuss the
destinies of nations, there may be as much of the milk of human
kindness and right feelings among them, as there was between
me and the labouring sawyer, Joe Brandon, the one being at the
top, and the other at the bottom of the wall.

The next Sunday, Brandon was again on the wall with a prodigious plum-cake. A regular cut-and-come-again affair: it fell to
the ground with a heaviness of sound that beat the falling of
Corporal Trim's hat all to ribbons.[2] To be sure, the Corporal's fell
as if there had been a quantity of 'clay kneaded in the crown of it,'
whilst mine was kneaded with excellent dough. The Sunday after

there was the same appearance varied with gingerbread, and then —for years, I neither saw, nor heard of him. Poor Joseph was threatened with the constable, and was put to no more expense for cakes for his foster-son.

CHAPTER XIII

Pray remember the fifth of November—Rumours of wars— —preceded by scholastic elocution, and succeeded by a cold dinner, darkness, and determination.

I SHALL now draw the dolorous recital of what I have termed my epoch of despondency to a close. The fifth of November was approaching; I had been at school nearly two years, and had learned little but the hard lesson 'to bear,' and that I had well studied. I had, as yet, made no friends. Boys are very tyrannical and very generous, by fits. They will bully and oppress the outcast of a school, because it is the fashion to bully and oppress him— but they will equally magnify their hero, and are sensitively alive to admiration of feats of daring and wild exploit. With them, bravery is the first virtue, generosity the second. They crouch under the strong for protection, and they court the lavish from self-interest. In all this they differ from men in nothing but that they act more undisguisedly. Well, the fifth of November was fast approaching, in which I was to commence the enthusiastic epoch of my schoolboy existence. I was now twelve years of age. Almost insensible to bodily pain by frequent magisterial and social thrashings, tall, strong of my age, reckless, and fearless. The scene of my first exploit was to be amidst the excitement of a 'barring out,' but of such a 'barring out,' that the memory of it remains in the vicinity in which it took place to this day.

I have before said that the school contained never less than two hundred and fifty pupils—sometimes it amounted to nearly three hundred. At the time of which I am about to speak, it was very full, containing, among others, many young men. The times are no more when persons of nineteen and twenty suffered themselves to be horsed, and took their one and two dozens with edification and humility. At this age, we now cultivate moustaches, talk of our

Joe Mantons,[1] send a friend to demand an explanation, and all that sort of thing. Oh! times are much improved! However, at that period, the birch was no visionary terror. Infliction or expulsion were the alternatives! and, as the form of government was a despotism—like all despotisms to my thinking, a most odious one—it was subject, at intervals, to great convulsions. I am going to describe the greatest under the reign of Root the First.

Mr. Root was capricious. Sometimes he wore his own handsome head well powdered; at others curled without powder; at others straight, without powder or curls. He was churchwarden; and then, when his head was full of his office, it was also full of flour, and full of ideas of his own consequence and infallibility. On a concert night, and in the ball-room, it was curled, and then it was full of amatory conquests—and, as he was captain in the —— cavalry volunteers, on field days his hair was straight and lank— martial ardour gave him no time to attend to the fripperies of the coxcomb. These are but small particulars, but such are very important in the character of a great man. With his hair curled, he was jocular, even playful—with it lank, he was a great disciplinarian—had military subordination strong in respect, and the birch gyrated freely. But when he was full blown in powder, he was unbearable. There was then combined all the severity of the soldier and the dogmatism of the pedagogue, with the self-sufficiency and domineering nature of the coxcomb and churchwarden.

On the memorable fifth of November, Mr. Root appeared in the school-room, with his hair elaborately powdered.

The little boys trembled. Lads by fifteens and twenties wanted to go out under various pretences. The big boys looked very serious, and very resolved. It was twelve o'clock—and some thirty or forty —myself always included—were duly flogged, it being 'his custom at the hour of noon.'[2] When the periodical operation was over, at which there was much spargefication of powder from his whitened head, he commanded silence. Even the flagellated boys contrived to hush up their sobs, the shuffling of feet ceased, those who had colds refrained from blowing their noses; and, after one boy was flogged for coughing, he thus delivered himself:

'Young gentlemen, it has been customary—customary it has been, I say, for you to have permission to make a bonfire in the lower field, and display your fireworks, on this anniversary of the fifth of November. Little boys, take your dictionaries, and look out for the word "anniversary."'

A bustle for the books, whilst Mr. Root plumes himself, and struts up and down. Two boys fight for the same dictionary; one of them gets a plunge on the nose, which makes him cry out—he is immediately horsed and flogged for speaking; and, rod in hand, Mr. Root continues.

'Young gentlemen, you know my method—my method is well known to you, I say,—to join amusement with instruction. Now, young gentlemen, the great conflagration—tenth, ninth, and eighth forms, look out the word "conflagration"—the great conflagration, I say, made by this pyrotechnic display—seventh, sixth, and fifth forms, turn up the word "pyrotechnic." Mr. Reynolds, (the head classical master) you will particularly oblige me by not taking snuff in that violent way whilst I am speaking, the sniffling is abominable.'

'Turn up the word "sniffling,"' cries a voice from the lower end of the school. A great confusion—the culprit remains undiscovered, and some forty, at two suspected desks, are fined three-halfpence a-piece. Mr. Root continues, with a good deal of indignation: 'I sha'n't allow the bonfire no more—no, not at all; nor the fireworks neither—no, nothing of no kind of the sort.' All this in his natural voice: then swelling in dignity and in diction, 'but, for the accumulated pile of combustibles, I say—for the combustible pile that you have accumulated, that you may not be deprived of the merit of doing a good action, the materials of which it is composed, that is to say, the logs of wood, and the bavins of furze, with the pole and tar-barrel, shall be sold, and the money put in the poor-box next Sunday, which I, as one of the churchwardens, shall hold at the church-porch; for a charity sermon will on that day be preached by the Reverend Father in God, the Lord Bishop of Bristol. It is our duty, as Christians, to give eleemosynary aid to the poor;—let all classes but the first and second, look out the word "eleemosynary." I say to the poor, eleemosynary aid should be given. You will also give up all the fireworks that you may have in your play-boxes, for the same laudable purpose. The servant will go round and collect them after dinner. I say, by the servants after dinner they shall all be collected. Moreover, young gentlemen, I have to tell you, that the churchwardens, and the authorities in the town, are determined to put down Guy Faux, and he shall be put down accordingly. So now, young gentlemen, you'd better take your amusements before dinner, for you will have no holiday in the afternoon, and I shall not suffer any one to go out after tea, for fear of mischief.' Having thus spoken, he dismissed the school, and strode forth majestically.

O reader! can you conceive the dismay, the indignation, and the rage that the Court of Aldermen would display, if, when sitting down hungrily to a civic feast, they were informed that all the eatables and potatories were carried off by a party headed by Mr. Scales?[1] Can you conceive the fury that would burn in the countenances of a whole family of lordly sinecurists, at being informed upon official authority, that henceforth their salaries would be equal to their services? No, all this you cannot conceive; nor turtle-desiring alderman, nor cate-fed sinecurist, could, under these their supposed tribulations, have approached in fury and hate, the meekest-spirited boys of Mr. Root's school, when they became fully aware of the extent of the tyrannous robbery about to be perpetrated. Had they not been led on by hope? Had they not trustingly eschewed banbury-cakes—sidled by longingly the pastry-cook's—and piously withstood the temptation of hard-bake, in order that they might save up their pocket-money for this one grand occasion? and even after this, their hopes and their exertions to end in smoke? Would that it were even that; but it was decided that there should be neither fire nor smoke. Infatuated pedagogue! Unhappy decision!

The boys did not make use of the permission to go out to play. They gathered together unanimously, in earnest knots—rebellion stalked on tip-toe from party to party—the little boys looked big, and the big boys looked bigger—and the young men looked magnificent. The half-boarders whispered their fears to the ushers, the ushers spoke under their breaths to the under-masters, the under-masters had cautious conversation with the head Latin, French, and mathematical tutors, and these poured their misgiving into the ears of the awful *Dominus* himself; but he only shook his powdered head in derision and disdain.

On that cold, foggy, fifth of November, we all sat down to a dinner as cold as the day, and with looks as dark as the atmosphere. Amidst the clatter of knives and forks, the rumour already ran from table to table, that a horse and cart was just going to remove the enormous pile of combustibles collected for the bonfire. We had good spirits amongst us. There was an air of calm defiance on a great many. The reason was soon explained, for before we rose from our repast, huge volumes of red flame rose from the field—the pile had been fired in twenty places at once, and, at this sight, a simultaneous and irrepressible shout shook the walls of the school-room. The maid-servants who were attending the table, shrieking, each in her peculiar musical note, hurried out in confusion and fear; and there was a rush towards the door by the scholars, and some few got down stairs. However, the masters soon closed the door, and those who had escaped were brought back. The shutters of the windows that looked out upon the fire were closed, and thus, in the middle of the day, we were reduced to a state almost of twilight.

Every moment expecting actual collision with their pupils, the masters and ushers, about sixteen in number, congregated at the lower end of the room, near the door, for the double purpose of supporting each other, and of making a timely escape. The half-suppressed hub-bub among three hundred boys, confined in partial darkness, grew stronger each moment; it was like the rumbling beneath the earth, that precedes the earthquake. No one spoke as yet louder than the other—the master-voice had not yet risen. That dulled noise seemed like a far-off humming, and had it not been so intense, and so very human, it might have been compared to the wrath of a myriad of bees confined in the darkness of their hives, with their queen lying dead amongst them.

CHAPTER XIV

*Hard words the precursors of hard blows—A turn-up to be
apprehended, but not merely of polysyllables—Ralph commences
raving—Root resisting—The latter gets the whip-hand of us.*

WHILST this commotion was going on in the school-room, Mr. Root was active in the field, endeavouring, with the aid of the men-servants, to pluck as much fuel from the burning pile as possible. The attempt was nearly vain. He singed his clothes, and burnt his hands, lost his hat in the excitement and turmoil, and sadly discomposed his powdered ringlets. Advices were brought to him (we must now use the phrase military) of the demonstration made by the young gentlemen in the school-room. He hurried with the pitchfork, in his hand, which he had been using, and appeared at the entrance of his pandemonium, almost, considering his demoniac look, in character. He made a speech, enforced by thumping the handle of the fork against the floor, which speech, though but little attended to, was marked by one singularity. He did not tell the lads to turn up any of his hard words. However, he hoped that the young gentlemen had yet sense of propriety enough left, to permit the servants to clear the tables of the plates, knives, forks, and other dinner appurtenances. This was acceded to by shouts of 'Let them in—let them in.' The girls and the two school servants came in, one of the latter being the obnoxious hoister, and they were permitted to perform their office in a dead silence. It speaks well for our sense of honour, and respect for the implied conditions of the treaty, when it is remembered that this abhorred Tom, the living instrument of our tortures, and on whose back we had most of us so often writhed, was permitted to go into the darkest corners of the room unmolested, and even uninsulted. When the tables were cleared, then rung out exultingly the shout of 'Bar him out—bar him out!'

'I never yet,' roared out Mr. Root, 'was barred out of my own premises, and I never will be!' He was determined to resist manfully, and if he fell, to fall like Cæsar, in the capitol, decorously: so as togæ are not worn in our unclassical days he retired to prepare himself for the contention, by getting his head newly powdered, telling his assistants to keep the position that they still held, at all hazards, near the door.

Before I narrate the ensuing struggle—a struggle that will be ever remembered in the town in which it took place, and which will serve any one that was engaged in it, as long as he lives, to talk of with honest enthusiasm, even if he has been happy enough to have been engaged in real warfare; it is necessary to describe exactly the battle-field. The school was a parallelogram, bowed at one end, and about the dimensions of a moderately-sized chapel. It was very lofty, and, at the bowed end, which looked into the fields, there were three large windows built very high, and arched after the ecclesiastical fashion. One of the sides had windows similar to those at the end. The school-room was entered from the house by a lobby, up into which lobby terminated a wide staircase, from the play-ground. The school-room was therefore entered from the lobby by only one large folding door. But over this end there was a capacious orchestra, supported by six columns, which orchestra contained a very superb organ. The orchestra might also be entered from the house, but from a floor and a lobby above that which opened into the school-room. Consequently, at the door end of the school-room, there was a space formed of about twelve or fourteen feet, with a ceiling much lower than the rest of the building, and which space was bounded by the six pillars that supported the gallery above. This low space was occupied by the masters and assistants—certainly a strong position, as it commanded the only outlet. The whole edifice was built upon rows of stone columns, that permitted the boys a sheltered play-ground beneath the school-room in inclement or rainy weather. The windows being high from the floor within doors, and very high indeed from the ground without, they were but sorry and dangerous means of communication, through which, either to make an escape, or bring in succours or munitions, should the siege be turned to a blockade. It was, altogether, a vast, and when properly fitted up, a superb apartment, and was used for the monthly concerts and the occasional balls.

Time elapsed. It seemed that we were the party barred in, instead of the master being the party barred out. The mass of rebellion was as considerable as any radical could have wished; and, as yet, as disorganized as any Tory commander-in-chief of the forces could have desired. However Mr. Root did not appear, and it having become completely dark, the boys themselves lighted the various lamps. About six or seven o'clock there was a stir among the learned guard at the door, when at length Mr. Reynolds, the head classical master, having rapped the silver top of his great horn snuff-box, in a speech, mingled, very appropriately, with Latin and Greek quotations, wished to know what it was precisely that the young gentlemen desired, and he was answered by fifty voices at once, 'Leave to go into the fields, and let off the fireworks.'

After a pause, a message was brought that this could not be granted; but, upon the rest of the school going quietly to bed, permission would be given to all the young gentlemen above fifteen years of age, to go down the town until eleven o'clock. The proposal was refused with outcries of indignation. We now had many leaders, and the shouts of 'Force the door!' became really dreadful. Gradually the lesser boys gave back, and the young men formed a dense front line, facing the sixteen masters, whose position was fortified by the pillars supporting the orchestra, and whose rear was strengthened by the servants of the household. As yet, the scholars stood with nothing offensive in their hands, and with their arms folded, in desperate quietude. At last, there was a voice a good way in the *rear*, which accounts for the bravery of the owner, that shouted, 'Why don't you rally, and force the door?' Here Monsieur Moineau, a French emigré, and our Gallic tutor, cried out lustily, 'You shall force that door, never—*jamais*, *jamais* —my pretty *garçons*, *mes chers pupils*, be good, be quiet—go you couch yourself—*les feux d'artifice!* bah! they worth noding at all— you go to bed. Ah, ah, *demain*—all have *congé*—one, two, half holiday—but you force this door—*par ma fois*, *loyauté*—*jamais*— you go out, one, two, three, *tout*—go over dis *corps*, of Antoine Auguste Moineau.'

We gave the brave fellow a hearty cheer for his loyalty; and, I have no doubt, had he been allowed to remain, he would have been trampled to death on his post. He had lost his rank, his fortune, everything but his self-respect, in the quarrel of his king, who had just fallen on the scaffold: he had a great respect for constituted authority, and was sadly grieved at being obliged to honour heroism in spite of himself, when arrayed against it.

Let us pause over these proceedings, and return to myself. As the rebellion increased, I seemed to be receiving the elements of a new life. My limbs trembled, but it was with a fierce joy. I ran hither and thither exultingly—I pushed aside boys three or four years older than myself—I gnashed my teeth, I stamped, I clenched my hands,—I wished to harangue, but I could not find utterance, for the very excess of thoughts. At that moment I would not be put down; I grinned defiance in the face of my late scorners; I was drunk with the exciting draught of contention. The timid gave me their fireworks, the brave applauded my resolution, and, as I went from one party to another, exhorting more by gesture than by speech, I was at length rewarded, by hearing the approving shout of 'Go it, Ralph Rattlin!'

I am not fearful of dwelling too much upon the affair. It must be interesting to those amiabilities called the 'rising generation,' the more especially as a 'barring out'[1] is now become matter of history. Alas! we shall never go back to the good old times in that

F

respect, notwithstanding we are again snugly grumbling under a Whig government. Let us place at least one 'barring out' upon record, in order to let the radicals see, and seeing hope, when they find how nearly extremes meet, what a slight step there is from absolute despotism to absolute disorganization.

Things were in this state, the boys encouraging each other, when, to our astonishment, Mr. Root, newly-powdered, and attended by two friends, his neighbours, made his appearance in the orchestra, and incontinently began a speech. I was then too excited to attend to it; indeed it was scarcely heard for revilings and shoutings. However, I could contain myself no longer, and I, even I, though far from being in the first rank, shouted forth, 'Let us out, or we will set fire to the school-room, and, if we are burnt, you'll be hung for murder.' Yes, I said those words—I, who actually now start at my own shadow—I, who when I see a stalwart, whiskered and moustached-fellow coming forward to meet me, modestly pop over on the other side—I, who was in a fit of the trembles the whole year of the comet![1]

'God bless me,' said Mr. Root, 'it is that vagabond Rattlin! I flogged the little incorrigible but eight hours ago, and now he talks about burning my house down. There's gratitude for you! But I'll put a stop to this at once—young gentlemen, I'll put a stop to this at once! I'm coming down among you to seize the ring-leaders, and that good-for-nothing Rattlin. Ah! the monitors, and the heads of all the classes, shall be flogged; the rest shall be forgiven, if they will go quietly to bed, and give up all their fireworks.' Having so said, he descended from above with his friends, and in about a quarter of an hour afterwards, armed with a tremendous whip, he appeared among his satellites below.

CHAPTER XV

Much excellent, and consequently useless, diplomacy displayed—
A truce, and many heads broken—the battle rages; and, at length
the pueriles achieve the victory.

THE reader must not suppose that, while masters and scholars
were ranged against each other as antagonists, they were quiet as
statues. There was much said on both sides, reasonings, entreaties,
expostulations, and even jocularity passed between the adverse,
but yet quiescent ranks. In this wordy warfare the boys had the
best of it, and I'm sure the ushers had no stomach for the fray—
if they fought, they must fight, in some measure, with their hands
tied; for their own judgment told them that they could not be
justified in inflicting upon their opponents any desperate wounds.
In fact, considering all the circumstances, though they asseverated
that the boys were terribly in the wrong, they could not say that
Mr. Root was conspicuously in the right.

When Mr. Root got among his myrmidons, he resolutely cried,
'Gentlemen assistants, advance, and seize Master Atkinson,
Master Brewster, Master Davenant, and especially Master Rattlin;'
the said Master Rattlin having very officiously wriggled himself
into the first rank. Such is the sanctity of established authority,
that we actually gave back, with serried files however, as our
opponents advanced. All had now been lost, even our honour, had
it not been for the gallant conduct of young Henry St. Albans,
a natural son of the Duke of Y——, who was destined for the army,
and, at that time, studying fortification, and to some purpose—
for, immediately behind our front ranks, and while Mr. Root was
haranguing and advancing, St. Albans had ranged the desks quite
across the room, in two tiers, one above the other; the upper tier
with their legs in the air, no bad substitute for *chevaux-de-frize*.
In fact, this manœuvre was an anticipation of the barricades of
Paris. When the boys came to the obstacle, they made no difficulty
of creeping under or jumping over it—but for the magisterial Mr.
Root, fully powdered; or the classical master, full of Greek; or
the mathematical master, conscious of much algebra, to creep
under these desks, would have been *infra dig.*, and for them to
have leapt over was impossible. The younger assistants might

certainly have performed the feat, but they would have been but scurvily treated for their trouble, on the wrong side of the barricade.

When two antagonist bodies cannot fight, it is no bad pastime to parley. St. Albans was simultaneously and unanimously voted leader, though we had many older than he, for he was but eighteen. A glorious youth was that St. Albans! Accomplished, generous, brave, handsome, as are all his race, and of the most bland and sunny manners that ever won woman's love or softened man's asperity. He died young—where? Where should he have died, since this world was deemed by Providence not deserving of him, but amidst the enemies of his country, her banners waving victoriously above, and her enemies flying before, his bleeding body?

Henry now stood forward as our leader and spokesman: eloquently did he descant upon all our grievances, not forgetting mouldy bread, caggy mutton, and hebdomadal meat pies. He represented to Mr. Root the little honour that he would gain in the contest, and the certain loss—the damage to his property, and to his reputation—the loss of scholars, and of profit; and he begged him to remember that every play-box in the school-room was filled with fireworks, and that they were all determined,—and sorry he was in this case to be obliged to uphold such a determination,—they were one and all resolved, if permission were not given to let off the fireworks out of doors, they would in—the consequences be on Mr. Root's head. His speech was concluded amidst continued 'bravos!' and shouts of 'Now, now!'

Old R——lds, our classic, quietly stood by, and, taking snuff by handfuls, requested, nay entreated Mr. Root to pass it all off as a joke, and let the boys, with due restrictions, have their will. Mr. Root, with a queer attempt at looking pleasant, then said, 'He began to enter into the spirit of the thing—it was well got up—there could be nothing really disrespectful meant, since Mr. Henry St. Albans was a party to it, (be it known that Henry was an especial favourite,) and that he was inclined to humour them, and look upon the school in the light of a fortress about to capitulate. He therefore would receive a flag of truce, and listen to proposals.'

The boys began to be delighted. The following conditions were drawn up, and a lad, with a white handkerchief tied to a sky-rocket stick, was hoisted over the bench into the besieging quarters. The paper, after reciting (as is usual with all rebels in arms against their lawful sovereign) their unshaken loyalty, firm obedience, and unqualified devotion, went on thus—but we shall, to save time, put to each proposition the answer returned:—

1. The young gentlemen shall be permitted, as in times past, to discharge their fireworks round what remains of the bonfire, between the hours of nine and eleven o'clock.

Ans. Granted, with this limitation, that all young gentlemen under the age of nine, shall surrender their fireworks to the elder boys, and stand to see the display without the fence.

2. That any damage or injury caused by the said display to Mr. Root's premises, fences, &c., shall be made good by a subscription of the school.

Ans. Granted.

3. It now being nearly eight o'clock, the young gentlemen shall have their usual suppers.

Ans. Granted.

4. That a general amnesty shall be proclaimed, and that no person or persons shall suffer in any manner whatever, for the part that he or they may have taken in this thoughtless resistance.

Ans. Granted, with the exception of Masters Atkinson, Brewster, Davenant, and Rattlin.

Upon the last article issue was joined, the flag of truce still flying during the debate. The very pith of the thing was the act of full amnesty and oblivion. Yet so eager were now the majority of the boys for their amusement, that had it not been for the noble firmness of St. Albans, the leaders, with poor Pilgarlick, would have been certainly sacrificed to their lust of pleasure. But the affair was soon brought to a crisis. All this acting the military pleased me most mightily, and the better to enjoy it, I crouched under one of the desks that formed the barricade, and, with my head and shoulders thrust into the enemy's quarters, sat grinning forth my satisfaction.

The last clause was still canvassing, when, unheard of treachery! Mr. Root, seeing his victim so near, seized me by the ears, and attempted to lug me away captive. My schoolfellows attempted to draw me back. St. Albans protested—even some of the masters said 'shame!' when Mr. Root, finding he could not succeed, gave me a most swinging slap of the face, as a parting benediction, and relinquished his grasp. No sooner did I fairly find myself on the right side of the barricade, than, all my terrors overcome by pain,

I seized an inkstand and discharged it point blank at the fleecy curls of the ferulafer with an unlucky fatality of aim! Mr. Root's armorial bearings were now, at least on his crest, *blanche* chequered *noir*.

'On, my lads, on!' exclaimed the gallant St. Albans; the barricades were scaled in an instant, and we were at fisty cuffs with our foes. Rulers flew obliquely, perpendicularly, and horizontally— inkstands made ink-spouts in the air, with their dark gyrations— books, that the authors had done their best to fasten on their shelves peacefully for ever, for once became lively, and made an impression. I must do Mr. Root the justice to say, that he bore him gallantly in the *mêlée*. His white and black head popped hither and thither, and the smack of his whip resounded horribly among the shins of his foes.

Old R——lds not, even in battle, being able to resist the inveteracy of habit, had the contents of his large snuff-mull forced into his eyes, ere twenty strokes were struck. He ran roaring and prophesying, like blind Tiresias, among both parties, and as a prophet we respected him. The French master being very obese was soon borne down, and there he lay sprawling and calling upon glory and *la belle France*, whilst both sides passed over him by turns, giving him only an occasional kick when they found him in their way. It is said of Mr. Simp—n, the mathematical master— but I will not vouch for the truth of the account, for it seems too Homeric—that being hard pressed, he seized, and lifted up the celestial globe, wherewith to beat down his opponents, but being a very absent man, and the ruling passion being always dreadfully strong upon him, he began, instead of striking down his adversaries, to solve a problem upon it, but, before he had found the value of a single tangent, the orb was beaten to pieces about his skull, and he then saw more stars in his eyes than ever twinkled in the Milky Way. In less than two minutes, Mr. Root to his crest added *gules* —his nose spouted blood, his eyes were blackened, and those beautiful teeth, of which he was so proud, were alarmingly loosened.

For myself, I did not do much—I could not—I could not for very rapture. I danced and shouted in all the madness of exhilaration. I tasted then, for the first time, the fierce and delirious poison of contention. Had the battle-cry been 'A Rattlin!' instead of 'A St. Albans!' I could not have been more elated. The joy

of battle to the young heart is like water to the sands of the desert
—which cannot be satiated.

In much less than three minutes the position under the gallery
was carried. Root and the masters made good their retreat through
the door, and barricadoed it strongly on the outside—so that, if
we could boast of having barred him out, he could boast equally
of having barred us in. We made three prisoners, Mr. R——lds,
Mr. Moineau, and a lanky, sneaking, turnip-complexioned under
usher, who used to write execrable verses to the sickly housemaid,
and borrow half-crowns of the simple wench, wherewith to buy
pomatum to plaister his thin, lank hair. He was a known sneak,
and a suspected tell-tale. The booby fell a-crying in a dark corner,
and we took him with his handkerchief to his eyes. Out of the
respect that we bore our French and Latin masters, we gave them
their liberty, the door being set a-jar for that purpose, but we
reserved the usher, that, like the American Indians, we might make
sport with him.

CHAPTER XVI

*An affecting appeal that effects nothing—The rebels commence
their rejoicings—They are suddenly damped—The firemen defeat
the fire-boys by means of water—The victors are vanquished, who
shortly find themselves covered with disgrace and the bed-clothes.*

When we informed the captive usher that he was destined for the
high honour of being our Guy Faux, and that he should be the
centre of our fireworks, promising him to burn him as little as we
could help, and as could reasonably be expected, his terror was
extreme, and he begged, like one in the agonies of death, that we
would rather bump him. We granted his request, for we determined to be magnanimous, and he really bore it like a stoic.

The beauty of the scene is to come yet. Scarcely had we finished
with the usher, than Mrs. Root, 'like Niobe, all in tears,'[1] appeared
with out-stretched arms in the gallery. Her out-stretched arms,
her pathetic appeals, her sugared promises, had no avail,—the
simple lady wanted us to go to bed, and Mr. Root, to use her own
expression, should let us all off to-morrow. We were determined to

stay up, and let all our fireworks off to-night. But we granted to her intercession, that all the little boys should be given up to her.

It now became a very difficult thing to ascertain who was a little boy. Many a diminutive urchin of eight, with a stout soul, declared that he was a big fellow, and several lanky lads with sops of bread for hearts, called themselves little boys. There was, as I said before, no communication from the school-room with the orchestra; we were therefore obliged to pile the desks as a platform, and hand up the chicken-hearted to take protection under the wing of the old hen.

Our captive usher respectfully begged to observe that, though he could not say that he was exactly a little boy, yet if it pleased us, he would much rather go to bed, as he had lately taken physic. The plea was granted, but not the platform. That was withdrawn, and he was forced to climb up one of the pillars; and as we were charitably inclined, we lent him all the impetus we could, by sundry appliances of switches and rulers, in order to excite a rapid circulation in those parts that would most expedite his upward propulsion, upon the same principles that cause us to fire one extremity of a gun, in order to propel the ball from the other. He having been gathered with the rest round Mrs. Root, she actually made us a curtsey in the midst of her tears, and smiled as she curtseyed, bidding us all a good night, to be good boys, to do no mischief, and, above all, to take care of the fire. Then, having obtained from us a promise that we would neither injure the organ, nor attempt to get into the orchestra, she again curtseyed, and left us masters of the field.

Now the debate was frequent and full. We had rebelled, and won the field of rebellion in order to be enabled to discharge our fireworks. The thought of descending by means of the windows was soon abandoned. We should have been taken in the detail, even if we escaped breaking our bones. We were compelled to use the school-room for the sparkling display, and, all under the directions of St. Albans, we began to prepare accordingly.

Would that I had been the hero of that night! Though I did not perform the deeds, I felt all the glow of one; and, unexpected honour! I was actually addressed by Henry St. Albans himself, as 'honest Ralph Rattlin, the brave boy who slept in the haunted room.' There was a distinction for you! Of course, I cannot tell how an old gentleman, rising sixty-five, feels when his sovereign places the blue ribbon over his stooping shoulders, but if he enjoys half the rapture I then did, he must be a very, very happy old man.

Revenons à nos moutons—which phrase I use on account of its originality, and its applicability to fireworks. Nails were driven into the walls, and Catherine wheels fixed on them; Roman candles placed upon the tables instead of mutton dips, and the upper parts of the school windows let down for the free egress of our flights of sky-rockets. The first volley of the last-mentioned beautiful fire-work went through the windows, amidst our huzzas, at an angle of about sixty-five degrees, and did their duty nobly; when— when—of course, the reader will think that the room was on fire. Alas! it was quite the reverse. A noble Catherine wheel had just begun to fizz, in all the glories of its many-coloured fires, when, horror, dismay, confusion! half a dozen firemen, with their hateful badges upon their arms, made their appearance in the orchestra, and the long leathern tube being soon adjusted, the brazen spout began playing upon us and the Catherine wheel, amidst the laughter of the men, in which even we participated, whilst we heard the clank, clank, clank, of the infernal machine working in the play-ground. Mr. Root was not simple enough to permit his house to be burned down with impunity; and, since he found he could do no better, he resolved to throw cold water upon our proceedings.

The school-room door was now thrown open, to permit us to go out if we pleased, but we chose to remain where we were, for the simple reason, that we did not know whom we might meet on the stairs. We had agreed, under the directions of St. Albans, to let off our fireworks with some order; but now, instead of play-things for amusement, they were turned into engines of offence. Showers of squibs, crackers, and every species of combustible were hurled at our opponents above us. It was the struggle of fire with water; but that cold and powerful stream played continuously; wherever it met us it took away our breath, and forced us to the ground, yet we bore up gallantly, and the rockets that we directed into the orchestra very often drove our enemies back, and would have severely injured the organ, had they not covered it with blankets.

We advanced our desks near the gallery, to use them as scaling-ladders to storm; but it would not do, they were not sufficiently high, and the stream dashed the strongest of us back. However, we plied our fiery missiles as long as they lasted; but the water never failed—its antagonist element did too soon. Whilst it lasted, considering there was no slaughter, it was a very glorious onslaught.

In one short half-hour we were reduced. Drowned, burnt, blackened—looking very foolish, and fearing very considerably, we now approached the door: it was still open—no attempt to capture any one—no opposition was offered to us; but the worst of it was, we were obliged to sneak through files of deriding neighbours and servants, and we each crept to bed, like a dog that had stolen a pudding, anything but satisfied with our exploits, or the termination of them.

St. Albans would not forgive himself. He heaped immeasurable shame upon his own head, because he had not secured the orchestra. He declared he had no military genius. He would bind himself an apprentice to a country carpenter, and make pigstyes—he would turn usher, and the boys should bump him for an ass—he would run away. He did the latter.

Leaving the firemen to see all safe, Mr. Root to deplore his defaced school-room and his destroyed property, Mrs. Root to prepare for an immensity of cases of cold, and burnt faces and hands,—I shall here conclude the history of the famous barring out of the fifth of November, of the year of grace, 18—. If it had not all the pleasures of a real siege and battle, excepting actual slaughter, I don't know what pleasure is; and the reader by-and-bye will find out that I had afterwards opportunities enough of judging upon this sort of kingly pastimes, in which the cutting of throats was not omitted.

CHAPTER XVII

Is full of moral and religious disquisitions, therefore it behoveth the general reader to look at and pass it by with that inattention that readers generally have for morality and religion.

IF we may judge from the expressed sentiments of the first general of any age, the feelings and retrospections after a splendid victory are anything but exhilarating. Indeed, our hero has not only fought many good battles, but said a few good things. When, after the achievement of Waterloo, he exclaimed that the victory was only less to be deplored than the defeat, he spoke at once with the sublimity of the Christian and the depth of the philosopher. If, then, seeing it involves so many distressing contingencies, even a victory gives but little satisfaction, a drawn battle must consequently give much less. We will not say one single word of a defeat. We, of the academy, would never acknowledge so much shame as that word expresses. It was a drawn battle in every sense. Had we not drawn the magisterial blood of Mr. Root? Had not Mr. Root, in return, drawn off all the disposable water on his premises? Had we not, at the end of the affray, drawn off our forces unmolested? Neither party occupied the field of battle, that incontestable proof of victory. Certainly it was a drawn battle.

The fastidious may call all this a mere quibbling upon words—but unjustly: did they ever read the despatches of two contending powers, neither of which has much to boast of excepting honourable blows—it will then be perceived that they make out their case in no manner more effectually than I have done mine. There is much virtue in the artful construction of words.

When the boys came down stairs there was as comfortless a scene displayed before them, as the most retributive justice could have wished to visit on the rebellious. The morning raw and cold, the floor saturated with water, and covered with cases of exploded fireworks; the school-room in horrible confusion, scarcely a pane of glass unshattered—the walls blackened, the books torn—and then the masters and ushers stole in, looking both suspicious and discomfited. Well, we went to prayers, and very lugubriously indeed did we sing the hymn,

> 'Awake, my soul, and with the sun
> Thy daily course of duty run.'

Now, that morning, no one could tell whether the sun had waked or not, at least he kept his bed-curtains of fog closely drawn; and about twenty-five of the scholars gave a new reading to 'thy daily course of duty run,' as, immediately after they had paid their doleful orisons, they took the course of running their duty by running away. There were no classes that day. Mr. Root did not make his appearance—and we had a constrained holiday.

On the 7th, to use a nautical expression, we had repaired damages, and we began to fall into the usual routine of scholastic business—but it was full a week before our master made his appearance in the school-room, and he did so then with a green shade over his eyes, to conceal the green shades under them. He came in at the usual hour of noon—the black list was handed up to him—and I expected, in the usual order of things, an assiduous flogging. But in this world we are the martyrs of disappointment. The awful man folded up the paper very melancholily, and thrust it into his waistcoat pocket, and thus saved me the expense of some very excellent magnanimity, which I had determined to display, had he proceeded to flagellation. It was my intention, very intrepidly, to have told him, that if he punished me, I also would run away. On the veracity of a schoolboy, I was disappointed at not receiving my three or four dozen.

I had now fairly commenced my enthusiastic epoch. I was somebody. I still slept in the haunted room. I had struck the first blow in the barring out—St. Albans had openly commended me for my bravery—I could no longer despise myself, and the natural consequence was, that others dared not. I formed friendships, evanescent certainly, but very sweet, and very sincere. Several of the young gentlemen promised to prevail upon their parents to invite me to their homes, during the approaching holidays; but either their memories were weak, or their fathers obdurate.

Well, the winter holidays came at last, and I was left sole inhabitant of that vast and lonely school-room, with one fire for my solace, and one tenpenny dip for my enlightenment. How awful and supernatural seemed every passing sound that beat upon my anxious ears! Everything round me seemed magnified—the massive shadows were as the wombs teeming with unearthly phantoms—the whistle of the wintry blasts against the windows, voiced the half unseen beings that my fears acknowledged in the deep darknesses of the vast chamber. And then that lonely orchestra,—often did I think that I heard low music from the organ, as if touched by ghostly fingers—how gladly I would have sunk down from my solitude to the vulgarity of the servants' hall—but that was now carefully interdicted. The consequences of all this seclusion to a highly imaginative, and totally unregulated mind, must have been much worse than putting me to sleep in the haunted room, for in that I had my counter spell—and long use had almost endeared me to it and its grotesque carvings—but this dismally large school-room, generally so instinct with life, so superabounding in animation, was painfully fearful, even from the contrast. Twenty times in the evening, when the cold blast came creeping along the floor, and wound round my ankles, did I imagine it was the chill hand of some corpse, thrust up from beneath, that was seizing me, in order to drag me downwards—and a hundred times, as the long flame from the candle flared up tremulously, and shook the deep shadows that encompassed me around, did I fancy that there were very hideous faces indeed mouthing at me amidst the gloom —and my own gigantic shadow—it was a vast horror of itself personified! It was a cruel thing, even in Mr. Root, to leave me alone so many hours in that stupendous gloom, but his wife— fie upon her!

Considering how my imagination had been before worked upon, even from my earliest childhood, and the great nervous excitability of my temperament, it is a wonder that my mind did not reel, if not succumb—but I now began to combat the approaches of one sort of insanity with the actual presence of another—*I wrote verses.* That was 'tempering the wind to the shorn lamb,'[1] as Sterne would have expressed it, after the prettiest fashion imaginable.

Had I not the reader so completely at my mercy—did I not think him or her not only the gentlest but also the most deserving of all the progeny of Japhet—did I not think that it would be the very acme of ingratitude to impose upon him or her, I would certainly transcribe a centaine, or so, of these juvenile poems. It is true, they are very bad—but then that is a proof that they are undeniably genuine. I really have, in some things, a greatness of soul. I will refrain—but in order that these effusions may not be lost to the world, I offer them to the annuals for 1837; not so much for the sake of pecuniary compensation, but in order to improve the reading of some of that very unreadable class of books.

Well, during these dismal holidays, I wrote verses, and began to take, or to make, my madness methodical. The boys came back, and having left me a very Bobadil, they now found me a juvenile Bavius;[2] not quite so bad as a juvenile Whig, however, for I could boast of being able to rhyme ghost with twelve words at most. Oh! but I became a lad of great consideration.

I wish much to hurry over this part of my life, but I should not be using those philosophical geniuses well, who love to study all the vagaries of the human mind, did I omit to describe a very peculiar hallucination that held the most despotic sway over me

for more than a month. This phase of mental associations was so
singular and so perfect, and will be viewed in such different lights
by persons as they are biassed by education or by prejudice, that
I shall merely confine myself to the fact, and leave others to pronounce an opinion upon it. I only beg leave most solemnly to
asseverate that what I am going to state is unexaggerated truth.

I was at this period nearly in my thirteenth year, and, what with
my rhyming and my fistical prowess,—my character for bravery,
and the peculiarity of my situation, as it regarded its mystery—
I became that absurd thing that the French call 'une tête montée.'
When persons act much, they soon find it necessary to reason.
I was thus forced, in order to preserve my position, to become
irrationally rational. Root had ceased to flog me. I could discover
that he even began to fear me—and just in proportion as he seemed
to avoid all occasion to punish me, I became towards him mild,
observant, and respectful. The consequence was, that, as I was
no longer frightened out of my wits at church; from very weariness,
and for the sake of variety, I began to attend to the sermons. What
a lesson ought not this to be to instructors! One Sunday, I returned
from church in a state of almost spiritual intoxication. The rector
was a pale, attenuated man, with a hollow, yet flashing eye—a man
who seemed to have done with everything in this world, excepting
to urge on his brethren to that better one, to which himself was fast
hastening; and, on this memorable day, that I fancied myself a
convert, he had been descanting on the life of the young Samuel.
Of course he, very appropriately, often turned to the juvenile part
of his congregation; and as I was seated in the front row, I felt as
if I were alone in the church—as if every word were individually
addressed to myself; his imploring yet impassioned glances seemed
to irradiate my breast with a sweet glory. I felt at once, that since
the goodness of the Creator was inexhaustible, the fault must rest
with man if there were no more Samuels, so I determined to be
one—to devote myself entirely to divine abstraction, to heavenly
glory, and to incessant worship—and, stupendous as the assertion
may seem, for six weeks I did so. This resolution became a passion
—a madness. I was as one walking in a sweet trance—I revelled in
secret bliss, as if I had found a glorious and inexhaustible treasure.
I spoke to none of my new state of mind—absorbed as I was, I yet
dreaded ridicule—but I wrote hymns, I composed sermons. If
I found my attention moving from heavenly matters, I grew angry

with myself, and I renovated my flagging attention with inward ejaculation. I had all the madness of the anchorite upon me in the midst of youthful society, yet without his asceticism, and certainly without his vanity.

My studies, of course, were nearly totally neglected, under this complete alienation of spirit, and Mr. Root, lenient as he had lately become towards me, began to flog again; and—shall I be believed when I say it?—I have been examining my memory most severely, and I am sure it has delivered up its record faithfully; but yet I hardly dare give it to the world—but, despite of ridicule, I find myself compelled to say, that those floggings I scarcely felt. I looked upon them as something received for the sake of an inscrutable and unfathomable love, and I courted them—they were pleasurable. I now can well understand the enthusiasm and the raptures of that ridiculous class of exploded visionaries, called flagellants. I certainly was in a state of complete oblivion to everything but a dreamy fanaticism, and yet that term is too harsh, and it would be impiety to call it holiness, seeing that it was a state of inutility,—and yet, many well-meaning persons will think, no doubt, that my infant and almost sinless hand, had hold of a blessed link of that chain of ineffable love, which terminates in the breast of that awful Being, who sits at the right hand of the throne of the Eternal. I give, myself, no opinion. I only state facts. But I cannot help hazarding a conjecture of what I might have been, had I then possessed a friend in any one of my instructors, who could have pointed out to me what were the precincts of true piety, what those of incipient insanity. At that time I had the courage to achieve anything. Let the cold-hearted and the old say what they will, youth is the time for moral bravery. The withered and the aged mistake their failing forces for calmness and resignation, and an apathy, the drear anticipator of death, for presence of mind.

However, this state of exalted feeling had a very ludicrous termination. I ceased fighting, I was humble, seeking whom I might serve, reproving no one, but striving hard to love all, giving, assisting, and actually panting for an opportunity of receiving a slap on one side of the face, that I might offer the other for the same infliction. The reader may be sure that I had the Bible almost constantly before me, when not employed in what I conceived some more active office of what I thought sanctification. But though the spirit may be strong, at times the body will be weak. I believe

I dozed for a few minutes over the sacred book, when a wag stole
it away, and substituted for it the 'renowned and veracious history
of the Seven Champions of Christendom.' There was the frontispiece, the gallant St. George, in green and gold armour, thrusting
his spear into the throat of the dragon, in green and gold scales.
What a temptation! I ogled the book coyly at first. I asked for my
Bible. 'Read that, Ralph,' said the purloiner; and oh! recreant
that I was, I read it.

I was cured in three hours of being a saint, of despising flogging,
and of aping Samuel.

CHAPTER XVIII

*Ralph receives an infusion of patriotism—Is himself drilled and
drills a touch-hole—He turns out a monstrous big liar—Somebody
comes to see him whom nobody can see, and the mystery ends in
another migration.*

It is the nature of men and boys to run into extremes. I have
carried the reader with me through my desponding and enthusiastic epochs. I now come to the most miserable of all, my
mendacious one. An avowed poet is entitled, *de jure*, to a good
latitude of fiction; but I abused this privilege most woefully.
I became a confirmed and intrepid liar—and this, too, was the
natural course of my education, or the want of it. I began to read
all manner of romances. There was a military and chivalrous spirit
strong in the school—the mania for volunteering was general, and
our numerous school were almost all trained to arms. The government itself supplied us with a half-dozen drill serjeants to complete
us in our manual and platoon exercise. We had a very pretty
uniform, and our equipments as infantry were complete in all
things, save and excepting that all the muskets of the junior boys
had no touch-holes. Mine was delivered to me in this innocent
state. Oh! that was a great mortification on field-days, when we
were allowed to incorporate with the united —— and ——
volunteers, whilst all the big lads actually fired off real powder, in
line with real men, to be obliged to snap a wooden flint against a
sparkless hammer. A mortification I could not, I would not, endure.

There was a regular contention between Mr. Root, my musket, and myself, and at last, by giving my serjeant a shilling, I conquered. Every day that our muskets were examined on parade, mine would be found with a touch-hole drilled in it; as certainly as it was found, so certainly was I hoisted. In that fever of patriotism, I, of all the school, though denied powder and shot, was the only one that bled for my country. However, I at length had the supreme felicity of blowing powder in the face of vacancy, in high defiance of Buonaparte and his assembled legions on the coast of Boulogne. Thus I had military ardour added to my other ardencies. Moreover, I had learned to swim in the New River, and, altogether, began to fancy myself a hero.

I began now to appreciate and to avail myself of the mystery of my birth. I did not read romances and novels for nothing. So I began my mendacious career. Oh! the improbable and impossible lies that I told, and that were retold, and all believed. I was a prince incognito; my father had coined money—and I gave my deluded listeners glimpses at pocket-pieces as proofs; if I was doubted, I fought. The elder boys shook their heads, and could make nothing of it. The ushers made what inquiries they dared, and found nothing which they could contradict positively, but much upon which to found conjecture.

Still, notwithstanding my success, my life began to grow burthensome. The lies became too manifold, too palpable, and, to me, too onerous. They had been extremely inconsistent—ridicule began to raise her hissing head. Shame became my constant companion—yet I lied on. I think I may safely say, that I would, at the time that I was giving myself out as a future king, have scorned the least violation of the truth, to have saved myself from the most bitter punishment, or to injure, in the least, my worst enemy; my lies were only those of a most inordinate vanity; begun in order to make a grand impression of myself, and persevered in through obstinacy and pride. But I was crushed beneath the stupendous magnificence of my own creations. I had been so circumstantial—described palaces, reviews, battles, my own chargers, and now—oh! how sick all these fabrications made me! It was time I left the school, or that life left me, for it had become intolerable. And yet this state of misery, the misery of the convicted, yet obstinately persevering liar, lasted nearly a year. Let me hurry over it; but, at the same time, let me hold it up as a picture

G

to youth, upon the same principle as the Spartans showed drunken slaves to their children. Could the young but conceive a tithe of the misery I endured, they would never after swerve from truth.

I have not time to expatiate on several droll mishaps that occurred to Mr. Root; how he was once bumped in all the glowing panoply of equine war; how, when one night, with his head well powdered, he crept upon all-fours, as was his wont, into one of the boys' bedrooms, to listen to their nightly conversations; and how such visit being expected, as his head lay on the side of the bedstead, it was there immovably fixed, by the application of a half-pound of warm cobbler's wax, and release could only be given by the Jason-like operation of shearing the fleecy locks. We must rapidly pass on. I was eager to get away from this school, and my desire was accomplished in the following very singular manner.

One fine sunshiny Sunday morning, as we were all arranged in goodly fashion, two by two, round the play-ground, preparatory to issuing through the house to go to church, the unusual cry was heard, of 'Master Rattlin wanted,' which was always understood to be the joyful signal that some parent or friend had arrived as a visitor. I was immediately hurried into the house, a whispering took place between Mr. and Mrs. Root, and the consequence was, that I was bustled up into the bedroom, and my second best clothes, which I then had on, were changed for the best, and, with a supererogatory dab with a wet towel over my face, I was brought down, and, my little heart playing like a pair of castanets against my ribs, I was delivered into the tender keeping of the pedagogue.

Having taken me by the hand, whilst he was practising all the amenities with his countenance, he opened the parlour-door, where the supposititious visitor was expected to be found, and lo! the room was empty. Mrs. Root and the servants were summoned, and they all positively declared, and were willing to swear to the fact, that a gentleman had gone into the room, who had never gone out. It was a front parlour, on the ground floor, and from the window he could not have emerged, as the area intervened between that and the foot pavement; and to see a gentleman scrambling through by that orifice into the principal street of ——, and from one of the principal houses of the town, whilst all the people were going to church, was a little too preposterous even for Mr. Root's matter-of-fact imagination. However, they all peeped up the chimney one after the other, as if an elderly, military-looking gentleman, encumbered with a surtout, for thus he was described, would have been so generous as to save my schoolmaster a shilling, by bustling up his chimney, and bringing down the soot. The person was not to be found; Root began to grow alarmed—a constable was sent for, and the house was searched from the attics to the cellar. The dwelling was not, however, robbed, nor any of its inmates murdered, notwithstanding the absconder could not be found.

Now, Mr. Root was a man wise in his own generation, yet was he, notwithstanding, a great fool. He was one of that class who can sometimes overreach a neighbour, yet, in doing so, inevitably loses his own balance, and tumbles into the mire. A sagacious ninny, who had an '*I told you so*,' for every possible event after it had happened. Indeed, he was so much in the habit of applying this favourite phrase upon all unhappy occasions, that he could not help using it to an unfortunate housemaid of his, one morning, who had delivered herself secretly of twins the previous night. Mrs. Root did not like the application of the sentence at all.

Instead of taking the common sense view of the affair of the missed gentleman, and supposing that the footman had been bribed to let him quietly out at the street-door, who, perhaps, had found his feelings too little under his control to go through the interview with me that he sought, Root set about making a miracle of the matter. It was astounding—nay, superhuman! It boded some misfortune to him; and so it really did, by the manner in which he treated it. I verily believe, that had the servants or Mrs. Root, who had seen the gentleman, averred to a cloven foot as peeping out from his military surtout, he would have given the assertion not only unlimited credence, but unlimited circulation also. However, as it was, he made himself most egregiously busy; there were his brother churchwardens and the curate summoned to assist him in a court of inquiry; evidence was taken in form, and a sort of *procès verbal* drawn out and duly attested. Mr. Root was a miracle-monger, and gloried in being able to make himself the hero of his own miracles.

Well, after he had solaced himself by going about to all his neighbours with this surprising paper in hand, for about the space of a fortnight, he thought to put the climax to his policy and his vain glory, by taking it and himself up to the banker's in town where he always got the full amount of his bills for my board and education paid without either examination or hesitation. The worthy money-changer looked grimly polite at the long and wonderful account of the schoolmaster, received a copy of the account of the mysterious visitor with most emphatic silence, and then bowed the communicant out of his private room with all imaginable etiquette.

Mr. Root came home on excellent terms with himself; he imposed silence upon his good lady, his attentive masters and ushers, and then wiping the perspiration from his brow, proceeded to tell his admiring audience of his great, his very great exertions, and how manfully through the whole awful business he had done his duty. Alas! he soon found to his cost that he had done something more. In cockney language, he had done himself out of a good pupil. A fortnight after I was again 'wanted.' There was a glass coach at the door. A very reserved sort of gentleman alighted, paid all demands up to the end of the ensuing half-year, answered no questions, but merely producing a document, handed me and all my worldly wealth into his vehicle, and off we drove.

To the best of my recollection, all the conversation that I heard from this taciturn person, was that sentence, so much the more remarkable for verity than originality, 'Ask no questions, and I shall tell you no stories.' Having nothing else to do in this my enforced *tête-à-tête*, I began to conjecture what next was going to become of me. At first I built no castles in the air; I had got quite sick of doing that aloud with my late school-fellows, and passing them all off as facts. Still it must be confessed, that my feelings were altogether pleasurable. It was a soul-cheering relief to have escaped from out of that vast labyrinth of lies that I had planted around me, and no longer to dread the rod-bearing Root; even novelty, under whatever form it may present itself, is always grateful to the young.

In the midst of these agitations I again found myself in town; and I began to hope that I should once more see my foster-parents. I began to rally up my 'little Latin and less Greek,' in order to surprise the worthy sawyer and his wife; and I had fully determined to work out for him what the amount of his daily wages came to in a week, firstly by simple arithmetic, secondly by fractions, thirdly by decimals, and fourthly by duodecimals; and then to prove the whole correct by an algebraical equation. But all those triumphs of learning were not destined for me. I found, at length, that the glass coach drove up the inn-yard of some large coachmaster; but few words were said, and I was consigned to the coachman of one of the country stages, with as little remorse and as little ceremony as if I had been an ugly, blear-eyed pug, forwarded in a basket labelled, 'this side uppermost,' to an old maiden aunt, or a super-annuated grandmother.

This was certainly unhandsome treatment to one who had been lately seriously telling his companions that he was a disguised prince of the blood, forced, for state reasons, to keep a strict incognito. It is true, that I travelled with four horses, and was attended by a guard; nay, that a flourish of music preceded my arrival at various points of my journey; but all these little less than royal honours I shared with a plebeian butcher, a wheezing and attenuated plumber and glazier, and other of his lieges, all very useful, but hardly deemed ornamental members of the body politic.

But let me now pause at this point of my life; and sum up in a few words, what I was at thirteen years of age; what I might have been, it is both useless and painful to conjecture. At that age, it is certain that the outlines of the character are traced in, unerasably so. If the youth's bursts of passion have not been counteracted, all his life he will be passionate; if his vindictive feelings have not been corrected, all his life he will be revengeful; if religious principles have not been cultivated, he will be either lukewarm in faith, or a sinner, or a sceptic; if habits of industry have not been formed, he will for ever after think labour to be ignoble, and exertion only laudable when its immediate aim is pleasure. Now, what was I at thirteen,—the child of desertion or neglect; by turns the footstool of oppression, or the shuttlecock of caprice; alternately kicked, cajoled, and flattered? I will tell the reader what I was. I was superstitious, with a degree of superstition that would have borne me within the drear realms of fatuity, had not a healthful tempera-ment, and an indomitable pride, made me, whilst I believed in all absurd horrors, brave them. I owed this to the Methodist preachers. I hated public worship; and all that associated with it, and for this feeling I was indebted to the church-observing disciplinarian, Mr. Root. I was idle, extravagant, and as inconstant as the summer wind; though I could, when the whim seized me, wander amongst the flowers of literature, unwearied, for successive hours. This was the consequence of the neglect I experienced at school. I was obdurate, obstinate, and cruel—the undoubted effects of my repeated floggings; and above all, I was a monstrous liar. But mine was not the lying of profit or of fear, but of ambition. I could not carve out for myself, young as I was, glory by my sword, so I vainly thought to create it to myself by my tongue. The consolation that I have in looking back upon this the shameful part of my character, was, that I did it heroically. If the axiom be true, that one murder makes a felon, a thousand a hero, surely I may say, one falsehood makes a grovelling liar, a thousand a magnificent inventor. But sound morality sees through and condemns the one and the other. There is nothing really great that is not true, even in those things that seem to take fiction for their basis. Let me earnestly advise every high-spirited youth, to be aware of romancing at school, or elsewhere. If he possess genius, he will not be able to stop himself, and the first pause that he will make will be, when he finds himself brought up suddenly, the standing-mark for the derision of fools whom he despises, but whose superiority he cannot dispute, because *they* have not lied.

CHAPTER XIX

A chapter of disappointments, which Ralph hopes the reader will not share—Some comparisons which he hopes will not be found odious, and some reflections which he thinks cannot be resented.

My friends will perceive, that at the time of which I am speaking, the stage coach contained, if not actually a bad character, a person on the very verge of being one—that I was that graceless, yet tolerated being, a scamp, was very certain—yet my gentle demeanour, my smooth, bright countenance, and never-ceasing placid smile, would have given a very different impression of my qualities. I have been thus liberal in my confessions, in order that parents may see that their duties do not terminate where those of the schoolmaster begin; that the schoolmaster himself must be taken to task, and the watcher watched. I had been placed in one of the first boarding-schools near town; a most liberal stipend had been paid with me; I had every description of master; yet, after all this outlay of money, which is not dross—and waste of time, which is beyond price precious, what was I at leaving this academy? Let the good folks withinside of the Stickenham stage testify; by one trick or another I had contrived to make them all tolerably un-comfortable before the journey was half over.

But where am I going? Cæsar and his fortunes are embarked in a stage coach. An hour and a half had elapsed when I perceived that the horses were dragging the vehicle slowly up a steep hill. The full-leaved trees are arching for us, over head, a verdant canopy; the air becomes more bracing and elastic; and even I feel its invigorating influence, and cease to drop slily the gravelly dirt I had collected from my shoes, down the neck and back of a very pretty girl, who sat blushing furiously on my left. Now the summit is gained, and in another moment, the coach thunders down the other side of the hill. But what a beautiful view is spread before my fascinated eyes! and then rose up in my young heart the long-sleeping emotions of love, and kindred affection. Into whose arms was I to be received? whose were to be the beautiful lips that were now longing to kiss me with parental, perhaps fraternal rapture? Had I a sister? Could I doubt it at that ecstatic moment? How I would love her! The fatted calf was not only killed, but cooked, to welcome the long lost. Nor Latin, nor French, nor Greek, nor Mathematics, should embitter the passing moments. This young summer, that breathed such aromatic joy around me, had put on its best smile to welcome me to my paternal abode. 'No doubt,' said I to myself—'no doubt, but that some one of the strange stories that I told of myself at Root's, is going to be realized.'

In the midst of these rapturous anticipations, each later one becoming more wild and more glorious than the previous one that begot it, it wanting still an hour of sundown, all at once the coach stopped before a house, upon a gentle elevation—stopped with a jerk, too, as if it were going to usher in some glorious event. I looked out, and behold! in hated gold letters, upon the hated blue board, the bitterly hated word 'academy' met my agonized sight.

I burst into tears. I needed no voice to tell me that I was the person to alight. I knew my doom. Farewell to all my glorious visions! I could have hurled back into the face of the laughing sun, my hate, and called him deceiver and traitor; for had he not, with other causes, conspired to smile me, five minutes ago, into a fool's paradise?

'Master Rattlin, won't you please to alight?' said one of those under-toned, gerund-singing voices, that my instinct told me to be an usher's.

'No thank'ee, sir,' said I, amidst my sobbings, 'I want to go home.'

'But you are to get down here, however,' said my evil-omened inviter. 'Your boxes are all off the coach, and the coachman wants to go forward.'

'So do I.'

'It's excessively droll this—hi, hi, hi! as sure as my name's Saltseller, it is excessively droll. So you want to get forward, Master Rattlin? why come to school then, that's the way—droll, isn't it? Why, you've been riding backwards all the way, too—time to change—droll that—hi, hi!'

'It's no change,' said I, getting out sulkily, 'from one school to another—and do you call this a school?' I continued, looking round contemptuously, for I found about twenty little boys playing upon a green knoll before the house, and over which we were compelled to walk to reach it, as the road did not come near the habitation. 'Do you call this a school? Well, if you catch me being flogged here, I'm a sop, that's all—a school! And I suppose you're the usher—I don't think those little boys bumped you last half-year.'

'I don't think they did,' said Mr. Saltseller, which was actually the wretch's name, and with whom I fell desperately in hate at first sight. 'Bump me!' he exclaimed soliloquising—and with that air of astonishment, as if he had heard the most monstrous impossibility spoken of imaginable. 'Bump me? droll, is'nt it—excessively? Where have you been brought up, Master Rattlin?'

'Where they bar out tyrannical masters, and bump sneaking ushers,' said I. 'That's where I was brought up.'

'Then that's what I call very bad bringing up.'

'Not so bad as being brought down here, any how.'

His next 'excessively droll, isn't it?' brought us to the door of the academy; but, in passing over the play-ground, I could see, at once, that I was with quite another class of beings, than those who composed my late schoolfellows. They were evidently more delicately nurtured; they had not the air of school-boy daring, to which I had been so much accustomed, and they called each other 'Master.' Everything, too, seemed to be upon a miniature scale. The house was much smaller, yet there was an air of comfort and of health around, that at first I did not appreciate, though I could not help remarking it.

No sooner was I conducted into the passage, than I heard a voice which I thought I remembered, exclaim, 'Show Master Rattlin in here, and shut the door.'

I entered; and the next moment I was in the arms of the mysterious and very beautiful lady that had called to see me the few times that I have recorded; and who, I conceived, was intimately connected with my existence. I think that I have before said, that she never avowed herself, either to my nurse or to myself, as more than my godmother. She evinced a brief, but violent emotion; and then controlled her features to a very staid and matronly expression. For myself, I wept most bitterly, from many mingled emotions; but, to the shame of human nature, and of my own, wounded pride was the most intolerable pang that I felt. In all my day-dreams I had made this lady the presiding genius. I gave her, in my inmost heart, all the reverence and the filial affection of a son; but it was the implied understanding between my love and my vanity, that in joining herself to me as a mother, she was to bestow upon me a duchess at least; though I should not have thought myself over-well used had it been a princess. And here were all these glorious anticipations merged, sunk, destroyed, in the person of a boarding-school mistress of about twenty boys, myself the biggest. It was no use that I said to myself over and over again, she is not less lovely—her voice less musical, her manner less endearing, or her apparel less rich. The startling truth was ever in my ear—she 'keeps a school,' and, consequently, she cannot be my mother.

She could not know what was passing in my mind; but it was evident that my grief was of that intensity that nearly approached to misery. She took me by the hand, showed me my nice little bed, the large garden, the river that ran at the bottom of it, and placed before me fruit and cakes; I would not be consoled; what business had she to be a schoolmistress? I had a thousand times rather have had Mrs. Brandon for a mother again—she had never deceived me. But I was soon aware that this lady, whom I now, for the first time, heard named, as Mrs. Cherfeuil, was as little disposed to grant me the honour of calling her mother, as I was to bestow it. I was introduced to her husband as the son of a female friend of hers of early life; that she had stood godmother to me, that my parentage was respectable; and, as he had before had sufficient references to satisfy him from the agent, who had called a week before my arrival, the good man thought that there was nothing singular in the affair.

But let us describe this good man, my new pedagogue. In all things he was the antithesis of Mr. Root. The latter was large, florid and decidedly handsome—Mr. Cherfeuil[1] was little, sallow, and more than decidedly ugly. Mr. Root was worldly wise, and very ignorant; Mr. Cherfeuil, a fool in the world, and very learned. The mind of Mr. Root was so empty, that he found no trouble in arranging his one idea and a half; Mr. Cherfeuil's was so full, that there was no room for any arrangement at all. Mr. Root would have thought himself a fool if he condescended to write poetry; but he supposed he could, for he never tried. Mr. Cherfeuil would have thought any man a fool that did not perceive at once that he, Cherfeuil, was born a great poet. Shall I carry, after the manner of Plutarch, the comparison any farther? No; let us bring it to an abrupt conclusion, by saying in a few words, that Mr. Root was English; Mr. Cherfeuil French; that the one had a large school, and the other a little one; and that both were immeasurably great men in their own estimation—though not universally so in that of others.

Mr. Cherfeuil was ambitious to be thought five feet high; his attitude, therefore, was always erect; and, to give himself an air of consequence, he bridled and strutted like a full-breasted pigeon, with his head thrown back, and was continually in the act of wriggling his long chin into his ample neckerchief. He could not ask you how you do, or say in answer to that question, 'I thank you, sare, very well,' without stamping prettily with his foot, as if cracking a snail, and tossing his chin into the air as if he were going to balance a ladder upon it. Then, though his features were compressed into a small monkeyfied compass, they were themselves, individually, upon a magnificent scale. It was as if there had been crowded half a dozen gigantic specimens of human ugliness into my lady's china closet, all of which were elbowing each other for room. The eyes would have been called large, had it not been for the vast proportions of the nose, and the nose would have been thought preposterous, had it not been for the horrible dimensions of the mouth. Yet the expression of all these anomalies, though very grotesque, was not unpleasing. You smiled with satisfaction when you saw how great the improvement was that baboonery had made toward manhood. You might call him, in a word, a queer, little ugly-looking box of yellow mortality, that contained some amiable qualities, and a great many valuable attainments. Of good sense, or of common sense, he was never known to show, during the whole period of his life, but one instance; and that was a most important one—a complete deference, in all things, to his stately and beautiful wife. Her dominion was undivided, complete, and unremitting. How she came to marry him was one of those human riddles that will never be satisfactorily resolved. He had been a French *émigré*, had had a most superior education—played on several instruments without taste—understood everything connected with the classics but their beauty, and was deeply versed in the mathematics, without comprehending their utility.

At this school my progress was rapid. All the care and attention that the most maternal of hearts could bestow upon me were mine; yet there was no approach to anything like familiarity on the part of Mrs. Cherfeuil. There lay a large wild common before the house— there was a noble collection of deep water in the vicinity, in which I perfected my natatory studies, (affected phraseology is the fashion) and my body strengthened, my mind improved, and I began to taste of real happiness.

It would be an amusing work, to write a biography of some of the most remarkable ushers. They seem to be the bats of the social scheme. Gentlemen will not own them, and the classes beneath reject them. They are generally self-sufficient; the dependency of their situation makes them mean, and the exercise of delegated power tyrannical. If they have either spirit or talent, they lift themselves above their situation; but when they cannot do this, they are, in my estimation, the most abject of all classes—gipsies and beggars not excepted. Mr. Cherfeuil was, in himself, a mine of learning: but he delivered it out from the dark cavities of his mind, encumbered with so much ore, and in such misshaped masses, that it required another person to arrange for use what he was so lavish of producing. A good usher or assistant was therefore necessary; but I do not recollect having more than one, out of the thirty or forty that came and went during the three years I was at the school.

This class of people are, alas! fatally susceptible of the tender impulses. They always find the rosy cheeks of the housemaid, or the *en bon point* of the cook, irresistible. And they have themselves such delicate soft hands, so white and so ashy. On Sundays, too, their linen is generally clean; so, altogether, the maidservants find them killing.

Mr. Saltseller, who found everything droll, and who used to paint his cheeks, lost his situation just at the precise moment that the housemaid lost her character. The two losses together were not of very great moment; then we had another, and another, and another; and more characters were lost—till at last there did come a man,

> 'take him for all in all,
> I ne'er shall look upon his like again.'

He was very tall, stout, of a pompous carriage, *un homme magnifique*. He wore a green coat, false hair, a black patch over his left eye, and was fifty, or rather fifty-five. His face was large, round, and the least in the world bloated. This Adonis of matured ushers, after school-hours, would hang a guitar from his broad neck, by means of a pale pink ribbon, and walk up and down on the green before the house, thrum, thrum, thrumming, the admiration of all the little boys, and the coveted of all the old tabbies in the village. O, he was the *beau idéal* of a *vieux garçon*. We recommend all school-assistants to learn the guitar, and grow fat—if they can; and then, perhaps, they may prosper, like Mr. Sigismund Pontifex. He contrived to elope with a maiden lady, of good property, just ten years older than himself: the sweet, innocent, indiscreet ones, went off by stealth one morning before daylight, in a chaise and four, and returned a week after, Mr. and Mrs. Pontifex.

The gentleman hung up his guitar, and for ever; and every fine day, he was found, pipe in mouth and tankard in hand, presiding at the bowling-green of the Black Lion, the acknowledged and revered umpire—cherished by mine host, and referred to by the players. I write this life for instruction. Gentlemen ushers, look to it—be ambitious—learn the guitar, and make your mouths water with ideas of prospective tankards of ale, and odoriferous pipes.

CHAPTER XX

Ralph groweth egregiously modest, and boasteth immoderately,
until he is beaten by one with one foot in the grave; with something
touching the feats of the man without feet.

I FIND myself in a dilemma. My modesty (?) is at variance with
my love of verity. O the inconvenience of that little pronoun, I!
Would that I had, in the first instance, imitated the wily conduct
of the bald-pated invader of Britain. How complacently might I
not then have vaunted in the beginning, have caracoled through
the middle, and glorified myself at the conclusion of this my auto-
biography! What a monstrous piece of braggadocio would not
Cæsar's Commentaries have been, had he used the first, instead
of the third person singular! How intolerable would have been the
presumption of his Thrasonical, 'I thrashed the Helvetians—I sub-
jugated the Germans—I utterly routed the Gauls—I defeated the
painted Britons!' And, on the contrary, for I like to place heroes
side by side, how decorously and ingeniously might I not have
written, 'Ralph Rattlin blackened Master Simpkin's left eye—
Ralph Rattlin led on the attack upon Farmer Russel's orchard, and
Ralph Rattlin fought three rounds, with no considerable dis-
advantage, with the long-legged pieman.' Alas! I cannot even
shelter myself under the mistiness of the peremptory *we*. I have
made a great mistake. But I have this consolation, in common with
other great men, that, for our mistake, the public will assuredly
suffer more than ourselves. Many a choice adventure, of which
I was the hero, must be suppressed. *I* should blush myself black
in the face, to say what *he* would relate with a very quiet smile of
self-satisfaction. However, as regrets are quite unavailing, unless,
like the undertaker's, they are paid for, I shall exclaim, with the
French soldier who found his long military queue in the hands of
a pursuing English sailor, 'Chivalry of the world, *toujours en avant.*'

En avant. Have I lingered too long over my school days? Ah,
no! In early spring are not the flowers more fresh? Are not the
waters of the river more pure, the nearer we go to their source?
Even the glorious sun is hailed with the greatest rapture at his
rising. It is at the commencement of everything, as well as of life,
that we must look for the greatest enjoyment. No scheme of

ambition, of grandeur, or of avarice, but contains its greatest elements of happiness in the conception and its prosecution. The last throb of exultation for success, is the sure herald of the first pang of satiety. The final chorus of fruition is, 'All is vanity and vexation of spirit.' It is the chorus of ages, of time, and of mortality. Let us then go back to the early and fresh days of young life, to the spring-tide of joyous existence, and what reader is there, however *blazé* by the world, that will not gladly attend us?

I have described a wretched schoolboy, let us now view a happy one. It is a fine and breezy summer morning, the sun about an hour old. Remark that tall youth springing over the garden railings. The gate is fastened only with a latch, but the exultation of health disdains to lift it. There is a vast and heathy common before him, bounded by lofty hills; behind, an immense expanse of champaign country; on his right is a lovely lake, crisping to the fragrant winds; and on his left, nestling in foliage of antique oaks and majestic elms, sleeps, in rural repose, the village. He pauses for one moment on the green sward—his eyes are upon the golden fretwork of the heavens. You may see, by the mantling cheek, that there is a gush of rapture thrilling through his bosom; and his glistening eyes are beautiful, for in them is silent worship. Perhaps the reverie is too joyous, the swelling sensation in his bosom too overpowering, for see, with a bound like that of a startled stag, he is off and away. He is racing with the winds—he is competing with the viewless messengers, that bring health upon their swift wings. He seems to have no object but the enjoyment of rapid motion. He leaps over bush and brake exultingly; and even while we admire him, he is down in the far vale. The cheruping lark rises from the dewy grass; he stops, and his unconscious voice bursts out into a shout of imitative rapture. At first he pours out his soliloquy in mere ejaculations of pleasure; by-and-bye, these bursts of feeling assume a more regular form; he walks more slowly, and before he has reached, on his return, the lake, he has composed a hymn of gratitude to the bountiful Author of all good, that hung the bright and gorgeous canopy above him, and spread the odoriferous and variegated carpet at his feet. He thinks himself unheard, and he shouts out his composition with honest joy. Now he plunges into the lake, and dives, and swims, and gambols amid the tiny waves. He is the personation of animal spirits. He is wild with the sweet and innocent intoxication of nature's beauty. It is six o'clock, and he hears the bell that summons him to his morning studies. The sound strikes him with no dismay. His Greek and Latin are prepared; and he well knows that the hour of his examination will be the hour of his triumph. He looks round, and he sees his master, proud of him and his talents; and school-fellows, that have all for him the greetings of a love that is not venal, and the homage of admiration that is sincere. Is not all this delightful? and this delight was all mine. Ah, my good sir—notwithstanding your bilious look, and pursed-up mouth, it, or something similar to it, was once yours. Notwithstanding the late fall in the funds, does not this description throw you back into yourself—into that close and secret arcanum of your seared heart, that you have always kept sacred for the holier feelings? I'm sure it does—I am almost inclined to believe with the Hebrews, that, though the rest of the mortal frame will perish, there is a minute and indestructible particle within us, a sort of heart of hearts, that shall last eternally, and about it will hang, for ever, all our virtues and all our youthful associations. It never grows old, though old age forgets it. Be it my office sometimes to remind the worldly, that they have that exhaustless storehouse of happiness within them.

I now began to commit the sin of much verse, and consequently acquired in the neighbouring village much notice. No chastising blow, or even word of reproof, fell upon me. My mind was fed upon praise, and my heart nourished with caresses. In the school I had no equal, and my vanity whispered that such was the case without. However, this vanity I did not show, for I was humble from excessive pride.

There are two animals that are almost certain to be spoiled— a very handsome young man, and the 'cock of the school.' Being certainly in the latter predicament, I was only saved from becoming an utter and egregious ass, by the advent of one, the cleverest, most impudent, rascally, agreeable scoundrel, that ever swindled man or deceived woman, in the shape of a wooden-legged usher. He succeeded my worthy friend of the guitar, Mr. Sigismund Pontifex. His name was Riprapton, and he only wanted the slight requisite of common honesty to have made himself the first man of any society in which fate might happen to cast him—and fate had been pleased to cast him into a great many. He was a short, compactly made, symmetrically-formed man, with a countenance deeply indented with the small pox, and, in every hole, there was visibly ensconced a little imp of audaciousness. His eyes were such intrepid and quenchless lights of impudence, that they could look even Irish *sang froid* out of countenance. And then that inimitable wooden leg! It was a perfect grace. As he managed it, it was irresistible. He did not progress with a miserable, vulgar, dot-and-go-one kind of gait; he neither hopped, nor halted, nor limped; and though he was wood from the middle of his right thigh downwards, his walk might almost have been called the poetry of motion. He never stumped, but he stole along with a glissade that was the envy and admiration—not exactly of surrounding nations—but of the dancing-master. It was a beautiful study to see him walk, and I made myself master of it. The left leg was inimitably formed; the calf was perhaps a little too round and Hibernian—a fault gracious in the eyes of the fair sex; his ancle and foot were exquisitely small and delicately turned; of course, he always wore shorts, with immaculate white cotton or silk stockings.

I shall not distinguish the two legs by the terms, the living and the dead one—it would be as great an injustice to the carved as to the calfed one. For the former had a graceful life, *sui generis*, of its own. I shall call them the pulsating and the gyrating leg, and now proceed to describe how they bore along, in a manner so fascinating, the living tabernacle of Mr. Riprapton. The pulsator, with pointed toe, and gently turned calf, would make a progress in a direct line, but as the sole touched the ground, the heel would slightly rise, and then fall, and whilst you were admiring the undulating grace of the pulsator, unobserved and silently, you would find the gyrator had stolen a march upon you, and actually taken the *pas* of its five-toed brother. One leg marched and the other swam, in the prettiest semicircle imaginable. When he stopped, the flourish of the gyrator was ineffable. The drum-stick in the hand of the big black drummer of the first regiment of foot guards, was nothing to it. Whenever Riprapton bowed, and he was always bowing, this flourish preluded and concluded the salutary bend. It was making a leg indeed.

Many a time, both by ladies and gentlemen, he had been offered a cork leg—but he knew better; had he accepted the treacherous gift, he would have appeared but as a lame man with two legs, now he was a perfect Adonis with one. I do believe, in my conscience, that Cupid often made use of this wooden appendage when he wished to befriend him, instead of one of his own arrows, for he was really a marvellous favourite with the ladies.

Well, no sooner had my friend with the peg made himself a fixture in the school, than he took me down, not one peg or two, but a good half dozen. He ridiculed my poetry—he undervalued my drawing—he hit me through my most approved guards at my fencing—he beat me hollow at hopping, though it must be confessed, that I had the advantage with two legs; but he was again my master at 'all fours.' He outtalked me immeasurably, he outbragged me most heroically, and outlied me most inconceivably. Knowing nothing either of Latin or Greek, they were beneath a gentleman's notice, fit only for parsons and pedants; and he was too patriotic to cast a thought away upon French. As he was engaged for the arithmetical and mathematical departments, it would have been perhaps as well, if he had known a little of algebra and Euclid; but, as from the first day he honoured me with a strict, though patronizing friendship, he made me soon understand that we were to share this department of knowledge in common. It was quite enough if one of the two knew anything about the matter; besides, he thought that it improved me so much to look over the problems and algebraical calculations of my schoolfellows.

With this man I was continually measuring my strength; and as I conceived that I found myself woefully wanting, he proved an excellent moral sedative to my else too rampant vanity. Few, indeed, were the persons who could feel themselves at ease under the withering sarcasms of his intolerable insolence. Much more to their astonishment than to their instruction, he would very coolly, and the more especially when ladies were present, correct the divinity of the parson, the pharmacy of the doctor, and the law of the attorney; and with that placid air of infallibility that carried conviction to all but his opponents.

Once, at a very large evening party, I heard him arguing strenuously, and very triumphantly, against a veteran captain of a merchant ship, who had circumnavigated the world with Cook, that the degrees of longitude were equal in length all over the world, be they more or less—for he never descended to details—and that the farther south you sailed, the hotter it grew, though the worthy old seaman pointed to what remained of his nose, the end of which had been nipped off by cold, and consequent mortification, in the antarctic regions. As Riprapton flourished his wooden index, in

H

the midst of his brilliant peroration, he told the honest seaman that he had not a *leg* to stand upon; and all the ladies, and some of the gentlemen too, cried out with one accord, 'O fie, Captain Headman, now don't be so obstinate—surely you are quite mistaken.' And the arch-master of impudence looked round with modest suavity, and, in an audible whisper, assured the gentleman that sat next to him, that Captain Headman's argument of the demolished proboscis went for nothing, for that there were other causes equally efficacious as cold and frost, for destroying gentlemen's noses.

In the sequel this very learned tutor had to instruct me in navigation. Nothing was too high or too low for him. Had any person wished to have taken lessons in judical astrology, Mr. Riprapton would not have refused the pupil. Plausible ignorance will always beat awkward knowledge, when the ignorant, which is generally the case, make up the mass of the audience.

CHAPTER XXI

Treateth of the amativeness of wooden members, and the folly of virgin frights—Ralph putteth his threat of versifying into actual execution, for which he may be thought worthy of being executed.

NOTWITHSTANDING the superciliousness of my friendly assistant, I still wrote verse, which was handed about the village as something wonderful. As Riprapton doubted, or rather denied my rhyming prowess, at length I was determined to try it upon himself, and he shortly gave me an excellent opportunity for so doing. Writers who pride themselves on going deeply into the mysteries of causes and effects will tell you, that in cold weather people are apt to congregate about the fire. Our usher, and a circle of admiring pupils, were one day establishing the truth of this profound theory. The timbered man was standing in the apex of the semicircle, his back to the fire-place, and his coat tails tucked up under his arms. He was enjoying himself, and we were enjoying him. He was the hero of the tale he was telling us—indeed, he never had any other hero than himself—and this tale was wonderful. In the energy of delivery, now the leg of wood would start up with an egotistical flourish, and describe with the leg of flesh, a right-angled triangle, and then down would go the peg, and up the leg, with the toe well pointed, whilst he greeted the buckle on his foot with an admiring glance.

Whilst this was proceeding in the school-room; in the back-kitchen, or rather breakfast-parlour, immediately below, in a very brown study, there sate a very fair lady, pondering deeply over the virtues of brimstone and treacle, and the most efficacious antidote to chilblains. She was the second in command over the domestic economy of the school. Unmarried of course. And ever and anon, as she plied the industrious needle over the heel of the too fragmental stocking, the low melody would burst unconsciously forth of, 'Is there nobody coming to marry me? Nobody coming to woo-oo-oo?' Lady, not in vain was the burden of that votive song. There *was* somebody coming.

Let us walk up stairs—Mr. Rip is in the midst of his narrative—speaking thus:—'And, young gentlemen, as I hate presumption, and can never tolerate a coxcomb, perceiving that his lordship was going to be insolent, up went thus my foot to chastise him, and down,'——a crash! a cry of alarm, and then one of derision, and behold the chastiser of insolence, or at least, that part of him that was built of wood, through the floor!

Mr. Cherfeuil opening the door at this moment, and perceiving a great noise, and not perceiving him who ought to have repressed it, for the boys standing round *what remained of him* with us, it was concealed from the worthy pedagogue, who exclaimed, 'Vat a noise be here! Vere ist Mr. Reepraaptong?'

'Just *stepped* down *below*, to Miss Brocade, in the breakfast-parlour,' I replied.

'Ah, bah! *c'est un veritable chevalier aux dames,*' said Mr. Cherfeuil, and slamming to the door, he hurried down stairs to reclaim his too gallant representative. We allowed Mr. Riprapton to inhabit for some time two floors at once, for he was, in his position, perfectly helpless; that admired living leg of his, stretched out at its length upon the floor. We soon, however, recovered him; but so much I cannot say of his composure, for he never lost it. I do not believe that he was ever discountenanced in his life.

'Nobody coming to woo-oo-oo,' sang Miss Brocade below—down into her lap come mortar, rubbish, and clouds of dust! And, when the mist clears away, there pointed down from above an inexplicable index. Her senses were bewildered, and being quite at a loss to comprehend the miracle, she had nothing else to do but faint away. When Mr. Cherfeuil entered, the simple and good-natured Gaul found his beloved manageress apparently lifeless at his feet, covered with the *débris* of his ceiling, and the wooden leg of his usher slightly tremulous above him. The fright, of course, was succeeded by a laugh, and the fracture by repairs, and the whole by the following school-boy attempt at a copy of verses, upon the never-to-be-forgotten occasion.

> Ambitious usher! there are few
>   Beyond you that can go,
> In double character, to woo
>   The lovely nymph below.
> At once both god and man you ape
>   To expedite your flame;
> And yet you find in either shape,
>   The failure just the same.
>
> Jove fell in fair Danaë's lap
>   In showers of glittering gold;
> By Jove! his Joveship was no sap!
>   How could *you* be so bold,
> To hope to have a like success,
>   Most sapient ciphering master,
> And think a lady's lap to bless
>   With show'rs of *lath* and *plaster?*
>
> That you should fail, when you essay'd
>   To act the god of thunder,
> In striving to enchant the maid,
>   Was really no great wonder;
> But when as *man* you wooing go,
>   Pray let me ask you whether
> You had no better leg to show,
>   Than one of wood and leather?

These verses are exactly as I wrote them, and I trust the reader will not think that I could now be guilty of such a line, as 'To *expedite* your flame,' or of the pedantic school-boyism of calling a house-keeper a nymph. In fact, it is by the merest accident, that I am now enabled to give them in their genuine shape. An old school-fellow, whom I have not seen since the days of syntax, and whose name I had utterly forgotten, enclosed them to me very lately.

However, such as they are, they were thought in a secluded village as something extraordinary. The usher himself affected to enjoy them extremely. They added greatly to my reputation, and what was of more consequence to me, my invitations to dinner and to tea. Truly, my half-holidays were no longer my own. I had become an object of curiosity, and I hope and believe, in many instances, of affection. I was quite cured of my mendacious propensities, by the pain, the horror, and the disgust that they had inflicted upon me at my last school. I invented no more mysteries and improbabilities for myself, but my good-natured friends did it amply for me.

Mrs. Cherfeuil asserted she knew scarcely anything about me—indeed, before I came to her school, she had hardly seen me four times during the whole space of my existence. She only knew that I was the child of a lady that accident had thrown in her way, a lady whom she knew but shortly, but for whom she acquired a friendship as strong as it proved short; that, from mere sympathy she had been induced to stand godmother to me; that she had never felt authorized, nor did she inquire into the particulars of my birth. Of course, there was a mystery attached to it, but to which she had no clue; however, she knew, that at least on one side, I came of good, nay, very distinguished, parentage. But this, her departed friend assured her, and that most solemnly, that whoever should stigmatize me as illegitimate would do me a grievous wrong.

Here was a subject to be canvassed in a gossiping village! Conjecture was at its busy work. I was quite satisfied with the place that the imaginations of my hospitable patrons had given me in the social scale. Nor in the country only did I experience this friendly feeling; most of my vacations were spent in town, at the houses of the parents of some of my school-fellows. I was now made acquainted with the scenic glories of the stage. I fought my way through crowds of fools, to see a child perform the heroic Coriolanus, the philosophical Hamlet, and the venerable and magnificent Lear. Master Betty was at the height of his reputation; and the dignified and classical Kemble had, for a time, to veil his majestic countenance from the play-going eye. Deeply infatuated, indeed, were the Molly-coddles with their Betty.

As the diplomatists say, mine was a curious, yet a pleasant position.

I felt myself shadowed from all evils by the guardian wings of an unavowed, yet fond and admiring mother; often, when in company, have I seen her eye glisten, and her face flush, with the mantling blush of triumph, as some one has praised me for some good quality, either real or imaginary. I alone felt and understood, and loved those emotions, that were to all others so mysterious. But she followed one unvarying policy: her's was constantly the language, let who would praise me, of gentle depreciation, but a depreciation always accompanied by a saving clause, that generally made it real commendation. And how very cautious she was of showing me anything like a preference! Hardly ever did I find myself alone with her, and on those rare occasions when it so happened, her manner was more than ordinarily cold. The words, 'who am I?' always when we were thus situated, burned upon my lips, yet such was the respect with which her deportment inspired me, that I could not utter what was so painful to suppress.

Whatever once there might have been, at this period, though perhaps placed in a most romantic situation, there was not a particle of romance in her character. How could there be, when her bosom was continually filled with suppressed tenderness, and per-adventure, fear? That she loved me with a surpassing affection I felt assured, from two little circumstances; the first was, every night, when she thought me soundly asleep, before she retired, her-self, to rest, she came and kissed me as I lay in bed, first ascertain-ing, by many little manœuvres, if I were not awake. She would stoop down, and as she eased the fulness of her maternal heart, she did it tremblingly and cautiously, like a guilty thing. Once or twice, I purposely let her see that I was awake, and then, as I watched her retire, she did so with a look of such sorrow and disappointment, that I was determined no more to inflict upon her so much pain,— and thus, whilst, in general, the expected benison kept me awake until she came and gave it, I always feigned sleep that I might ensure it, and a sweet night's rest in the bargain, to myself. How she would have comforted herself, had I been seriously ill, I can-not conjecture, for that trial was never put upon her; as, notwith-standing my weakly infancy, and excepting during the low fever flogged into me by Mr. Root, I was never confined, during the whole course of my life, by any malady, for a single day. Of course I do not reckon the infliction of wounds and the effects of external accidents as sicknesses.

CHAPTER XXII

Ralph describeth a rare character, a noble and a good man—He goeth to fish without a rod, and suffereth more than fifty rods could inflict, and is not reconciled to the honour of the sun riding him a pick-a-back.

IT is now my duty, as well as my greatest pleasure, to put on record the true kindness, the considerate generosity, and the well-directed munificence of a family, a parallel to which can only be found in our own soil—a superior nowhere. By the heads of this family, I was honoured with particular notice. Perhaps they never gave a thought about my poetical talent, or the wonderful progress that my master said that I had made in my classics, and my wooden-legged tutor in my mathematics. Their kind patronage sprang from higher motives,—from benevolence; they had heard that I had been forsaken—their own hearts told them that the sunshine of kindness must be doubly grateful to the neglected, and, indeed, to me they were very kind.

Perhaps it may be thought, that I had a quick eye to the failings and the ridiculous points of those with whom chance threw me in contact. I am sure that I was equally susceptible to the elevation of character that was offered to me, in the person of Mr. ——, the respected father of the family of which I have just made mention.[1] As the noble class to which he belonged, and of which he was the first ornament, are fast degenerating, I will endeavour to make a feeble portrait of a man, that at present finds but too few imitators, and that could never have found a superior. He was one of those few merchant princes, that was really, in all things, princely. Whilst his comprehensive mind directed the commerce of half a navy, and sustained in competence and happiness hundreds at home, and thousands abroad, the circle immediately around him felt all the fostering influence of his well-directed liberality, as if all the energies of his powerful genius had been concentrated in the object of making those only about him prosperous. He was born for the good of the many, as much as for the elevation of the individual. Society had need of him, and it confessed it. When its interests were invaded by a short-sighted policy, it called upon his name to advocate its violated rights, and splendidly

did he obey the call. He understood England's power and greatness, for he had assisted in increasing it; he knew in what consisted her strength, and in that strength he was strong, and in
his own.

As a senator, he was heard in the assembled councils of his
nation, and those who presided over her mighty resources and
influenced her destinies, that involved those of the world, listened
to his warning counsel, were convinced that his words were the
dictates of wisdom, and obeyed. This is neither fiction nor fulsome
panegyric. The facts that I narrate have become part of our history;
and I would narrate them more explicitly, did I not fear to wound
the susceptibilities of his still existing and distinguished family.
How well he knew his own station, and preserved, with the blandest
manners, the true dignity of it! Though renowned in parliament for
his eloquence, at the palace for his patriotic loyalty, and in the city
for his immense wealth, in the blessed circle, that he truly made
social, there was a pleasing simplicity and joyousness of manner,
that told, at once, the fascinated guest, that though he might earn
honours and distinctions abroad, it was at home that he looked for
happiness—and, uncommon as such things are in this repining
world—there, I verily believe, he found it. His was a happy lot:
he possessed a lady, in his wife, who at once shared his virtues and
adorned them. The glory he won was reflected sweetly upon her,
and she wore with dignity, and enhanced those honours, that his
probity, his talents, and his eloquence had acquired. At the time
of which I am speaking, he was blessed with daughters, that even
in their childhood had made themselves conspicuous by their
accomplishments, amiability of disposition, and gracefulness of
manners, and plagued with sons who were full of wildness,
waggishness, and worth.

It is too seldom the case that the person accords with the high
qualification of the mind. Mr. —— was a singular and felicitous
exception to this mortifying rule. His deportment was truly dignified, his frame well-knit and robust, and his features were almost
classically regular. His complexion was florid, and the expression of
his countenance serene, yet highly intelligent. No doubt but that his
features were capable of a vast range of expression; but, as I never
saw them otherwise than beaming with benevolence, or sparkling
with wit, I must refer to Master James, or Master Frank, for the
description of the austerity of his frown, or the awfulness of his rebuke.

This gentleman's two elder sons, at the time to which I allude, had already made their first step in the world. James was making a tour of the West Indies, the continent being closed against him; and Frank had already begun his harvest of laurels in the navy under a distinguished officer. The younger sons, my juniors, were my school-fellows. Master Frank was two or three years my senior, and before he went to sea, not going to the same school as myself, we got together only during the vacations; when, notwithstanding my prowess, he would fag me desperately at cricket, out-swim me on the lake, and out-cap me at making Latin verses. However, I consoled myself by saying, 'As I grow older all this superiority will cease.' But when he returned, after his first cruise, glittering in his graceful uniform, my hopes and my ambition sank below zero. He was already a man, and an officer—I a schoolboy, and nothing else.

Of course he had me home to spend the day with him—and a day we had of it. It was in the middle of summer, and grapes were ripe only in such well-regulated hot-houses as were Mr. ——'s. We did not enact the well-known fable as it is written—the grapes were not *too* sour—nor did we repeat the fox's ill-natured and sarcastic observation, 'That they were only fit for blackguards.' We found them very good for gentlemen—though, I fear, Mr. ——'s dessert some time after owed more to Pomona than to Bacchus for its embellishments. And the fine mulberry-tree on the lawn—we were told that it must be shaken, and we shook it: if it still exist, I'll answer for it, it has never been so shaken since.

The next day we went fishing. Though our bodies were not yet fully grown, we were persons of enlarged ideas; and to suppose that we, two mercurial spirits, could sit like a couple of noodles, each with a long stick in our hands, waiting for the fish to pay us a visit, was the height of absurdity. No, we were rather too polite for that; and as it was we, and not the gentlemen of the finny tribe that sought acquaintance, we felt it our duty as gentlemen to visit them. We carried our politeness still farther, and showed our good breeding in endeavouring to accommodate ourselves to the tastes and habits of those we were about to visit. 'Do at Rome as the Romans do,' is the essence of all politeness. As our friends were accustomed to be *in naturalibus—vulgice*, stark naked, we adopted their Adamite fashion, and, undressing, in we plunged. Our success was greater with the finny, than was that of any exquisite, with the fair tribe. We captivated and captured pailfuls. We drove our entertainers into the narrow creeks in shoals, and then with a net extended between us, we had the happiness of introducing them into the upper air. The sport was so good, that we were induced to continue it for some hours, but whilst we were preparing for a multitudinous fry, the sun was actually all the while enjoying a most extensive broil. Our backs, and mine especially, became one continuous blister. Whilst in the water, and in the pursuit, I did not regard it—indeed, we were able to carry home the trophies of our success—and then—I hastened to bed. My back was fairly peeled and repeeled. I performed involuntarily Mr. St. John's curative process to a miracle. No wonder that I've been ever since free from all, even the slightest symptoms of pulmonary indisposition. However, my excruciating torments gained me two things—experience, and a new skin.

When I had fresh skinned myself, and it took me more than a week to do it, I found that my fellow-labourer had flown. I heard that he had suffered almost as severely as myself, but, as he looked upon himself as no vulgar hero, he was too manly to complain, and next Sunday he actually went to church, whilst I lay in bed smarting with pain—yet I strongly suspect that a new sword, that he had that day to hang by his side, made him regardless to the misery of his back.

That Sunday fortnight I dined with Mr. ——, and of course he did me the honour to converse upon our fishing exploit, and its painful consequences.

'So, Master Rattlin,' said the worthy gentleman, 'you think that you and Frank proved yourselves excellent sportsmen?'

'Yes, sir,' said I; 'I will answer for the sport, if you will only be pleased to answer for the men.'

'Well said, my little man!' said Mrs. —— to me, smiling kindly.

'You see, sir, with all submission, I've gained the verdict of the lady; and that's a great deal.'

'But I think you lost your hide. Was your back very sore?' said my host encouragingly.

'O dear—very sore indeed, sir! Mrs. Cherfeuil said that it looked quite like a new cut steak.'

'O it did, did it? but Frank's was not much better' said the senator turning to his lady.

'Indeed it was not,' said she compassionately.

'Very well,' said Mr. ——, very quietly. 'I'll tell you this, Master Ralph, sportsmen as you think yourselves, you and Frank, after all, whatever you both were when you went into the lake, you turned out two *Johnny Raws*.'

'Why, Master Rattlin,' said the lady, 'Mr. —— uses you worse than the sun—that did but scorch—but he roasts you.'

'No wonder, madam, as he considers me *raw*,' replied I.

CHAPTER XXIII

Reminiscences—A friend found and a line lost—Ralph makes a new acquaintance and a hearty supper, both of which do him much good.

OPENLY admired abroad, and secretly cherished by a love, the more intense because concealed, at home, the course of my days was as happy as the improvement in the various branches of my education was rapid. Nor was I wholly unnoticed by men who have since stood forward, honoured characters, in the van of those who have so nobly upheld the fame of England. The bard who began his career in the brightest fields of Hope,[1] and whose after-fame has so well responded to his auspicious commencement, read many portions of my boyish attempts, and pronounced them full of promise, and the author possessed of *nous*. It was the term he himself used, and that is the only reason why I have recorded it. Indeed, this deservedly great man was, in some sense, my school-fellow, for he came in the evening to learn French of M. Cherfeuil. He was then engaged to translate an epic, written by one of the Buonapartes, into English verse. I believe that engagement never was carried into effect, notwithstanding the erudite pains Mr. —— took to qualify himself to perform it successfully. No man could have laboured more to make himself master of the niceties of the Gallic idiom, and the right use of its very doubtful subjunctive.

At the time to which I allude, the inspired author wore a wig[2]—not that his then age required one. Perhaps, the fervid state of his brain, like a hidden volcano, burnt up the herbage above—perhaps, his hair was falling off from the friction of his laurels—perhaps growing prematurely grey from the workings of his spirit; but without venturing upon any more conjectures, we may safely come to the conclusion, that the hair that God gave him did not please him so well as that which he bought of the perruquiers. Since we cannot be satisfied with the causes, we must be satisfied with the fact—he wore a wig; and, in the distraction of mental perplexity, when M. Cherfeuil was essaying to get the poet out of the absent into the conditional mood, the man of verse staring abstractedly upon the man of tense, would thrust his hand under his peruke, and rub, rub, rub his polished scalp, which all the while effused a divine ichor—(poets never perspire)—and, when he was gently reminded that his wig was a little awry towards the left side, he would pluck it, resentfully, equally as much awry on the right; and then, to punish the offending and displacing hand, he would commence gnawing off the nails of his fingers, rich with the moisture from above. We have recorded this little personal trait, because it may be valuable to the gentleman's future biographers; and also because it is a convincing proof to the illiterate and the leveller, that head work is not such easy, sofa-enjoyed labour, as is commonly supposed; and finally, that the great writer's habit, *vivos ungues rodere*, proves him to be, tooth and nail, *homo ad unguem factus*.

I was also honoured with the friendship and monitory familiarity of Dr. ——, a retired head-master of one of our principal public schools.[1] He was a man who had seen much of the highest circles, had been a courtier, and was once upon a most intimate footing with the third George. This gentleman gave me lessons, better than any I have ever heard or read, upon the *practicability* of true Christianity in every grade of life. He impressed upon my mind, that Christianity, though a creed, was as essentially a virtue as courage, and as necessary to the fulfilment of the duties of life. He showed me that it could go with the labourer to the plough, with the lawyer to the bar, and even with the soldier to battle. He proved to me that it might be courtly with the polished gentleman, gainful with the merchant, and even rough with the sailor; and yet, be not only in all truth itself unchanged, yet continually changing those who possessed it really, into better and higher beings. I owe him much that I ought to have treasured with a better memory, and to have repaid with a better life.

I feel, also, that there are many other persons to whom I ought to pay a passing tribute of gratitude for much kindness shown to me; but, as my first duty is to my readers, I must not run the risk of wearying them even by the performance of a virtue. But there was one, to omit the mention of whom would be, on my part, the height of ingratitude, and, as concerns the public, something very like approaching to a fraud; for by the implied contract between it and me, I am, in this my auto-biography, bound to supply them with the very best materials, served up to them in my very best manner. The gentleman whom I am going to introduce to the notice of my readers, was the purest personation of benevolence that perhaps ever existed. His countenance was a glowing index of peace with himself, goodwill to man, and confidence in the love of God. There was within him that divine sympathy for all around him, that brings man, in what man can alone emulate the angels, so near to his Creator. But with all this goodness of soul there was nothing approaching to weakness, or even misjudging softness; he had seen, had known, and had struggled with the world. He left the sordid strife triumphantly, and bore away with him, if not a large fortune, a competence; and what also was of infinitely more value, that 'peace of mind which passeth all understanding.'

Mr. R——[1] was, in his person, stout, tall, florid in his countenance, and, for a man past fifty, the handsomest that I have ever beheld. I do not mean to say that his features possessed a classical regularity, but that soul of benevolence transpired through, and was bound up with them, that had a marble bust fitly representing them been handed down to posterity from some master-hand of antiquity, we should have reverenced it with awe as something beyond human nature, and gazed on it at the same time with love, as being so dearly and sweetly human. These are not the words of enthusiasm, but a mere narrative of fact. He wore his own white and thin hair, that was indeed so thin, that the top of his head was quite bald. A snuff-coloured coat, cut in the olden fashion, knee-breeches, white lamb's-wool stockings, and shoes of rather high quarters, gave a little of the primitive to his highly respectable appearance.

I first saw him as he was pretending to angle in the river that runs through the village. Immediately I had gazed upon his benignant countenance, I went and sate down by him. I could not help it. At once I understood the urbanity and the gentlemanliness that must have existed in the patriarchal times. There was no need of forms between us. He made room for me as a son, and I looked up to him as to a father. He smiled upon me so encouragingly, and so confidently, that I found myself resting my arm upon his knee, with all the loving familiarity of long-tried affection. From that first moment of meeting until his heart lay cold in the grave—and cold the grave alone could make it—a singular, unswerving, and, on my part, an absorbing love was between us. We remained for a space in this caressing position, in silence; my eyes now drinking in the rich hues of the evening, now the mental expression of the 'good old man.' 'O! it is very beautiful,' said I, thinking as much of his mild face as of the gorgeousness of the sky above me.

'And do you *feel it?*' said he. 'Yes, I see you do; by your glistening eyes and heightened colour.'

'I feel very happy,' I replied; 'and have just now two very, very strange wishes, and I don't know which I wish for most.'

'What are they, my little friend?'

'O! you will laugh at me so if I tell you.'

'No, I will not, indeed. I never laugh at anybody.'

'Ah, I was almost sure of that. Well, I was wishing when I looked up into the sky, that I could fly through and through those golden clouds like an eagle; and when I looked at you, I wished that I were just such a good-natured old gentleman.'

'Come, come, there is more flattery than good sense in your wishes. Your first is unreasonable, and your second will come upon you but too soon.'

'I did not mean to flatter you,' I replied, looking proudly; 'for I would neither be an eagle nor an old man, longer than those beautiful clouds last, and the warm sunset makes your face look so—so——'

'Never mind—you shall save your fine speeches for the young ladies.'

'But I have got some for the gentlemen too: and there's one running in my head just now.'

'I should like to hear it.'

'Should you? Well, this fine evening put me in mind of it; it is Mrs. Barbauld's Ode.'[1] And then putting myself into due attitude, I mouthed it through much to my own, and still more to Mr. R.'s satisfaction. That was a curious, a simple, and yet a cheering scene. My listener was swaying to and fro, with the cadences of the poetry; I with passionate fervour ranting before him; and, in the mean time, his rod and line, unnoticed by either, were navigating peacefully, yet rapidly, down the river. When I had concluded, his tackle was just turning an eddy, far down below us, and the next moment was out of sight.

Without troubling ourselves much about the loss, shortly after, we were seen hand in hand, walking down the village in earnest conversation. I went home with him—I shared with him and his amiable daughters a light and early supper, of fruit and pastry; and such was the simultaneous affection that sprung up between us—so confiding was it in its nature, and so little worldly, that I had gained the threshold, and was about taking my leave, ere it occurred to him to ask, or myself to say, who I was, and where I resided.

From that evening; excepting when employed in my studies, we were almost inseparable. I told him my strange story; and he seemed to love me for it a hundredfold more. He laid all the nobility, and even the princes of the blood, under contribution, to procure me a father. He came to the conclusion firmly, and at once, that Mrs. Cherfeuil was my mother. Oh! this mystery made him superlatively happy. And when he came to the knowledge of my poetical talents, he was really in an ecstacy of delight. He rhymed himself. He gave me subjects—he gave me advice—he gave me emendations, and interpolations. He re-youthed himself. In many a sequestered nook in the beautiful vicinity of the village, we have sat, each with his pencil and paper in his hand—now ranting, now conversing—and in his converse the instruction I received was invaluable. He has confirmed me in the doctrine of the innate goodness of human nature. Since the period to which I am alluding, I have seen much of villany. I have been the victim, as well as the witness, of treachery. I have been oftentimes forced to associate with vice in every shape; and yet when, in misery, when oppressed, when writhing under tyranny, I have been sometimes tempted to curse my race, the thought of the kind, the good old man, has come over me like a visitation from heaven, and my malediction has been changed into a prayer, if not into a blessing.

CHAPTER XXIV

*A disaster by water is the first cause of all Ralph's future disasters
upon it—He gets with his tutor out of his depth, in latitude and
longitude; and finds himself rivalled by the man with the peg.*

OF course, Mr. R. sought and soon gained the friendship of Mrs.
Cherfeuil—and then he commenced operations systematically.
Now he would endeavour to take her by surprise—now to overcome by entreaty, and then to entrap by the most complex cross
questions. He would be, by turns, tender, gallant, pathetic,
insinuating; but all was of no avail—her secret, whatever it was,
was firmly secured in her own bosom. With well-acted simplicity
she gave my worthy friend the same barren account about me that
was at the service of all interrogators.

What poems did not Mr. R—d—n and myself write together—
how he prophesied my future greatness, and how fervently he set
about to convince any one of his mistake, who could not see in me
the future glory of the age! The good man! His amiable *self-
deception* was to him the source of the purest happiness; and never
was happiness more deserved. Even at that early age, I often could
not help smiling at his simplicity, that all the while he was doing
his best to make me one of the vainest and most egregious coxcombs, by his unfeigned wonder at some puny effort of my puny
muse, and by his injudicious praises, he would lecture me parentally,
by the hour, upon the excellence of humility, and the absolute
necessity of modesty, as a principal ingredient to make a great
character.

However, I had my correction at home, in my wooden-legged
preceptor; if I returned from R—d—n's, in my own imagination,
like poor Gil Blas, the eighth wonder of the world, he would soon,
in his own refined phraseology, convince me that I was 'no great
shakes.' Being now nearly sixteen, I began to make conjectures
upon my future destiny; and a sorrowful accident at once determined in what line I should make my ineffectual attempts upon
fame.

I have mentioned a noble piece of water that lay adjacent to the
school. It was during the holidays, when the rest of the young
gentlemen were at their respective homes, that I, accompanied by

some young acquaintances who resided in the village, repaired to the water to swim. It was a fine summer's afternoon, and both Mr. and Mrs. Cherfeuil were in town. There was a little boy named Fountain, also staying with me at school during the vacation, and he too stole after us unperceived, and when I and my companions had swam to the middle of the lake, the imprudent little fellow also stripped, and went into the water. There were some idle stragglers looking on, and, when I was far, very far from the spot, the fearful shout came along the level surface, of 'Help, help, he is drowning!' and with dreadful distinctness, as if the voice had been shrieked into my very ears, I heard the poor lad's bubbling and smothered cry of 'Ralph Rattlin!' Poor fellow, he thought there was safety wherever I was, for I had often borne him over the lake out of his depth, as I taught him to swim, at which art he was still too imperfect. I immediately turned to the place, and strove, and buffetted, and panted, but the distance was great; and, though a rapid and most expert swimmer, when I arrived at the spot that the lookers on indicated, not a circle, not a ruffle appeared to show where a human soul was struggling beneath, to free itself from its mortal clay. Four or five times I dived, and stayed below the water with desperate pertinacity, and ploughed up the muddy bottom, but they had pointed out to me the wrong spot.

Finding my efforts useless, naked as I was, with the fleetness of a greyhound I started into the village and gave the alarm, and immediately that I saw the people running to the lake, I was there before them and again diving. Mrs. ——, the lady of the M.P. whom I have before mentioned, who was always the foremost in every work of humanity, was soon on the banks, accompanied by many of the most respectable inhabitants in the vicinity. Mrs. ——, who never lost her presence of mind, immediately suggested that a boat that lay on the neighbouring river, and which belonged to the landlord of the principal inn, should be conveyed, on men's shoulders, across the space of land that divided one water from the other. The landlord refused—yes, actually refused—but Mrs. ——, who from her station, and her many virtues, possessed a merited and commanding influence in the place, ordered the boat to be taken by force, and she was promptly and cheerfully obeyed. Whilst this was going forward, I was astonishing everybody by the length of time I stayed underneath the water; and a last effort almost proved fatal to me, for, when I arose, the blood gushed

I

from my mouth and nose; and, when I got on shore, I felt so weak, that I was obliged to be assisted in dressing myself. The boat now began to sweep the bottom with ropes, but this proved as ineffectual to recover the body as were my own exertions.

It was the next day before it was found, and then it was brought up by a Newfoundland dog, very far from the spot in which we had searched for it. Had the frightened spectators, who stood on the shore, but have shown me correctly where the lad had disappeared, I have no doubt but that I should have brought the body up in time for resuscitation. To persons who have not seen what can be done by those who make water, in a manner, their own element, my boyish exertions seemed almost miraculous. My good old friend was present, betraying a curious mixture of fear and admiration; big, as I then was, he almost carried me in his arms home, that is, to the school-house, and there we found all in confusion: Mrs. Cherfeuil had just arrived, and hearing that one of the boys was drowned, had given one painful shriek and fainted. When we came into the room she was still in a state of insensibility, and, as we stood around, she slowly opened her eyes; but the moment that they became conscious of my presence, she leaped up with frantic joy and strained me in her arms, and then, laying her head upon my shoulder, burst into a passion of tears. Mr. R. cast upon me a most triumphant smile, and, as he led me away from the agitated lady, she took a silent farewell of me, with a look of intense fondness, and a depth of ineffable felicity, which I hope will be present to me in my dying hour; for assuredly it will make light the parting pang.

All this may seem very vain-glorious, but I cannot help it—the truth is dearer to me than my bashfulness—and I believe so well of the most cynical that may condemn this egotism, as to think that, under similar circumstances, they would have acted in a similar manner. However, this affair changed the whole current of Mr. R—d—n's ideas, and altered his plans for me. I was no longer to be the future poet laureate; I was no more enticed to sing great deeds, but to do them. The sword was to displace the pen, the hero the poet. Verse was too effeminate, and rhyme was severely interdicted, and to be forgiven only when it was produced by accident.

He was some time before he brought Mrs. Cherfeuil over to his opinions. It was in vain that she protested the direction of my fate was in other hands, he would not listen to it for a moment; he was obstinate, and I suppose, by what occurred, he was in the right. He declared that the navy was the only profession that deserved my spirit and my abilities. This declaration, perhaps, was not unacceptable at head quarters, wherever they might have been. For myself, I was nothing loath, and the gallant bearing and the graceful uniform of my gallant young friend, Frank ——, who had already seen some hard fighting, added fresh stimulants to my desires. My friend Riprapton had now the enviable task to impart to me the science of navigation, and, with his peculiar notions of longitude and latitude, there can be no question as to the merits of the tuition that I received from that very erudite person.

Shortly after I had commenced navigation under his auspices, or, more properly speaking, that he was forced to attend to it a little under mine, the harmony of our friendship was broken by a quarrel; yes, a heart-embroiling quarrel—and, strange to say, about a lady. I concede to this paragon of ushers that he was a general favourite with the sex. I was never envious of him. All the world knows that I ever did sufficient honour to his attractions—I acknowledged always the graces that appertained to his wooden progression—but still, he was not omnipotent. Wilkes, that epitome of all manner of ugliness, often boasted that he was only an hour behind the handsomest man that ever existed, as far as regarded his position with the fair. Rip was but twenty-five minutes and a fraction. In ten minutes he would talk the generality of women into a good opinion of themselves—an easy matter some may think, for the ladies have one ready made—but it is a different thing from having it and daring to own it. In ten minutes he would make his listener, by some act or word, avow her opinion of her own excellence, in ten more he would bring her to the same opinion as regarded himself, and the remaining five he used to occupy with his declaration of love; for he was very rapid in his execution—and the thing was done; for if he had not made a conquest, he chronicled one—and that was the same thing. He looked more for the glory than the fruition of his passions. In one respect, he followed Chesterfield's advice with wonderful accuracy; he hazarded a declaration of love to every woman between sixteen and sixty, a little under and over also; for, with his lordship, he came to the very pertinent conclusion, that, if the act were not taken as a sincerity, it would be as a compliment. This ready-made adorer, for every new-comer, was as jealous as he was universal in his attachments.

Let the imaginative think, and, running over with their mind's
eye all the beautiful sculptures of antiquity, endeavour to picture
to themselves a personation of that commanding goddess that the
ancients venerated under the title of Juno. The figure must be tall,
in proportion faultless, in majesty unrivalled, in grace enchanting;
all the outlines of the form must be full yet not swelling—and, as
far removed from the modern notions of *en bon point* as possible—
let us add to these the bust of Venus ere she weaned her first born,
the winged-boy god; and then we may have an adequate idea of the
figure of Mrs. Causand. Her face was of that style of beauty that
those women who think themselves delicate are pleased to slander
under the name of bold—a style of beauty, however, that all men
admire and most men like. Thirty-five years had only written in
a stronger hand those attractions which must have undergone every
phase of loveliness, and which now, without appearing matronly,
seemed stamped with the signs of a long-enduring maturity. The
admiration she excited was general; as she passed, men paused to
look upon her, and women whispered to each other behind her
back. Never, till this paragon had made her appearance, had I heard
of ladies wearing supposititious portions of the human frame—
now I found that envy, or the figure maker, had improved almost
every member of Mrs. Causand's body. It was voted by all the
female scandal of the village that such perfection could not be
natural—but, since if all were true that was said upon the subject,
the object of their criticism must have been as artificial as Mr.
Riprapton's left leg, and she must have been nothing more than an
animated lay figure, I began to disbelieve these assertions, the more
especially as the lady herself was as easy under them as she was in
every gesture and motion. Whenever she made her appearance, so
did my old friend Mr. R—d—n; he entertained a platonic attachment for her, and that the more strongly, as each visit enabled him
to entertain every one who would listen to him, with a long story
about the king of Prussia. And every lady expects attention and
politeness as a matter of course, equally as a matter of course did she
expect the assiduities and some manifestation, even stronger than
gallantry—and treated it merely as a matter of course. Really, without an hyperbole, she was a woman to whom an appearance of
devotion might be excusable, and looked upon more as a tribute
to the abstract spirit of beauty and its divine Creator, than as
a sensual testimony to the individual.

Her first appearance even silenced the hitherto dauntless loquacity of Rip—for half a minute. But he made fearful amends for this involuntary display of modesty afterwards. *Secundum artem*, he opened all the batteries of his fascination upon her. He rolled his eyes at her with a violence approaching to agony; he bowed; he displayed in every possible and captivating attitude his one living leg—but his surpassing strength was in the adulation of his serpent tongue—and she bore it all so stoically; she would smile upon him when he made a good hit, as upon an actor on the boards —she would, at times, even condescend to improve some of his compliments upon herself; and when her easy manners had perchance overset him at the very *début* of one of his finest speeches, she would begin it again for him; taking up the dropped sentence, and then settle herself into a complacent attitude for listening.

CHAPTER XXV

Evidences of good taste in favour of Master Ralph—Jealousy ushers in revenge, revenge retaliation, which he is compelled to chronicle on the usher's face, and what punishment thereupon ensued.

WHEN Mrs. Causand came to Stickenham, she made universal jubilee. The orderly routine of scholastic life had no longer place. She almost ruined Riprapton in clean linen, perfumes, and Windsor soap. Cards and music enlivened every evening; and the games she played were those of the fashion of the day, and she always played high, and always won. Her ascendancy over Mrs. Cherfeuil was complete. The latter was treated with much apparent affection, but still with the airs of a patroness. I do not know that the handsome schoolmistress lent her money, for I do not think that she stood in need of it; but I feel assured that her whole property was at her disposal. She stood in awe of her. *She knew her secret.*

With his usual acuteness, my good old friend discovered this immediately, and he began to woo her also, more for her secret than for her heart. But she was a perfect mystery—I never knew till her death who she was. Her residence was at no time mentioned, and I believe that no one knew it but the lady of the house and myself, when Mrs. Causand herself gave it me at the eve of my departing for my ship. She came without notice, staid as long as she chose, and departed with an equal disregard to ceremony.

She loved me to a folly. She would hold me at her knees by the hour, and scan every feature of my countenance, as Ophelia said[1] of Hamlet, 'as she would draw it.' And then she smiled and looked grave, and sighed and laughed; and I, like a little fool, set all these symptoms of perturbation down to my own unfledged attractions, whilst during their perusal she would often exclaim, 'So like him! —so like him!' I do not know whether I ought to mention it, for it is a censorious world; but, as I cannot enter into, or be supposed to understand, the feelings of a fine woman of thirty-five caressing a lad of fifteen, I have a right to suppose all such demonstrations of fondness highly virtuous and purely maternal; though, perhaps, to the fair bestower a little pleasant. I found them exquisitely so. I bore all her little blandishments with a modest pleasure; for, observing the high respect in which she was generally held, I looked upon these testimonials of affection as a great honour, sought them with eagerness, and remembered them with gratitude.

Manner is perhaps more seducing than mere beauty; but where they are allied, the captivation is irresistible. That subduing alliance was to be found in perfection in the person of Mrs. Causand. As she always dressed up to the very climax of the fashion, possessed a great variety of rich bijouterie, and never came down to us in the stage, but always posted it, I concluded that she was in very easy circumstances.

I cannot speak as to the extent of her mental powers, as her surface was so polished and dazzling, that the eye neither could nor wished to look more deeply into her. I believe that she had no other accomplishment but that gorgeous cloak for all deficiency—an inimitable manner. Her remarks were always shrewd, and replete with good sense; her language was choice; her style of conversation varying, sometimes of that joyous nature that has all the effect, without the pedantry of wit, upon the hearer, and, at times, she could be really quite energetic. This is, after all, but an imperfect description of one who took upon herself the task of forming my address, revising my gait after the dancing-master, and making me to look the gentleman.

This person quite destroyed Riprapton's equanimity. During

her three or four first visits he was all hope and animation. She permitted him, as she did everybody else, as far as words were concerned, to make love as fast as he pleased. But beyond this, even his intrepid assurance could not carry him. So his hope and animation gradually gave place to incertitude and chagrin; and then, by a very natural transition, he fell into envy and jealousy. Though but fifteen, I was certainly taller than the man who thought he honoured me by considering me as his rival. Though affairs remained in this unsatisfactory state as far as he was concerned, for certain very valid reasons he had not yet chosen to vent upon me any access of his spleen. But this procrastination of actual hostilities was terminated in the following manner.

Mrs. Causand and I were standing, one fine evening, lovingly, side-by-side, in the summer-house that overhung the river at the bottom of the garden. Mr. Riprapton, washed, brushed, and perfumed—for the scholastic duties of the day were over—was standing directly in front of us, enacting most laboriously the agreeable, smiling with a sardonic grin, and looking actually yellow with spite, in the midst of his complimentary grimaces. As Mrs. Causand and I stood contemplating the tranquil and beautiful scene, trying to see as little of the person before us as possible, one of her beautiful arms hung negligently over my shoulder, and now she would draw me with a fond pressure to her side, and now her exquisite hand would dally with the ringlets on my forehead, and then its velvety softness would crumple up and indent my blushing cheek, that burned certainly more with pleasure than with bashfulness. I cannot say that the usher bore all this very stoically, but he betrayed his annoyance by his countenance only. His speech was as bland as ever. His trials were not yet over: at some very silly remark of mine the joyous widow pressed some half dozen rapid kisses on the cheek that was glowing so near her own. Either this act emboldened Riprapton, or he egregiously mistook her character, and judged that a mere voluptuary stood before him, for he immediately went on the vacant side and endeavoured to possess himself of her hand.

Face, neck, and arms flushed up in one indignant crimson of the most unsophisticated anger I ever beheld. She threw herself back with a perceptible shudder, as if she had come unexpectedly in contact with something cold, or dead, or unnatural.

'Mr. Riprapton,' she exclaimed, after a space of real emotion,

'I never yet boxed the ears of a gentleman: but had you been one, I should most assuredly have so far forgotten my feminine dignity, as to have expressed my deep resentment by a blow. I cannot touch anything so mean. While you confined your persecution to words, I bore with it. Sir, I only speak from my own sensations; but, judging by these, any female who could abide your touch without repugnance, must have long lost all womanly feelings; and now that we are upon this subject, let me give you a little friendly advice. When you are permitted to sit at the same table with ladies, and wish by the means of your feet to establish a secret intercourse with any one, take care, in future, that you do not use the wooden leg. Females may be more tender in the toes than in their hearts. You may go, sir; and remember, if you wish to preserve your station in this house—know it. When you behave as a gentleman, that title may be conceded to you: but the moment your conduct is inconsistent with that character, those around you will not forget that you are no more than a hired servant, and but one degree above a menial. Here, Ralph,' she continued, giving me the violated hand, 'cleanse it from that fellow's profanation.' I brought it to my mouth very gallantly, and covered it with kisses.

For the first-time, I saw my usher-friend not only confounded, but dumb with consternation, and his whitened face became purple even into the depths of his deep pock-marks, with an emotion that no courtesy could characterise as amiable. He moved off with none of his usual grace; but retired like a very common place, wooden-legged man; in a truly miserable dot-and-go-one style. What Mrs. Causand and I said to each other on the subject, when she went and seated herself in the summer-house to recover from her excitement, would, I am sure, have formed the ground-work and arguments of twelve good moral essays; but unfortunately I have forgotten everything about it, except that we staid there till not only the dews had fallen upon the flowers, but the shades of evening upon the dews.

As my stay at school was to be so short, I was treated more as a familiar friend by all than as a pupil. I staid up with the family and took tea and supper with them. Rip made no appearance the evening after his lecture, but retired to his chamber much indisposed. While Mrs. Causand was on her visits I always breakfasted with her *tête-à-tête* in the little parlour, whose French windows opened upon the garden, and it was on those occasions that I found her most amusing. She knew every one and every thing connected with fashionable life. Private and piquant, and I am sure authentic, anecdotes of every noble family, she possessed in an exhaustless profusion. Nor was this knowledge confined to the nobility: she knew more of the sayings and doings of some of the princes of the blood, than any other person living, out of their domestic circle, and she knew many things with which that circle were never acquainted. I am sure she could have made splendid fortunes for twelve fashionable novel-writers.

I have, at times, endeavoured to recollect some of her *morceaux*; but though I have succeeded, it has been so imperfectly, that I do not feel authorized in making them public. In the proper place I may be tempted to violate this secrecy as respects his late Majesty, the more especially, as in the singular transaction to which I allude, his character came off, through a fiery proof of no common temptations, and through circumstances of extreme hazard and difficulty, resplendently as a man of honour and as a gentleman. Obloquy enough has been flung at that which rather deserved panegyric; but it is a too common feeling to endeavour to daub over that lustre with mud, that the rampant cannot emulate.

I had breakfasted with Mrs. Causand the morning after Rip's discomfiture, and then went to prosecute my studies in the school-room. This was the first time that my tutor and I had met since his rebuff. Mr. Cherfeuil had not yet taken his place at his desk. As I passed the assistant who assisted me so little, I gave him my usual smile of greeting: but his countenance, instead of the good-humoured return, was black as evil passions could make it. However, I paid but little attention to this unfriendly demonstration, and taking my seat, began, as I was long privileged to do, to converse with my neighbour.

'Silence!' vociferated the man in authority. I conversed on. 'Silence! I say.'

Not supposing that I was included in this authoritative demand, or not caring if I were, I felt no inclination to suspend the exercise of my conversational powers. After the third order for silence, this sudden disciple of Harpocrates[1] left his seat, cane in hand, and coming behind me, I dreaming of no such temerity on his part, he applied across my shoulders one of the most hearty *con amore* swingers that ever left a wale behind it, exclaiming, at the same time, 'Silence, Master Rattlin.'

Here was a stinging degradation to me, almost an officer on the quarter-deck of one of his Majesty's frigates! However, without taking time to weigh exactly my own dignity, I seized a large slate, and turning sharply round, sent it hissing into his very teeth. I wish I had knocked one or two of them out. I wished it then fervently, and of that wish, wicked though it be, I have never repented. He was for some time occupied with holding his hand to his mouth, and in a rapid and agonizing examination of the extent of the damage. When he could spare an instant for me, he was as little satisfied with the expression of my features, as with the alteration in his, so he hopped down to Mr. Cherfeuil, while the blood was streaming between his fingers, to lay his complaint in form against me. I had two sure advocates below, so he took nothing by his motion, but a lotion to wash his mouth with; and after staying below for a couple of hours, he came up with a swelled face, but his teeth all perfect.

That morning Mr. Cherfeuil, in very excellent bad English, made a most impressive speech; the pith of it was, that, had I not taken the law into my own hands, he would most certainly have discharged Mr. Riprapton, for having exceeded his authority in striking me! but as my conduct had been very unjustifiable, I was sentenced to transcribe the whole of the first book of the Æneid. Before dinner my school-fellows had begged off one half of the task—Mrs. Cherfeuil at dinner begged off one half of that half; when things had gone thus far, Mrs. Causand interfered, and argued for a commutation of punishment; the more especially, as she thought an example ought to be made for so heinous an offence. As she spake with a very serious air, the good-natured Frenchman acquiesced in her wishes, and pledged himself to allow her to inflict the penalty, which she promulgated to the following effect: 'That I should be forced to swallow an extra bumper of port for not having knocked out, at least, one of the wretch's teeth,' and she then related enough of his conduct to bring Mr. Cherfeuil into her way of thinking upon the subject.

CHAPTER XXVI

A reconciliation—a walk planned, and a man planted—The latter found to grow impatient—Ralph at length rigged out as a reefer.

FOR two days Mr. Rip and myself were not upon speaking terms. On the third day a Master Barnard brings me up a slate full of plusses, minusses, x, y, z's, and other letters of the alphabet, in a most amiable algebraical confusion.

'Take it to Mr. Riprapton,' said I. The lad took it, and the mathematical master looked over it with a perplexed gravity, truly edifying. 'Take it to Master Rattlin—I have no time,' was the result of his cogitations.

It was brought to me again. 'Take it to the usher,' said I.

'It is of no use; he don't know anything about it.'

'Take it then to Mr. Cherfeuil, and tell him so.'

This advice was overheard by the party most concerned, and he called the boy to him, who shortly returned to me with a note, full of friendship, apology, and sorrow; ending with an earnest request that I would again put him right with Mrs. Causand, as well as the sum on the slate. I replied, for I was still a little angry, that he was very ungrateful, but that, as we were so soon to part, perhaps for ever, I accepted the reconciliation. So far was well. I told Mrs. Causand what had passed, and then interceded with her for her forgiveness; for her anger debarred him from many comforts, as it obliged him to take his solitary tea and supper in the school-room. She consented, as she did to almost everything that I requested of her, and that afternoon I brought up to her the penitent hand-presser. Her natural good temper, and blandness of manner, soon put him again at his ease, and his love-speeches flowed as fluently as ever.

We proposed a walk, and, accompanied by some half dozen of the elder boys, we began to stroll upon the common. By some *gaucherie* the conversation took a disagreeable turn on our late misunderstanding, and I could not help repeating what I had said in my note, that Mr. Rip had proved himself ungrateful, considering the many difficulties from which I had extricated him. At this last assertion before the lady, he took fire, and flatly denied it. I was too proud to enumerate the many instances of scholastic assistance that he had received at my hands, so I became sullen and silent, my opponent in an equal degree brisk and loquacious. My fair companion rather enjoyed the encounter, and began to rally me.

'Come, come,' said I, 'I'll lay him a crown that he will beg me to extricate him from some difficulty before the week's over.'

The wager was accepted with alacrity, and Mrs. Causand begged to lay an equal stake against me, which I took. I then purposely turned the conversation, and after some time, when we were fairly in the hollow made by the surrounding hills, I exclaimed, 'Rip, if you'll give me five-and-twenty yards, I'll run you three hops and a step a hundred yards for another crown.'

'Done, done!' exclaimed the usher, joyously, chuckling with the idea of exhibiting so triumphantly his prowess before the blooming widow. The ground was duly stepped, and the goal fixed, whilst my antagonist, all animation and spirits, was pouring his liquid nonsense into the lady's ear. I took care that, in about the middle of the distance, our race-ground should pass over where some rushes were growing. Now Riprapton had a most uncommon speed in this manner of progressing. He would, with his leg of flesh, take three tremendous hops, and then step down with his leg of wood one, and then three live hops again, and one dead step, the step being a kind of respite from the fatigue of the hops.

All the preliminaries being arranged, off we started, I taking, of course, my twenty-five yards in advance. The exhibition and the gait were so singular, that Mrs. Causand could scarcely stand for laughter, whilst the boys shouted, 'Go it, Ralph!'—'Well done, peg!'—'Dot-and-go-one will beat him.'

In the midst of these exhilarating cries, what I had calculated upon happened. Rip, before we had gone half the distance, was close behind me; but lo! after three of his gigantic hops, that seemed to be performed with at least one seven-leagued boot turned into a slipper, he came down heavily upon his step with his wood among the rushes. The stiff clay there being full of moisture and unsound, he plunged up to his hip nearly, in the adhesive soil, and there he remained, as much a fixture, and equally astonished, as Lot's wife. First of all, taking care to go the distance, and thus win the wager, we all, frantic with laughter, gathered round the man thus firmly attached to his mother earth. Whilst the tears ran down Mrs. Causand's cheeks, and proved that her radiant colour was quite natural, she endeavoured to assume an air of the deepest commiseration, which was interrupted, every moment, by involuntary bursts of laughter. For himself, no wretch in the pillory ever wore a more lugubrious aspect, and his sallow visage turned first to one, and then to another, with a look so ridiculously imploring that it was irresistible.

'I am sorry, very sorry,' said the lady, 'to see you look so pale— I may say, so livid—but, poor man, it is but natural, seeing already that you have *one foot in the grave*.'

The mender of pens groaned in the spirit.

'I say,' said the schoolboy wag of the party, applying an old Joe Miller to the occasion, 'why is Mr. Riprapton like pens, ink, and paper?'

'Because he is stationary,' vociferated five eager voices at once in reply.

The caster-up of sums cast a look at the delinquent, the tottle of the whole of which was, 'you sha'n't be long on the debit side of our account.'

'But what is to be done?' was now the question.

'I am afraid,' said I, 'we must dig him up like a dead tree, or an old post.'

'It is, I believe, the only way,' said the tutor despondingly; 'I was relieved once that way before in the bog of Ballynawashy.'

'O, then you are from Ireland after all,' said the lady.

'Only on a visit, madam!' said the baited fixture, with much asperity.

'But really,' said she, 'if I may judge from the present occasion, you must have made a *long stay*.'

'I hope he won't take cold in his feet,' said a very silly, blubber-lipped boy.

His instructor looked hot with passion.

'But really, now I think of it,' chimed in the now enraptured widow, 'a very serious alarm has seized me. Suppose that the piece of wood, so nicely planted in this damp clay, were to take root and throw out fibres. Gracious me! only suppose that you should begin to vegetate. I do declare that you look quite *green* about the eyes already!'

'Mercy me!' whispered the wag, 'if he should grow up, he'll certainly turn to a *plane* tree; for really, he is a very plain man.'

The wielder of the ruler gave a tremendous wriggle with the whole body, which proved as ineffectual as it was violent.

'But don't you think, Ralph,' said his tormentor, 'as the evening is drawing in, that something should be done for the poor gentleman; he will most certainly take cold if he remain here all night; couldn't you and your schoolfellows contrive to build a sort of hut over him? I am sure I should be very happy to help to carry the boughs—if the man won't go to the house the house must go to the man.'

'What a fine cock-shy he would make!' said Master Blubberlips.

'O, I should so like to see it,' said the lady. 'It will be the first time he has been made *shy* in his life.'

He was certainly like an Indian bound to the stake, and made to suffer mental torture—but he did not bear it with an Indian's equanimity. As a few stragglers had been drawn to the funny scene, and more might be expected, I, and I only, of all the spectators, began to feel some pity for him; the more especially, as I heard a stout, grinning chaw-bacon say to the baker's boy of the village, who asked him what was the matter, 'Whoy, Jim, it ben't nothink less than Frenchman's usherman ha drawn all Thickenham common on his'n roight leg for a stocking loike.'

'Come,' thought I, 'it's quite time, after that, for the honour of the academy, to beat a retreat, or we shall be beaten hollow by this heavy-shod clodpole. Mr. Riprapton,' said I, 'I don't bear you any malice—but I recollect my wager. If I extricate you out of the difficulty, will you own that I have won it?'

'Gladly,' said he, very sorrowfully.

'Come here, my lads, out knives and cut away the turf.' We soon removed the earth as far down as to where the bole of the wooden leg joined to the shank. 'Now, my lads,' said I, 'we must unscrew him.' Round and round we twirled him, his outstretched living leg forming as pretty a fairy-ring on the green sod, with its circumgyrations, as can be imagined. At last, after having had a very tolerable foretaste of the pillory, we fairly unscrewed him, and he was once more disengaged from his partial burial-place. I certainly cannot say that he received our congratulations with the grace of a Chesterfield,[1] but he begged us to continue our exertions to recover for him his shank, or otherwise he would have to follow Petruchio's orders[2] to the tailor—to 'hop me over every kennel home.' For the sake of the quotation, we agreed to assist, and, as many of us catching hold of it as could find a grip, we tugged, and tugged, and tugged. Still the stiff clay did not seem at all inclined to relinquish the prize it had so fairly won. At length, by one tremendous and simultaneous effort, we plucked it forth; but, in doing so, those who retained the trophy in their hands were flung flat on their backs, whilst the newly-gained leg pointed upwards to the zenith. Having first wiped a little of the deep yellow adhesion away from it, we joined the various parts of the man together; and, he taking singular care to avoid those spots where rushes grew, we all reached our home, with one exception, in the highest glee—as to the two wagers, he behaved like a gentleman, and *acknowledged* the debt—which was a great deal more than I ever expected.

After having worked some fifty problems out of Hamilton Moore,[1] of blessed memory, and having drawn an infinity of triangles with all possible degrees of incidence, with very neat little ships, now upon the base, now upon the hypothenuse, and now upon the perpendicular, my erudite usher pronounced me to be a perfect master of the noble science of navigation in all its branches, for the which he glorified himself exceedingly. As I had made many friends there was no difficulty in procuring for me a ship, and I was to have joined the Sappho, a first class brig of war, as soon as she arrived, and she was expected almost immediately. However, as at that particular time we were relieving the Danes from the onerous care of their navy,[2] the sloop was sent as soon as she arrived to assist in the amiable action. I was much grieved at this disappointment, as the Sappho was commanded by the son of that dignified divine who took so much interest in my welfare.

Having many who interested themselves about me, some apparent and others hidden, a ship was soon found for me, but by what chain of recommendation, I never could unravel. As far as the ship was concerned, I certainly had nothing to complain of. She was a fine frigate, and every way worthy to career over the ocean, that was, at that time, almost completely an English dominion. The usual quantity of hopes and wishes were expressed, and my final leave was taken of all my village friends. Mr. R. enjoining me to correspond with him on every opportunity, gave me his blessing, and some urgent advice to eschew poetry, and prophesied that he should live to see me posted. There was nothing outwardly very remarkable in the manner of Mrs. Cherfeuil on the eve of my departure. I went to bed a school-boy and was to rise next morning an officer—that is to say, I was to mount my uniform for the first time. I believe that I was already on the ship's books; for at the time of which I am writing, the clerk of the cheque was not so very frequent in his visits, and so particular when he visited, as he is at present. Notwithstanding the important change that was about to take place in everything connected with myself, I did sleep that night, though I often awoke,—there was a female hovering round my bed almost the whole of the night.

CHAPTER XXVII

Ralph commences his public career by accepting an I. O. U., he hardly knows why—He finds his future Captain based on a bottle—He is not taken by the hand.

So ignorant were those few, on whom devolved my fitting out, of what my station required, that I had made for me three suits of uniform, all of which had the lion upon the buttons instead of the anchor, and from which the weekly account[1] was absent. My transmission from school to town was by the stage; at town I was told to call on a lawyer in the King's-bench Walk, in the Temple, who furnished me with twenty pounds, and a letter for my future captain, telling me I might draw upon him for a yearly sum, which was more than double the amount I ought to have been entrusted with; then coldly wishing me success, he recommended me to go down that evening by the mail, and join my ship immediately, and wished me a good morning.

I certainly was a little astonished at my sudden isolation in the midst of a vast city. I felt that, from that moment, I must commence man. I knew several persons in London, parents of my school-fellows, but I was too proud to parade my pride before them, for I felt, at the same time, ashamed of wearing ostentatiously, whilst I gloried in, my uniform.

I dined at the inn where I alighted on coming to town, called for what I wanted in a humble semi-tone, said 'If you please, sir,' to the waiter, paid my bill without giving him a gratuity, for fear of giving him offence, took my place in the mail, and got down without accident to Chatham, and slept at the house where the coach stopped. On account of my hybrid uniform and my asserting my-self of the navy, the people of the establishment knew not what to make of me. I wished to deliver my credentials immediately; but my considerate landlord advised me to take time to think about it —and dinner. I followed his advice.

It is uncertain how long I should have remained in this un-certainty, had not a brother midshipman, in the coffee-room, accosted me, and kindly helped me out with my pint of port, which I thought I showed my manliness in calling for. He did not roast me very unmercifully, but what he spared in gibes he made up in drinking. I abstained with a great deal of firmness from following his example; he warmly praised my abstinence, I suppose with much sincerity, as it certainly appeared to be a virtue which he was incapable of practising. About seven o'clock my ready-made friend began to be more minute in his inquiries. I showed him my intro-ductory letter, and he told me directly at what hotel the captain was established, and enforced upon me the necessity of immediately waiting upon him; telling me I might think myself extremely lucky in having had to entertain only one officer, when so many thirsty and penniless ones were cruizing about to sponge upon the Johnny Raws. For himself, he said, he was a man of honour, quite a gentle-man, and insisted upon paying his share of the two bottles of port consumed, of which I certainly had not drunk more than four glasses. Secretly praising my man of honour for his disinterested-ness, for I had asked him to take a glass of wine, which he had read as a couple of bottles, I ordered my bill, among the items of which stood conspicuously forth, 'two bottles of old crusted port, four-teen shillings.'

'D——d imposition!' said my hitherto anonymous friend. 'Of all vices, I abominate imposition the most. I shall pay for all this wine myself. Here, wai-*terre*, pen and ink. Banking hours are over now; I have nothing but a fifty-pound bill about me. However, you shall have my I. O. U. You see that I have made it out for one pound—you'll just hand me the difference, six shillings. Your name, I think you said, was Rattlin—Ralph Rattlin. A good name, a very good purser's name[1] indeed. There, Mr. Rattlin, you have only to present that piece of paper when you get on board to the head swabwasher, and he'll give you either cash for it, or slops.'[2]

I gave the gentleman who so much abhorred imposition, six shillings in return for his paper, which contained these words:

'I. O. U. twenty shillings. Josiah Cheeks, Major-General of the Horse-Marines, of his Majesty's Ship, the Merry Dun, of Dover. —To Mr. Ralph Rattlin.'

I carefully placed this precious document in my pocket-book, among my one-pound notes, at that time the principal currency of the country; yet could not help thinking that my friend cast an awfully hungry eye at the pieces of paper. He had already commenced a very elaborate speech prefatory to the request of a loan, when I cut him short, by telling him that I had promised my god-mamma not to lend any one a single penny until I had been on board my ship six months, which was really the case. He commended my sense of duty, and said it was of no manner of consequence, as next morning he should be in possession of more than he should have occasion for, and then a five or a ten pound note would be at my service. After vainly endeavouring to seduce me to the theatre, he made a virtue of my obstinacy, and taking me by the arm, showed me to the door of the hotel, where Captain Reud of H.M.S. Eos[1] was located.

I was announced, and immediately ushered into a room, where I saw a sallow-visaged, compact, well-made little man, apparently not older than two or three-and-twenty, sitting in the middle of the room, upon a black quart bottle, the neck of which was on the floor, and the bottom forming the uneasy and unstable seat. Without paying much attention to me, every now and then he would give himself an impetus, and flinging out his arms, spin round like a turnstile. It certainly was very amusing, and, no doubt, so thought his companion, a fine, manly, handsome-looking fellow, of thirty-five or thirty-eight, by his long-continued and vociferous applause. The little spinner was habited in a plain but handsome uniform, with one gold epaulet on his right shoulder, whilst the delighted approver had a coat splendid with broad white casimere[2] facings.

I could observe that both parties were deeply immersed in the many-coloured delirium of much drink. I looked first at one, then at the other, undecided as to which of the two was my captain. However, I could not augur ill of one who laughed so heartily, nor of the other, who seemed so happy in making himself a teetotum. Taking advantage of a pause in this singular exhibition, I delivered my credentials to the former and more imposing-looking of the two, who immediately handed them over to Captain Reud. I was graciously received, a few questions of courtesy asked, and a glass of wine poured out for me.

My presence was soon totally disregarded, and my captain and his first lieutenant began conversing on all manner of subjects, in a jargon to me entirely incomprehensible. The decanter flew across and across the table with wonderful rapidity, and the flow of assertion increased with the captain, and that of assentation with his lieutenant. At length, the little man with the epaulet commenced a very prurient tale. Mr. Farmer cast a look full of meaning upon myself, when Captain Reud addressed me thus, in a sharp, shrill tone, that I thought impossible to a person who told such pleasant stories, and who could spin so prettily upon a quart bottle. 'Do you hear, younker, you'll ship your traps in a wherry the first thing tomorrow morning, and get on board early enough to be victualled that day. Tell the commanding officer to order the ship's tailor to clap the curse of God[1] upon you—(I started with horror at the impiety)—to unship those poodles[2] from your jacket, and rig you out with the foul anchor.'[3]

'Yes, sir,' said I; 'but I hope the tailor won't be so wicked, because I am sure I wish the gentleman no harm.'

'Piously brought up,' said the captain.

'We'll teach him to look aloft, any how,' said the lieutenant, striving to be original.

'A well-built young dog,' said the former, looking at me approvingly.

'Who is he, may I ask?' said the latter, in a most sonorous aside.

'Mum,' said Captain Reud, putting his finger to his nose, and endeavouring to look very mysterious, and full of important meaning; 'but when I get him in blue water—if he were the king's son —heh! Farmer?'

'To be sure. Then he is the son of somebody, sir?'

'More likely the son of nobody—according to the law of the land,—whoever launched him: but I'll never breathe a word, or give so much as a hint that he is illegitimate. I scorn, like a British sailor, to do that by a side-wind, Farmer, that I ought not to do openly; but there are two sides to a blanket. A Popish priest must not marry in England. Norman Will was not a whit the worse because his mother never stood outside the canonical rail. Pass your wine, Farmer; I despise a man, a scoundrel, who deals in innuendoes. O it's despicable, d—d despicable. I don't like, however, to be trusted by halves—shall keep a sharp look out on the joker—with me, a secret is always perfectly safe.'

'O, then there is a secret, I see,' said Mr. Farmer. 'You had better go now, Mr. Rattlin, and attend to the Captain's orders to-morrow.' The word Mister sounded sharply, yet not unpleasingly, to my ear: it was the first time I had been so designated or so dignified. Here was another evidence that I had, or ought to, cast from me the slough of boyhood, and enact, boldly, the man. I therefore summoned up courage to say that I did not perfectly understand the purport of the captain's order, and solicited an explanation.

'Yes,' said he; 'the service has come to a pretty pass, when the youngest officer of my ship asks me to explain my orders, instead of obeying them.'

'I had better give him a note to the commanding officer, for I may not happen to be on board when he arrives.'

A note was written and given me.

'Good night, Mr. Rattlin,' said the captain.

'Good night, sir,' said I, advancing very amiably to shake hands with my little commander. My action took him more aback than a heavy squall would have done the beautiful frigate he commanded. The prestige of rank, and the pride of discipline struggled with his sense of the common courtesies of life. He half held out his hand; he withdrew it—it was again proffered and again withdrawn! He really looked confused. At length, as if he had rallied up all his energies to act courageously, he thrust them resolutely into his pocket; and then said, 'There, younker, that will do. Go and turn in.'

'Turned out,' I muttered, as I left the room. From this brief incident, young as I was, I augured badly of Captain Reud. I at once felt that I had broken some rule of etiquette, but I knew that he had sinned against the dictates of mere humanity. There was a littleness in his conduct, and an indecision in his manner, quite at variance with my untutored notions of the gallant bearing of a British sailor.

As I lay in bed at my inn, my mind re-enacted all the scenes of the previous day. I was certainly dissatisfied with every occurrence. I was dissatisfied with the security of my friend Josiah Cheeks, the Major-General of the Horse Marines, of His Majesty's Ship the Merry Dun of Dover. I was dissatisfied with my reception by Captain Reud, of His Majesty's ship Eos, notwithstanding his skill at spinning upon a bottle; nor was I altogether satisfied with the blustering, half-protecting, half-overbearing conduct towards me, of his first lieutenant, Mr. Farmer. But all these dissatisfactions united were as nothing to the disgust I felt at the broad innuendoes, so liberally flung out, concerning the mystery of my birth.

END OF VOLUME I

VOLUME II

▬

CHAPTER I

*Ralph's heart still at home—His coffee-room friend all abroad—
Gets his I O U cashed, and sees the giver exalted to every body's
satisfaction but his own.*

BEFORE I plunge into all the strange adventures, and unlooked-
for vicissitudes, of my naval life, I must be indulged with a few
prefatory remarks. The royal navy, as a service, is not vilified, nor
the gallant members who compose it insulted, by pointing out the
idiosyncrasies, the absurdities, and even the vices and crimes of
some of its members. Human nature is human nature still, whether
it fawn in the court or philander in the grove. The man carries with
him on the seas the same predilections, the same passions, and the
same dispositions, both for good and for evil, as he possessed on
shore. The ocean breeze does not convert the coward into the hero,
the passionate man into the philosopher, or the mean one into
a pattern of liberality. It is true, that a coward in the service seldom
dares show his cowardice; that in the inferior grades, passion is
controlled by discipline, and in all, meanness is shamed by intimate, and social communion, into the semblance of much better
feelings. Still, with all this, the blue coat, like charity, covereth
a multitude of sins, and the blue water is, as yet, inefficacious to
wash them all out.

We have said here briefly what the service will not do. It will
not change the nature of man, but it will modify it into much that
is exalted, that is noble, and that is good. It almost universally
raises individual character; but it can never debase it. The world
is too apt to generalize—and this generalization has done much
disservice to the British navy. It forms a notion, creates a beau
ideal—a very absurd one truly—and then tries every character by
it. Even the officers of this beautiful service have tacitly given in

to the delusion; and, by attempting to frown down all *exposés* of the errors of individuals, vainly endeavour to exalt that which requires no such factitious exaltation.

If I am compelled to say that this captain was a fool and a tyrant, fools indeed must those officers be who draw the inference that I mean the impression to be general, that all captains are either fools or tyrants. Let the cavillers understand, that the tyranny and the folly are innate in the man, but, that the service abhors and represses the one, and despises and often reforms the other. The service never made a good man bad, or a bad one worse: on the contrary, it has always improved the one, and reformed the other. It is, however, no libel to say, that more than a quarter of a century ago (of course, now, it is all perfection) it contained some bad men among its multitude of good. Such as it then was I will faithfully record.

Oh! I left myself in bed. My reflections affording me so little consolation, when they were located in the vicinity of Chatham, I ordered my obedient mind to travel back to Stickenham, whilst I felt more than half inclined to make my body take the same course the next morning. Not that my courage had failed me; but I actually felt a disgust at all that I had heard and seen. How different are the sharp, abrading corners that meet us at every turn in our passage through real life to the sunny dreams of our imagination! Already my dirk had ceased to give me satisfaction in looking upon it, and my uniform, that two days before I thought so bewitching, I had, a few hours since, been informed was to be soiled by a foul anchor. How gladly that night my mind revelled among the woods and fields and waters of the romantic village that I had just left! Then its friendly inhabitants came thronging upon the beautiful scene; and pre-eminent among them stood my good schoolmistress, and my loving godmother. Of all the imaginary group, she alone did not smile. It was then, and not till then, that I felt the bitterness of the word 'farewell.' My conscience smote me that I had behaved unkindly towards her. I now remembered a thousand little contrivances, all of which, in my exalted spirits, I had pertinaciously eluded, that she had put in practice in order to be for a few minutes alone with me. I now bitterly reproached myself for my perversity. What secrets might I not have heard! And then my heart told me in a voice I could not doubt, that it was she who had hovered round my bed the whole night previous to my departure. My schoolfellows had all slept soundly, yet I, though wakeful, had the folly to appear to sleep also. Of one thing I felt convinced, that I could never again act unkindly, without myself suffering much more than my victim. I then remembered it distinctly, though I noticed it but little at the time, when she uttered her tremulous 'Good bye—God bless you!' that her sickly smile was accompanied by certain very pathetic twitchings in the face, which added but little to her personal beauty. All these things I now called to mind with a most tantalizing exactitude! and when I compared them to my new captain's hard, heartless, and sneering expression, 'Piously brought up,' I felt far from comfortable. Whilst I was considering how people could be so unkind, sleep came kindly to me, and I awoke next morning in good spirits, and laughed at my dejection of the preceding evening.

Whilst I was at breakfast in the coffee-room, I was a little surprised and a good deal flattered by the appearance of Lieutenant Farmer. He accosted me kindly, told me not again to attempt to offer first to shake hands with my captain, for it was against the rules of the service; and then he sat down beside me, and commenced very patiently *à me tirer les vers du nez.*[1] He was a fine, gallant fellow, passionately desirous of promotion, which was not surprising, for he had served long and with considerable distinction, and was still a lieutenant, whilst he was more than fourteen years above his captain, both in length of service and in age. Was I related to my Lord A——?[2] Did I know any thing of Mr. Rose?[3] Had I any connexions that knew Mr. Perceval, &c.? I frankly told him that I knew no one of any note, and that it had been directly enjoined upon me, by the one or two friends that I possessed, never to converse about my private affairs with any one.

Mr. Farmer felt himself rebuked, but not offended; he was a generous, noble fellow, though a little passionate, and too taut a disciplinarian. He told me that he had no doubt we should be good friends, that I had better go to the dock-yard, and inquire for the landing-place, and for the Eos' cutter, which was waiting there for stores. That I was to make myself known to the officer of the boat, who would give me two or three hands to convey my luggage down to it, and that I had better ship myself as soon as I could. He told me, also, that he would probably be on board before me, but, at all events, if he were not, that I was to give to the commanding officer the letter, with which he had furnished me on the night before.

He left me with a more favourable impression on my mind than I had before entertained. I paid my bill, and found my way to Chatham Dock-yard. I was struck with the magnitude of the works, at the order, cleanliness, and regularity that every where appeared, and at the gigantic structures of the vessels on the stocks.

I had just gained the landing-place, to which I had been directed by a gentleman, who wore some order of merit upon his ancles, and who kindly offered me a box of dominoes for sale, when I saw a twelve-oared barge pull in among the other boats that were waiting there. The stern sheets were full of officers, distinguishable among whom was one with a red round face, sharp twinkling eyes, and an honest corpulency of body truly comfortable. He wore his laced cocked hat, with the rosetted corners, resting each on one of his heavily epauletted shoulders. His face looked so fierce and rubescent under his vast hat, that he put me in mind of a large coal, the lower half of which was in a state of combustion. He landed with the other officers, and I then perceived that he was gouty and lame, and walked with a stick, that had affixed to it a transverse ivory head, something like a diminutive ram's horn. Amidst this group of officers, I observed my coffee-room friend, the major-general of the horse marines, who seemed excessively shy, and at that moment absorbed in geological studies, for he could not take his eyes from off the earth. However, pushing hastily by the port-admiral, for such was the ancient podagre,[1] 'Ah! major-general,' said I to the abashed master's mate, 'I am very glad to meet with you. Have you been to the bank this morning to cash your fifty pound bill?'

'Don't know ye,' said my friend, giving me more than the cut direct, for, if he could have used his eyes as a sword, I should have had the cut decisive.

'Not know me! well—but you are only joking, General Cheeks!'

The surrounding officers began to be very much amused, and the port-admiral became extremely eager in his attention.

'Tell ye, don't know ye, younker,' said my gentleman, folding his arms, and attempting to look magnificent and strange.

'Well, this is cool. So, sir, you mean to deny that you drank two bottles of my port wine yesterday evening, and that you did not give me your I O U for the twenty shillings you borrowed of me? I'll trouble you, if you please, for the money,' for I was getting angry; 'as I am quite a stranger to the head swabwasher, and should not like to trouble the gentleman either for cash or slops, without a formal introduction.'

At this juncture, the fiery face of the port-admiral became more fiery, his fierce small eye more flashing, and his ivory-handled stick was lifted up tremblingly, not with fear, but rage. 'Pray, sir,' said he to me, 'who is he?' pointing to my friend; 'and who are you?'

'This gentleman, sir, I take to be, either a swindler or Josiah Cheeks, Major-General of the Horse Marines, of his Majesty's ship, the Merry Dun of Dover,' handing to the admiral the acknowledgment; 'and I am, sir, Ralph Rattlin, just come down to join his Majesty's ship the Eos.'

'I'll answer for the truth of the latter part of this young gentleman's assertion,' said Captain Reud, now coming forward with Lieutenant Farmer.

'Is this your writing, sir?' said the admiral, to the discomfited master's mate, in a voice worse than thunder; for it was almost as loud, and infinitely more disagreeable. 'I see by your d—d skulking look, that you have been making a scoundrel of yourself, and a fool of this poor innocent boy.'

'I hope, sir, you do not think me a fool for believing an English officer incapable of a lie?'

'Well said, boy, well said—I see—this scamp has turned out to be both the scoundrel and the fool.'

'I only meant it for a joke, sir,' said the *soi-disant* Mr. Cheeks, taking off his hat, and holding it humbly in his hand.

'Take up your note directly, or I shall expel you the service for forgery.'

The delinquent fumbled for some time in his pocket, and at length could produce only threepence farthing, a tobacco-stopper, and an unpaid tavern bill. He was forced to confess he had not the money about him.

'Your fifty pound bill,' said I. 'The bank must be open.'

The major-general looked at me.

It was a good thing fot the giver of I O Us, that the mirth the whole transaction created, did not permit the old admiral to be so severe with his 'whys,' as he would have been. He, however, told the culprit's captain, whom he had just brought on shore in the barge, to give me the twenty shillings, and to charge it against him, and then to give him an airing at the mast-head till sunset; telling him, at the same time, he might feel himself very happy at not being disrated and turned before the mast.

I was departing, very well satisfied with this summary method of administering justice, when I found that I was not altogether to escape, for the old gentleman commenced opening a broadside upon me, for not wearing the Admiralty uniform. Lieutenant Farmer, however, came very kindly to my rescue, and offered the admiral a sufficient explanation.

I was then directed to the Eos' boat, the coxswain and a couple of men went with me for my luggage, and in less than half an hour, I was being rowed down the Medway towards the ship. As we passed by what I looked upon as an immense and terrifically lofty seventy-four, I looked up, and descried Major-General Cheeks slowly climbing up the newly-tarred main topmast rigging, 'like a snail unwillingly,'[1] to the topmast cross-trees. It was a bitterly cold day, at the end of November, and there is no doubt but that his reflections were as bitter as the weather. Practical jokes have sometimes very bad practical consequences.

CHAPTER II

Ralph is shipped, hulked and overcome—A dark hall and an ebony servitor—A tailor's politeness, and a master's mate, who sighs to be mated, yet does not see that he is outmatched.

I FOUND the Eos[2] all rigged and strong in the breeze, with the not very agreeable aroma of dock-yard paint. The ship's company was not, however, on board of her. They were hulked on board of the Pegasus. A very brief introduction to the officers of the watch, and I was shown down, with my sea-chest, my shore-going trunk, and quadrant, cocked hat, &c. to the midshipmen's berth in the hulk. One of the after-guard performed for me the office of gentleman usher. It was a gloomy, foggy, chilly day, and the damp of the atmosphere was mingled with the reeking, dank, animal effluvia that came up, thick and almost tangible, from the filthy receptacle of crowded hundreds.

As I descended into darkness, and nearly felt overpowered by the compound of villainous smells, I was something more than sick at heart. My pioneer, at length, lifted up the corner of a piece of dirty canvas, that screened off a space of about six feet square from the rest of the ship's company. This I was given to understand was the *young gentlemen's* quarters, their dining-room and their drawing-room combined. Even I, who had not yet attained my full growth, could not stand erect in this saloon of elegance. I am stating nothing but literal facts. On an oaken table, still more greasy than the greasy decks over which I had slipped in my passage to this den, stood a flickering, spluttering, intensely yellow candle, of very slender dimensions, inserted in a black quart bottle. Beside it was placed a battered breadbasket, containing some broken biscuit; and a piece of villainously-scented cheese, distinguished by the name of purser's, lay near it, in company with an old, blood-stained, worn-out tooth-brush, and a shallow pewter wash-hand basin, filled with horridly dirty water. For seats round this table there were no other substitutes than various chests of various dimensions.

Of such sordid penury as I then witnessed I had read, but never supposed I should be compelled to witness, much less to share. Notwithstanding the closeness of this hole, it was excessively cold. There was not a soul there to welcome me, the petty officers being all away on dock-yard duty. It might have been ten o'clock when I was first ushered into this region of darkness, of chill and evil odours. I remained with my surtout coat on, sitting on my chest, with my hands clasped before me, stiff with cold, and melancholy almost to tears. How much then I panted for the breeze that blew over the heathy common where I had lately wantoned, leaped and laughed!

As I there sat, I fell into a deep and dream-like reverie. I could not, after a pause, convince myself that all I saw around me was real. The light that the single unsnuffed candle gave, became more dim and smoky. I began to think that my spirit had most surely stepped into the vestibule of the abode of shadows; and I wished to convince myself that my body was far, far away sleeping in a pure atmosphere, and under a friendly roof. Minute after minute dropped its weight heavily, like so many pellets of lead upon my disordered brain. I became confused—perhaps I was nearly upon the point of syncope from the sudden change to bad air. I felt that all I saw about me, if not real, would prove that I was mad; and I feared that I should become so, if the scene turned out to be no illusion. At last I jumped up, as I felt my stupor and my sickness increasing, exclaiming—'This is hell—and there's the devil!' as I observed a hideous, shining black face peering at me over the top of the screen, grinning in such a manner, with a row of white teeth, that reminded me of so many miniature tombstones stretching right across a dark churchyard.

'No debbel, sar—my name, sar, Lillydew—vat you please vant, sar?—steward to young gentlemen, sar. Will young massa have a lilly white bit soft tommy,[1] sar,—broil him a sodger, sar—bumboat along side, get a fresh herring for relish, sar.'

'Get me a little fresh air—take me up stairs.'

'O Gemminnie! hi! hi! hi!—young gentleman, Massa Johnny Newcome. This way, sar.'

Conducted by this angel of darkness, I regained the deck and daylight, and the nausea soon left my chest, and the pain my head. I then made this reflection, that whatever glory a naval officer may attain, if he went through the ordeal I was about essaying, he richly deserved it. The captain and some of the other officers now came on board. I was introduced to most of them, and the skipper made himself very merry with an account of my recent adventure with the master's mate, who was still at the mast-head, as a convincing proof of the accuracy of the story, and was plainly distinguishable some half mile higher up the Medway.

I soon entered into conversation with one of the young gentlemen who was destined to be, for so long, my messmate. I told him that the air below would kill me. He acknowledged that it was bad enough to kill a dog, but that a reefer could stand it. He also advised me not to have my uniforms altered by the ship's tailors, as it would be done in a bungling manner; but to get leave to go on shore, and that he would introduce me to a very honest tradesman who would do me justice. I expressed my hopes to him, in a dry manner, that he did not belong to the regiment of horse marines. He understood me, and said, upon his honour, no; that it was all fair and above board; and as a recommendation, which he thought would be irresistible, he added that this tailor had a very pretty daughter, with the very pretty name of Jemima.

As the latter information was very satisfactory evidence as to the skill and honesty of the tradesman, I could not be guilty of such a *non sequitur* as not to promise to employ him. I then told him to make haste and come on shore with me. I now was made painfully sensible that before I could enjoy my wishes a little ceremony was needful. In fact, that my powers of locomotion were no longer under my own control, excepting for about one hundred and twenty feet, in one direction, and about thirty-five in another. As I was passing over the star-board of the quarter-deck to ask leave to go on shore, the captain accosted me, and did me the honour to request my company to dinner at his table. Finding him in so bland a humour, I preferred my request to live on shore till the ship sailed. He smiled at the enormity of my demand, and asked what induced it. I frankly told him the filth and bad smell of my accommodations; and also my wish not to be seen on board until my uniforms were complete.

'He's an original,' said the captain to the first lieutenant, 'but there is some sense in his request. I suppose *you* have no objection, Mr. Farmer. Young gentleman,' he continued, turning to me, 'you must always ask the first lieutenant, in future, for leave. Mind, don't be later than four o'clock.'

My messmate, with all manner of humility, now made his request, which being granted, we went down together to my chest, and making a bundle of all the clothes that required alteration, we placed that and ourselves in a shore boat, and made our way to the tailor's. I was there introduced to the lovely Jemima. She looked like a very pretty doll, modelled with crumbs of white bread; she was so soft, so fair, and so unmeaning. After the order was given, my maker of the outward man hazarded a few inquiries, in a manner so kind and so obliging, that quite made me lose sight of their impertinence. When he found that I had leave to remain on shore, and that my pocket-book was far from being ill-furnished, he expatiated very feelingly upon the exactions of living at inns, offered me a bed for nothing, provided only that I would pay for my breakfast, and appoint him my tailor in ordinary; and declared that he would leave no point unturned, to make me comfortable and happy. As this conversation took place in the little parlour at the back of the shop, Jemima—Miss Jemima—was present, and, as I seemed to hesitate, the innocent-looking dear slily came up beside me, and taking my hand pressed it amorously, stealing at me a look with eyes swimming with a strange expression. This by-play decided the business. The agreement was made, the terms being left entirely to Mr. Tapes. Covering my inappropriate dress with my blue surtout, I was about leaving with my messmate, when the young lady said to her father, 'Perhaps Mr. Rattlin would like to see his room before he goes out?'

'Not particularly.'

'Oh, but you must. You may come in, and I and the servant may be out—this way—you must not come up, Mr. Pridhomme, *your* boots are so abominably dirty. There, isn't it a nice room?—you pretty, pretty boy,' said she, jumping up, and giving me a long kiss, that almost took my breath away. 'Don't tell old leather-chops, will you, and I *shall* love you so.'

'Who is old leather-chops—your father?'

'Dear me, no, never mind him. I mean your messmate, Mr. Pridhomme.'

'I'm stepping into life,' thought I, as I went down stairs, 'and with no measured strides either.'

'What do you think of Jemima?' said Mr. Pridhomme, as we walked arm-in-arm towards the ramparts.

'Pretty.'

'Pretty—why she's an angel! If there was ever an angel on earth it is Jemima Tapes. But what is mere beauty? Nothing compared sincerity and innocence—she is all innocence and sincerity.'

'I am glad that you believe so.'

'Believe so—why look at her! She is all innocence. She won't let her father kiss her.'

'Why?'

'She says it is so indelicate.'

'How does she know what is, or what is not, indelicate?'

'D—n it, younker, you'd provoke a saint. She assures me, when she is forced to shake hands with a grown-up man, that it actually gives her a cold shudder all over. I don't think that she ever kissed any body but her mother, and that was years ago.'

'Perhaps she does not know how.'

'I'm sure she don't. If I had a fortune, I'd marry her to-morrow, only I'm afraid she's too modest.'

'Your fear is very commendable. Are the ladies at Chatham so remarkable for modesty?'

'No—and that's what makes Jemima so singular.'

I like to make people happy if they are not so, and if they are, even though that happiness may be the creation of a delusion, I like to leave them so. I, therefore, encouraged Mr. Pridhomme to pour all his raptures into, what he thought, an approving ear, and Jemima was the theme, until he left me at the door of the hotel at which I was to dine with Captain Reud. Whatever the reader may think of Jemima, I was, at this period, perfectly innocent myself, though not wholly ignorant. I should have deemed Miss Jemima's osculatory art as the mere effect of high spirits and hoydenly playfulness, had it not been for the hypocrisy that she was displaying towards my messmate. I had translated Gil Blas at school, and I therefore set her down for an intrepid coquette, if not *une franche aventurière*. However, though I pitied my messmate, that was no reason why I should not enjoy my dinner.

That day, I liked my little saffron-coloured captain much better. He played the host very agreeably. He made as many inquiries as he dared, without too much displaying his own ignorance, as to the extent of my acquirements, and, when he found them so far beyond his expectations, he seemed to be struck with a sudden respect for me. The tone of his conversation was more decorous than that of the preceding evening; he gave me a great deal of nautical advice, recommended me to the protection particularly of the first and second lieutenants, who were also his guests, approved of my plan of sleeping at the tailor's, and dismissed me very early, no doubt with a feeling of pleasure at having removed a restraint, for, as I left the room, I just caught the words—'Make a d—d sea lawyer[1] by-and-by.'

CHAPTER III

Jealousy cooled by a watering—Ralph exhorteth, and right wisely.— The boatswain sees many things in a new light—and, though he causeth crabs to be caught, he bringeth them to a wrong market.

PRIDHOMME had been lying in wait for me, and picked me up as I left the hotel. We went to the theatre, a wretched affair certainly, the absurdities of which I should have much enjoyed, had I not been bored to death by the eternal Jemima. That lady was like Jemima, and that was not. Was the person in the blue silk dress as tall as Jemima; or the other in the white muslin quite as stout? Jemima was all he could talk about, till at length, I was so horribly Jemimaed that I almost audibly wished Jemima jammed down his

throat; but, as every thing must have an end, even when a midshipman talks about Jemima, we, at length, got to the tailor's door,
which was opened by the lovely Jemima in *propriâ personâ*. Not
a step beyond the step of the door was the lover admitted, whilst
the poor wretch was fain to feast on the ecstasies of remembering
that he was permitted to grasp the tip of her fore-finger whilst he
sighed forth his fond good night.

In a few days the Eos being perfectly equipped, dropped down
to Sheerness, and I, for the first time, slept under the roof provided
for me by his Britannic Majesty. That is to say, I was coffined and
shrouded in a longitudinal canvas bag, hung up to the orlop deck
by two cleets, one at each end, in a very graceful curve, very useful
in forming that elegant bend in the back so much coveted by the
exhibitors in Regent Street.

I had taken a rather sentimental leave of Jemina, who had somehow or another persuaded me to exchange love tokens with her.
That which I gave her was a tolerably handsome writing-desk,
which I could not help buying for her, as she had taken a great
fancy to it; indeed, she told me it had annoyed her for some
months, because it stood so provokingly tempting in the shop-
window just over the way; and besides, 'She should be so—so
happy to write me such pretty letters from it.' The last argument
was convincing, and the desk was bought; in return for which she
presented me with a very old silver pencil-case—its age, indeed,
she gave me to understand, ought to be its greatest value in my
eyes—she had had it so long; it was given to her by her defunct
mother. So I promised to keep it as long as I lived. Really there was
no chance of my ever wearing it out by use, for it was certainly
quite useless; but love dignifies things so much! After having split
it up by shoving a piece of black-lead pencil into it, I put it into
my waitcoat pocket, saying to the heiress of the Chatham tailor—

'*Rich* gifts prove poor when givers prove unkind.'

'Ah, Edward!' said the giver of rich gifts, '*I* shall never prove
unkind.' So we parted, and, as I walked down the street, she waved
her hand, which would have been really white, had she not scored
her forefinger in a most villainous manner by her awkward method
of using her needle, when her father was short of hands.

When I afterwards heard of Chatham as being the universal
dépôt of 'ladies who love wisely and not too well,' rogues, and Jews,

I could not help thinking of my writing-desk, and adding to the list, Jewesses also.

About a week after, as we were still lying at Sheerness, and I had totally forgotten the innocent-looking Jemima, Mr. Pridhomme was smoking in a lover-like and melancholy fashion, against orders, a short pipe in the midshipmen's berth. As the ashes accumulated, he became at a loss for a tobacco-stopper, and I very good-naturedly handed him over the broken, broad-topped, vulgar-looking pencil-case, the gift of the adorable Jemima. His apathy, at the sight of this relic of love, dispersed like the smoke of his pipe.

'Where did you get this, younker?' he cried, swelling with passion in the true turkey-cock style.

'It was given me as a keepsake by Miss Jemima,' said I very quietly.

'It's a lie—you stole it.'

'You old scoundrel!'

'You young villain!'

'Take that!' roared my opponent, and the bread-basket, with its fragmental cargo of biscuits, came full in my face, very considerately putting bread into my mouth for his supposed injury.

'Take that!' said I, seizing the rum bottle.

'No, he sha'n't,' said Pigtop, the master's mate, laying hold of the much-prized treasure, 'let him take any thing but that.'

So I flung the water-jug at his head.

We were just proceeding to handycuffs, when the master-at-arms, hearing the riot, opened the door. We then cooled upon it, and a truce ensued. Explanations followed the truce, and an apology, on his part, the explanation; for which apology I very gladly gave him the pencil-case, that I had promised to keep as long as I lived, and a heartache at the same time.

The poor fellow had given the faithful Jemima this mutable love-gift three days before it came into my possession, on which occasion they had broken a crooked sixpence together. I moralized upon this, and came to the conclusion, that, whatever a tailor might be, a sailor is no match for a tailor's daughter, born and bred up at Chatham.

Now, I have nothing wherewith to amuse the reader about the mischievous tricks that were played upon me in my entrance into naval life. The clues of my hammock were not reefed. I was not lowered down by the head into a bucket of cold water, nor sent any where with a foolish message by a greater fool than myself. The exemptions from these usual persecutions I attribute to my robust and well-grown frame; my disposition so easily evinced to do battle on the first occasion that offered itself; and, lastly, my well-stocked purse, and the evident consideration shown to me by the captain and the first lieutenant.

As I write as much for the instruction of my readers, as for their amusement, I wish to impress upon them, if they are themselves, or if they know any that are, going to enter into the navy, the necessity, in the first instance, of showing or recommending a proper spirit. Never let the debutant regard how young or how feeble he may be—he must make head against the first insult—he must avenge the first hoax. No doubt he will be worsted, and get a good beating; but that one will save him from many hundreds hereafter, and, perhaps, the necessity of fighting a mortal duel. Your certain defeat will be forgotten in the admiration of the spirit that provoked the contest. And remember, that the person who hoaxes you is always in the wrong, and it depends only upon yourself to heap that ridicule upon him, that was intended for your own head; to say nothing of the odium that must attach to him for the cruelty, the cowardice, and the meanness, of fighting with a lad weaker than himself. This I will enforce by a plain fact that happened to myself. A tall, consequential, thirty-years-old master's mate, threatened to beat me, after the manner that oldsters are accustomed to beat youngsters. I told him, that if he struck me, I would strike again as long as I had strength to stand, or power to lift my hand. He laughed and struck me. I retaliated: it is true that I got a sound thrashing; but it was my first and last, and my tyrant got both his eyes well blackened, his cheek swollen—and was altogether so much defaced, that he was forced to hide himself in the sick-list for a fortnight. The story could not be told well for him, but it told for me gloriously; indeed, he felt so much annoyed by the whole affair, that he went and asked leave to go and mess with the gunner, fairly stating to the captain that he could not run the risk of keeping order—for he was our caterer—if he had to fight a battle every time he had to enforce it.

But I cannot too much caution youngsters against having recourse, in their self-defence, to deadly weapons. I am sorry to say, it was too common when I was in the navy. It is un-English and assassin-like. It rarely keeps off the tyrant; the knife, the dirk, or whatever else be the instrument, is almost invariably forced from the young bravo's hand, and the thrashing that he afterwards gets is pitiless, and the would-be stabber finds no voice lifted in his favour. He also gains the stigma of cowardice, and the bad reputation of being malignant and revengeful. Indeed, so utterly futile is the drawing of murderous instruments in little affrays of this sort, that, though I have known them displayed hundreds of times, yet I never knew a single wound to have been inflicted—though many a heavy beating has followed the atrocious display. By all means, let my young friends avoid it. Now this preachment is finished, I will on with my adventures.

On the day before we sailed from Sheerness, the captain had an order conveyed to the first lieutenant to send me away on duty immediately, for two or three hours. I was bundled into the pinnace with old canvas, old ropes, and old blocks, condemned stores, to the dock-yard, and, as I approached the landing-place appropriated for the use of admirals *in posse*, I saw embark from the stairs, exclusively set apart for admirals and post-captains *in esse*, my captain and the port-admiral in the admiral's barge, and, seated between these two awful personages, there sat a civilian, smiling in all the rotundity and fat of a very pleasant countenance, and very plain clothes, and forming a striking contrast to the grim complacency, and the iron-bound civility, of the two men in uniform.

The boat's crew were so much struck with this apparent anomaly, for to them, any thing in the civilian's garb to come near an officer, and that officer a naval one, was hardly less than portentous, and argued the said civilian to be something belonging to the *genus homo* extraordinary—and the fat specimen in the boat with the port-admiral, they thought, was one of the Lords of the Admiralty, or even Mr. Croker himself[1]—the notion of whose dimly-understood attributes was, with them, of a truly magnificent nature. Whoever this person was, he was carefully assisted up the side of our ship, and remained on board for about an hour, whilst we were burning with curiosity and eagerness to be on board to satisfy it, and forced to do our best to allay this tantalizing passion, by hauling along tallied bights of rope, and rousing old hawsers out, and new hawsers into the boat—a more pleasant employment may be easily imagined for a raw, cold, misty day in winter.

I regarded all these operations very sapiently, knowing as yet
nothing of the uses, or even of the names, of the different stores
that I was delivering and receiving. The boatswain was with me of
course: but notwithstanding that I had positive orders not to let
the men stray away from the duty they were performing—as this
official told me, after we had done almost every thing that we had
come on shore to perform, that he must borrow two of the men to
go up with him to the storekeeper's private house, to look out for
some strong fine white line with which to bouse up the best bower
anchor to the spanker-boom-end, when the ship should happen
to be too much down by the stern—I could not refuse to disobey
my orders upon a contingency so urgent. And there he left me, for
about two hours, shivering in the boat; and, at length, he and the
men came down, with very little white line in exchange for his not
very white lie; and truly, they had been bousing up something; for
Mr. Lushby, the respectable boatswain,[1] told me, with great condescension, that he was a real officer, whilst I was nothing but a
living walking-stick, for the captain to swear at when he was in
a bad humour; and that he had no doubt but that I should get mast-
headed when I got on board, for allowing those two men, who were
catching crabs, to get so drunk.

Similar tricks to this, every young gentleman entering the service
must expect—tricks that partake as much of the nature of malice
as of fun. Now, in the few days that I had been in the service, I very
well understood that the care of the men, as respected their
behaviour and sobriety, devolved on me, the delivering of old,
and the drawing of new stores, on the boatswain; yet, for the conduct of those men that he took from under my eye, I felt that, in
justice, he was answerable. I therefore made no reply to the vaunt-
ings and railings of Mr. Lushby, but had determined how to act.
The boat came alongside. There was nobody on board but the
officer of the watch, and Mr. Lushby tumbled up the side and down
the waist in double-quick time, sending the chief boatswain's mate
and the yeoman of the stores to act as his deputy. He certainly did
his duty in that respect, as two sober deputies are worth more than
is a drunken principal.

However, I walked into the gun-room to report myself and boat
to the first lieutenant. The officers were at their wine. I was
flattered and surprised at the frank politeness of my reception,
and the welcome looks that I received from all. I was invited to sit,

and a glass placed for me. When I found myself tolerably comfortable, and had answered some questions put to me by Mr. Farmer, our first lieutenant, the drift of which I did not then comprehend, and putting a little wilful simplicity in my manner, I asked with a great deal of apparent innocence, if all the sailors caught crabs when they were drunk.

'Catch crabs, Mr. Rattlin!' said Mr. Farmer, smiling. 'Not always; but they are sure to catch something worse—the cat.'

'With white line—how strange!' said I, purposely misunderstanding the gallant officer. 'Now I know why Mr. Lushby took up the two men—and why all three came down in a state to catch crabs. I thought that white line had something to do with it.'

'Yes, Mr. Rattlin, white line has.' Mr. Farmer then motioned me to stay where I was, took up his hat, and went on deck. I need not tell my naval readers that the boatswain was sent for, and the two men placed aft. It was certainly a very cruel proceeding towards the purveyor of white line, who had just turned his cabin into a snuggery, and had taken another round turn, with a belay over all, in the shape of two more glasses of half-and-half. When he found himself on the quarter-deck, though the shades of evening were stealing over the waters, (I like a poetical phrase now and then) he saw more than in broad daylight—that is to say, he saw many first lieutenants, who seemed, with many wrathful countenances, with many loud words, to order many men to see him down many ladders, safely to his cabin.

The next morning this 'real officer' found himself in a very uncomfortable plight; for, with an aching head, he was but too happy to escape with a most stinging reprimand: and he had the consolation then to learn, that, had he not endeavoured to play upon the *simplicity* of Mr. Rattlin, he would most surely have escaped the fright and the exposure.

The simplicity!

Now, I have mentioned this trifling incident, merely to show how easy it is for a youth just entered, by a little manœuvring, to make it a very dangerous thing to play tricks upon him, avoiding on the one hand, the odium of tale-bearer, and, on the other, that *ultima ratio*, of kings as well as midshipmen, war, in the repelling of insult.

CHAPTER IV

*Another mystery—all overjoyed because the Eos is under weigh; she
works well—through the water—her officers through their wine—
Ralph refraineth, and self glorifieth—a long shore man makes
a short stay on board—because he won't go on the wrong tack.*

BUT I must now explain why I had become so suddenly a favourite
in the ward-room. The very stout gentleman, who came off with
the admiral and captain, undertook the aquatic excursion on my
account. He made every inquiry as to my equipment, my messmates, and my chance of comfort. Yet I, the person most concerned, was sent out of the way, lest by accident I should meet with
him. I never knew who he was, nor do I think the captain did. My
shipmates had their conjectures, and I had mine. They took him
to be what is usually called, not a person, but a personage. I believe
that he was nothing more than a personage's fat steward, or some
other menial obesity—for it was very plain that he was ashamed
to look me in the face! and I understand he gave himself many
second-hand airs. If now living, I hope this may meet his eye.

And now we are off in earnest. The Nore-light is passed; the pilot
is on the hammock nettings. The breeze takes the sails, the noble
frigate bends to it, as a gallant cavalier gently stoops to receive the
kiss of beauty—the blocks rattle as the ropes fly through them—
the sails court the wind to their embrace, now on one side, now on
the other. I stand on the quarter-deck, in silent admiration at the
astonishing effects of this wonderful seeming confusion. I am
pushed here, and ordered there—I now jump to avoid the eddy
of the uncurling ropes as they fly upwards, but my activity is vain,
a brace now drags across my shins, and now the bight of a lee-
spanker-brail salutes me, not lovingly, across the face. The captain
and officers are viewing the gallant vessel with intense anxiety, and
scrutinizing every evolution that she is making. How does she
answer her helm? Beautifully. What lee-way does she make? Scarce
perceptible. The log is hove repeatedly—seven, seven and a half,
close hauled. Stand by, the captain is going to work her himself.
She advances head to the wind bravely, like a British soldier to the
breach—she is about! she has stayed within her own length—she
has not lost her way! 'Noble! excellent!' is the scarcely suppressed

cry; and then arose in the minds of that gallant band of officers visions of an enemy worthy to cope with; of the successful manœuvre, the repeated broadsides, the struggle and the victory; their lives, their honour, and the fame of their country they now willingly repose upon her—she is at once their home, their field of battle, and their arena of glory. See how well she behaves against that head sea! There is not a man in that noble fabric who has not adopted her—who has not a love for her—they refer all their feelings to her, they rest all their hopes upon her. The Venetian Doge may wed the sea in his gilded gondola, ermined nobles may stand near, and jewelled beauty around him—religion too may lend her overpowering solemnities;—but all this display could never equal the enthusiasm of that morning, when above three hundred true hearts wedded themselves to that beauty of the sea, the Eos, as she worked round the North Foreland into the Downs.

The frigate behaved so admirably in all her evolutions, that, when we dropped anchor in the roadstead, the captain, to certify his admiration and pleasure, invited all the wardroom officers to dine with him, as well as three or four midshipmen, myself among the rest.

It was an animated scene, that dinner party. The war was then raging. Several French frigates of our own size and class, and many much larger, were wandering on the seas. The republican spirit was blazing forth in their crews—and ardently we longed to get among them. As yet, no one knew our destination. We had every stimulant to honourable excitement, and mystery threw over the whole that absorbing charm, that impels us to love and to woo the unknown.

But this meeting, at first so rational, and then so convivial, at length permitted its conviviality to destroy its rationality. Men who spoke and thought like heroes one hour, the next spoke what they did not think, and made me think what I did not speak. No one got drunk except the purser, who is always a privileged person; yet they were not the same men as when they began their carouse, nor I the same boy when they had finished it. On that evening I made a resolution never to touch ardent spirits, and, whilst I was in the navy, that resolution I adhered to. It is a fact—I am known to too many, to make, on this subject, a solemn assertion falsely. I did not lay the same restriction on wine—yet, even that I always avoided, when I could do so without the appearance of affectation.

My reason, such as it was, never in the slightest degree tottered on her throne, either with a weakness or a strength not her own. The wine-cup never gladdened or sorrowed me. Even when the tepid, fœtid, and animalized water, was served out to us in quantities so minute, that our throats could count it by drops, I never sought to qualify its nauseous taste, or increase its quantity, by the addition of spirits, when spirits were more plentiful than the much-courted water. This trait proves, if it proves nothing else, that I had a good deal of that inflexibility of character, which we call in others obstinacy, when we don't like it, firmness when we do—in ourselves, always, decision.

And all my messmates,—where are they? I shall not quote the trite phrase and say, 'Echo answers, "where,"' which, by-the-by, must have been an Irish sort of echo; but my echo shall, as echoes usually do, repeat the last two syllables, and by a question, answer, 'Are they?' It is a melancholy question—and I must answer, 'Alas! I know not.' Indeed, after the lapse of five-and-twenty years, we can put the question to ourselves only with heaviness upon our hearts. Yet some there are, but how many more that are not!

Tempus edax rerum. I deny the assertion. The old mumbler is continually defrauded. How few are there of those gallant fellows who will fall ripe into his gumless jaws! Food for Time! Alas! they have been food for almost everything else. 'Food for powder, food for powder,' according to honest Jack, as many of them have been! some have been food for another Jack, whose prefix is yellow. More than one have been food for sharks. Yes, Time has been defrauded of them, and they of time. How many have been buried in the sea!

When at the last trumpet they shall arise from the vast and blue depths, and they shake from them the salt wave, may it wash away with it one half of their sins—and in the beneficence of the Creator they may fearlessly trust for the remission of the other; for who among them, through a wild life, has not suffered in the performance of a hard, and died in the execution of a sacred, duty? For this numberless, this unuttered dead, there have been but few tears, and there is no trophy. No trophy! yes, there is one, the best, the most imperishable. The past and the present glory of that country, for which they have died. This can be never taken from them. Even should England bend to the general law that destroys men and ruins empires, or fall to pieces by internal faction, still the glory of the past is theirs irrevocably. May England ever foster and honour the race, and while she does, though her prosperity may fluctuate, independence and superiority will never leave her ship-defended shores.

I give the incident that I am about to relate, to show in what way, five-and-twenty years ago, a man-of-war was made the alternative of a jail; and to prove, generally speaking, of what little use this kind of recruiting was to the service; and, as it made a great impression on me at the time, though a little episodical, I shall not hesitate to place it before my readers.

After remaining at anchor in the Downs during the night, we sailed next morning down the channel without stopping at Spithead, our ultimate destination being still a profound secret. As we proceeded, when we were off a part of the coast, the name of which I do not remember, about noonday it fell calm, and the tide being against us, we neared the shore a little, and came to an anchor. We had not remained long in our berth before we descried a shore boat pulling off to us, which shortly came alongside, with a very singular cargo of animals, belonging to the genus *homo*. In the stern sheets sate a magistrate's clerk, swelling with importance. On the after thwart, and facing the Jack in office, were placed two constables, built upon the regular Devonshire, chaw-bacon model, holding upright between their legs each an immense staff, headed by the gilded initials of our sovereign lord the King.

Seated between these imposing pillars of the state, sate in tribulation dire, a tall, awkward young man, in an elaborately-worked white smockfrock, stained with blood in front and upon the shoulders. He was the personification of rural distress. He blubbered *à pleine voix*, and lifted up and lowered his hand-cuffed wrists with a seesaw motion really quite pathetical. Though the wind had fallen, yet the tide was running strongly, and there was a good deal of sea, quite enough to make the motion in the boat very unpleasant. As they held on alongside by the rope, the parties in the stern sheets began bobbing at each other, the staves lost and resumed, and then lost again, their perpendicular—so much indeed, as to threaten the head of the clerk, whose countenance 'began to pale its effectual fire.'[1] The captain and many of the officers looking over the gangway, the following dialogue ensued, commenced by the officer of the watch. 'Shore-boat, ho-hoy!'

'In the name of the king,' replied the clerk, between many

minacious hiccoughs, and producing a piece of paper, 'I have brought you a *volunteer*, to serve in his majesty's fleet;' pointing to the blubberer in the smockfrock.

'Well,' said the captain, 'knock off his irons, and hand him up.'

'Dare not, sir—as much as my life is worth. The most ferocious poacher in the country. Has nearly beaten in the skull of the squire's head gamekeeper.'

'Just the sort of man we want,' said the captain. 'But you see he can't get up the side with his hands fast; and I presume you cannot be in much danger from the volunteer, whilst you have two such staves held by two such constables.'

'Yes,' said the now seriously affected clerk; 'I do not think that I incur much danger from the malefactor, since I am under the protection of the guns of the frigate.' So, somewhat re-assured by this reflection, the brigand of the preserves was unmanacled, and the whole party, clerk, constables, and prisoner, came up the side, and made their appearance on the break of the quarter-deck.

But this was not effected without much difficulty, and some loss, a loss that one of the parties must have bewailed to his dying day, if it did not actually hasten that awful period. One of the constables in ascending the side, let fall his staff, his much-loved staff, dear to him by many a fond recollection of riot repressed, and evil doer apprehended, and away it went, floating with the tide, far, far astern. His unmitigated horror at this event was comic in the extreme, and the keeper of the king's peace could not have evinced more unsophisticated sorrow than did the late keeper of his conscience at the loss of the seals, the more especially as the magistrate's clerk refused to permit the boat to go in pursuit of it, not wishing the only connecting link between him and the shore to be so far removed from his control.

CHAPTER V

*The volunteer and his fate, showing how a great rogue,
notwithstanding that he may appear to be born to be hung, will
sometimes happen to drown.*

THE group on the quarter-deck was singular and ludicrous.
Reuben Gubbins, for such was the name of the offender, was the
only son of a small farmer, who, it appeared, had even gone the
length of felony, by firing upon and wounding the gamekeeper of
the lord of the manor. He was quite six feet high, very awkwardly
built, and wore under his frock a long-tailed blue coat, dingy buck-
skin nether garments, and top-boots, with the tops tanned brown
by service. His countenance betrayed a mixture of simplicity,
ignorance, and strong animal instinct. He was the least suited being
that could be possibly conceived of whom to make a sailor. His
limbs had been long stiffened by rustic employments, and he had
a dread of the sea, and of a man-of-war, horrifying to his imagination. In this dread it was very evident that his companions largely
participated, not excepting the pragmatical clerk. The constable
with the staff, and the constable without, ranged themselves on
either side of the still sobbing Arcadian. Indeed, the staffless man
seemed to be but little less overcome than the prisoner. He felt as
if all strength, value, and virtue, had gone out of him; and ever and
anon he glared upon the baton of his brother officer with looks
felonious and intent on rapine.

The business was soon concluded. Reuben, rather than see himself tried for his life, determined to make trial of the sea, and thus
became, perhaps, the most unwilling volunteer upon record.

Poor fellow! his sufferings must have been great! The wild
animal of the forest, when pining, for the first time, in a cage, or the
weary land-bird, blown off, far away upon the restless sea, could
not have been more out of their elements than tall and ungainly
Reuben Gubbins on the deck of his Majesty's ship Eos. I do not
know how it was, for I am sure that I ought to have despised him
for his unmanly and incessant weeping, I knew that he had
offended the laws of his country, yet, when the great lout went
forward disconsolately, and sat himself down, amidst the derision
of the seamen, upon a gun-carriage on the forecastle, I could not

help going and dispersing the scoffers, and felt annoyingly inclined to take his toil-embrowned hand, sit down beside, and cry with him. However, I did not so far commit myself. But a few hours afterwards I was totally overcome.

Strict orders were given not to allow Gubbins to communicate with any one from the shore. A little before dusk, there was a boat ordered by the sentinels to keep off, that contained, besides the sculler, a respectable-looking old man, and a tall, stout, and rather handsome, young woman. Directly they caught the eye of Reuben, he exclaimed, 'Woundikins! if there bean't feyther and our sister Moll.' And running aft, and putting his hat between his knees, he thus addressed the officer of the watch, 'Please Mr. Officer, zur, there's feyther and our Moll.'

'Well!'

'Zur, mayn't I go and have my cry out with 'em, for certain I ha' behaved mortal bad?'

'Against orders.'

'But, sure-ly, you'll let him come up to comfort loike his un-dutiful son.'

'No, no, impossible.'

'Whoy, lookee there, zur—that's feyther with the white hair, and that's sister crying like mad. Ye can no' ha' the hard heart.'

'Silence! and go forward.'

I looked over the side, and there I saw the old man standing up reverently, with his hat in one hand, and a bag, apparently full of money, in the other. Undoubtedly, the simple yeoman had supposed that money could either corrupt the captain, or buy off the servitude of his guilty son. It was a fine old countenance, down the sides of which that silver hair hung so patriarchally and gracefully; and there that poor old man stood, bowing in his wretchedness and his bereavement, with his money extended, to every officer that he could catch a glimpse of, as his hat or head appeared above the hammock nettings or the bulwarks. The grief of his sister was common-place and violent; but there was a depth and a dignity in that of the old man that went to my very heart. I could not help going up to the lieutenant and entreating him to grant the interview.

'It won't do, Mr. Rattlin. Don't you know that the fellow was put on board with C.P.[1] before his name? I anticipate what you are going to say, but humanity is a more abstract thing than you are aware of, and orders must be obeyed.'

'But, zur,' said Gubbins, who had again approached, 'I can see that feyther has forgi'en me, and he's the mon I ha' most wronged arter all. Besides sistur wull break her heart if she doan't say "Good bye, Reuben"—if feyther has made it up, sure other folk mought by koind. Oh, ay—but I've been a sad fellow!' And then he began to blubber with fresh violence.

The officer was a little moved—he went to the gangway, hailed the boat, and when she came near enough, he told the old farmer kindly, that his orders to prevent personal communication were strict; that any parcel or letter should be handed up, but that he would do well not to let his reprobate son have any money. During this short conference, Reuben had placed himself within sight of his relatives, and the sacred words of 'My father,' 'My son,' were, in spite of all orders, exchanged between them. By this time the tide had turned, the wind had risen, and precisely from the right quarter; so the hands were turned up, 'up anchor.' The orders for the boat to keep off were now reiterated in a manner more impera- tive; but it still hung about the ship, and after we were making way, as long as the feeble attempts of the boatman could keep his little craft near us, the poor old man and his daughter, with a constancy of love that deserved a better object, hung upon our wake, he stand- ing up with his white hair blown about by the wind, to catch a last glimpse of a son whom he was destined to see no more, and who would without doubt, as the scripture beautifully and tenderly expresses it, 'bring his grey hairs with sorrow to the grave.'[1]

Long, long after the stolid and sullen son had ceased, apparently, to interest himself about the two that were struggling after us, in their really frail boat, I watched, from the taffrail, the vain and loving pursuit; indeed, until the darkness and the rapidly-increasing distance shrouded it from my view, I did not leave my post of observation, and the last that I could discern of the mourners, still showed me the old man standing up, in the fixed attitude of grief, and the daughter with her face bent down upon her knees. To the last, the boat's head was still towards the ship—a touching emblem of unswerving fatherly love.

I could not away with the old man's look, it was so wretched, so helpless, yet so fond—and was typed to my fancy so strongly by his little boat pursuing with a hopeless constancy over waves too rough for it, the huge and disregarding ship; so, with my breast full, even to suffocation with mingled emotions, I went down to my berth, and, laying my head upon the table, and covering my face with my hands, I pretended to sleep. The cruel torture of that half hour! I almost thought the poacher, with all his misery, still blessed in having a father's love—'twas then that I felt intensely the agony of the desertion of my own parent—the love that had been denied to me to give to my own father, I lavished upon the white-headed old man. In imagination, I returned with him to his desolate home; I supported his tottering steps over the threshold, no longer musical with an only son. I could fancy myself placing him tenderly and with reverence in his accustomed chair, and speaking the words of comfort to him in a low voice, and looking round for his family bible—and the sister, doubtless she had many sources of consolation; youth was with her—life all before her—she had companions, friends, perhaps a lover; but,—for the poor old man! At that moment, I would have given up all my anticipations of the splendid career that I fancied I was to run, in order to have gone and have been unto the bereaved sire as a son, and to have found in him a father.

But nobody could make a sailor of Reuben Gubbins, and Reuben had no idea of making a sailor of himself. It was in vain that the boatswain's-mate docked the long tails of his blue coat, (such things were done in the navy at that time,) razeed his top-boots into seaman's shoes, and that he had his smock-frock reduced into a seaman's shirt. The soil hung upon him, he slouched over the deck, as if he were walking over the furrows of ploughed land, and looked up into the rigging as if he saw a cock-pheasant at roost upon the rattlins. Moreover, he could talk of nothing else except-ing 'feyther,' and 'our Moll,' and he really ate his bread (*subintellige* biscuit) moistened with his tears, (if tears can moisten such flinty preparations) for he was always whimpering. For the sake of the fit of romance that I had felt for his father, I took some kind notice of this yokel afloat. I believe, as much as it lay in his nature, he was grateful for it, for to every one else on board he was the con-stant butt.

Mr. Farmer, our first lieutenant, was a smart and a somewhat exacting officer. He used to rig the smoke-sail some twelve feet high across the mizen mast, and make the young gentlemen just caught, and the boys of the ship, lay out upon it, in order that they might practise furling after a safe method. At first, nothing could persuade Reuben to go a single step up the rigging—not even the

rope's end of the boatswain's-mate. Now this delicacy was quite at
variance with Mr. Farmer's ideas; so, in order to overcome it by
the gentlest means in the world, Reuben had the option given him
of being flogged, or of laying out on the smoke-sail yard, just to
begin with, and to get into the way of it. It was a laughable thing to
see this huge clown hanging with us boys upon the thin yard, and
hugging it as closely as if he loved it. He had a perfect horror of
getting to the end of it. At a distance, when our smoke-sail yard
was *manned*, we looked like a parcel of larks spitted, with one great
goose in the midst of us. 'Doey get beyond me, zur; doey, Mr.
Rattlin,' he would say. 'Ah! zur, I'd climb with any bragger in this
ship for a rook's nest, where I ha' got a safe bough to stand upon;
but to dance upon this here seesawing line, and to call it a horse too,
ben't christian loike.'

But his troubles were soon to cease. He was made a waister, and,
at furling sails, stationed on the main yard. I will anticipate a little
that we may have done with him. The winter had set in severely,
with strong gales, and much frost and snow. We were not yet clear
of the chops of the channel, and the weather became so bad, that
it was found necessary to lie to under try-sails, and close-reefed
maintop-sail. About two bells in the first dog watch the first
lieutenant decided upon furling the main sail. Up on the main yard
Reuben was forced to go; he went to leeward, and the seamen, full
of mischief, kept urging him farther and farther away from the
bunt. I was with one of the oldsters in the maintop; the maintop-
sail had just been close reefed. I had a full view of the lads on the
main yard, and the terror displayed in Reuben's countenance was
at once ludicrous and horrible. It was bitterly cold, the rigging was
stiffened by frost, and the cutting north-east wind came down upon
the men on the lee yardarm out of the belly of the topsail with
tremendous force, added to which, the ship, notwithstanding the
pressure of the last-mentioned sail, surged violently, for there was
a heavy though a short sea. The farmer's son seemed to be gradually petrifying with fear: he held on upon a fold of the sail instinc-
tively, without at all assisting to bundle it up. He had rallied all his
energies into his cramped and clutching fingers. As I looked down
upon him, I saw that he was doomed. I would have cried out for
assistance, but I knew that my cry would have been useless, even if
I had been able, through the roar of the winds and the waters, to
have made it heard.

M

But this trying situation could not last long. The part of the sail on which Reuben had hung, with what might be truly termed his death-clutch, was wanted to be rolled in with the furl, and, by the tenacity of his grasp, he impeded the operation.

'Rouse up, my lads, bodily, to windward,' roared the master's-mate, stationed at the bunt of the sail.

'Let go, you lubber,' said the sailor next to windward of Reuben, on the yard.

Reuben was now so lost, that he did not reply to the man even by a look. 'Now, my lads, now. One, two, three, and a——.' Obedient to the call of the officer, with a simultaneous jerk at the sail, the holdfast of the stupified peasant was plucked from his cracking fingers; he fell back with a loud shriek from the yard, struck midway on the main rigging, and thence bounding far to leeward in the sea, disappeared, and for ever, amid the white froth of the curling wave that lapped him up greedily. He never rose again. Perhaps, in her leeway, the frigate drifted over him—and thus the violated laws of his country were avenged. I must confess, that I felt a good deal shocked at the little sensation this (to me) tragical event occasioned. But we get used to these things, in this best of all possible worlds; and if the poacher died unwept, unprayed, unknelled for, all that can be said of the matter is—that many a better man has met with a worse fate.

CHAPTER VI

Symptoms of sickness, not of the sea, but of the land beyond it.—
Our M.D. wishes to write D. I. O., and prepares accordingly.—
Ralph is about to reap his first marine laurels on the rocks of Cove.

I DO not get on with this life at all. The vast Atlantic, with its tranquil and tempestuous wonders, the new world, venerable in its natural antiquities, and the Mediterranean, in all the extent of its classic shores, are before me, and I have not yet reached the Cove of Cork. Clap on more sail. It is bitterly cold, however, and here we are now safely moored in one of the petals of the 'first flower of the sea.'

In making this short passage, Captain Reud was very affable

and communicative. He could talk of nothing but the beautiful coast of Leghorn, the superb Bay of Naples; pleasant trips to Rome, visits to Tripoli, and other interesting spots on the African coast; and, on the voluptuous city of Palermo, with its amiable ladies and incessant festivities, he was quite as eloquent as could reasonably be expected from a smart post-captain of four-and-twenty.

We were all in a fool's paradise. For myself, I was enraptured. I was continually making extracts from Horace, Virgil, and other school-books, that I still carried with me, which referred, in the least, to those places that we were at all likely to see. But visions of this land of promise, of this sea flowing with gentle waves and rich prizes, were soon dispersed before a sad reality, that, without the aid of the biting weather, now made most of the officers and men look blue, as soon as our anchors had nipped the ground of the Green Island. We found ourselves in the middle of a convoy of more than two hundred vessels of all descriptions, that the experienced immediately knew to be West Indiamen.

The sarcastic glee with which Captain Reud rubbed his skinny, yellow hands, when he ordered additional sentries, and a boat to row guard round the ship from sunset to sunrise, weather permitting, to prevent desertion, gave me a strong impression of the malignity of his disposition. Certainly, the officers, from the first lieutenant downwards, looked, when under the influence of the first surprise, about as sage as we may conceive did those seven wise men of Gotham, who put to sea in a bowl. Some of them had even exchanged into the ship, for certain unlawful considerations, because she was so fine a frigate, and the captain possessed so much interest, being a very near and dear relation[1] of the then treasurer of the navy. With this interest they thought, of course, that he would have the selection of his own station. And so he had. They either did not know, or had forgotten, that Captain Reud was a West Indian creole, and that he had large patrimonial estates in Antigua.

'Not loud but deep[2] were the curses in the gun-room, but both 'loud and deep' were those in the midshipmen's berth, for the denizens thereof were never proverbial for the niceties of their expressions, when the appalling certainty broke on the comminators, of three years' roasting in the West Indies, with accompaniments of misgivings about Yellow Jack,[3] and the palisades,[4] merely because the captain wished to go and see why the niggers did not make quite so much sugar and rum as they used to do. But, after all, we had a sage ship's company, officers included, for there was scarcely a man in the ship, who, after our destination was ascertained, did not say, 'Well, I thought as much;' and they derived much consolation from the consciousness of their foresight.

The knowledge of our station had a most decided effect upon two of our officers, the master and surgeon; the former of whom, a weather-beaten, old north-countryman, who had been all his life knocking about the north sea, and our channels at home, immediately gave himself up for lost. He made his will, took a decidedly serious turn, and came into the midshipmen's berth with a case bottle of rum under one arm, and a Bible under the other, in order to see if he could not establish a sort of periodical prayer-meeting. He was made heartily welcome; but, as we occupied so much time in properly discussing the preliminaries, we did not even open the principal subject, which he perceiving, came next day with the Bible only; and then, never was there a set of young gentlemen more assiduous in their duties. Those whose watch it was on deck, though we were safely moored, could not think of being off their posts, notwithstanding the inclemency of the weather; and those who had the middle and first watches, were anxious to turn in, that they might relieve punctually, and in an officer-like manner, when it should be their turn to be on deck. One very devout young gentleman told Mr. Shields, for that was the master's name, that he thought it very impious for any one to read the Bible, excepting either in church or on Sundays, without such reader were a parson.

This second attempt of the good man closed the subject. Whether his fit of devotion wore off, or his attachment to the bottle increased, I cannot say; but it is certain, that his nose grew daily more red, and we heard nothing more of prayer-meetings, after Mr. Shields had got over the first quizzing upon the matter. I must do him also the justice to state, that, the very evening after his devotional failure, when his piety was, by the marine officer, very illiberally ascribed to his fears, Mr. Shields, over his fourth glass of half-and-half, asserted, with an imprecation that might well have split a deal board, that he was moved to his sanctimonious undertaking solely by his care for the welfare of the puir souls of the benighted and scripture-denying young ne'er-do-wells, and swearing blackguards; meaning, of course, my very respectable self, and my much-to-be-respected messmates. Now, I would not have it thought that there was anything approaching to pusillanimity in the conduct and deportment of this hard-a-weather sailor, for a braver man never carried a ship into action; but he had a great predilection for Northumbrian worms; and, as he believed all his ancestors had been, from time immemorial, decorously devoured by them, he thought it something indecent, shocking, and profane, that he, the last of the Shields, should be macerated by the unholy-looking mandibles of land-crabs, a species of animal that he could nowhere find mentioned in the Bible. Moreover, he knew that all flesh was grass; and, as he had been credibly informed, that persons dying in the West Indies were always buried in the sands, he thought it, in some way, flying in the face of Providence; for he asserted that, however fructifying his body might be, there, at least, it would never again turn to grass. He had no great objection to dying, in a general way, for he had a vile shrew of a wife, who, it was plain, had no intention of dying herself; but he objected strongly, for the above-mentioned reasons, to dying at Port Royal, and at having his obsequies performed within the palisades.

But there was another person, who viewed the West India station not religiously like our master, or joyously like our captain, or grumblingly like the marine officer, or despitefully like all the lieutenants, or detestably like my messmates, or indifferently like myself. He took the matter into consideration discreetly, and so, in order to enjoy a long life, he incontinently fell sick unto death. Of course he knew, more than any man on board, how ill he was, for he was the doctor himself. He was not merely a naval surgeon, but a regular M. D., and with an English diploma. He could appreciate, as much as any man, the value of life, and hard indeed did he struggle to preserve the means of prolonging it. He was a short, round, and very corpulent person, with a monstrously large and pleasantly-looking face, with a very high colour—a colour, not the flush of intemperance, but the glow of genuine health. This vast physiognomy was dug all over with holes; not merely pock-marks, but pock-pits. Indeed, his countenance put you in mind of a vast tract of gravelly soil on a sunny day, dug over with holes; it was so red, so cavernous, and withal, so bright. I need not mention that he was a *bon vivant*, a most joyous, yet a most discreet one. Even on board of ship he contrived to make his breakfasts dinners, his dinners feasts, and his suppers, though light, delicacies.

He was no mean proficient in the culinary art, and as refined a gourmand as the dear departed Dr. Kitchener[1]—a man, to whose honour I have a great mind to devote an episode, and would do so, were not my poor shipmate, Dr. Thompson, just now waiting for me to relieve him from his illness.

No sooner did our clever medical attendant understand his destination, than he sent away his plate untouched at dinner—refused his wine—talked movingly of broken constitutions, a predisposition to anasarca,[2] and the deceitful and dangerous appearances of florid health. At supper, he pronounced himself a lost man, held out his brawny fist to whomsoever would choose to feel his pulse, and sent for the first assistant-surgeon to make him up a tremendous quantity of prescriptions, to be exhibited the ensuing night—to whatever fish might be so unfortunate as to be swimming alongside. After this display, and whilst he was languidly sipping a tumbler of barley-water, the Hon. Mr. B., our junior luff,[3] was loud in his complaints of being, what he called, fairly entrapped; when Dr. Thompson, in a feeble and tremulous voice, read him a long lecture on patriotism, obedience to the dictates of duty, and self-devotion, finishing thus:—'By heaven, show me the man that flinches from his duty, and I'll show you, whatever may be his outward bearing, a craven at heart! I am very ill—I feel that I am fast sinking into a premature grave—but what of that? I should be but too happy if I could make my dying struggles subservient to my country. My body, Mr. Farmer—Mr. Wade, this poor temple of mine contains an insidious enemy—a strange, a dreadful, and a wasting disease. It is necessary for the sake of medical science, for my country's good, for the health of the world at large, that my death, which will speedily happen, should take place in England, in order that after dissolution I may be dissected by the first operators, viewed by the most intelligent of the faculty, and thus another light be placed on the present dark paths of curative knowledge. My symptoms are momentarily growing worse. Gentlemen, messmates, friends, I must leave you for the night, and too soon, I fear, for ever; but never shirk your duty. If they be the last words that I shall utter to you—humble though I be—I may venture to hold myself up to you as a pattern of self-devotion. God bless you all—good night—and never shirk your duty.'

Of course, the company to whom this was addressed, were infinitely amused at this display, and the third lieutenant observed mournfully, 'Now there's no chance for me. The fat rogue is going to invalide himself. I suppose that I need not trouble my liver to be diseased just now, for the hypocrite won't allow another man in the ship to be sick but himself.'

The gentleman guessed rightly. All the next day Dr. Thompson kept his cot, and was duly reported to the captain as dangerously ill. Now, our first lieutenant was a noble, frank, yet sensible and shrewd fellow, and the captain was as mischief-loving, wicked little devil, as ever grinned over a spiteful frolic. They held a consultation upon the case, and soon came to a more decided opinion on it, than the gentlemen of the faculty generally do on such occasions. Now, whilst the doctor is plotting to prove himself desperately and almost hopelessly sick, and the captain and Mr. Farmer, to make him suddenly well, in spite of himself, I shall take the opportunity of displaying my own heroic deeds, when placed in the first independent command ever conferred upon me. Jason, with his Argonauts, went to bear away the Golden Fleece; Columbus, and his heroes, to give a world to the sovereign of Spain; and I, with two little boys, pushed out of the Cove, perilously to procure some sand in the dingy. Nothing elevates a biography like appropriate comparisons. But I doubt whether either Jason or Columbus felt a more enthusiastic glow pervade their frames when each saw himself fairly under sail for unknown seas, than did I, when I seized the tiller of the dingy, which was, by-the-bye, a stick not at all bigger than that which I had, not many months before, used in trundling my hoop.

CHAPTER VII

A little boat with a large cargo—Worse than the drift of a dull argument, Ralph finds drifting across the Atlantic—He meets with land at length, and a real Irish welcome—Potatoes and poteen, and much more fur than furniture.

BUT this little boat, as it so often bore Cæsar and his fortunes, and our surgeon and his fat, deserves and shall have a more than passing notice. It was perhaps one of the smallest craft that ever braved the seas. Such a floating miniature you may have conceived

Gulliver to be placed in, when he was sighed across the tub of water by his Brobdignag princess. Wofully and timorously, many's the time and oft, did the obese doctor eye it from the gangway; when, asking for a boat, the first lieutenant, smiling benignantly, would reply, 'Doctor, take the dingy.' It was all that the dingy could do, to take the doctor. Then the care with which he gently deposited himself, precisely in the centre of the very small stern-sheets, would have afforded a fine moral lesson to those who pretend to watch over the safety of states. As the little craft, laden with this immense pharmacopœian depositary, hobbled over the seas, it seemed almost to progress upright, and 'walked the waters like a thing of life;'[1] for it had a shrewd likeness to a young monkey learning to go upright, with its two long arms steadying its uncertain gait, the oars making all this resemblance. Indeed, it was so diminutive, that it often kept the two boys that belonged to it from the fresh as well as the salt water, they clapping it over their heads, by way of an umbrella, whenever the clouds poured down a libation too liberal. To those curious in philology, I convey the information, that in the word *dingy*, the *g* was pronounced hard. This explanation is also necessary to do justice to the pigmy floater, as it was always painted in the gayest colours possible. It was quite a pet of the first lieutenant's. Indeed, he loved it so much, that he took care never to oppress it with his own weight.

The Cove of Cork is a fine harbour, entered by the means of a somewhat narrow strait. I have forgotten the names of all the headlands and points, and I am so sick of Irish affairs,[2] that I do not choose to go into the next room and get the map to refer to, for on it there is scarcely a spot that could meet my eye, that would not give rise to disagreeable associations. So I prefer writing from memory, magic memory, that gives me now the picture of five-and-twenty years ago, all green, and fresh, and beautiful.

On entering the Cove, there were, on the left hand of the strait, fortifications and military barracks. Beyond these, to the seaward, and just on the elbow of the land, that formed the entrance to the strait, our first lieutenant discovered from the taffrail of the frigate, a white patch of sand. The rest of the shore was rocky, iron-bound, and unapproachable from the sea. Mr. Farmer took me aft, pointed out to me the just visible spot, told me to fetch off as much sand as the dingy could bear, and return with all expedition. Proud of the commission, about four P. M., the tide running out furiously,

I ordered the *dingees* to be piped away, and walking down the side with due dignity, with a bucket and a couple of spades, we pushed off, and soon reached the spot. The boat was loaded, but in the mean time the tide had left, and, light and small, as she was, three little boys could not launch her till almost all the sand had been returned to its native soil. All this occupied much time. It was nearly dusk when we got her afloat, and the wind had got up strongly from off the land. It came on to rain, and we had not got far from the shore, before the tide swept us clean out into the Atlantic. We were shortly in a situation sufficiently perilous for the heroic. There we were, three lads, whose united years would not have made up those of a middle-aged man, in a very little boat, in a very high sea, with a strong gale that would have been very favourable for us, if we had wished to steer for New York. As we could not make head at all against the combined strength of an adverse wind, tide, and sea, we left off pulling, and threw all the sand out of the boat. We knew the tide would turn, we hoped that the sea might go down, and trusted that the wind would change. Before it was quite dark, we had lost sight of the land, and I began to feel a little uncomfortable, as my boat's crew from stem to stern, (no great distance) assured me that we should certainly be swamped. In this miserable position of our affairs, and when we should have found ourselves very cold, if we had not been so hungry, and very hungry if we had not been so cold, an Hibernian mercantile vessel passed us, laden with timber and fruit, viz. potatoes and birch-brooms, and they very kindly and opportunely threw us a tow-rope. This drogher,[1] that was a large, half-decked, cutter-rigged vessel, made great way through the water, and, as we were dragged after her, we were nearly drowned by the sea splashing over us, and, had it not been for our sand-bucket, it is probable that we should have filled. In the state of the sea, to get on board the drogher from the dingy, was an operation too dangerous to be attempted.

But, before this assistance came, what were my feelings? No situation could be more disconsolate, and, apparently, more hopeless. Does not the reader suppose that there was a continual rushing through my bosom of agonized feelings? Can he not understand that visions of my lately-forsaken green play-ground came over the black and massive waves, and seemed to settle on them, as in mockery? But were I to dilate upon these horrors, would he not weary of them? Had I been the son of a king thus situated, or even the acknowledged offspring of a duke, there might have been sympathy. But the newly emancipated schoolboy, drowned with two lads just drafted from the Marine Society,[1] in a small boat off the Irish coast, may be thought a melancholy occurrence, but involving nothing of particular interest. I see my error: if I wish to create an effect, I must first prove that I am the son of a duke or a king. I have begun at the wrong end.

However, let the reader sneer as he will at my predicament, there was something sublime in the scene around me. The smallness of the craft magnified the greatness of the waves. I literally enjoyed the interesting situation which naval writers, who are not nautical, of 'seas running mountains high,' so rejoice to describe. One wave on either hand bounded my horizon. They were absolutely mountain waves to me; and when our little walnut-shell got on the top of one, it is no great stretch of metaphor to say, that we appeared ascending to the clouds. We could not look down upon one wave, until we were fairly on the back of another. Now, in a vessel of tolerable size, let the sea rage at its worst, from the ship's decks you always look down upon it, excepting now and then, when some short-lived giant will poke up its overgrown head. But I must remember that I am in tow of the potato craft.

Though she lay well up for the harbour's mouth, she could not fetch it, so she tacked and tacked again, until nearly ten o'clock, at which time, we, in the dingy, were half frozen, and almost wholly drowned. The moon was now up, though partially obscured by flying rack, and in making a land board, the honest Pat, in the command of the sloop, shortened the tow-rope, and hailed us, telling us when we were well abreast of a little sandy bight, to cast off, pull in, and haul up our boat above high-water mark. We took his advice, and, without much difficulty, found ourselves, once more, on terra firma.

I cannot help, in this place, making the reflection, of the singular events that the erratic life of a sailor produces. Here were evidently three lives saved, among which was that of the future paragon of reefers, and neither the saved nor the saviours knew even the names, or saw distinctly the faces of each other. How many good and brave actions we sailors do, and the careless world knows nothing about them. The sailor's life is a series of common-place heroisms.

Well, here we were, landed on the coast of Ireland, but in what part we knew not, and with every prospect of passing the night under the grandest, but, in winter, the most uncomfortable roof in the world. The two lads begged for leave to go up and look for a house; but, as I had made up my mind that, if a loss took place, we should be all lost together, I would not run the risk of *losing* my boat's crew, and *finding* myself—alone. I refused my consent, telling them that it was my duty to stay by my boat, and theirs to stay by me. Now this was tolerably firm, considering the ducking that I had enjoyed, and the hunger, cold, and weariness that I was then enjoying—enjoying? yes, enjoying. Surely I have as much right to enjoy them, if I like, as the ladies and gentlemen of this metropolis have to enjoy bad health.

But this epicene state of enjoyment was not long to last. A fresh-coloured native, with a prodigious breadth of face, only to be surpassed by his prodigious breadth of shoulders, approached, and addressed us in a brogue so strong, that it would, like the boat-swain's grog, have floated a marling-spike, and in a stuttering so thick, that a horn spoon would have stood upright in it. The consequence was, that though fellow subjects, we could not understand each other. So he went, and brought down with him a brawny brother, who spoke 'Inglis iligantly any how.' Well, the proverbial hospitality of the Irish suffered no injury in the persons of my Irish friends. A pressing invitation to their dwelling and to their hospitality, was urged upon us in terms, and with looks, that I felt were the genuine offspring of kindness and generosity of soul. But I still demurred to leave my boat. When they understood the full force of my objection, my frieze-coated friend, who spoke the 'iligant Inglis,' explained.

'O, by Jasus, and aint she welcome intirely? Come along, ye little undersized spalpeen, with your officer, won't you?'

And, before I could well understand what they were about, the two 'jontlemen' had taken up his majesty's vessel under my command, had turned it bottom up, with several shakes, to clear it of the water and sand, and with as little difficulty as a farmer's boy would have turned upside down a thrush's cage, in order to cleanse it. After this operation had been performed, they righted it, and one laying hold of the bow, and the other the stern, they swung it between them, as two washerwomen might a basket of dirty clothes. I must confess, that I was a great deal mortified at seeing my command treated thus slightingly, which mortification was not a little increased by an overture that they kindly made to me, saying, that if I were at all tired, they would, with all the pleasure in the world, carry me in it. I preferred walking.

Officer, boat's crew, guides, boat and oars, proceeded in this manner for more than half a mile up into the country. At length, by the moonlight, I discovered a row of earthy mounds, that I positively, at first, thought was a parcel of heaps, such as I had seen in England, under which potatoes are buried for the winter.

I was undeceived, by being welcomed to the town of some place, dreadful in 'as,' and 'ghas,' and with a name so difficult to utter, that I could not pronounce it when I attempted, and which, if I had ever been so fortunate as to retain, I should, for my own comfort, have made haste to forget.

I hope that the 'finest pisintry in the world,' are better located now than they were a quarter of a century ago, for they are, or were, a fine peasantry, as far as physical organization can make them, and deserve at least to be housed like human beings; but what I saw, when on that night I entered the mud edifice of my conductors, made me start with astonishment. In the first place, the walls were mud all through, and as rough on the inside as the out. There was actually no furniture in it of any description; and the only implement I saw, was a large globular iron pot, that stood upon spikes, like a carpenter's pitch kettle, which pot, at the moment of my entrance, was full of hot, recently boiled, unskinned, fine mealy praties. Round this there might have been sitting some twelve or fourteen persons of both sexes, and various ages, none above five-and-twenty. But it must be remembered, that the pot was upon the earth, and the earth was the floor, and the circle was squatted round it. At the fire-place, each on a three-legged stool, sate an elderly man and woman. These stools the fastidious may call furniture if they please; but were any of my readers placed upon one of them, so rough and dirty were they, that he or she must have been very naughty, did not the stool of repentance prove a more pleasant resting-place.

Among the squatted circle there were a bandy-legged drummer, and a blotched-faced fifer, from the adjacent barracks, both in their regimentals. They rose, and capped to my uniform. We were welcomed with shouts of congratulations. My boat was brought in and placed bottom up along one side of the hovel, and immediately the keel was occupied by a legion of poultry, and half a score pigs, little and big, were, at the same time, to be seen dubbing their snouts under the gunnel, on voyages of alimentary discovery. I was immediately pulled down between two really handsome lasses in the circle, and, with something like savage hospitality, had my cheeks stuffed with the burning potatoes.

Never was there a more hilarious meeting. I, and my Tom Thumb of a boat, and my minikin crew, I could well understand, though my hosts spoke in their mother tongue, were the subjects of their incessant and uncontrollable bursts of laughter. But with all this, they were by no means rude, and showed me that sort of respect that servants do to the petted child of their master: that is to say, they were inclined to be very patronizing, and very careful of me, in spite of myself, and to humour me greatly. My two boys, whom I have so often dignified with the imposing title of my boat's crew, though treated with less, or with no respect at all, were welcomed in a manner equally kind.

CHAPTER VIII

Ralph figureth at a ball, excelleth, and afterwards sleepeth—
He returneth on board, and hath both his toils and his sand
undervalued, and thus discovereth the gratitude of first lieutenants.

Not yet having sufficiently Hibernized my taste to luxuriate on Raleigh's root, plain, with salt, I begged them to procure me something more placable to an English appetite. I gave money to my hosts, and they procured me eggs and bacon. I might also have had a fowl, but I did not wish to devour guests, to whom on my boat's keel I had given such recent hospitality. They returned me my full change, and, though there was more than enough of what they cooked for me to satisfy myself and boys, they would not partake of the remains until I assured them, that if they did not I would throw them away. At this intimation they disappeared in a twinkling.

Then came the whiskey—the real dew. I never touched it. I have before stated, that for three years, I abstained from all spirituous liquors. My lads had made no such resolution. The big iron pot was now, like an honest old sailor, that had done his duty, kicked aside in the corner; the drummer and fifer seating themselves on the keel of the inverted dingy, struck up a lilt, and

'Off they went so gaily O!'

More lads and lasses came in, and jigs and reels succeeded each other with such rapidity, that, notwithstanding the copious supplies of whiskey, the drummer's arms failed him, and the fifer had almost blown himself into an atrophy. Did I dance? To be sure I did, and right merrily too. I had such pleasant, fair-haired, rosy, Hebe-like instructresses, ready to tear each other's eyes out to get me for a partner. Then, they talked Irish so musically, and put the king's English to death so charmingly, that, notwithstanding the heat and smoke of the cabin was upon them, and the whiskey did more than heighten the colour on their lips, they were really enchanting, though stockingless creatures. It has been truly said, that in the social circle, the extremes, as to manners, almost meet. These ladies, I suppose, had gone so far beyond vulgarity, that they were now converging to the superior tone and frank dégagement of the upper classes. Positively, it never struck me, that I was in vulgar company. I then, of course, could have been but an indifferent judge. But I have thought of it often since, and must say, that, in the degrading sense of the word, my company of that night was not vulgar. It was pastoral, and perhaps barbarous, but every thing was natural, and every thing free from pretension. I did not often again, though I have danced with spirits as unwearied, dance with a heart so light. During this festive evening I saw no indications of that pugnacity so inseparable with Irish hilarity, though there were assembled a dozen of as pretty 'broths of boys,' as ever practised skull salutation at Donnybrook fair.

At length, about one in the morning, the whiskey had overpowered my boat's crew, and the whisking myself. They made up a lair for me with abundant great coats in the corner of the room, and my eyes gradually closed in sleep, catching, till they were finally sealed up, every now and then, twinklings of bare legs and well-turned ancles, mingling with the clatter of heavy brogues, and the drone of a bagpipe, that had now superseded the squeak of the fife, and the rattle of the drum.

I certainly did dream, I suppose about an hour after I had fallen asleep, of the clattering of sticks, the squalling of women, and the cursing of men; and I felt an indistinct sensation, as if people were practising leaping over my body, and finally, as if some soft-rounded figure had caught me in her arms. I was so terribly oppressed with fatigue, that I could not awake; and, as the last part of my dream gave me so sweet an idea of happiness and security, if I may use the expression, I shall say, as every novelist has a right to do once in his three volumes—'I was lapped in Elysium.'

Every thing was oblivion until I was awakened by one of my lads, at eight in the morning, and I arose refreshed, though a little stiff. The hardened clay, which composed the floor, was neatly swept up, the pigs and the poultry were driven out, and a good fire was blazing under the chimney. Of all the party of the night before, there remained only the two fine young men who brought me and my boat up; the elderly couple, and two blooming girls, with the youngest of whom I had danced almost the whole of the previous evening. I observed on one of the young men a tremendous black eye, that certainly was not there the day before, and the other had his temples carefully bandaged, and both my boat-boys complained of being kicked and trampled on during the night, yet, I am not so ungrateful, upon such slender evidence, as to assert that the dance had ended in a skrimmage, or so presumptuous as to say in what manner I thought that I had been protected during the row, if there had been one.

My hosts had nothing to offer me for breakfast but a thin, and by no means tempting pot of hot meal and water. I certainly did taste a little, that I might not seem to disrespect the pretty Norah, who had prepared it for me, and strove to make it palatable by a lump of butter, a delicacy that was offered to no one else. As I was impatient to be off, I kissed the girls heartily, yes, heartily, shook hands with the sons, and prepared for my departure, after having, with considerable difficulty, forced a half-guinea upon my hosts. I begged to know the names of those to whose hospitality I was so much indebted, and, as well as memory will serve me at this distance of time, I think they were specimens of what excellent O'Tooles potatoes are capable of producing. We then resumed our procession down to the beach, I walking first, bearing the boat-hook pikeways, followed by the boat itself, borne between the two athletic Tooles, and the procession was closed by the boat's crew, each with his oar upon his shoulder. We were soon launched, and instructed as to the course we were to take. The wind and sea had gone down, and the tide was favourable. We had to pull about five miles to get round the bluff, when we arrived at the sandy little nook, from which we had made our involuntary excursion to sea the night before. The spirit of obedience to orders was strong upon me, and in spite of the remonstrance of the boys, I went in, and loaded the dingy nearly down to the gunnel with the sand, for which we had been so much perilled. After all my dangers, I got safely on board before noon, much to the surprise of all on board, who had given us up as lost, and there had already been a coolness between the captain and the first lieutenant on my account. This coolness promised a warm reception for myself, and I got it.

So occupied had Mr. Farmer been all the day before in taking in Irish beef and pork, for the West Indian storehouses, and extra water to supply any of the convoy that might fall short of that necessary article, that he had totally forgotten the sand expedition, and it was eight in the evening, just at the time that I was, in the words of the song, 'far, far at sea,' that he was reminded of it. Mr. Silva, the second lieutenant, begged, as a favour, that a boat might be lent him, just to put him alongside the Roebuck, one of the two eighteen-gun brigs that was to accompany us as whippers-in to the convoy. As the captain was not expected on board till late, Mr. Farmer had not much hesitation in granting the request, with his usual 'Take the dingy, Mr. Silva.' But just then the Atlantic had been beforehand with him. The dingy had not returned. She had been last seen at the sandy nook to which she had been sent. The barge and cutter were immediately manned and sent to look for me. They easily got to the place where I was seen loading, and found the sand disturbed, but nothing else. They returned with some difficulty against the head-wind, and, of course, made a most disheartening report. When the captain returned he was dreadfully angry.

Well, as I crept up the side sneakingly, not very well knowing whether I were to enact the hero or the culprit, I concocted a speech that was doomed to share the fate of 'the lost inventions.' I saw the captain and Mr. Farmer pacing the deck, but both decidedly with their duty faces on. Touching my hat very submissively, I said, sheepishly, 'I've come on board, sir, and——'

'You young blackguard! I've a great mind——'

'To do what, Mr. Farmer?' said Captain Reud, interposing.

Now, I can assure the reader, twenty-five years ago, when we had nearly cleared the seas of every enemy, and the British pennant was really a whip, which had flogged every opponent off the ocean, the 'young gentlemen' were sometimes flogged too, and more often called young blackguards, than by any other title of honour. All this is altered for the better now. We don't abuse each other, or flog among ourselves so much—and, the next war, I make no doubt, what we have spared to ourselves, we shall bestow upon our enemies. I mention this, that the reader may not suppose that I am coarse in depicting the occasional looseness of the naval manners of the times.

'To punish him for staying out all night without leave.'

'That's a great fault, certainly,' said the captain, slily. 'Pray Mr. Rattlin, what *induced* you to commit it?'

'Please, sir, I wasn't induced at all. I was regularly blown out, and now I am as regularly b——'

'Come, sir, I'll be your friend, and not permit you to finish your sentence. If it's a fair question, Mr. Rattlin, may I presume to ask where you slept last night?'

'With the two Misses O'Tooles,' said I; for really the young ladies were uppermost in my thoughts.

'You young reprobate! What, with both?' said the captain, grinning.

'Yes, sir,' for I now began to feel myself safe; 'and Mr. and Mrs. O'Toole, and Mr. Cornelius O'Toole, who has red hair, and Mr. Phelim O'Toole, who has a black eye,—and the poultry, and the pigs, and the boat's crew.'

'And where was the boat all this time?'

'Sleeping with us too, sir.'

I then shortly detailed what had happened to me, which amused the captain much. 'And so,' he continued, 'after all, you have brought off the sand. I really commend your perseverance.'

A bucket of sand was handed up, and Mr. Farmer contemptuously filtered it through his fingers; then turning to me wrathfully, exclaimed, 'How dare you bring off for sand, such shelly, pebbly, gritty stuff as this, sir?'

'If you please, sir, I had no hand in putting it where I found it, and I only obeyed orders in bringing it off.' For I really felt it to be very unjust to be blamed for the act of nature, and especially as three lives had been endangered to procure a few buckets of worthless earth.

N

The captain thought so too; for he said to Mr. Farmer, very coldly, 'I think you should have ascertained the quality of the sand before you sent for it; and I don't think that you should have sent for it at all towards nightfall, and at the beginning of ebb tide. Youngster, you shall dine with me to-day, and give me a history of the O'Tooles.'

CHAPTER IX

An invaliding suit—The cards well played, and by a trump; the odd trick, however, in much danger—The doctor finesses with a good heart, but diamonds are cutting articles.

Two days had elapsed after my incursions upon the 'wild Irishers,' during which our surgeon had kept himself closely to his cabin, when he wrote a letter on service to the captain, requesting a survey upon his self-libelled rotundity of body. The captain, according to the laws of the service, 'in that case made and provided,' forwarded the letter to the port-admiral, who appointed the following day for the awful inspection. As I said before, the skipper and his first lieutenant had laid down a scheme of a counterplot, and they now began to put it into execution. Immediately that Dr. Thompson had received his answer, he began to dose himself immoderately with tartarised antimony, and other drugs, to give his round and hitherto ruddy countenance the pallor of disease. He commenced getting up his invaliding suit.

It had been a great puzzle to his brother officers, to understand what two weasan-faced mechanical-looking men, from the shore, had been doing in his cabin the greater part of the night. They did not believe, as the doctor intimated, that they were functionaries of the law, taking instructions for his last will and testament; though the astute surgeon had sent a note to Mr. Farmer, the first lieutenant, with what he thought infinite cunning, to know, in case of any thing fatal happening immediately to the writer, whether his friend would prefer to have bequeathed to him the testator's double-barrelled fowling-piece, or his superb Manton duelling pistols. Mr. Farmer replied, 'that he would very willingly take his chance of both.'

At twelve o'clock every thing was ready. The survey was to take place in the captain's cabin. Dr. Thompson sends for his two assistants, and then, for the first time for three days, he emerges, leaning heavily upon both his supporters.

Can this be the jovial and rubicund doctor? Whose deadly white face is that, that peers out from under the shadow of an immense green shade? The lips are livid—the corners of the mouth drawn down—and yet there is a triumphant sneer in their very depression. The officers gather round him, he lifts up his head slowly, and then looks round and shakes it despondingly. His eyes are dreadfully bloodshot. His messmates, the young ones especially, begin to think that his illness is real. There is the real sympathy of condolence in the greetings of all but the hard-a-weather master, the witty purser and the obdurate first. The invalid was apparelled in an ancient roast-beef uniform coat, bottle-green from age; the waistcoat had flaps indicative of fifty years' antiquity, and the breeches were indescribable. He wore large blue-worsted stockings folded up outside above the knee, but carefully wrinkled and disordered over the calf of the leg, in order to conceal its healthy mass of muscle. Big as was the doctor, his clothes were all, as Shakspeare has it, 'a world too big,'[1] though we cannot finish the quotation, by adding, 'for his shrunk shank.' Instead of two lawyer's-clerks, the sly rogue had had two industrious snips closeted with him, for the purpose of enlarging this particular suit of clothes to the utmost.

'In the name of ten thousand decencies, doctor,' exclaimed Mr. Farmer, 'who made you that figure?'

'Disease,' was the palsied and sepulchral reply.

'But the clothes—the clothes—these incomprehensible clothes!'

'Are good enough to die in.'

'But I doubt,' said the purser, 'whether either they or their wearer are good enough to die.'

There was a laugh, but it was not infectious as respected the occasion of it. He shook his head mournfully, and said, 'The flippancy of rude health—the inconsiderate laugh of strong youth!'

With much difficulty he permitted himself to be partly carried up the ladder, and seated in all the dignity of suffering in a chair in the fore-cabin, the two assistants standing, one on each side of him, in mute observance.

It is twelve o'clock—half-past twelve—one—two. The captain is coming on board—tell the officers—the side is manned—the boatswain pipes—and the little great man arrives, and, attended by Mr. Farmer, enters the cabin. Prepared as he was for a deception, even he starts back with surprise at the figure before him.

With one hand upon a shoulder of each of his assistants, the doctor, with an asthmatical effort, rises.

'Well, doctor, how are you?'

The doctor shook his head.

'Matters have gone a great length, I see.'

Another shake eloquent with suffering and despondency.

'I understand from my friend here,' (Mr. Farmer and he *were* friends sometimes for half an hour together) 'that with Christian providence you have been making your will. Now, my dear doctor, it is true, that we have hardly been three months associated; but that time, short as it is, has given me the highest opinion of your convivial qualities, your professional skill, and the great *depth* of your understanding. Deep—very deep! You must not class me among the mean herd of legacy-hunters; but I would willingly have some token by which to remember so excellent a man, and an officer so able, and so *unshrinking* in the performance of his duties.'

'There is my tobacco-box,' said the doctor with a feeble malice; 'for though chewing the weed cannot cure, it can conceal, a bad breath.'

The captain winced. It was a thrust with a double-edged sword. He was what we now call, an exquisite, in person, and one to whom the idea of chewing tobacco was abhorrent, whilst he was actually and distressingly troubled with the infirmity hinted at. For a moment, the suavity of his manner was destroyed, and he forgot the respect due to the dying.

'D—n the tobacco-box—and d—n that—never mind—no, no, doctor, you had better order the box to be buried with you, for no body *could* use it after you; but if I might presume so far—might use the very great liberty to make a selection, I would request, entreat, nay, implore you to leave me the whole *suit of clothes* in which you are now standing; and if you would be so considerate, so kind, so generous, by G—d I'll have them stuffed and preserved as a curiosity.'

'Captain Reud, you are too good. Mr. Staples,' turning helplessly to his assistant, 'get me immediately an effervescing draught. Excuse my sitting—I am very faint—you are so kind—you quite *overcome* me.'

'No, not yet,' said the captain in a dry tone, but full of meaning. 'I may perhaps by-and-by, when you know more of me; but now—O no! However, I'll do my best to make you grateful. And I'm sorry to acquaint you, that the admiral has put off the survey till twelve o'clock to-morrow, when I trust that you will be as well *prepared* as you are now. Don't be dejected, doctor, you have the consolation of knowing, that if you die in the mean time, all the annoyance of the examination will be saved you. In the interim, don't forget the old clothes—the invaliding suit. My clerk shall step down with you into the cabin, and tack a memorandum on, by way of codicil, to your will: don't omit those high-quartered, square-toed shoes, with the brass buckles.'

'If you would promise to wear them out yourself.'

'No, no; but I promise to put them on when I am going to invalid; or to lend them to Mr. Farmer, or any other friend, on a similar occasion.'

'I hope,' said Mr. Farmer, 'that I shall never stand in the doctor's shoes.'

'I hope you never will—nor in Captain Reud's either.'

The gallant commander turned from yellow to black at this innuendo, which was, for many reasons, particularly disagreeable. Seeing that he was lagging to leeward, like a west-country barge laden with a haystack, in this sailing-match of wits, he broke up the conference by observing, 'You had better, doctor, in consideration of your weakness, retire to your cabin. I certainly cannot, seeing my near prospect of your invaluable legacy, in any honesty wish you better.'

With all due precautions, hesitations, and restings, Dr. Thompson reached his cabin, and I doubt not as he descended, enervated as he was, but that he placed, like O'Connell, a vow in heaven, that if ever Captain Reud fell under his surgical claws, the active operations of Dr. Sangrado[1] should be in their celerity even as the progress of the sloth, compared with the despatch and energy with which he would proceed on the coveted opportunity.

When he was alone he was overheard to murmur, 'Stand in my shoes—the ignorant puppies! I shall see one of them, if not both, in their shrouds yet. Stand in my shoes! it is true, the buckles are but brass, but they are shoes whose latchets they are not worthy to unloose.'

There was then another day for the poor doctor, of fasting,

tartarised antimony, and irritating eye-salve. And the captain, no doubt in secret understanding with the admiral, played off the same trick. The survey was deferred from day to day, for six days, and until the very one before the ship weighed anchor. It must have been a period of intense vexation and bodily suffering to the manœuvring doctor.

Each day as he made his appearance at noon in the captain's cabin, he had to wait in miserable state his hour and a-half, or two hours, and then to meet the gibing salutation of the captain, of, 'Not dead yet, doctor?' with his jokes upon the invaliding suit. The misery of the deception, and the sufferings that he was forced to self-impose to keep it up, as he afterwards confessed, had nearly conquered him on the third day: that he was a man of the most enduring courage to brave a whole week of such martyrdom, must be conceded to him. Had the farce continued a day or two longer, he would have had the disagreeable option forced upon him, either of being seriously ill, or of returning *instanter* to excellent health.

CHAPTER X

Valid reasons for invaliding—The patient cured in spite of himself—
And a lecture on disease in general, with a particular case of
instruments as expositors.

AT length, the important day arrived on which the survey did assemble. The large table in the cabin was duly littered over with paper and medical books, and supplied with pens and ink. Three post-captains, in gallant array, with swords by their sides, our own captain being one, and three surgeons, with lancets in their pockets, congregated with grave politeness, and taking their chairs according to precedency of rank, formed the Hygeian court. A fitting preparation was necessary, so the captains began to debate upon the various pretensions of the beautiful Phrynes of Cork— the three medical men, whether the plague was contagious or infectious, or both—or neither. At the precise moment when Captain Reud was maintaining the superiority of the attractions of a blonde Daphne against the assertions of a champion of a dark Phyllis, and the eldest surgeon had been, by the heat of the argument, carried so far as to maintain, in asserting the non-infectious and non-contagious nature of the plague, that you could not give it a man by inoculating him with its virus, the patient, on whose case they had met to decide, appeared.

In addition to the green shade, our doctor had enwrapped his throat with an immense scarlet comforter, so that the reflection of the green above, and the contrast with the colour below, made the pallor of his face still more lividly pale. He was well got up. Captain Reud nodded to the surgeons to go on, and he proceeded with his own argument.

Thus there were two debates at this time proceeding with much heat, and with just so much acrimony as to make them highly interesting. With the noble posts it was one to two, that is, our captain, the Daphneite, had drawn upon him the other two captains, both of whom were Phyllisites. When a man has to argue against two, and is not quite certain of being in the right either, he has nothing for it but to be very loud. Now men, divine as they are, have some things in common with the canine species. Go into a village, and you will observe that when one cur begins to yelp, every dog's ear catches the sound, bristles up, and every throat is opened in clamorous emulation. Captain Reud talked fast as well as loud, so he was nearly upon a par with his opponents, who only talked loud.

At the other end of the table the odds were two to one, which is not always the same as one to two. That is, the two older surgeons were opposed to the youngest. These three were just as loud within one note—the note under being the tribute they unconsciously paid to naval discipline—as the three captains. Both parties were descanting upon plagues.

'I say, sir,' said the little surgeon, who was the eldest, 'it is *not* infectious. But here comes Dr. Thompson.'

Now the erudite doctor, from the first, had no great chance. Captain Reud had determined he should not be invalided.[1] The two other captains cared nothing at all about the matter, but, of course, would not be so impolitic as to differ from their superior officer; an officer, too, of large interest, and the Amphitryon[2] of the day; for, when they had performed those duties for which they were so well fitted, their medical ones, they were to dine on the scene of their arduous labours. The eldest surgeon had rather a bias against the doctor, as he could not legally put M. D. against his own name. The next in seniority was entirely adverse to the invaliding, as, without he could invalide too, he would have to go to the West Indies in the place of our surgeon. The youngest was indifferent just then to any thing but to confute the other two, and prove the plague infectious.

'But here comes Dr. Thompson—I'll appeal to him,' said non-infection; but the appeal was unfortunate, both for the appealer and the doctor. The latter was an infectionist, so there was no longer any odds, but two against two, and away they went. Our friend in the wide coat forgot he was sick, and his adversaries that they had to verify it. They sought to verify nothing but their dogmas. They waxed loud, then cuttingly polite, then slaughter-ingly sarcastic, and, at last, exceeding wroth.

'I tell you, sir, that I have written a volume on the subject.'

'Had you no friend near you,' said Dr. Thompson, 'at that most unfortunate time?'

'I tell you, sir, I will never argue with any one on the subject, unless he have read my Latin treatise "De Natura Pestium et Pestilentiarum."'

'Then you'll never argue but with yourself,' said the stout young surgeon.

Then arose the voices of the men militant over those of the men curative.

'The finest eye,' vociferated our skipper, 'Captain Templar, that ever beamed from mortal. Its lovely blue, contrasted with her white skin, is just like—'

'A washer-woman's stone-blue bag among her soapsuds—stony enough.'

Here the medical voices preponderated, and expressions such as these became distinct—'Do you accuse me of ignorance, sir-r-r?'

'No, sir-r-r. I merely assert that you know nothing at all of the matter.'

In the midst of this uproar I was walking the quarter-deck with the purser.

'What a terrible noise they are making in the cabin,' I observed. 'What can they be doing?'

'Invaliding the surgeon,' said the marine officer, who had just joined us, looking wise.

'Doubted,' said the purser.

'What a dreadful operation it must be,' said a young Irish young gentleman (all young gentlemen in the navy are not *young*) 'but, for the honour of the service, he might take it aisy any how, for the life of him.'

'The very thing he is trying to do,' was the purser's reply.

But let us return to the cabin and collect what we can hear, and record the sentences as they obtain the mastery, at either end of the table.

'Look at her step,' said a captain speaking of his lady.—'Tottering, feeble, zig-zag,' said a surgeon, speaking of one stricken with the plague.—'Her fine open ivory brow'—'Is marked all over with disgusting pustules.'—'Her breath is—oh! her delicious breath!' 'Noisome, poisonous, corruption.'—'In fact, her whole lovely body is a region of . . .'—'Pestilent discolorations, and foul sores.' —'And,' roared out Captain Templar, 'if you would but pass a single hour in her company . . .'—'You would assuredly repent of your temerity,' said the obstinate contagionist.

This confusion lasted about a quarter of an hour, a time sufficient, in all conscience, to invalide a West Indian regiment.

'Well, gentlemen,' said Captain Reud, rising, a little chafed, 'have you come to a conclusion upon this very plain case? I see the doctor looks better already, his face is no longer pale.'

'I tell you what,' said the senior surgeon, rising abruptly with the others, 'since you will neither listen to me, to reason, nor to my book, though I will not answer for the sanity of your mind, I will for that of your body. My duty, sir, my duty, will not permit me to invalide you.'

'Never saw a healthier man in my life,' said the second surgeon.

'Never mind, doctor,' said the third, 'we have fairly beaten them in the argument.'

The gallant captains burst out into obstreperous laughter, and so the survey was broken up, and the principal surgeons declared that our poor doctor was in sound health, because they found him unsound in his opinions.

The three surgeons took their departure, the eldest saying, with a grim smile to Thompson, 'It may correct some errors, and prepare you for next invaliding day. Shall I send you my book, "De Natura Pestium et Pestilentiarum?"'

The jolly doctor, with a smile equally grim, thanked him, and formally declined the gift, assuring him 'that, at the present time, the ship was well stocked with emetics.'

Now the good doctor was a wag, and the captain, for fun, a very monkey. The aspirant for invaliding sate himself down again at the one end of the table, as the captains did at the other. Wines, anchovies, sandwiches, oysters, and other light and stimulating viands were produced to make a relishing lunch. Captain Reud threw a triumphant and right merry glance across the table on the silent and discomfited doctor. The servant had placed before him a cover and glasses unbidden.

'Bring the doctor's plate,' said the captain. The doctor was passive—the plate was brought, filled with luxuries, and placed directly under his nose. The temptation was terrible. He had been fasting and macerating[1] himself, for eight or nine days. He glared upon it with a gloomy longing. He then looked up wistfully, and a droll smile mantled across his vast face, and eddied in the holes of his deep pock-marks.

'A glass of wine, doctor?' The decanter was pushed before him, and his glass filled by the servant. The doctor shook his head and said, 'I dare not, but will put it to my lips in courtesy.'

He did so, and when the glass reached the table it was empty. He then began gradually to unwind his huge woollen comforter, and when he thought himself unobserved, he stole the encumbrance into his ample coat-pocket. He next proceeded to toss about, with a careless abstraction, the large masses of cold fowl and ham in his plate, and, by some unimaginable process, without the use of his knife, he contrived to separate them into edible pieces. They disappeared rapidly, and the plate was almost as soon empty as the wine glass. The green shade, by some unaccountable accident, now fell from his eyes, and, instead of again fixing it on, it found its way to the pocket, to keep company with the comforter. Near him stood a dish of delicious oysters, the which he silently coaxed towards his empty plate, and sent the contents furtively down his much wronged throat.

The other gentlemen watched these operations with mute delight, and, after a space, Captain Templar challenged him to a bumper, which was taken and swallowed without much squeamishness. The doctor found that he had still a difficult task to play; he knew that his artifice was discovered, and that the best way to repair the error was to boldly throw off the transparent disguise. The presence of the two stranger captains was still a restraint upon him. At length, he cast his eyes upon Captain

Reud, and putting into his countenance the drollest look of deprecation mingled with fun, said plaintively, 'Are we friends, Captain Reud?'

'The best in the world, doctor,' was the quick reply, and he rose and extended his open hand. Doctor Thompson rose also and advanced to the head of the table, and they shook hands most heartily. The two other captains begged to do the same, and to congratulate him on his rapid convalescence.

'To prove to you, doctor, the estimation in which I hold you, you shall dine with us, and we'll have a night of it,' said the skipper.

'Oh! Captain Reud, Captain Reud, consider—really I cannot get well so fast as that would indicate.'

'You must, you must. Gentlemen, no man makes better punch. Consider the punch, doctor.'

'Truly, that alters the case. As these dolts of surgeons could not fully understand the diagnostics of my disease, I suppose I must do my duty for the *leetle* while longer that I have to live. I *will* do my duty, and attend you punctually at five o'clock, in order to see that there be no deleterious ingredients mingled in the punch.' Saying which he bowed and left the cabin, without leaning on the shoulder of either of his assistants.

But he had yet the worst ordeal to undergo—to brave the attack of his messmates—and he did it nobly. They were all assembled in the ward-room, for those that saw him descend, if not there before, went immediately and joined him. He waddled to the head of the table, and when seated, exclaimed in a stentorian voice, 'Steward, a glass of half-and-half. Gentlemen, I presume you do not understand a medical case. Steward, bring my case of pistols and the cold meat. I say, you do not understand a medical case.'

'But we do yours,' interrupted two or three voices at once.

'No, you don't; you may understand that case better,' shoving his long-barrelled Manton duellers on to the middle of the table. 'Now, gentlemen—I do not mean to bully—I am only, God help me, a weak civil arm of the service,'—and whining a little—'still very far from well. Now, I'll state my case to you, for your satisfaction, and to prevent any little mistakes. I was lately afflicted with a sort of nondescript atrophy, a stagnation of the fluids, a congestion on the small blood-vessels, and a spasmodic contraction of the finitesimal nerves, that threatened very serious consequences. At the survey, two of the surgeons, ignorant quacks that they are,

broached a most ridiculous opinion—a heterodox doctrine—
a damnable heresy. On hearing it, my indignation was so much
roused, that a reaction took place in my system, as instantaneous
as the effects of a galvanic battery. My vital energies rallied, the
stagnation of my fluids ceased, the small blood-vessels that had
mutinied returned to their duty; and I am happy to say, that,
though now far from enjoying good health, I am rapidly approaching it. That is my case. Now for yours. As, gentlemen, we are to
be cooped up in this wooden inclosure, for months, perhaps years,
it is a duty that we owe to ourselves to promote the happiness of
each other by good temper, politeness, mutual forbearance, and
kindness. In none of these shall you find me wanting, and, to prove
it, I will say this much—singular cases will call forth singular
remarks; you must be aware that if such be dwelt on *too* long, they
will become offensive to me, and disturb that union which I am so
anxious to promote. So let us have done with the subject at once—
make all your remarks now—joke, quiz, jeer, and flaunt, just for
one half hour'—taking out his watch, and laying it gently on the
table—'by that time I shall have finished my lunch, which, by-the-
bye, I began in the cabin; there will be sufficient time for you to
say all your smart things on the occasion; but if after that I hear
any more on the subject, by heavens that man who shall dare to
twit me with it, shall go with me immediately to the nearest shore
if in harbour—or shoot me, or I him, across the table, if at sea. Now,
gentlemen, begin if you please.'

'The devil a word will I ever utter on the matter,' said Farmer,
'and there's my hand upon it.'

'Nor I.'

'Nor I.'

And every messmate shook him heartily by the hand, and by
them the subject was dropped, and for ever. That evening Dr.
Thompson made the captain's punch, having carefully locked up,
in his largest sea-chest, his invaliding suit.

Whatever impression this anecdote may make on the reader, if
it be one injurious to the doctor, we beg to tell him, that he proved
a very blessing to the ship—the kind friend as well as the skilful
and tender physician, the promoter of every social enjoyment, the
soother of conflicting passions, the interceder for the offending,
and the peacemaker for all.

CHAPTER XI

Paving-stones sometimes prove stumbling-blocks—A disquisition on the figurative, ends by Ralph figuring at the mast-head, thus extending his views upon the subject.

THE next morning, at daylight, we weighed, and by the aid of much firing of guns, and the display of unmeasured bunting, we got the whole of the convoy out of the cove by noon, with two men-of-war brigs bringing up the rear. Shortly after losing sight of land, bad weather came on, in which poor Gubbins was drowned, as I have before narrated.

By the time that we had reached Madeira, the ship's company had settled into good order, and formed that concentrated principle which enabled them to act as one man. It was a young and fine crew, made up of drafts of twenties and thirties, from different vessels, thanks to the nepotism of the treasurer of the navy.

We also began to understand each other's characters, and to study the captain's. Mischief was his besetting sin. Naturally malignant he was not, but inconsiderate to a degree that would make you think that his heart was really bad. One of his greatest pleasures was that of placing people in awkward and ludicrous situations. He very soon discovered the fattest men among the masters of the merchant vessels; and, when we had run far enough to the southward to make sitting in an open boat very unpleasant, he would, in light winds, make a signal for one of his jolly friends to come on board, the more especially if he happened to be far astern. Then began Captain's Reud's enjoyment. After two hours' hard pulling, the master would be seen coming up astern, wiping his brows, and, when within hail, Reud would shout to him to give away—and, just as he reached the stern ladder, the main-topsail of the frigate would be shivered, and the boat again be left half a mile astern. Another attempt, and another failure, the captain meanwhile gloating over the poor man's misery with the sup-pressed chuckle of delight, in which you would fancy a monkey to indulge after he had perpetrated some irreparable mischief.

However, he would generally tease his victim no longer than dinner-time. The ship would then be effectually hove-to, the half-melted skipper would get on board, and the captain receive him

with studied politeness. Much would I admire the gravity with
which he would deplore the impossibility of stopping his Majesty's
ship Eos, by anything short of an anchor and good holding ground.
No, she would not be hove-to—go a-head, or go astern she must—
but stand still she could not. During this harangue, the mystified
mariner would look at his commodore, much wondering which of
the two was the fool.

'But, Mister Stubbs,' the tormentor would continue, 'it is now
nearly six bells—you have not dined, I presume; how long have
you been making this little distance, Mister Stubbs?' with a slow
accent on the word Mister. 'Six hours!—bless me—I would
certainly rope's-end those lubbers in your boat. You *must* be
hungry—so must they, poor fellows! Here, Mr. Rattlin, call them
up, put a boat-keeper in the boat, and let her drop astern—tell my
steward to give them a good tuckout and a glass of grog. Mister
Stubbs, you'll dine with me.' And the affair would end by the
gratified hoaxed one being sent on board his own vessel about the
end of twilight, seeing more stars in the heavens than astronomers
have yet discovered.

But these skippers were, though very plump, but very humble
game for our yellow-skinned tormentor. He nearly drove the third
lieutenant mad, and that by a series of such delicate persecutions,
annoyances so artfully veiled, and administered in a manner so
gentlemanly, that complaint on the part of the persecuted, instead
of exciting commiseration, covered him with ridicule. This officer
was a Portuguese nobleman, of the name of Silva—the Don we
could never bring our English mouths to use—who had entered
our service at a very early age, and consequently spoke our language
as naturally as ourselves. He was surnamed 'the Paviour,' and,
when off duty, generally so addressed. It must not be supposed
that he acquired this sobriquet on account of the gentlemen in
corduroys laying by their rammers when he walked the street,
bidding God bless him, for he was a light and elegant figure, and
singularly handsome. At this time, I was the youngster of his watch,
and a great favourite with him. The misfortune of his life was, that
he had written a book—only one single sin—but it never left him
—it haunted him through half the ships in the service, and finally
drove him out of it. He had written this book, and caused it to be
printed—and he *published* it also—for nobody else could. His
bookseller had tried, and failed lamentably. Now Don Silva was

always publishing, and never selling. His cabin was piled up with several ill-conditioned cases of great weight, which cases laboured under the abominable suspicion of containing the unsold copies.

As much as ever I could learn of the matter, no one ever got farther than the middle of the second page of this volume, excepting the printer's devils, the corrector of the press, and the author. The book was lent to me, but, great reader as I am, I broke down in attempting to pass the impassable passage. The book might have been a good book, for aught I, or the world, knew to the contrary: but there was a fatality attending this particular part, that was really enough to make one superstitious—nobody could break the charm, and get over it. I wish that the thought had occurred to me at that time, of beginning it at the end, and reading it backwards; surely, in that manner, the book might have been got through. It was of a winning exterior, and a tolerable thickness. Never did an unsound nut look more tempting to be cracked, than this volume to be opened and read. It had for its title the imposing sentence of, 'A Naval and Military *Tour up and down* the Rio de la Plate, by Don Alphonso Ribidiero da Silva.'

I have before stated that my shipmates were all strangers to each other. We had hardly got things to rights after leaving Cork, when Mr. Silva began, 'as was his custom in the afternoon,' to *publish* his book. He begged leave to read it to his messmates after dinner, and leave was granted. With bland frankness, he insisted upon the opinions of the company as he proceeded. He began—but the wily purser at once started an objection to the first sentence—yea, even to the title. He begged to be enlightened as to what sort of *tour* that was that merely went *up* and *down*. However, the doctor came at this crisis to the assistance of the Don, and suggested that the river might have *turns* in it. The reader sees how critical we are in a man-of-war.

However, in the middle of the second page appeared the fatal passage, 'After having *paved* our way up the *river*.' Upon which, issue was immediately joined, and hot argument ensued. The objector, of course, was the purser, and, on this point, the doctor went over to the enemy. All the lieutenants followed, the master stood neuter, and the marine officer fell asleep—thus poor Silva stood alone in his glory, to fight the unequal battle; and, in doing so, after the manner of authors, lost his temper.

Five, six, seven times was the book begun, but, like the hackney coaches, the audience could not get off the stones. The book and the discussion were always closed together in anger, just as the author was *paving his way*. As he adopted the phrase with a parental fondness, the father was called the '*paviour*.'

All this duly reached the ears of the captain. He immediately wrote to Don Silva, requesting his company to dinner, particularly soliciting him to bring his excellent work. Of course, the little man took care to have the doctor and purser. The claret is on the table, the Amphytrion settles himself into a right critical attitude, but with a most suspicious leer in the corner of his eye. Our friend begins to read his book exultingly, but, at the memorable passage, as was previously concerted, the hue and cry is raised.

During the jangling of argument, Reud seems undecided, and observes that he can only judge the matter from well understanding the previous style and the context, and so, every now and then, requests him, with a most persuasive politeness, to begin again from the beginning. Of course, he gets no farther than the paving. After the baited author had re-read his page and-a-half about six or seven times, the captain smiles upon him lovingly, and says, in his most insinuating tones, 'Just read it over again once more, and we shall never trouble you after—we shall know it by heart.'

As it was well understood that the author was never to get beyond that passage until he had acknowledged it absurd and egregiously foolish, any body who knows any thing about the *genus irritabile*, will be certain, that if he lived till 'the crack of doom,' Don Silva would never have passed the Rubicon. It was thus that the poor fellow was tormented: and every time that he was asked to dine in the cabin, he was requested to bring his Tour, in order that the *whole* of it might be read.

The best and most imposing manner of writing, is to lay down some wise dogma, and afterwards prove it by example. I shall follow this august method.—It is unwise for a midshipman to argue with the lieutenant of the watch, whilst there are three lofty mastheads unoccupied. Q. E. D.

One morning, after a literary skirmish in the captain's cabin overnight, Mr. Silva smiled me over to him on his side of the quarter-deck, just as day was breaking. The weather was beautiful, and we had got well into the trade winds.

'Mr. Rattlin,' said he, 'you have not yet read my book. You are very young, but you have had a liberal education.'

I bowed with flattered humility.

'I will lend it to you—you shall read it: and, as a youthful, yet a clever scholar, give me your opinion of it—be candid. I suppose you have heard the trivial, foolish, spiteful objection started against a passage I have employed in the second page,' and he takes a copy out of his pocket, and begins to read it to me until he comes to, 'After having *paved* our way up the *river*;' he then enters into a long justificatory argument, the gravamen of which was to prove, that in figurative phrases a great latitude of expression was not only admissible, but often elegant.

I begged leave, in assenting to his doctrine, to differ from his application of it, as we ought not to risk, by using a figurative expression, the exciting of any absurd images, or catachrestical[1] ideas. The author began to warm, and terminated my gentle representation by ordering me over to leeward, with this pompous speech, 'I tell you what, sir, your friends have spent their money, and your tutors their time, upon you to little purpose; for know, sir, that when progress is to be made anywhere, in any shape, or in any manner, a more appropriate phrase than paving your way cannot be used—send the topmen aloft to loose the top-gallant sails.'

Checked, though not humbled, I repeat the necessary orders, and no sooner do I see the men on the rattlings, than I squeak out at the top of my voice, '*Pave your way* up the rigging—*pave your way*, you lubbers.' The men stop for a moment, grin at me with astonishment, and then scamper up like so many party-coloured devils.'

'Mr. Rattlin, pave your way up to the mast-head, and stay there till I call you down,' said the angry lieutenant; and thus, through my love for the figurative, for the first time I tasted the delights of a mast-heading.

O

CHAPTER XII

Ralph regenerateth himself, and becometh good, for half an hour—
Singeth one verse of a hymn, escheweth telling one lie, and getteth
his reward in being asked to breakfast.

WHAT a nice, varied, sentimental, joyous, lachrymose, objurgatory, laudatory, reflective volume might be made, entitled, 'Meditations at the Mast-head!'

When I found myself comfortably established in my aëry domicile, I first looked down upon the vessel below with a feeling nearly akin to pity, then around me with a positive feeling of rapture, and, at length, above me with a heart-warming glow of adoration. Perched up at a height so great, the decks of the frigate looked extremely long and narrow; and the foreshortened view one has of those upon it, makes them look but little bigger, or more important, than so many puppets. Beneath me I saw the discontented author of my elevation, and of 'A Tour up and down the Rio de la Plate,' skipping actively here and there, to avoid the splashing necessary in washing the decks. I could not help comparing the annoyance of this involuntary dance, with the afterguard, this *croissez* with clattering buckets, and *dos à dos*ing with wet swabs, with my comfortable and commanding recumbency upon the cross-trees. I looked down upon Lieutenant Silva, and pitied him. I looked around me, and my heart was exceeding glad. The upper rim of the sun was dallying with a crimson cloud, whilst the greater part of his disc was still below the well-defined, deep blue horizon. All above him, to the zenith, was chequered with small vapours, layer over layer, like the scales of a breastplate of burnished gold. The little waves were mantling, dimpling, and seemed playfully striving to emulate the intenser glories of the heavens above. They now flashed into living light, now assumed the blushing hue of a rose-bud, and here and there wreathed up into a diminutive foam, mocking the smile of youth when she shows her white teeth between her beauty-breathing lips. As I swung aloft, with a motion gentle as that of the cradled infant, and looked out upon the splendours beneath and around me, my bosom swelled with the most rapturous emotions. Every where, as far as my eye could reach, the transparent and beryl-dyed waters were speckled with white sails, actually 'blushing rosy-red'[1] with the morning beams. Far, far astern, hull down, were the huge, dull sailers, spreading all their studding sails to the winds, reminding me of frightened swans with expanded wings. Conspicuous among these were the two men-of-war brigs, obliquely sailing, now here, and then there, and ever and anon firing a gun, whose mimic thunder came with melodious resonance over the waters, whilst the many coloured signals were continually flying and shifting. They were the hawks among the covey of the larger white-plumed birds.

At this moment our gallant frigate, like a youthful and a regal giant, more majestic from the lightness of her dress, walked in conscious superiority in the midst of all. She had, as I before mentioned, just set her topgallant sails, in order to take her proud station in the van. We now passed vessel after vessel, each with a different quantity of canvass set, according to her powers of sailing. It was altogether a glorious sight, and, to my feelings, excelled in quiet and cheerful sublimity any review, however splendid might be the troops, or imposing their numbers. Then the breeze came so freshly and kissingly on my cheek, whispering such pleasant things to my excited fancy, and invigorating so joyously the fibres of my heart—I looked around me, and was glad.

When the soul is big with all good and pure feelings, gratitude will be there; and, at her smiling invitation, piety will come cheerfully and clasp her hand. Surely not that sectarian piety, which metes out wrath instead of mercy to an erring world; not that piety, dealing 'damnation round the land,'[2] daily making the pale, within which the only few to be saved are folded, more and more circumscribed; nor even that bigoted, sensuous piety, which floats on the frankincense that eddies round the marble altar, and which, if unassisted by the vista of the dark aisle, the dimly-seen procession, the choral hymn, the banner, and the relic, faints, and sees no God: no, none of these will be the piety of a heart exulting in the beneficence of the All-Good. Then and there, why should I have wished to have crept and grovelled under piled and sordid stone? Since first the aspiring architect spanned the arch at Thebes, which is *not* everlasting, and lifted the column at Rome, which is *not* immortal, was there ever dome like that which glowed over my head imagined by the brain of man? 'Fretted with golden fires,'[3] and studded with such glorious clouds, that it were almost sinful not to believe that each veiled an angel; the vast concave, based all around upon the sapphire horizon, sprang upwards, terminating above me in that deep, deep, immeasurable blue, the best type of eternity;—was not this a fitting temple for worship? What frankincense was ever equal to that which nature then spread over the wave and through the air? All this I saw—all this I felt. I looked upwards, and I was at once enraptured and humbled. Perhaps then, for the first time since I had left my schoolboy's haunts, I bethought me that there was a God. Too, too often I had heard his awful presence wantonly invoked, his sacred name taken in vain. Lately, I had not shuddered at this habitual profanation. The work of demoralisation had commenced. I knew it then, and, with this knowledge, the first pang of guilty shame entered my bosom. I stood up with reverence upon the cross-trees. I took off my hat; and though I did not even whisper the prayers we had used at school, mentally I went through the whole of them. When I said to myself, 'I have done those things that I ought not to have done, and have *left undone* those things that I *ought* to have done,' I was startled at the measure of sin that I had confessed. I think that I was contrite. I resolved to amend. I gradually flung off the hardness that my late life of recklessness had been encrusting upon my heart. I softened towards all who had ever shewn me kindness; and, in my mind, I faithfully retraced the last time that I had ever walked to church with her whom I had been fond to deem my mother. These silent devotions, and these home-harmonized thoughts, first chastened, and then made me very, very happy. At last, I felt the spirit of blissful serenity so strong upon me, that, forgetting for a moment to what ridicule I might subject myself, I began to sing aloud that morning hymn that I had never omitted, for so many years, until I had joined the service—

'Awake, my soul, and with the sun.'

And I confess that I sang the whole of the first verse.

I am sure that no one will sneer at all this. The good will not—the wicked dare not. The worst of us, even if his sin have put on the armour of infidelity, must remember the time when he believed in a God of love, and loved to believe it. For the sake of that period of happiness, he will not, cannot condemn the expression of feelings, and the manifestation of a bliss that he has himself voluntarily, and, if he would ask his own heart, and record the answer, miserably, cast away.

However, it will be long before I again trouble the reader with any thing so *outré* as that which I have just written. Many were the days of error, and the nights of sin, that passed before I again even looked into my own heart. The feelings with which I made my mast-head orisons are gone, and for ever. How often, and with what bitterness of spirit, have I said, 'Would that I had then died!' If there is mercy in heaven—I say it with reverence—I feel assured that then to have passed away, would have been but the closing of the eyes on earth to awaken immediately in the lap of a blissful immortality. Since then the world's foot has been upon my breast, and I have writhed under the opprobrious weight: and, with sinful pride and self-trust, have, though grovelling in the dust, returned scorn for scorn, and injury for injury—even wrong for wrong.

I have been a sad dog, and that's the truth; but——

I have been forced to hunt, and to house, and to howl with dogs much worse than myself, and that's equally true.

'Maintopmast head there,' squeaked out the very disagreeable treble of Captain Reud, who had then come on deck, as I was trolling, 'Shake off dull sloth, and early rise.'[1] 'Mr. Rattlin, what do you say?'

'Ay, ay, sir.'

'Ay, ay, sir! what were you saying? How many sails are there in sight?'

'I can't make out, sir.'

'Why not? Have you counted them?'

Now, as I before stated, I had taken off my hat, and was standing up in a fit of natural devotion; and the captain, no doubt, thought that I was bareheaded, and shading my eyes, the better to reckon the convoy. To lie would have been so easy, and I was tempted to reply to the question, that I had. But my better feelings predominated; so, at the risk of a reprimand, I answered, 'Not yet, sir.'

At this moment Mr. Silva, the lieutenant of the watch, placed the mast-head look-outs, and sent the signalman up to assist me in counting the convoy; and, at the same time, the latter bore me a quiet message, that when the number was ascertained I might come down.

I came on deck and gave the report.

'I am very glad, Mr. Rattlin,' said the captain, approvingly, 'to see you so attentive to your duty. No doubt you went up of your own accord to count the convoy?'

'Indeed, sir,' said I, with a great deal of humility, 'I did not.'

'What—how? I thought when I came on deck I heard you singing out.'

'I was mast-headed, sir.'

'Mast-headed! How—for what?'

At this question, revenge, with her insidious breath, came whispering her venom into my ear; but a voice, to the warnings of which I have too seldom attended, seemed to reverberate in the recesses of my heart, and say, 'Be generous.' If I had told the truth maliciously, I should have assuredly drawn ridicule, and perhaps anger, on the head of the lieutenant, and approbation to myself. I therefore briefly replied, 'For impertinence to Mr. Silva, sir.'

And I was amply repaid by the eloquent look that, with eyes actually moistened, my late persecutor cast upon me. I read the look aright, and knew, from that moment, that he was deserving of better things than a continued persecution, for having unfortunately misapplied an expression. I immediately made a vow that I would read the 'Tour up and down the Rio de la Plate' with exemplary assiduity.

'I am glad,' said the captain, 'that you candidly acknowledge your offence, instead of disrespectfully endeavouring to justify it. I hope, Mr. Silva, that it is not of that extent to preclude me from asking him to breakfast with us this morning?'

'By no means,' said Silva, his features sparkling with delight; 'he is a good lad: I have reasons to say, a very good lad.'

I understood him; and though no explanations ever took place between us, we were, till he was driven from the ship,[1] the most perfect friends.

'Well,' said the captain, as he turned to go down the quarter-deck ladder, 'you will, at the usual time, both of you, *pave your way into the cabin.* I am sure, Mr. Silva, you won't object to that, though I have not yet made up my mind as to the propriety of the expression, so we'll have the purser, and talk it over in a friendly, good-humoured way.' And saying this, he disappeared, with a look of merry malignancy that no features but his own could so adequately express.

The scene at the breakfast-table was of the usual description. Authority, masking ill-nature under the guise of quizzing, on the one hand, and literary obstinacy fast resolving itself into deep personal hostility on the other.

CHAPTER XIII

*How to make a day's work easy—Ralph avoideth trouble by
anticipating land, but is anticipated by the enemy—A chapter
altogether of chasing, which it is hoped will pleasantly chase away
the reader's ennui.*

WE now had the usual indications of approaching the land. In fact,
I had made it, by my reckoning, a fortnight before. The non-
nautical reader must understand, that the young gentlemen are
required to send into the captain daily, a day's work, that is, an
abstract of the course of the ship for the last twenty-four hours,
the distance run, and her where-abouts exactly.

Now, with that failing that never left me through life, of feeling
no interest where there was no difficulty to overcome, after I had
fully conquered all the various methods of making this calculation,
to make it at all became a great bore. So I clapped on more steam,
and giving the ship more way, and allowing every day for forty or
fifty miles of westerly currents, I, by my account, ran the Eos high
and dry upon the Island of Barbadoes, three good weeks before
we made the land. Thus, I had the satisfaction of looking on with
placid indolence, whilst my messmates were furiously handling
their Gunter's scales, and straining their eyes over the small
printed figures in the distance and departure columns of John
Hamilton Moore,[1] of blessed (cursed?) memory, in a cabin over
90 degrees Fahrenheit, that was melting at the same time the youthful navigator, and the one miserable purser's dip that tormented
rather than enlightened him with its flickering yellow flame.

As we neared the island, greater precautions were taken to preserve the convoy. We sailed in more compact order, and scarcely
progressed at all during the night. The whippers-in were on the
alert, for it was well known that this part of the Atlantic was
infested with numerous small French men-of-war, and some
privateer schooners.

That morning at length arrived, when it was debated strongly
whether the faint discolouration that broke the line of the western
horizon as seen from the mast-head, were land or not. As daylight
became more decided, so did the state of our convoy. The wolves
were hovering round the sheep. Well down to the southward there

was a large square-rigged, three-masted vessel, fraternizing with
one of our finest West Indiamen. The stranger looked tall, grim,
and dark, with his courses up, but his top-gallant sails and royals
set. The white sails of the merchant vessel, and she was under
a press of sail, were flying in all directions; she was hove to, with
her studding-sails set, and many of her tacks and sheets were
flapping to the wind. Both vessels were hull down from the deck,
and we well understood what was going forward. Right astern,
and directly in the wind's eye of us, was a flat, broad schooner,
running before the wind, with nothing set but her fore stay-sail.
As she lifted to the sea, at the edge of the horizon, her breadth of
beam was so great, and her bulwarks so little above the water, that
she seemed to make way broadside on, rather than to sail in the
usual position. There was no vessel particularly near her. Those of
the mercantile navy that most enjoyed her propinquity, did not
seem, by the press of sail that they were carrying, to think the situation very enviable. However, the Falcon, one of our men-of-war
brigs, was between this schooner and all the convoy, with the
signal flying, 'May I chase?'

But this was not all; as a whitish haze cleared up to the northward there was a spanking felucca, with her long lateen sails brailed
up, and sweeping about in the very centre of a knot of dull sailing
merchant vessels, four of which, by their altered courses, had
evidently been taken possession of. Reversing the good old adage,
first come first served, we turned our attention to the last appearance. We made the signal to the other man-of-war brig, the Curlew,
to chase and capture the felucca, she not being more than two
miles distant from her.

No sooner did the convoy generally begin to find out how matters
stood, than like a parcel of fussy and frightened old women, they
began to pop, pop, pop, firing away their one and two pounders in
all directions, and those farthest from the scene of action serving
their guns the quickest, and firing the oftenest. It seemed to them
of but little consequence, so long as the guns were fired, where the
shot fell. Now this was a great nuisance, as it prevented, by the
smoke it raised, our signals from being distinguished, even if these
belligerents in a small way, had not been so occupied by these
demonstrations of their valour from attending to them. Indeed, the
volumes of smoke the popping created, became very considerable.
I do not now know if there be any convoy signal in the merchant

code, equivalent to 'cease firing.' If there were at that time, I am sure it was displayed, but displayed or not, the hubbub was on the increase. We were at last compelled to fire shot over these pugnacious tubs to quiet them, and there was thus acted the singular spectacle of three vessels capturing the convoy, whilst the artillery of its principal protector appeared to be incessantly playing upon it.

Having our attention so much divided, there was a great deal of activity and bustle, though no confusion, on our decks. We were hoisting out the boats to make the re-captures, and dividing the marines into parties to go in each. In the midst of all this hurry, when Mr. Farmer, our gallant first lieutenant, was much heated, a droll circumstance occurred, the consequence of the indiscriminate firing of the convoy. A boat pulled alongside, and a little swab man, with his face all fire, and in an awfully sinful passion, jumped on the quarter-deck, with something rolled up in a silk handkerchief. He was so irritated, that whilst he followed the first lieutenant about for two or three minutes, he could not articulate.

'Out of my way, man. Mr. Burn, see that all the small arms are ready, and handed down into the boat in good order. Out of my way, man—what the devil do you want? Muster the pinnace's crew on the starboard gangway—move all these lubberly marines. Mr. Silva, if that stupid fool don't cease firing, send a shot right into him. Man, man, what do you want—why don't you speak?'

'There, sir,' at last stammered out the little angry master of a brig, unfolding his handkerchief, and exhibiting a two pound shot in a most filthy condition, 'What—what do you think of that, sir? Slap on board of me, from the Lady Jane, sir—through, clean through my bulwarks into the cook's slush tub. There's murder and piracy for you on the high seas—my slush tub, sir—my bulwarks, sir.'

'D—n you and your slush tub too—out of my way! Sail trimmers, aloft, and get ready the topmast and top-gallant studding sails.'

'Am I to have no redress, sir? Is a British subject to have his slush tub cannonaded on the high seas, and no redress, sir? Sir, sir, I tell you, sir, if you don't do me justice, I'll go on board and open my fire upon that scoundrelly Lady Jane.'

Now this was something like a gasconade, as our irritated friend happened to have but three quakers (wooden guns) on each side, that certainly were not equal to the merits of that apocryphal good dog, that could bark, though not bite—however, they looked as if they could.

'You had better,' said Captain Reud, 'go on board the Lady Jane, and, if you are man enough, give the master a hiding.'

'If I'm man enough!' said he, jumping with his shot into his boat, with ireful alacrity. Shortly after, taking my glass, I looked at the Lady Jane, and sure enough there was a pugilistic encounter proceeding on her quarter-deck, with all that peculiar *goût* that characterizes Englishmen when engaged in that amusement.

In answer to the signal of the Falcon, which was astern of all the convoy, and between it and the gigantic schooner, 'Shall I chase?' we replied, 'No.' By this time we had thrashed our convoy into something like silence and good order. We then signalled to them to close round the Falcon, and heave to. To the Falcon, 'to protect convoy.'

We had now been some time at quarters, and every thing was ready for chasing and fighting. But the fun had already begun to the northward. Our second man-of-war brig, the Curlew, had closed considerably upon the felucca, which was evidently endeavouring to make the chase a windward one. The brig closed more upon her than she ought. It certainly enabled her to fire broadside after broadside upon her, but, as far as we could perceive, with little or no effect. In a short time the privateer contrived to get in the wind's eye of the man-of-war and away they went. After the four ships that had been taken possession of, and which were each making a different course, we sent three of the boats—the barge, yawl, and pinnace—under the command of Mr. Silva, in order to recapture them, of which there was every prospect, as the breeze was light, and would not probably freshen before ten o'clock; for however the captured vessels might steer, their courses must be weather ones, as, if they had attempted to run to leeward, they must have crossed the body of the convoy.

Having now made our arrangements, we turned all our attention to leeward upon the large dark three-masted vessel, that still remained hove to, seeming to honour us with but little notice. She had taken possession of the finest and largest ship of the convoy.

Long as I have been narrating all these facts, I assure the reader they did not occupy ten minutes in action, including the episodical monomachia on board of the Lady Jane. Just as we had got the ship's head towards the stranger, with every stitch of canvass crowded upon her, and the eight-oared cutter, manned, armed, and marined, towing astern, they had got the captured West Indiaman before the wind, with every thing set. The stranger was not long following this example; but steered about a S.W. and by W. course, whilst his prize ran down nearly due south.

I have always found in the beginning, that the size of the chase is magnified, either by the expectations or the fears of the pursuers. At first, we had no doubt but that the flying vessel was a French frigate, as large, or nearly as large, as ourselves. We knew from good authority, that a couple of large frigate-built ships had, evading our blockading cruisers, escaped from Brest, and were playing fine pranks among the West India islands. Every body immediately concluded the vessel in view to be one of them. If this conjecture should turn out true, there would be no easy task before us, seeing how much we had crippled ourselves, by sending away, in the boats, so many officers and men.

It now became a matter of earnest deliberation, to which of the two ships we should first turn our attention, as the probabilities were great against our capturing both. The Prince William, the captured West Indiaman, I have before said, was the largest and finest ship of the convoy. Indeed, she was nearly as large as ourselves, mounted sixteen guns, and we had made her a repeating ship, and employed her continually in whipping in the bad sailors.

The chase after her promised to be as long as would have been the chase after the Frenchman.

Mr. Farmer, who was all for fighting, and getting his next step of promotion, was for nearing the West Indiaman a little more, sending the cutter to take possession, and then do our best to capture the frigate. Now, the cutter pulled eight oars, there were two good looking jollies with their muskets between their knees stuck up in the bows, six in the stern sheets, Mr. Pridhomme, the enamoured master's mate, and the Irish young gentleman, who had seen as much service and as many years as myself, with the cock-swain, who was steering. Mr. Farmer, of course, measured every body's courage by his own; but I think it was taxing British intrepidity a little too much, to expect that nineteen persons, in broad daylight, should chase in an open boat, and which must necessarily pull up a long stern pull of perhaps two or three hours, exposed to the fire of those on board, and then afterwards, supposing that nobody had been either killed or wounded by the ball practice that would have been certainly lavished on the attacking party, to get alongside, and climb up the lofty side of a vessel, as high out of the water as a fifty gun ship. We say nothing of the guns that might have been loaded by the captors with grape, and the number of men that would infallibly be placed to defend and to navigate so noble a vessel.

Captain Reud weighed all this, and decided upon making, with the frigate, the re-capture first, and then trusting to Providence for the other: for which decision, which I thought most sound, he got black looks from the first lieutenant and some of the officers, and certain hints were whispered of *dark* birds sometimes showing white feathers.

The sequel proved that the captain acted with the greatest judgment. To our utter astonishment, we came up hand over hand with a vessel, which we before had shrewd suspicions, could, going free, sail very nearly as well as ourselves. Of course, we were now fast leaving the convoy; we found that the felucca had worked herself dead to windward, and was, by this time, nearly out of gun-shot of the Curlew, and, that the *fainéant* strange schooner had now made sail, and on such a course as approximated her fast to the other privateer.

The large vessel, perceiving our attention solely directed to the capture, shortened sail and made demonstrations of rescue. At this, Mr. Farmer grinned savage approbation, and, not yet having had a good view of her hull, we all thought, from her conduct, that she was conscious of force. We were, therefore, doubly on the alert in seeing every thing in the very best order for fighting. The bulk-heads of the captain's cabin were knocked down, and the sheep, pigs, and poultry, gingerly ushered into the hold, preparatory to the demolition of their several pens, styes, and coops, on the main deck. All this I found very amusing, but I must confess to a little anxiety, and younker as I was, I knew, if we came to action, that the eighty or ninety men, away in the boats, would be very severely felt. I was also sorry for the absence of Mr. Silva, as I had a great, yet puerile curiosity to see how a man that had written a book would fight.

The run of an hour and a half brought us nearly alongside the Prince William, when we expected, at the least, a ten hours' chase. It was well we came up so soon; the Frenchman had clapped forty as ill-looking, savage vagabonds on board of her, as ever made a poor fellow walk the plank. They had fully prepared themselves for sinking the cutter, as soon as she should come alongside, and their means for doing so were most ample.

As our prisoners came up the sides, we soon discovered by the shabby, faded, and rent uniforms of the two officers among them, that they belonged to the French imperial service. They bore their reverse of fortune, notwithstanding they belonged to a philosophical nation, with a very despicable philosophy. They stamped with rage, and ground their *sacrés* unceasingly between their teeth. They could not comprehend how so fine a looking vessel should sail so much like a haystack. The mystery was, however, soon solved. The third mate, with about half a dozen men, had been left on board of her; and the provident and gallant young fellow had, whilst the Frenchmen were so pre-occupied in preparing to resist the threatened attack of the boat, contrived to pass, unobserved, overboard from the bows, a spare sail, loaded with shot, that effectually had checked the ship's way. Had the Frenchmen turned their attention to that part of the vessel, without they had examined narrowly, they would have perceived nothing more than a rope towing overboard. He certainly ought to have shared with us prize-money for the recapture; but, after all, he sustained no great loss by not having his name down on the prize-list, as nobody but the captain ever got any thing for what we did that day. He, lucky dog, got his share in advance, many said much more, for appointing the Messrs. Isaiahsons and Co. as our agents. They got the money, and then, as the possession of much cash (of other people's) is very impoverishing, they became bankrupts, paid nothing-farthing in the pound, were very much commiserated, and the last that we heard of them was, that they were living like princes in America, upon the miserable wreck of their (own?) property.

We made, of course, most anxious and most minute inquiries of Messieurs les François, as to the class of vessel to which they belonged, and which we were, in turn, preparing to pursue. As might be expected, we got from them nothing but contradictory reports, but they all agreed in giving us the most conscientious and disinterested advice, not to think of irritating her, as we should most certainly be blown out of the water. We read this backwards. If she were strong enough to take us, it was their interest that we should engage her, and thus their liberation would be effected.

As it was, notwithstanding these many occurrences, only eight A.M., when we made the recapture, and as the convoy were all still in sight, we only put six men in the Prince William, which, in addition to the English still on board, were sufficient to take her to the Curlew, near which vessel the merchantmen had all nestled, and orders were transmitted to her commanding officer to see that men enough were put on board the recapture to insure her safety.

CHAPTER XIV

Ralph maketh acquaintance with bloody instruments, and boweth to the iron messengers of death; and is taught to stand fire, by being nearly knocked down.

WE now pressed the ship with every stitch of canvass that we could set. We had already learned the name of our friend in the distance; it was the Jean Bart. Indeed, at this time, almost every fourth French vessel in those seas, if its occupation was the cutting of throats, was a 'Jean Bart.'[1] However, Jean Bart, long before we had done with the Prince William, had spread a cloud of canvass, a dark one it is true, and had considerably increased his distance from us. It was a chase dead before the wind. By nine o'clock the breeze had freshened. I don't know how it could be otherwise, considering the abundance of wishing and votive whistling. At ten, we got a good sight of Johnny Crapaud's[2] hull from the maintop, and found out that she was no frigate. I was not at all nervous before, but I must confess, at this certainty, my courage rose considerably. I narrowly inspected the condition of the four after-quarter-deck guns, my charge, and was very impressive on the powder-boys as to the necessity of activity, coolness, and presence of mind.

Dr. Thompson now came on deck, very much lamenting the disordered rites of his breakfast. The jocular fellow invited me down into the cockpit to see his preparations, in order, as he said, to keep up my spirits, by showing me what excellent arrangements he had made for trepanning my skull, or lopping my leg, should any accident happen to me. I attended him. What with the fearnought*

* An amazingly thick cloth, of a woollen texture.

screens, and other precautions against fire, it was certainly the hottest place in which I had yet ever been. The dim, yellow, yet sufficient light from the lanterns, gave a lurid horror to the various ghastly and blood-greedy instruments that were ostentatiously displayed upon the platform. Crooked knives, that the eye alone assured you were sharp, seemed to be twisting with a living anxiety to embrace and separate your flesh; and saws appeared to grin at me, which to look upon, knowing their horrid office, actually turned my teeth on edge. There were the three assistant surgeons, stripped to their shirts, with their sleeves tucked up ready, looking anxious, keen, and something terrified. As to the burly doctor, with his huge, round, red face, and his coarse jokes, he abstracted something from the romantic terrors of the place; but added considerably to the disgust it excited, as he strongly reminded me of a carcass butcher in full practice.

No doubt, his amiable purpose, in bringing me to his den, was to frighten me, and enjoy my fright. Be that as it may, I took the matter as coolly as the heat of the place would permit me. The first lesson in bravery is to assume the appearance of it; the second, to sustain the appearance, and the third will find you with all that courage 'that doth become a man.'[1]

By noon we had a staggering breeze. We could now perceive that we were chasing a large corvette, though from the end-on view we had of her, we could not count her ports. The Eos seemed to fly through the water. She bowed not to the waves before her, but dashed them indignantly aside. She appeared, in her majestic spirit, to say to the winds, 'I obey not your impulse. I await not your assistance. I lead you. Follow.' To the sea, 'Level before me your puny waves. Let them rush after in my path—let them bow down as I pass on.' To the clouds, 'Come, we will run a race—we will strive together in the pride of our speed. The far-off isles of the south shall be our goal, and the rainbow the coronet of triumph.' Well she bore herself and right gallantly on that day.

At one o'clock the spars began to complain—preventer braces were rove, but no one thought of shortening sail. Away! away! Is not this hunting of a flying foe glorious? Achilles, throbbed not with irrepressible exultation thine iron-bound breast as thou chasedst the flying Hector round the walls of his deserted Troy? But canst thou, heaven-descended warrior that thou art, compare thy car to ours? The winged winds are our coursers—the

ocean waves our chariot wheels—and unbounded space our unlimited course. Away! away!

At two o'clock we had risen the Jean Bart, so as to clear her
broadside from the water's edge, as seen from our decks. The
appetites of the doctor and purser had risen in proportion. They
made a joint and disconsolate visit to the galley. All the fires were
put out. The hens were cackling and the pigs grunting in dark
security among the water-casks. Miserable men! there was no
prospect of a dinner. They were obliged to do detestable penance
upon cold fowl and ham, liquefied with nothing better than claret,
burgundy, and the small solace derivable from the best brandy,
mixed with filtrated water in most praiseworthy moderation.

At three o'clock we had the Jean Bart perfectly in sight, and we
could, from the foreyard, observe well the motions of those on deck.
The master was broiling his very red nose over his sextant in the
forestay-sail netting, when it was reported that the Frenchman
was getting aft his two long brass bow chasers; and, in half an
hour after, we had the report from the said brass bellowers themselves, followed by the whistling of the shot, one wide of the ship,
but the other smack through our foresail, and which must first
have passed very near the nose of our respectable master.

Most of the officers, myself with the rest, were standing on the
forecastle. Though not the first shot that I had seen fired in anger,
it certainly was the first that had ever hissed by me. This first salute
is always a memorable epoch in the life of a soldier or sailor. By
the rent the shot made in the foresail, it could not have passed more
than two yards directly over my head. I was taken by surprise.
Every body knows that the rushing that the shot makes is excessively loud. As the illustrious stranger came on board with so much
pomp and ceremony, I, from the impulse of pure courtesy, could
not do otherwise than bow to it; for which act of politeness the
first lieutenant gave me a very considerably tingling box of the ear.

My angry looks, my clenched fists, and my threatening attitude,
told him plainly that it was no want of spirit that made me duck to
the shot. Just as I was passionately exclaiming, 'Sir—I—I—I—'
Captain Reud put his hand gently on my shoulder, and said, 'Mr.
Rattlin, what are you about? Mr. Farmer, that blow was not
deserved. I, sir,' said he, drawing himself up proudly, 'ducked to
the first shot. Many a fine fellow that has bobbed to the first has
stood out gallantly to the last. What could you expect, Mr. Farmer,

from such a mere boy? And to strike him! Fie upon it! That blow, if the lad had weak nerves, though his spirit were as brave as Nelson's, and as noble as your namesake's,[1] that foul blow might have cowed him for ever.'

'They are getting ready to fire again,' was now reported from the foreyard.

'Here, Rattlin,' continued the captain, 'take my glass, seat yourself upon the hammock-cloths, and tell me if you can make out what they are about.'

Two flashes, smoke, and then the rushing of the shot, followed by the loud and ringing report of the brass guns, and of the reverberation of metal, was heard immediately beneath me. One of the shot had struck the fluke of the anchor in the forechains.

'There, Mr. Farmer,' said the captain exultingly, 'did you mark that? I knew it—I knew it, sir. He neither moved nor flinched—even the long tube that he held to his eye never quivered for an instant. Oh! Mr. Farmer, if you have the generous heart I give you credit for, never, never again strike a younker for bobbing at the first, or even the fifth shot.'

'I was wrong, sir,' was the humble reply; 'I am sorry that I should have given you occasion to make this *public* reprimand.'

'No, Farmer,' said the little Creole very kindly; 'I did not mean to reprimand, only to remonstrate. The severest reprimand was given you by Mr. Rattlin himself.'

I could, at that moment, have hugged the little yellow-skinned captain, wicked as I knew him to be, and stood unmoved the fire of the grape of a twenty-gun battery.

But was I not really frightened at the whistling of the shot?

Yes; a little.

P

CHAPTER XV

It's well to have a long spoon when one sips soups with the devil—
The captain's shot seldom misses—It is not always pleasant to have
a clean shirt to one's back, very amply proved—And the best
method of viewing an affair is to see it to your own advantage.

IT is always a greater proof of courage to stand fire coolly than to
fire. Captain Reud, I must suppose, wished to try the degree of
intrepidity of his officers, by permitting the chase to give us several
weighty objections against any more advance of familiarity on our
parts. A quarter of a century ago there were some very strange
notions prevalent in the navy, among which none was more
common, than that the firing of the bow guns *materially* checked
the speed of the vessel. The captain and the first lieutenant both
held this opinion. Thus we continued to gain upon the corvette,
and she, being emboldened by the impunity with which she
cannonaded us, fired the more rapidly and with greater precision,
as our rent sails and ravelled running rigging began to testify.

I was rather impatient at this apparent apathy on our parts.
Mr. Burn, the gunner, seemed to more than participate in my feelings. Our two bow guns were very imposing-looking magnates.
They would deliver a message at three miles' distance, though it
were no less than a missive of eighteen pounds avoirdupois; and
we were now barely within half that distance. Mr. Burn was particularly excellent at two things,—a long shot, and the long bow. In
all the ships that I have sailed, I never yet met with his equal at
a cool, embellished, intrepid lie, or at the accuracy of his ball
practice. Baron Munchausen would have found no mean rival in
him at the former; and, were duels fought with eighteen pounders,
Lord Camelford[1] would have been remarkably polite in the company of our master of projectiles.

I was upon the point of writing that Mr. Burn was *burning* with
ardour. I see it written—it is something worse than a pun—therefore, *per omnes modos et casus*—heretical and damnable—consequently, I beg the reader to consign it to the oblivion with which
we cover our bad actions, and read thus:—The gunner was burning
with impatience to show the captain what a valuable officer he
commanded. The two guns had long been ready, and, with the

lanyard of the lock in his right hand, and the rim of his glazed hat in his left, he was continually saying, 'Shall I give her a shot now, Captain Reud?'

The answer was as provokingly tautologous as a member of parliament's speech, who is in aid of the whipper-in,[1] speaking against time. 'Wait a little, Mr. Burn.'

'Well, Mr. Rattlin,' said the fat doctor, blowing himself up to me, 'so you have been knighted—on the deck of battle too—knight banneret of the order of the light bobs.'[2]

I was standing with the captain's glass to my eye, looking over the hammocks. In order to get near me he had been obliged to cling hold of the hammock-rails with both hands, so that his huge, round, red face, just peeped above the tarpaulin hammock-cloths, his chin resting upon them, no bad type of an angry sun showing his face above the rim of a black cloud, through a London November fog.

'Take care, doctor,' I sang out, for I had seen the flashings of the enemy's guns.

'Light bobs,' said the jeering doctor; when away flew the upper part of his hat, and down he dropped on the deck, on that part which nature seems to have purposely padded in order to make the fall of man easy.

'No light bob, however,' said I.

The doctor arose, rubbing with an assiduity that strongly reminded me of my old schoolmaster, Mr. Root.

'To your station, doctor,' said the captain harshly.

'Spoilt a good hat in trying to make a bad joke;' and he shuffled himself below.

'Your gig, Captain Reud, cut all to shivers,' said a petty officer.

This was the unkindest cut of all. As we were approaching Barbadoes, the captain had caused his very handsome gig to be hoisted in from over the stern, placed on the thwarts of the launch, and it had been in that position, only the day before, very elaborately painted. The irritated commander seized hold of the lanyard of one of the eighteen-pounders, exclaiming, at the same time, Mr. Burn, when you have got your sight, fire!'

The two pieces of artillery simultaneously roared out their thunders, the smoke was driven aft immediately, and down toppled the three topmasts of the corvette. The falling of those masts was a beautiful sight. They did not rush down impetuously, but stooped themselves gradually and gracefully, with all their clouds of canvass. A swan in mid air, with her drooping wings broken by a shot, slowly descending, might give you some idea of the view. But after the descent of the multitudinous sails, the beauty was wholly destroyed. Where before there careered gallantly and triumphantly before the gale a noble ship, now nothing but a wreck appeared painfully to trail along laboriously its tattered and degraded ruins.

'What do you think of that shot, Mr. Farmer?' said the little captain, all exultation. 'Pray, Mr. Rattlin, where did Mr. Burn's shot fall?'

'*One* of the shot struck the water about half a mile to port, sir,' said I, for I was still at my post watching the proceedings.

'O Mr. Burn! Mr. Burn! what could you be about? It is really shameful to throw away his Majesty's shot in that manner. Oh, Mr. Burn!' said the captain, more in pity than in anger.

Mr. Burn looked ridiculously foolish.

'O Mr. Burn!' said I, 'is this all you can show to justify your bragging?'

'If ever I fire a shot with the captain again,' said the mortified gunner, 'may I be rammed, crammed, and jammed in a mortar, and blown to atoms.'

In the space of a quarter of an hour we were alongside of the Jean Bart. She mounted twenty-two guns, was crowded with a dirty crew, and, after taking out most of them, and sending plenty of hands on board, in two hours more we had got up her spare topmasts.

Before dark, every thing appeared to be as if nothing had occurred, with the exception of the captain's gig and the doctor's hat; and hauling our wind, in company with our prize, we made sail towards that quarter in which we had left our convoy.

I am going to mention a very trivial anecdote; but, as it is one of those curious coincidences upon which are grounded so much superstition, I may be pardoned for narrating it. After the top-masts of the prize had fallen, every body had run below in the Jean Bart, with the exception of the captain, and two or three of the officers. The captain had taken the wheel, and still kept his vessel before the wind. When we were close upon her, we had hailed him several times to broach to; but either not hearing, or not under-standing, there was no attention paid to our commands. The consequence was, a half dozen marines were ordered to fire into her. This had the desired effect. Of the four or five persons still on her decks, the captain was the only one struck. The ball passed through his right arm. He then let go the wheel immediately, and the ship came, with her yards all square, and the wreck hanging about her, right into the wind.

When the French commander was having his wound dressed in the gun-room, he continued sacré-ing between his teeth, *cette maudite chemise*. The ball had passed clean through his arm, and not half an inch from the spot there were two scars, the marks that showed the passage of another ball, and on the shirt that he had on were the corresponding orifices.

This is the story of the shirt, which we had from his own mouth, and which he told the officers without much appearance of shame. The few French vessels then upon the seas were hunted about without intermission. They could rarely make any of the few friendly ports that were open to them; and, in the West Indies, every harbour was in the hands of their enemies. Consequently, linen of any sort was a great luxury. About two years before, the French captain had boarded and taken possession of an English merchant vessel, on board of which there was the body of a young gentleman, who had, the day before, died of a consumption. He was attended by an old black woman; indeed, her age was almost as much beyond belief as were her activity and strength. She had nursed this young gentleman's father, and his father, and felt a sort of canine devotion for every one bearing the family name. She had dressed out the body in the best linen shirt that she could find.

As the French captain had no idea of running into Antigua in order that the rites of sepulture should be paid to the departed plantation proprietor, he ordered the corpse, amidst the imprecations of the old negress, to have a shot attached to it, and to be thrown overboard. Not wishing to lose a good shirt, when shirts were so very scarce, he had it removed from the body, as he thought any old canvass was good enough to sink a corpse in. The horror of the negress at this profanation was intense, and she cursed him with all the bitterness of hate and revenge. Among other things, she wished that every time he put it on, it might bring disgrace and ruin upon his head, wither the strength of his right arm, and be stained with his best blood. Protected as this shirt was by the maledictions of the venerable of years, he had put it on but twice, at the interval of a year. Each time he had been wounded in the right arm, each time been ruined, and each time lost his ship.

Three times is generally considered fatal in similar affairs; but whether he experienced this fatality, I know not. I can only vouch for as much as I have related. Methinks a very pretty nautical drama might be made out of this anecdote, entitled 'The Fatal Shirt,' or 'The Curse of the Oboe Woman.' If any manager is inclined to be liberal, my tale and my talents are entirely at his service.

At daylight, next morning, we found ourselves again with our convoy. Mr. Silva had recaptured the four vessels taken by the felucca. The Falcon hove in sight about mid-day. She had chased the felucca well to windward, when the immense large schooner had intruded herself as a third in the party, and she and the felucca, as well as I could understand, had united, and gave the man-of-war brig a pretty considerable tarnation licking, as brother Jonathan hath it.

She certainly made a very shattered appearance, and had lost several men. However, in the official letter of the commander to Captain Reud, all this was satisfactorily explained. He had beaten them both, and they had struck; but owing to night coming on before he could take possession of them, they had most infamously escaped in the darkness. However, it did not much signify, as they were now, having struck, lawful prizes to any English vessel that could lay hold of them. I thought at the time that there was no doubt of *that*.

The next day we made the land. The low island of Barbadoes had the appearance of a highly-cultivated garden, and the green look so refreshing in a hot country, and so dear to me, as it reminded me of England.

CHAPTER XVI

A naval dinner, with its consequences—A naval argument, with its consequences, also—The way down the river paved at last, and the progress and the person of the unfortunate pavier finally arrested.

I HAVE no intention of repeating the oft repeated description of the West India islands. What is personal to me I shall relate: of course, incidentally, I may be drawn in to describe what has struck me as peculiar to these very favoured regions. We made but a short stay at 'little England,' as the Barbadians fondly call their verdant plat, and then ran down through all the Virgin islands, leaving parts of our convoy at their various destinations. Our recaptured vessels, with a midshipman in each, also went to the ports to which they were bound. When we were abreast of the island of St. Domingo, our large convoy was reduced to about forty, all of which were consigned to the different ports of Jamaica. Our prize corvette was still in company, as we intended to take her to Port Royal.

We were all in excellent humour: luxuriating in the anticipation of our prize-money, and somewhat glorious in making our appearance in a manner so creditable to ourselves and profitable to the admiral on the station. All this occupied our minds so much, that we had hardly opportunity to think of persecution. But some characters can always find time for mischief, especially when mischief is but another name for pleasure. The activity which Mr. Silva had displayed in making the recaptures, had gained him much respect with his messmates, and seemed to *pave the way* for a mutual good understanding.

What I am now going to relate could not, by any possibility, happen in the naval service of the present day. Let no one, therefore, suppose that in recording things that actually occurred, I am disseminating a libel against the profession, amongst the members of which I passed the happiest days of my life, in whom I have ever found the most chivalrous honour, the most unbounded generosity, and feelings the most remote from that all-pervading selfishness, which is the bane of the social circle, and the besetting sin of the times, at least in England. The little that is good, the very little upon which I pride myself, that my character gathered up, was gained amidst the toils, the dangers, and the constantly occurring privations, of my ocean life: had the profession, however, been then improved, in many particulars, to what it now is, I make no doubt that it would have had a beneficial effect upon me. But no profession, drill the body, and awe the mind as it may, can destroy identity of character. Discipline and coercion will, and always do, modify it; but the more the submission of the lower grades of any social pact is complete, the controlling power must necessarily be the more haughty, the more wilful, and, too often, becomes the more insolent.

To show the navy as it was, and to point out some of its insolences of office, instead of being a libel, is a compliment to the navy that now is. The affair that drove poor Silva out of the service can never recur; but it may not be amiss to relate it, as it is, in some measure, a justification for that curtailment of the mere wantonness of power in the commanding officer, that now, much to the annoyance of many worthy old tars, exists. It will, also, show to those who delight in tracing the philosophy of the mind, the rampant course of the passions, when an individual supposes himself above the consideration of the feelings of others, and released from every responsibility, even that of opinion; for opinion dared not make itself heard on board of a man-of-war then, and even now, and properly too, is wholesomely checked by the contemplation of danger.

The second lieutenant was invited to dinner with his two constant quizzers, the fat doctor and the acute purser, just as we had made the east end of Jamaica. I, it having been my forenoon watch, was consequently invited with the officer of it. We had lately been too much occupied to think of annoying each other; but those who unfortunately think that they have a prescriptive right to be disagreeable, and have a single talent that way (the most common talents), seldom violate the advice of the Scripture, that warns us, not to hide that one talent in a napkin.

We found our sarcastic little skipper in the blandest and most urbane humour. He received me with a courtesy that almost made me feel affection for him. We found Mr. Farmer, the first lieutenant, with him, and had it not been for a sly twinkling of the eye of the captain, and very significant looks that now and then stole from Mr. Farmer, as he caught the expression of his commander's countenance, I should have thought that that day there was no 'minching malicho,' or any thing like mischief meant. There were but five of us sat down to table, yet the dinner was superb. We had, or rather the captain, supplied himself now with all the luxuries of a tropical climate, and those of the temperate were, though he could boast of little temperance, far from exhausted. We had turtle dressed different ways, though our flat friend made his first appearance in the guise of an appetising soup. We had stewed guana, a large sort of delicious lizard, that most amply repairs the offence done to the eye by his unsightly appearance, in conciliating in a wonderful manner all those minute yet important nerves that Providence has so bountifully and so numerously spread over the palate, the tongue, and the uvula. The very contemplation of this beneficent arrangement is enough to make a swearing boatswain pious.

We lacked neither fish, beef, nor mutton; though it is true, that the carcasses of the sheep, after having been dressed by the butcher and hung up under the half deck, gave us the consolation of knowing, that while there was a single one on board, we should never be in want of a poop lantern, so delicately thin and transparent were the teguments that united the ribs. Indeed, when properly stretched, the body would have supplied the place of a drum, and but little paring away of flesh would have fitted the legs and shoulders for drumsticks. Of fowls we had every variety, and the curries were excellent. Reud kept two experienced cooks; one was an Indian, well versed in all the mysteries of spices and provocatives; the other a Frenchman, who might have taken a high degree in Baron Rothschild's kitchen, which Hebrew kitchen is, we understand, the best appointed in the Christian world. The rivals sometimes knocked a pot or so over, with its luscious contents, in their contests for precedency, for cooks and kings have their failings in common; but, I must confess, that their Creole master always administered even-handed justice, by very scrupulously flogging them both.

Well, we will suppose the dinner done, and the West Indian dessert on the table, and that during the repast the suavity of our host had been exemplary. He found some means of putting each of us on good terms with himself. At how little expense we can make each other happy!

The refreshing champagne had circulated two or three times, and the pine-apples had been scientically cut by the sovereign hand of the skipper, who now, in his native regions, seemed to have taken to himself an increased portion of life. All this time, nothing personal or in the least offensive had been uttered. The claret, that had been cooling all day, by the means of evaporation, in one of the quarter galleries, was produced, and the captain ordered a couple of bottles to be placed to each person, with the exception of myself. Having thrown his legs upon another chair than that on which he was sitting, he commenced, 'Now, gentlemen, let us enjoy ourselves. We have the means before us, and we should be very silly not to employ them. In a hot country, I don't like the trouble of passing the bottle.'

'It is a great trouble to me when it is a full one,' said Dr. Thompson.

'Besides, the bustle and the exertion destroys the continuity of high-toned and intellectual conversation,' said Captain Reud, with amiable gravity.

'It is coming now,' thought I. Lieutenant Silva looked at first embarrassed, and then a little stern: it was evident, that that which the captain was pleased to designate as highly-toned intellectual conversation was, despite his literary attainments, and the *pas* of superiority the publishing a book had given him, no longer to the author's taste.

'I have been thinking,' said Captain Reud, placing the fore finger of his left hand, with an air of great profundity, on the left side of his nose, 'I have been thinking of the very curious fatality that has attached itself to Mr. Silva's excellent work.'

'Under correction, Captain Reud,' said Silva, 'if you would permit this unfortunate work to sink into the oblivion that perhaps it too much merits, you would confer upon me, its undeserving author, an essential favour.'

'By no means. I see no reason why I may not be proud of the book, and proud of the author (Mr. Silva starts), providing the book be a good book; indeed, it is a great thing for me to say, that I have the honour to command an officer who has printed a book; the mere act evinces great *nerve*.' (Mr. Silva winces.)

'And,' said the wicked purser, 'Captain Reud, you must be every way the gainer by this. The worse the book, the greater the courage. If Mr. Silva's wit——'

'You may test my wit by my book, Mr. ——, if you choose to read it,' and the author looked scornfully, 'and my courage, when we reach Port Royal,' and the officer looked magnificently.

'No more of this,' said the captain. 'I was going to observe, that perhaps I am the only officer on the station, or even in the fleet, that has under my command a live author, with the real book that he has published. Now, Mr. Silva, we are all comfortable here——no offence is meant to you—only compliment and honour; will you permit us to have it read to us at the present meeting? we will be all attention. We will not deprive you of your wine—give the book to the younker.'

'If you will be so kind, Captain Reud, to promise for yourself and the other gentlemen, to raise no discussion upon any particular phrase that may arise.'

The captain did promise. We shall presently see how that promise was kept. The book was sent for, and placed in my hands. Now, I fully opined, that at least we should get past the second page. I was curiously mistaken.

'Here, steward,' said the skipper, 'place half-a-bottle of claret near Mr. Rattlin. When your throat is dry, younker, you can whet your whistle; and when you come to any particularly fine paragraph, you may wash it down with a glass of wine.'

'If that's the case, sir, I think, with submission, I ought to have my two bottles before me also; but, if I follow your directions implicitly, Captain Reud, I may get drunk in the first chapter.'

Mr. Silva thanked even a midshipman, with a look of real gratitude, for this diversion in his favour. I had begun to like the man, and there might have been a secret sympathy between us, as one day it was to be my fate to write myself, author.

Having adjusted ourselves into the most comfortable attitudes that we could assume, I began, as Lord Ogleby[1] hath it, 'with good emphasis and good discretion,' to read the 'Tour up and down the Rio de la Plate.' Before I began, the Captain had sent for the master, and the honourable Mr. B——, so I had a very respectable audience.

I had no sooner finished the passage, 'After we had paved our way down the river,' than with one accord, and evidently by preconcert, every one, stretching forth his right hand, as do the witches in Macbeth, roared out, 'Stop!' It was too ludicrous. My eyes ran with tears, as I laid down the book, with outrageous laughter. Mr. Silva started to his feet, and was leaving the cabin, when he was *ordered* back by Captain Reud. An appearance of amicability was assumed, and to the old argument they went, baiting the poor author like a bear tied to a stake. Debating is a thirsty affair; the two bottles to each, and two more, quickly disappeared; the wine began to operate, and with the combatants, discretion was no longer the better part of valour.

Whilst words fell fast and furious, I observed something about eight feet long and one high, on the deck of the cabin, covered with the ensign. It looked much like a decorated seat. Mr. Silva would not admit the phrase to be improper, and consequently his associates would not permit the reading to proceed. During most of this time the captain was convulsed with laughter, and whenever he saw the commotion at all lulling, he immediately, by some ill-timed remark, renewed it to its accustomed fury. At length, as the seamen say, they all had got a cloth in the wind—the captain two or three, and it was approaching the time for beating to quarters. The finale, therefore, as previously arranged, was acted. Captain Reud rose, and steadying himself on his legs, by placing one hand on the back of his chair, and the other on the shoulder of the gentleman that sat next to him, spoke thus:—'Gentlemen—I'm no scholar—that is—you comprehend fully—on deck, there—don't keep that d——d trampling—and put me out—where was I?'

'Please sir,' said I, 'you were saying you were no scholar.'

'I wasn't—couldn't have said so. I had the best of educations—but all my masters were dull—d——d dull—so they couldn't teach a quick lad, like me, too quick for them—couldn't overtake me with their d——d learning. I'm a straightforward man. I've common sense—com——common sense. Let us take a common sense view of this excruciation—ex—ex—I mean exquisite argument. Gentlemen, come here,' and the captain between two supporters, and the rest of the company, with Mr. Silva, approached the mysterious-looking, elongated affair, that lay, like the corpse, covered with the Union Jack, of some lanky giant, who had run himself up into a consumption by a growth too rapid. The doctor and purser, who were doubtlessly in the secret, wore each a look of the most perplexing gravity, the captain one of triumphant mischief; the rest of us, one of the most unfeigned wonder.

'If,' spluttered out Captain Reud, see-sawing over the yet concealed thing. 'If, Mr. Pavier, you can pave your way down a river——'

'My name, sir, is Don Alphonso Ribidiero da Silva,' said the annoyed lieutenant, with a dignified bow.

'Well, then, Don Alphonso Ribs-are-dear-o damned Silva, if you can pave your way down a river, let us see how you can pave it in a small way down this *hog-trough* full of water,' plucking away, with the assistance of his confederates, the ensign that covered it.

'With fools' heads,' roared out the exasperated, and I fear, not very sober, Portuguese.

Though I was close by, I could not fully comprehend the whole manœuvre. The captain was head and shoulders immersed in the filthy trough, which, uncleaned, was taken from the manger, that part of the main deck directly under the forecastle, and filled with salt water. The doctor and purser had taken a greater lurch, and fallen over it, sousing their white waistcoats, and well-arranged shirt frills, in the dirty mixture. The rest of us contrived to keep our legs. The ship was running before the wind, and rolling considerably, and the motion aided by the wine, and the act of plucking aside the flag, *might* have precipitated the captain into his unenviable situation—he thought otherwise. No sooner was he placed upon his feet, and his mouth sufficiently clear from the salt water decoction of hog-wash—than he collared the poor victim of persecution, and spluttered out, 'Mutiny—mu—mu—mutiny—sentry. Gentlemen, I call you all to witness, that Mr. Silva has laid violent hands upon me.'

The 'pavier of ways' was immediately put under arrest,[1] and a marine, with a drawn bayonet, placed at his cabin door, and the captain had to repair damages, vowing the most implacable vengeance for having been shoved into his own hog-trough. *Did ever any body know any good come of hoaxing?*

CHAPTER XVII

The palisade banquet, and Major Flushfire's anthem to Yellow Jack—Who's afraid?—The sands of life's hour-glass will run out rapidly, unless well soaked with wine.

WE will despatch the object of persecution in a few words. Lieutenant Silva was given the option of a court-martial, or of exchanging into a sloop of war. He chose the latter. The captain and his messmates saw him over the side, two days after we had anchored in Port Royal. The spiteful commander purposely contrived, when his effects were whipped into the boat, that one of the heavy, suspicious-looking cases should be swung against the gun and smashed. The result was exactly what we all expected. The water was strewed with copies, in boards, of the 'Tour up and down the Rio de la Plate.' They must certainly have been light reading, as they floated about triumphantly. 'I wonder whether they will pave their way up to Kingston,' said the captain, with a sneer.

As the author would not suffer them to be picked up, they sank, one by one, and disappeared, like the remembrance of their creator in the minds of his companions. We heard, a few weeks after, that he had died of the yellow fever; and thus he, with his books, was consigned to oblivion, or is only rescued from it, if haply this work do not share his fate, by this short memento of him.

Yellow fever! malignant consumer of the brave! how shall I adequately apostrophise thee? I have looked in thy jaundiced face, whilst thy maw seemed insatiate. But once didst thou lay thy scorched hand upon my frame, but the sweet voice of woman startled thee from thy prey, and the flame of love was stronger than even thy desolating fire. But now is not the time to tell of this, but rather of the eagerness with which most of my companions sought to avoid thee.

Captain Reud had got, apparently, into his natural, as well as native, climate. The hotter it was, like a cricket, he chirped the louder, and enjoyed it the more. Young and restless, he was the personification of mischievous humour and sly annoyance. The tales he told of the fever were ominous, appalling, fatal. None could live who had not been seasoned, and none could outlive the seasoning. For myself, I might have been frightened, had I not been so constantly occupied in discussing pine-apples. But the climax was yet to be given to the fears of the fearful.

All the officers that could be spared from the ship were invited to dine with the mess of the 60th regiment, then doing duty at Kingston and Port Royal. That day, Captain Reud having been invited to dine with the admiral at the Penn, we were consequently deprived of his facetiousness. All the lieutenants and the wardroom officers, with most of the midshipmen, were of the party. The master took charge of the frigate. Suppose us all seated at the long table, chequered red and blue, with Major Flushfire, the officer in command of the garrison, at the top of the table, all scarlet

and gold, and our own dear Doctor Thompson, all scarlet and
blue, at the bottom. These two gentlemen were wonderfully alike.
The major's scarlet was not confined to his regimentals: it covered
his face. There was not a cool spot in that flame-coloured region;
the yellow of his eyes was blood-shot, and his nose was richly
Bardolphian. The expression of his features was thirst; but it was
a jovial thirst withal—a thirst that burned to be supplied, encouraged,
pampered. The very idea of water was repugnant to it. Hydro-
phobia was written upon the major's brow.

We have described our rubicund doctor before. He always
looked warm, but since his entrance into the tropics, he had been
more than hot, he had been always steaming. There was almost
a perceptible mist about him. His visage possessed not the adust
scorch of the major's; his was a moist heat; his cheeks were constantly parboiling in their own perspiration. He was a meet *croupier*
for our host.

Ranged on each side of this noble pair were the long lines of very
pale and anxious faces, (I really must except my own, for my face
never looked anxious till I thought of marrying, or pale till I took
to scribbling,) the possessors of which were experiencing a little the
torment of Tantalus. The palisades, those graves of sand, turned
into a rich compost by the ever-recurring burial, were directly
under the windows, and the land-breeze came over them, chill and
dank, in palpable currents, through the jalousies, into the heated
room; and, had one thrust his head into the moonlight and looked
beneath, he would have seen hundreds of the shell-clad vampires,
upon their long and contorted legs, moving hideously round, and
scrambling horribly over newly made mounds, each of which contained the still fresh corpse of a warrior, or of the land, or of the
ocean. In a small way, your landcrab is a most indefatigable resur-
rectionist. But there is retribution for their villainy. They get eaten
in their turn. Delicate feeding they are, doubtlessly; and there can
be no manner of question, but that, at that memorable dinner
a double banquet was going on, upon a most excellent principle of
reciprocity. The epicure crab was feeding upon the dish, man,
below, whilst epicure man was feeding upon the dished-up crab
above. True, the guests knew it not; I mean those who did not
wear testaceous armour: the gentlemen in the coats of mail knew
very well what they were about. It was, at the time of which I am
speaking, a standing joke to make Johnny Newcome eat land-crab

disguised in some savoury dish. Thank God, that was more than
a quarter of a century ago. We trust that the social qualities and
the culinary refinements of the West Indians do not now march
à l'ecrevisse[1] and progress à reculons.[2]

There we all sat, prudence coqueting with appetite, and the
finest yellow curries contending with the direst thoughts of yellow
fever. Ever and anon some amiable youth would dash off a bumper
of claret with an air of desperate bravery, and then turn pale at the
idea of his own temerity. The most cautious were Scotch assistant-
surgeons, and pale young ensigns who played the flute. The
midshipmen feasted and feared. The major and the doctor kept
on the 'even tenor of their way,'[3] that is, they ate and drank
à l'envie.

We will now suppose the king's health drank, with the hearty
and loyal, God bless him? from every lip—the navy drank, and
thanks returned by the doctor, with his mouth full of vegetable
marrow—the army drank, and thanks returned by the major, after
clearing his throat with a bumper of brandy—and after 'Rule
Britannia' had ceased echoing along the now silent esplanade, that
had been thundered forth with such energy by the black band, an
awful pause ensues. Our first lieutenant of marines rises, and, like
conscience, 'with a still small voice,' thus delivers himself of the
anxiety with which his breast was labouring.

'Major Flushfire, may I claim the privilege of the similar colour
of our cloth to entreat the favour of your attention? Ah! heh!—
but this land-breeze—laden, perhaps, with the germs of the yellow
—fever—mephitic—and all that—you understand me, Dr.
Thompson?'

'As much as you do yourself.'

'Thank you—men of superior education—sympathy—and all
that—you understand me fully, major. Now this night-breeze
coming through that half-open jalousie—miasmata—and all that.
Dr. Armstrong, Dr. Thompson—medical pill—"pillars of the
state"—you'll pardon the classical allusion——'

'I won't,' growled out the doctor.

'Ah—so like you—so modest—but don't you think the draught
is a little dangerous?'

'Do you mean the doctor's, or this?' said the inattentive and
thirsty major, fetching a deep breath, as he put down the huge
glass tumbler of sangaree.

'O dear no!—I mean the night draught *through* the window.'

'The best way to dispose of it,' said the purser, nodding at the melting Galen.

'No,' replied Major Flushfire, courteously; 'there's no danger in it at all—I like it.'

'Bless me, major,' said the marine, 'why it comes all in *gusts*.'

'Like it all the better,' rejoined the major, with his head again half buried in the sangaree glass.

'*De gustibus non est disputandum*,' observed Thompson.

'Very true,' said the marine officer, looking sapiently. 'That remark of yours about the *winds* is apposite. We ought to *dispute* their entrance, as you said in Latin. But is it quite fair, my dear doctor, for you and me to converse in Latin? We may be taking an undue advantage of the rest of the company.'

'Greek! Greek!' said the purser.

'Ay, certainly—it was Greek to Mr. Smallcoates,' muttered Thompson.

'To be sure it was,' said the innocent marine. 'Major Flushfire,' continued he, once more on his legs, 'may I again entreat the honour of your attention. Dr. Thompson has just proved, by a quotation from a Greek author, Virgil or Paracelsus, I am not certain which, that the entrance of the night air into a hot room is highly injurious, and in—in—and all that. You understand me perfectly—would it be asking too much to have all the windows closed?'

'Ovens and furnaces!' cried out the chairman, starting up. 'Look at me and worthy Doctor Thompson. Are we persons to enjoy a repetition of the Blackhole of Calcutta? The sangaree, Quasha—suffocation! The thought chokes me!' and he recommenced his devotions to the sangaree.

'It melts me,' responded the doctor, swabbing his face with the napkin.

'Are you afraid of taking cold?' said the purser to Mr. Smallcoates.

'Taking cold—let the gentleman take his wine,' said the major.

'I must confess I am not so much afraid of cold as of fever. I believe, major, you have been three years in this very singularly hot and cold climate. Now, my dear sir, may I tax your experience to tell us which is the better method of living? Some say temperance, carried out even to abstemiousness, is the safer; others, that the fever is best repelled by devil's punch, burnt brandy, and high

Q

living. Indeed, I may say that I speak at the request of my messmates. Do, major, give us your opinion.'

'I think,' said the man of thirst, 'the medical gentlemen should
be applied to in preference to an old soldier like myself. They have
great practice in disposing of fever cases.'

'But if we must die, either of diet or the doctor, I am for knowing,' said the purser, 'not what doctor, but what sort of diet, is
most dilatory in its despatch.'

'Well, I will not answer the question, but state the facts. My
messmates can vouch for the truth of them. Five years ago, and not
three, I came out with a battalion of this regiment. We mustered
twenty-five officers in all. We asked ourselves the very same
question you have just asked of me. We split into two parties,
nearly even in number. Twelve of us took to water, temperance,
and all manner of preservatives; the other thirteen of us led a
harum-scarum life, ate whenever we were hungry, and when we
were not hungry; drank whenever we were thirsty, and when we
were not thirsty; and, to create a thirst, we qualified our claret with
brandy; and generally forgot the water, or substituted madeira for
it, in making our punch. This portion of our body, like Jack
Falstaff, was given to sleeping on bulkheads on moonlight nights,
shooting in the midday sun, riding races, and sometimes, hem!
assisting—a—a—at drinking matches.'

Here the worthy soldier made a pause, appeared more thirsty
than ever, scolded Quasha for not brandying his sangaree, and
swigging it with the air of Alexander when he proceeded to drain
the cup that was fatal, he looked round with conscious superiority.
The pale ensign looked more pale—the sentimental lieutenants
more sentimental—many thrust their wine and their punch from
before them, and there was a sudden competition for the water-
jug. The marine carried a stronger expression than anxiety upon
his features—it was consternation—and thus hesitatingly delivered
himself:

'And—so—so—sir—the bon vivants—deluded—poor deluded
gentlemen! all perished—but—pardon me—delicate dilemma—
but *yourself*, my good major.'

'Exactly, Mr. Smallcoates; and within the eighteen months.'

There was a perceptible shudder through the company, military as well as naval. The pure element became in more demand
than ever, and those who did not actually push away their claret,

watered it. The imperturbable major brandied his sangaree more potently.

'But,' said Mr. Smallcoates, brightening up, 'the temperate gentlemen all escaped the contagion—*undoubtedly!*'

'I beg your pardon—*they all died within the year*. I alone remain of all the officers to tell the tale. The year eight was dreadful. Poor fellows!' The good major's voice faltered, and he bent over his sangaree much longer than was necessary to enjoy the draught.

Blank horror passed her fearful glance from guest to guest. Even the rubicund doctor's mouth was twitched awry. I did not quite like it myself.

'But I'm alive,' said the major, rallying up from his bitter recollections, 'and the brandy is just as invigorating, and the wine just as refreshing, as ever.'

'The major *is* alive,' said the marine officer, very sapiently. 'Is that brandy before you, Mr. Farmer? I'll trouble you for it—I really feel this claret very cold upon my stomach. Yes,' he repeated, after taking down a tumbler full of half spirits, half wine, 'the major *is* alive—and—so am I.'

'The major is alive,' went round the table; 'let us drink his health in bumpers.'

The major returned thanks, and volunteered a song. I begged it, and the reader may sing it as he pleases, though I shall please myself by recording how the major was pleased to have it sung.

'Gentlemen,' said he, 'you will do me the favour to fill a bumper of lemonade, and when I cry chorus, chorus me standing, with the glasses in your hands; and at the end of each chorus you will be pleased to remember, that the glass is to be drained. No heel-taps after, and no daylight before. Now for it, my lads!' and with a voice that must have startled the land crabs from their avocations, he roared out—

'Yellow Jack! Yellow Jack! hie thee back! hie thee back!
  To thy damp, drear abode in the jungle;
    I'll be sober and staid,
      And drink LEMONADE,
  Try and catch me—you'll make a sad bungle,
                    Yellow Jack!

'But he came, the queer thief, and he seized my right hand,
And I writh'd and I struggled, yet could not withstand
His hot griping grasp, though I drank lemonade,—
He grinn'd and he clutch'd me, though sober and staid.

CHORUS, (*with increasing loudness.*)

'Yellow Jack! Yellow Jack! hie thee back! hie thee back!
To thy damp, drear abode in the jungle;
  We'll be sober and staid,
  And we'll drink lemonade,
Try and catch us—you'll make a sad bungle,
       Yellow Jack! (*tremendously.*)

'Bumpers of sangaree!' roared the major, and sang,

'Yellow Jack! Yellow Jack! hie thee back! hie thee back!
To thy pestilent swamp quickly hie thee;
  For I'll drink SANGAREE,
  Whilst my heart's full of glee,
In thy death-doing might I'll defy thee,
       Yellow Jack!

'But the fiend persever'd and got hold of my side,
How I burn'd, and I froze, and all vainly I tried
To get rid of his grasp—though I drank sangaree,
No longer my bosom exulted with glee.

CHORUS, (*still more loudly.*)

'Yellow Jack! Yellow Jack! hie thee back! hie thee back!
To thy pestilent swamp quickly hie thee;
  For we'll drink sangaree,
  Whilst our hearts throb with glee,
In thy death-doing might we defy thee,
       Yellow Jack!'

After the sangaree, strong and highly spiced, had been quaffed, the excitement grew wilder, and the leader of our revels exclaimed at the top of his voice, 'Wine, gentlemen, wine—brimmers!' and thus continued—

'Yellow Jack! Yellow Jack! hie thee back! hie thee back!
Begone to thy father, old Sootie;
  Pure WINE now I'll drink,
  So Jack, I should think,
Of me thou wilt never make booty,
       Yellow Jack!

'But a third time he came, and seized hold of my head;
'Twas in vain that the doctor both blister'd and bled;
My hand, and my side, and my heart too, I think,
Would soon have been lost, though pure wine I might drink.

CHORUS.

'Yellow Jack! Yellow Jack! hie thee back! hie thee back!
Begone to thy father, old Sootie,
    Pure wine now we'll drink,
    So Jack, we should think,
Of us thou wilt never make booty,

                                  Yellow Jack!'

'Brandy!' shouted the major. 'Brandy—he's a craven who shirks
the call.' There was no one there craven but myself. My youth
excused my apostasy from the night's orgies. The major resumed,
his red face intensely hot and arid.

'Yellow Jack! Yellow Jack! hie thee back! hie thee back!
To the helldam, Corruption, thy mother;
    For with BRANDY I'll save
    My heart, and thus brave
Thee, and fell Death, thine own brother,

                                  Yellow Jack!

'To brandy I took, then Jack took his leave,
Brandy-punch and neat brandy drink morn, noon, and eve,
At night drink, then sleep, and be sure, my brave boys,
Naught will quell yellow Jack, but neat brandy and noise.

THE CHORUS, (*most uproariously.*)

'Yellow Jack! Yellow Jack! hie thee back! hie thee back!
To the helldam, Corruption, thy mother;
    For with brandy we'll save
    Our hearts, and thus brave
Thee, and fell Death, thine own brother,

                                  Yellow Jack!'

At last 'Yellow Jack' was thundered out loud enough to awake
his victims from the palisades. The company were just then fit
for any thing, but certainly most fit for mischief. Our first lieutenant
intimated to me that the jolly-boat was waiting to take the junior
officers on board—considerate man—so I took the hint, marvelling
much upon the scene that I had just witnessed.

Whether or not there was any mystic virtue in the exorcisory
cantation of the previous night I cannot determine; but it is certain,
that next morning, though headaches abounded among our officers,
indications of the yellow fever there were none.

CHAPTER XVIII

Insubordination followed by elevation—A midshipman triced up in mid-air, and affording a practical lesson on oscillation— All truck and no barter.

BUT as it is not my intention to write a diary of my life, which was like all other midshipmen's lives in the West Indies, I shall pass over some months, during which we remained tolerably healthy, took many prizes, cut out some privateers, and spent money so rapidly gained, in a manner still more rapid.

Of my own messmates I remember but little. They were generally shockingly ignorant young men, who had left school too early, to whom books were an aversion, and all knowledge, save that merely nautical, a derision. I had to go more often to fisty-cuffs with these youths, in defending my three-deckers—words of Latin or Greek derivation—than on any other occasion. I remember well that the word 'idiosyncrasy' got me two black eyes, and my opponent as 'pretty a luxation' of the shoulder by being tumbled down the main hatchway at the close of the combat, as any man of moderate expectations might desire. I was really obliged to mind my parts of speech. I know, that instead of using the obnoxious word, idiosyncrasy, I should have said, that Mr. So-and-so had 'a list to port in his ideas.' I confess my error—my sin against elegance was great; but it must be said in extenuation, that then I was young and foolish.

However, I really liked my mode of life. Notwithstanding my occasional squabbles with my messmates upon my inadvertently launching a first-rate, I can safely say, I was beloved by every body—nor is the term too strong. The captain liked me because I was always well dressed, of an engaging appearance, and a very handsome appendage to his gig, and aide-de-camp in his visits on shore; perhaps from some better motives—though certainly, amidst all his kindness to me, he once treated me most tyrannously.

The doctor and the purser liked me, because I could converse with them rationally upon matters not altogether nautical. The master almost adored me, because, having a good natural talent for drawing, I made him plans of the hold, and the stowage of his tiers of watercasks, and sketches of headlands in his private log-book, to all which he was condescending enough to put his own name. The other superior officers thought me a very good sort of fellow, and my messmates liked me, because I was always happy and cheerful—and lent them money.

The crew, to a man, would have done any thing for me, because —(it was very foolish, certainly)—I used, for some months to cry heartily when any of them were tied up. And afterwards, when I got rid of this weakness, I always begged as many of them off from the infliction of the lash of Mr. Farmer, the first lieutenant, as I could. With him I could take the liberty if I found him in a good humour, though I dared not with the captain; for, though the latter had some attachment for me, it was a dreadfully wayward and capricious feeling.

The longer I sailed with him the more occasion I had to dread, if not hate him. The poor man had no resources; it is not, therefore, surprising, that he began to have recourse to habitual ebriety. Then, under the influence of his wine, he would be gay, mischievous, tyrannical, and even cruel, according to the mood of the moment. Yet, at the worst, though his feet faltered, when in his cups, his tongue never did. He even grew eloquent under the vinous influence. It sharpened his cunning, and wonderfully increased his aptitude for mischief. It was a grievous calamity to all on board the ship, that we could not give his mind healthful occupation. I said that he was fond of me; but I began to dread his affection, and to feel myself as being compelled to submit to the playful caresses of a tiger. As yet, not only had we not had the slightest difference, but he had often humoured me to the detriment of the service, and in defiance of the just discipline Mr. Farmer wished to maintain. If I presumed upon this, who shall blame such conduct in a mere boy? And then, Captain Reud was necessary to me. I found that I could not avail myself of my too ample allowance until he had endorsed my bills of exchange.

However, the concealed fang of the paw that had so often played with and patted me into vanity, was to wound me at length. It came upon me terribly, and entered deeply into my bosom.

I was learning to play chess of the purser—the game had already become a passion with me. It was also my turn to dine in the ward-room, and, consequently, I was invited. The anticipated game at chess enhanced the value of the invitation. That same forenoon, the captain and I had been very sociable. He gracious, and I, facetious as I could. I had been giving him a history of my various ushers, and he had been pleased to be wonderfully amused. I was down in the midshipmen's berth: a full hour after I had received the ward-room invitation, the captain's steward shoved his unlucky head within the door, and croaked out, 'Captain Reud's compliments to Mr. Rattlin, and desires his company to dinner to-day.'

I answered, carelessly, rather flippantly, perhaps, 'Tell the captain I'm going to dine in the ward-room.' I meant no disrespect, for I felt none. Perhaps the fellow who took back my answer worded it maliciously. I had totally forgotten, as soon as I had uttered my excusal, whether I had or had not used the word 'compliments,' or 'respects,'—perhaps, thoughtlessly, neither one nor the other.

I dined in the ward-room, enjoyed my chess, and, good easy youth, with all my blushing honours thick upon me, of having given mate with only trifling odds in my favour, the drum beat to evening quarters. I was stationed to the four aftermost carronnades on the quarter-deck. I had run up in a hurry; and at that period, straps to keep down the trousers not having been invented, my white jeans were riddled a good deal up my leg. I passed the captain, touched my hat, and began to muster my men. Unconscious of any offence, I stole a look or two at my commander, but met with no good-humoured glance in return. He had screwed up his little yellow physiognomy into the shape of an ill-conditioned and battered face on a brass knocker. He had his usual afternoon wine-flush upon him; but a feeling of vindictiveness had placed his feelings of incipient intoxication under complete mastery.

'So, you dined in the ward-room, Mr. Rattlin?'

'Yes, sir,' my hat reverently touched, not liking the looks of my interrogator.

'And you did not even condescend to return the compliments I sent you, with my misplaced invitation to dinner.'

'Don't recollect, sir.'

'Mr. Rattlin, in consideration of your ignorance, I can forgive a personal affront—damme—but, by the living G—d, I cannot overlook disrespect to the service. You young misbegotten scoundrel! what do you mean by coming to quarters undressed? Look at your trousers, sir.'

'The captain is in a passion, certainly,' thought I; as I

quietly stooped to pull the offending garment down to my shoes.

'Mr. Farmer, Mr. Farmer, do you see the young blackguard?' said the commander. 'Confound me, he is making a dressing-room of my quarter-deck—and at quarters, too—which is the same as parade. Hither, sirrah; ho—ho—my young gentleman. Young gentleman, truly—a conceited little bastard!'

The word burnt deeply into my young heart, and caused a shock upon my brain, as if an explosion of gunpowder had taken place within my skull; but it passed instantaneously, and left behind it an unnatural calm.

'Pray sir,' said I, walking up to him, deliberately and resolutely, 'how do *you* know that I am a bastard?'

'Do you hear the impudent scoundrel? Pray, sir, who is your father?'

'Oh! that I knew,' said I, bursting into tears. 'I bless God that it is not you.'

'To the mast-head! to the mast-head! Where's the boatswain? start him up! start him up!'

The boatswain could not make his way aft till I was some rattlings up the main rigging, and thus, his intentional and kind dilatoriness saved me from the indignity of a blow. Twice I gazed upon the clear blue, and transparent water, and temptation was strong upon me, for it seemed to woo me to rest; but when I looked in-board and contemplated the diminutive, shrivelled, jaundiced figure beneath me, I said to myself, 'Not for such a thing as that.'

Before I had got to the main-top, I thought, 'This morning he loved me!—poor human nature!'—and when I had got to the topmast-cross-trees, I had actually forgiven him. It has been my failing through life, as Shakspeare expresses it, 'to have always lacked gall.'[1] God knows how much I have forgiven, merely because I have found it impossible to hate.

But I was to be tried still more. I had settled myself comfortably on the cross-trees, making excuses for the captain, and condemning my own want of caution, and anticipating a reconciliatory breakfast with my persecutor, when his shrill voice came discordantly upon my ears.

'Mast-head, there!'

'Sir.'

'Up higher, sir—up higher.'

I hesitated—the order was repeated with horrid threats and imprecations. There were no rattlings to the top-gallant rigging. It had been tremendously hot all day, and the tar had sweated from the shrouds; and I was very loath to spoil my beautiful white jean trousers by swarming up them. However, as I perceived that he had worked himself into a perfect fury up I went, and to the top-gallant-mast-head, embracing the royal pole with one arm, and standing on the bights of the rigging. My nether apparel, in performing this feat, appeared as if it had been employed in wiping up a bucket of spilled tar.

But I was not long to remain unmolested in my stance on the high and giddy mast. My astonishment and dismay were unbounded at hearing Captain Reud still vociferate, 'Up higher, sir.'

The royal pole stood naked, with nothing attached to it but the royal and the signal-halyards, the latter running through the truck. My lady readers must understand that the truck is that round thing at the top of all the masts, that looks so like a button. I could not have got up the well-greased pole if I had attempted it. A practised seaman could, certainly, and, indeed, one of those worthies who climb for legs of mutton at a fair, might have succeeded to mount a few inches.

'What!' said I, half aloud, 'does the tyrant mean? He knows that this thing I cannot do: and he also knows that if I attempt it, it is probable I shall lose my hold of this slippery stick, and be rolled off into the sea. If he wishes to murder me, he shall do so more directly. Forgive him—never. I'll brave him first, and revenge myself after.'

Again that deadly calm came over me, which makes soft dispositions so desperate, and to which light-haired persons are so peculiarly subject. In these temperaments, when the paleness becomes fixed and unnatural, beware of them in their moods. They concentrate the vindictiveness of a life in a few moments, and, though the paroxysm is usually short, it is too often fatal to themselves and to their victims. I coolly commenced descending the rigging, whilst the blackest thoughts crowded in distinct and blood-stained array upon my brain. I bethought me from whence I could the most readily pluck a weapon, but the idea was but instantaneous, and I dismissed it with a mighty effort. At length, I reached the deck, whilst the infuriated captain stood mute with surprise at my outrageously insubordinate conduct. The men were still at their quarters and partook of their commander's astonishment; but, I am convinced, of no other feeling.

When I found myself on the deck I walked up to Captain Reud, and between my clenched teeth I said to him slowly and deliberately, 'Tyrant, I scorn you. I come premeditately to commit an act of mutiny: I give myself up as a prisoner: I desire to be tried by a court-martial. I will undergo any thing to escape from you; and I don't think that, with all your malice, you will be able to hang me. I consider myself under an arrest.' Then turning upon my heel I prepared to go down the quarter-deck hatchway.

Captain Reud heard me to the end in silence; he even permitted me to go down half the ladder unmolested, when, rousing himself from his utter astonishment, he jumped forward and spurning me with his foot violently on my back, dashed me on the main deck, I was considerably bruised, and, before I got to the midshipman's berth, two marines seized me and dragged me again to the quarter-deck. Once more I stood before my angry persecutor, looking hate and defiance.

'To the mast-head, sir, immediately.'

'I will not. I consider myself a prisoner.'

'You refuse to go?'

'I do.'

'Quarter-masters, the signal halyards. Sling Mr. Rattlin.' Mr. Rattlin was slung. 'Now run the mutinous rascal up to the truck.'

In a moment I was attached to a thin white line, waving to and fro in mid air, and soon triced up to the very top of the royal pole, and jammed hard to the truck. Is this believed? Perhaps not; yet no statement was ever more true.[1] At the time when this atrocity was perpetrating not an officer interfered. My sufferings were intense. The sun was still hot, my hat had fallen off in my involuntary ascent, and, as the ship was running before the wind under her topsails, the motion at that high point of elevation was tremendous. I felt horribly seasick. The ligature across my chest became every moment more oppressive to my lungs, and more excruciating in torture: my breathing at each respiration more difficult, and, before I had suffered ten minutes, I had fainted. So soon as the captain had seen me run up he went below, leaving strict orders that I should not be lowered down.

Directly that the captain was in his cabin, the first-lieutenant, the doctor, purser, and the officers of the watch, held a hurried consultation on my situation. But the good-natured doctor did not stop for the result, but immediately went below, and told Reud if I remained where I was I should die. Those who knew the navy at that time will anticipate the answer—no others can—'Let him die and be damned!' The good doctor came on deck desponding. Mr. Farmer then hailed me once, and again, and again. Of course he received no answer: I heard him, but, at that moment, my senses were fast leaving me. The sea, with its vast horizon, appearing so illimitable from the great height where I was swaying, rocked, to my failing sight, awfully to and fro: the heavens partook of the dizzying motion. I only, of all the creation, seemed standing still: I was sick unto death; and as far as sensation was concerned, then and there I died.

Upon receiving no reply, Mr. Farmer sent one of the top-men up to look at me. No sooner had he reached the topgallant rigging than he reported me dead. A cry of horror escaped from all on deck. The captain rushed up: he needed no report. He was frantic with grief. He wept like a child, and assisted with his own hands to lower me down: they were his arms that received, himself that bore me to his cabin. Like a wilful boy who had slain his pet lamb, or a passionate girl her dove, he mourned over me. It was a long time before my respiratory organs could be brought into play. My recovery was slow, and it was some time before I could arrange my ideas. A cot was slung for me in the cabin, and, bewildered and exhausted, I fell into a deep sleep.

I awoke a little after midnight perfectly composed, and suffering only from the wale that the cord had made across my chest. Before a table, and his countenance lighted by a single lantern, sate the captain. His features expressed a depth of grief and a remorse that were genuine. He sate motionless, with his eyes fixed upon my cot: my face he could not see, owing to the depth of the shadow in which I lay. I moved: he advanced to my cot with the gentleness of a woman, and softly uttered:

'Ralph, my dear boy, do you sleep?'

The tones of his voice fell soothingly upon my ear like the music of a mother's prayer.

'No, Captain Reud; but I am very thirsty.'

In an instant he was at my side with some weak wine and water. I took it from the hand of him whom, but a few hours before, in my animosity I could have slain.

'Ralph,' said he, as he received back the tumbler, 'Ralph, are we friends?'

'Oh! Captain Reud, how could you treat a poor lad thus, who respected, who loved you so much?'

'I was mad—do you forgive me, Ralph?' and he took my not unwilling hand.

'To be sure, to be sure; but do me one little favour in return.'

'Any thing, any thing, Ralph—I'll never mast-head you again.'

'Oh, I was not thinking of that; I ought not to have put you in a passion. Punish me—mast-head me—do any thing, Captain Reud, but call me not bastard.'

He made no reply: he pressed my hand fervently; he put it to his lips and kissed it—on my soul he did: then, after a pause, gently murmured 'Good night;' and, as he passed into the after-cabin to his bed, I distinctly heard him exclaim, 'God forgive me—how I have wronged that boy!'

The next day we were better friends than ever; and for the three years that we remained together, not a reproachful word or an angry look ever passed between us.

I must be permitted to make three observations upon this, to me, memorable transaction. The first is, that at that time I had not the power of retention of those natural feelings of anger, which all should carry with them as a preservation against, or a punishment for, injury and insult. I know that most of my male, and many of my female readers, will think my conduct throughout pusillanimous or abject. My mother's milk, as it were, still flowed in my veins, and with that no ill blood could amalgamate. All I can say is, that now I am either so much better or so much worse, that I should have adopted towards Captain Reud a much more decided course of proceedings.

My second remark is, that this captain had really a good heart, but was one of the most striking instances that I ever knew of the demoralizing effect of a misdirected education, and the danger of granting great powers to early years and great ignorance. With good innate feelings, no man ever possessed moral perceptions more clouded.

And lastly, that this statement is not to be construed into a libel on the naval service, or looked upon, in the least, as an exaggerated account. As to libel, the gentlemanly deportment, the parental care of their crews, and the strict justice of thousands of captains, cannot in the least be deteriorated by a single act of tyranny by a solitary member of their gallant body; and, as to exaggeration, let it be remembered that, in the very same year, and on the very same station that my tricing up to the truck occurred, another post-captain tarred and feathered one of his young gentlemen, and kept him in that state, a plumed biped, for more than six weeks in his hen-coop. This last fact obtained much notoriety, from the aggrieved party leaving the service, and recovering heavy damages from his torturer in a court of civil law. My treatment never was known beyond our own frigate.

CHAPTER XIX

Ralph entereth into the regions of romance and privateering—
Carried thither by a French pilot, malgré lui—*An inopportune visit.*

SHORTLY after the illegal suspension of the Habeas Corpus that I recorded in the last chapter, the portion of the navy stationed in the West Indies became actively employed in the conquest of those islands still in the possession of the French. Some fell almost without a struggle, others at much expense of life, both of the military and naval forces. As every one, who could find a publisher, has written a book on all these events, from the capture of the little spot Deseada, to the subduing the magnificent island of Gaudaloupe, and the glorious old stone-built city of Domingo, I may well be excused detailing the operations.

Among other bellicose incidents that varied the dull monotony of my life, was the beating off a frigate equal in force to our own; though I believe that we were a little obliged to her for taking leave of us in a manner so abrupt, though we could not certainly complain of the want, on her part, of any attention for the short and busy hour that she stayed with us, for she assisted us to shift all our topmasts, and as, before she met us, we had nothing but old sails to display, she considerately decorated us with a profusion of ribands gaily fluttering about our lower masts and the topmasts that were still standing gracefully hanging over our sides.

We were too polite and well bred not to make some return for all these *petits soins.* As, between the tropics, the weather is generally very warm, we evinced a most laudable anxiety that she should be properly ventilated, so we assiduously began drilling holes through and through her hull; and, I assure the reader, that we did it in a surpassingly workmanlike manner. But, in the midst of this spirited exchange of courtesies, our Gallic friend remembered that he had, or might have, another *engagement*, so he took his leave; and, as he had given us so many reasons to prevent our insisting to attend upon him, we parted, *en pleine mer*, leaving us excessively annoyed that we were prevented from accompanying him any further.

In Captain Reud's despatches he stated, and stated truly, that we beat him off. Why he went, I could not understand; for, excepting in the shattered state of his hull, and more particularly in a sad confusion of his quarter gallery with his two aftermost main-deck ports, he sailed off with his colours flying, and every sail drawing, even to his royals. But the French used to have their own method of managing these little matters.

But let us rapidly pass over these follies, and hasten to something more exquisitely foolish. And yet I cannot. I have to clear away many dull weeds, and tread down many noxious nettles, before I can reach the one fresh and thornless rose, that bloomed for a short space upon my heart, and the fragrance of which so intoxicated my senses, that, for a time, I was under the blessed delusion of believing myself happy.

I had now been two years and a half in the West Indies, and I was fast approaching my nineteenth year. At this period, we had taken several English West Indiamen. There was a fearful, a soul-harrowing, yet a tender tale, connected with one of these recaptures. It should be told, for the honour of that sex, whom to honour is man's greatest glory; but not now—nor in this life. Yet it ought to be narrated; and I here record my vow, that if I live, and I have the heart to go through it, and my dear —— will resolve me that one incubus of a doubt that has hung heavily on my heart for these five-and-twenty years, that that tale shall be told, that man may admire, and wonder, and weep.

In one of these retaken merchant vessels there was found, as the French prize-master, and now of course our prisoner, a mercurial little fellow of the name of Messurier. He was very proud of the glory of his nation, and still prouder of his own. As France possessed many historians, and Monsieur Adolphe Sigismund

Messurier but one, and that one himself, of course, he had the duty of, at least, three hundred savans thrown upon his own shoulders: he performed it nobly, and with an infinite relish. Now, when a person who is given to much talking is also given to much drinking, it generally happens, injurious as is the vice of the grog bottle, that the vice of the voluble tongue is still worse. When in his cups, he told us of the scores that he had slain, counting them off by threes and fives upon his fingers, his thumbs indicating captains, his forefingers first-lieutenants, and so on with the various grades in our service, until the *aspirants*, or middies, were merely honoured by his little finger as their representative, we only laughed; and asked him, if he had been so destructive to the officers, how many men had fallen by the puissance of his arm. It seemed that these latter were too numerous and too ignoble to be counted; for that question was always answered with a *bah!* and a rapidly passing over the extended palm of his left hand with his open right one.

But when, one evening, he mentioned that he could pilot a frigate into the inland waters from whence swarmed the crowd of schooner-privateers that infested the islands, and by their swift sailing to windward, eluded our fastest ship, we laughed still, and I did something more; I reported this boast to Captain Reud.

'Then,' exclaimed my valorous little creole, 'by all the virtues of a long eighteen, he shall take in his Majesty's frigate, Eos.'

Whenever he protested by a long eighteen, in the efficacy of whose powers he had the most implicit reliance, we might look upon the matter as performed.

The next morning, whilst Monsieur Messurier was solacing his aching head with his hands, oblivious of the events of the preceding evening, he was feelingly reminded of his consummate skill in pilotage. He then became most unnaturally modest, and denied all pretensions to the honour. Now Captain Reud had no idea that even an enemy should wrap up his talent in a napkin, so he merely said to him, 'You must take my ship in.' When the captain had made up his mind, the deed generally trod upon the heels of the resolve. Poor man! he was always in want of something to do, and thus he was too happy to do any thing that offered excitement. Monsieur Messurier was in despair; he prayed and swore alternately; talked about sacrificing his life for the good of his country; and told us, in a manner that convinced us that he wished us to believe the absurdity, that honour was the breath of his nostrils.

However, the captain was fully intent upon giving him the glorious opportunity of exclaiming with effect, *Dulce et decorum est pro patriâ mori.*

Not knowing the strength of the stronghold that it was our intention to surprise, Captain Reud cruised about for a few days, until he had collected another frigate, a sloop of war, and two eighteen gun-brigs, the commanders of all being, of course, his juniors. Having made all necessary arrangements, one beautiful morning we found ourselves close off the iron-bound and rocky shores of the east end of St. Domingo. We ran along shore for a couple of hours, when we perceived an opening in the lofty piles of granite, that frowned over the blue ocean. This was the entrance into the harbour where lay our destined prizes.

Captain Reud, taking the responsibility into his own hands, had determined to lead in. The charts were minutely examined, but they gave us no hope. The soundings laid down were so shallow, and the path so intricate, that, by them, we wondered much, how even a privateer-schooner could make the passage in safety. To a frigate drawing three-and-twenty feet of water, the attempt seemed only a precursor to destruction.

We hove-to; the captains of the other vessels were signalled on board, and, with them and our first-lieutenant and master, a sort of council of war was held; and, as every one present gave his voice against the attempt, our skipper's mind was made up directly. He resolved to go in, trusting to the chapter of accidents, to a gracious Providence, and Monsieur Messurier upon the fore-yard, with a seaman with a pistol at each ear, to scatter his brains the moment the ship struck. The weather was brilliant, the wind moderate and fair, when we bore up for the mouth of the passage. It was something at once ludicrous and painful to witness the agony of our pilot in spite of himself. Between oaths, protestations, and tremors, the perspiration of terror flowing down his face, mingled with his tears, he conned the ship with a precision that proved, at least in that matter, that he was no vain boaster.

But we had scarcely advanced a few hundred yards within the gorge, than I had eyes only for the sublimity of the scenery that opened itself in succession as we passed. The water was as smooth as the cheek, as bright as the smile, and as blue as the eye of our first love. Indeed, it was '*deeply*, beautifully blue,'[1] as Lord Byron saith—to that *deeply* we owed every thing. The channel was so

R

narrow, that, in many places, there was not sufficient room to tack
the ship, even if she could have turned within her own length, and,
in two remarkable points, we had not sufficient width to have
carried our studding-sails. At one singularly romantic spot of this
pass, the rocks far above our mast-heads leant over towards each
other, and the ancient forest trees that crowned the heights,
mingled their feathery branches, and permitted us to get a sight
of the vaulted blue above us only at intervals, between the
interstices of the dark-green foliage.

The seamen regarded their situation with wonder, not unmixed
with awe. But the view was not the unvaried one of two gigantic
walls festooned with flowers and crowned with trees. At intervals,
we found the channel open into wide lagunes, with shelving and
verdant shores, studded with white stone buildings, and well-
cultivated plantations, and then the passage would narrow again
suddenly, and the masses of rock rose so high on each side of us,
as almost to exclude the light of the day. The way was tortuous,
but not abruptly so; and, as we wound through it, ever and anon
we came to some picturesque inlet, some cool grotto, so beautiful
that its very beauty must have peopled it with nymphs, for none
could look upon them, without feeling, for a time, like poets. At
the entrance, the heaving water rose and fell with a heavy moaning
against the eternal bases of the rocks, though the surface in mid
channel was perfectly smooth; but, as we advanced, this dull
undulation gradually subsided, and its measured splash no longer
echoed among the cliffs. The silence, as we proceeded, grew strange
to us. An awe crept over us, like that which is felt upon the first
entrance into a vast cathedral: and the gentle wind came to us
noiselessly, and, dying away at intervals, left the ship silently
stealing on, impelled for a space, by no visible means.

The hush throughout the ship was tomb-like, and the few words
of command, that from time to time, broke upon the ear, sounded
hollow and unearthly from the reverberations of the over-hanging
precipices.

But quickly the scene would change; the jutting promontories
and overtopping walls would recede, and a fairy spot encircled by
forest-land would open upon us, studded with green islands,
glorious in all the beauties of an eternal spring, and crowded and
crowned with flowers of every hue, and of a brilliancy the most
intense. We proceeded in this delightful manner for more than

twelve miles, yet no one had appeared, in the least, to notice our approach. Had the most trivial attempt at defence been made, we could not have proceeded a quarter of the distance; for I verily believe that we passed by points so over hanging, that a couple of pounds of gunpowder, properly applied and fired at the right moment, would have tumbled fragments of solid rock upon us, that would have crushed us to the bottom in an instant, to mention nothing of the several protruding corners of this singular pass, on which two or three guns could have raked an approaching vessel for half an hour with impunity: as I have before stated that it would be impossible in those straitened passages to have turned a broadside to bear on any impediment. On we came, and at last a noble bay, or rather salt-water lake opened upon us, with two wide rivers delivering their waters into the bottom of it. On our right lay the town of Aniana,[1] with a fort upon a green mount overlooking the houses, and rising much higher than our floating pennant.

Our unexpected *entrée*, like all other mistimed visits, caused the visited a terrible degree of confusion. Twelve or thirteen beautiful schooners had their sweeps out, and all their sails set immediately. We having anchored opposite the town about noon, the breeze fell away into almost a perfect calm, and off they went, making the best of their way up the rivers. There were several other craft lying off the town, into which the inhabitants were crowding, with all their effects of any value, no doubt intending to go a little way up into the country also, to avoid the inconvenience of inopportune calls. The signal was made for our little squadron to get out their boats, chase and capture.

CHAPTER XX

Treats of kind intentions frustrated—A visiting party prevented by one ball too many having been given—And ready-made domestic happiness for strangers.

WE first of all brought out the heavily laden craft that were still near the town, and anchored them under our guns. To the privateers that shewed their heels, the larger boats gave chase, and coming up with them, one after another, they were finally all captured. Had they but acted in combination, I think they might have resisted the boats with success; but their commanders seemed to have lost all presence of mind, in the confusion and astonishment into which our sudden appearance had thrown them.

Now, all this was very pleasant to us, *Messieurs les concernés*. We calculated upon having the whole wealth of the French town, and the little French fleet, converted into lawful prize-money. The deeply laden poop-encumbered brigs and schooners, so ungracefully down by the stern, we imagined to be full of treasure. Visions of gold glittered before our mind's eye. We were about to recover the plunder of ages, for it must be confessed, that this same Aniana was no better than a haven for pirates. One of us was cruelly undeceived in one respect. As yet, we had met with no manner of resistance whatever—it was ten o'clock in the evening, the full moon giving us a very excellent imitation of daylight, when all the commanders who had dined with our yellow skipper came on deck, in the highest possible glee, delightedly rubbing their hands, and calculating each his share of the prize-money. All this hilarity was increased, every now and then, by some boats coming on board, and reporting to us, as commodore, another privateer or some fugitive merchantmen taken, and then immediately shoving off in chase of others.

'Well, gentlemen,' said our skipper, 'I'll tell you what we'll do. We'll send the marines on shore to-morrow, and take possession of the town. However, we will be very civil to the ladies;—we will, by Venus! As commanding officer, I'll permit of no rudeness.'

'None whatever: who could think of frightening them? I suppose, Captain Reud, there could be no harm in going ashore now and paying them a visit, just to alleviate their fears,' was the reply of one of the commanders.

'Not to-night, not to-night. Depend upon it, all the best of the beauty, and the best of the wealth is safely stowed in this numerous fleet, quietly anchored about us: we have them all safe. There might be some villains lurking about the town with their cane knives in their belts: let us have all clear, and daylight before us. Not that I think there is any pluck among them—they have not spirit enough to throw a stone at a dog.'

Hardly had these taunting words escaped his lips, than 'bang, crash,' and a four-and-twenty pound shot came reeking through the waist-hammocks, for they had not yet been piped down, and covered us over with horse-hair, and an abominable composition called flock. The ball took a slanting direction through the main and orlop decks, and came out just below the water-line, making instantly a leak that we could not affect to despise.

'Droll,' said Reud, shaking the dust from his person.

'Very,' said his well-dined echoes around him.

If this be jesting, thought I, the cream of the joke is to come yet.

'Beat to quarters, Mr. Rattlin.' The lieutenants and more than half of the crew were away in the boats. The men were soon at their guns, and, as they had been only slightly secured, they were ready to return the fire almost immediately. Upon looking up at the source of our annoyance, we found that it was a hopeless case. The height was so great, and so immediately above us, that, without heeling the frigate over, not a gun could be brought to bear. Another shot from the battery served to quicken our deliberations. There was no time to be lost.

Captain Reud sent the various commanders on board their respective vessels, with orders, as fast as any of their boats came in, to send them to us immediately, with their marines. For ourselves, all our boats were away except the gig. Into that I jumped, followed by the captain and six marines. Every man, except a quarter-master and a couple of look-outs, was piped down below, with strict orders that they were to stay there and not expose themselves, and the ship was left in charge of the gunner, whilst the carpenter and his crew were actively employed in the wings, in plugging the shot-holes; for every ball that was fired came in somewhere upon the decks, and made its way through the ship's sides, low under the water.

However, annoying as this was, there were but two guns playing upon us, which, though served with admirable precision, fired but slowly. We had not lain on our oars a quarter of an hour between the ship and the shore, a space of not more than forty yards, when we were joined by seven boats of various dimensions, crammed as full of jollies as they could possibly hold. We were on shore in a moment, and, without much care as to forming, we all scrambled up the hill as fast as we could. It was very steep indeed, but we were not fired upon by any small arms whatever, and the guns could not be sufficiently depressed from the embrasures to be made to bear upon us. They certainly must have perceived us, for the moon was shining with singular splendour; but they

seemed to take no notice of our advance, but fired twice upon the
frigate as we were climbing or rather scrambling up.

This assault was an affair got up with so little premeditation, that
Captain Reud had no other arms than his regulation sword; and
his aide-de-camp, my redoubtable self, no other weapon of offence
than a little crooked dirk, so considerately curved, that it would not
answer the purpose of a dagger to stab with, and so blunt, that I am
sure, though it might separate, it could not *cut* through a plum-
pudding. Though I was approaching *pari passu* with my commander to a parapet, where there was *no* 'imminent deadly breach,'
I was so much ashamed of my side-arms, that I would not expose
them to the night air.

Up we tumbled close under the low, turf-constructed battle-
ment, and, as we were in the act of scrambling over it, we received
a straggling and ill-directed fire of musketry.

One hurrah from our party, and we were into the fort in a
moment, and that on the two flanks as well as the front. For all
the service that I could render, I might as well have charged, as
a midshipman usually walks the deck, with my hands in my pockets.
However, there we were face to face with our opponents, on the
planked floor of the fort, just as they were making up their minds
to run away. But they did not go quite so soon as they ought. In
jumping over the turfy mound, it must be supposed, as was really
the case, that it took us an instant or two to recover our equilibrium
and ascertain the surety of our footing, but that instant was a very
annoying one, for the Frenchman directly opposed to Captain
Reud deliberately put his musket against the said captain's face,
and though I, unarmed as I was, actually did strike up this musket
as much as I was able, it had only the effect of making the bayonet
at the end of it score a deep wound from the bridge of his nose to
the top of his forehead, when the trigger was pulled, and the whole
crown of Captain Reud's skull completely blown away.[1] The shot
turned him round like a weathercock; I naturally half turned also,
giving the enemy the advantage of studying my profile, whilst
I endeavoured to support my captain in my arms, and then the
same man, being bent on mischief, thrust his bayonet right through
the back of my neck, grazing the vertebra, and entering on the right
and coming out on the left side. Having in this manner a sheath
for his weapon, the blackguard left it there, and thus, having
trussed me as with a skewer, shewed me his back and fled. The

butt-end of the musket falling to the ground, gave me a terrible wrench of the head, but relieved me at the same time of my incumbrance.

That was the first time I ever *bled* for my country. Indeed, I bled much more than my poor captain. However, the gentlemen of the fort rushed out as we rushed in, and rolled head over heels down the other side of the hill. Three or four were killed on the platform; among whom, at the time I devoutly wished, was the inflicter of my wound; some were shot as they ran down the inland side of the hill, and the fort was ours, with the loss of one man killed, and, I think, six wounded. My hurt was very trifling: a piece of adhesive plaster on the two orifices was all the surgical assistance that I either had or required. But the case with poor Reud was very different. I detest giving a revolting description of wounds; I shall only say, that this was a most dreadful one. He lay for a month almost in a state of insensibility; and though he lived for more than half a year with his head plated with silver, I know that he was never afterwards perfectly sane.[1]

Walking about for a couple of days with a stiff neck, which was all the inconvenience I experienced, I assumed no little upon my firmness in storming, and on my honourable scars. The next morning all the prizes were secured, the town formally taken possession of, and, whilst Captain Reud lay in the torpor of what was all but death, it was deliberated that we should do with our conquest. It was a matter of some difficulty to decide upon. At this period, the two factions of the blacks, Petion's and Christophe's, held the western parts of the fine island of St. Domingo. The Spaniards had large possessions in the centre of the island, and the French still held a sway over the city of St. Domingo, and had a precarious footing in the eastern division, where we now were.

The place was too insignificant to garrison for a permanent conquest for the English. Many of our officers, and all the men, wished very naturally to plunder it; but the captain of the other frigate, now the commander, would not listen to the proposal for a moment. However, we totally destroyed their small dock-yard, burned three fine schooners on the stocks, demolished the fort that had been so pernicious to Captain Reud, and which commanded the town; and then, the officers, and small parties of the ship's company were permitted to go on shore, and to live at free quarters upon the inhabitants. Strict orders were given to respect life and limb, and the honour of the ladies; and these orders were generally well enforced. It was certainly a pleasant thing to go on shore and walk into any house that pleased you, call for what you wanted, be very protecting, and, after having eaten and drunk to satiety, to depart without having to cast up the items of a bill.

These brigands were treated much too leniently, for I verily believe, that, for a vast number of years, all the male population were born, bred, lived, and had died pirates. They were of all nations of the earth; and, I must say, that this blending of the various races, had produced a very handsome set of men, and very beautiful women. There were many English females among them, who had been captured in our merchant vessels, and had been forced into marriages with their lawless captors. They were, for the most part, like the Sabine women, reconciled to their lot, and loath to leave their lords, their mansions, and their children.

The governor of the place, a French colonel, was captured as he endeavoured to make his escape in one of the schooner privateers. We had him on board of our ship for some time, and he confessed that the place flourished only by means of what he was pleased to designate as free trading.

The prizes, deeply laden, left the port one after the other, and then the men-of-war brigs, afterwards the sloop of war, and, at length, our consort, the frigate. We now lay alone in these quiet waters, and there we remained for nearly three months. All this time our captain could hardly be said to be living. No one was allowed to come aft beyond the mizen-mast. We always spoke with hushed voices, and walked about stealthily upon tip-toe. The bells ceased to be struck, and every precaution was taken to preserve the most profound silence. But our amusements on shore were more than commensurate for our restraints on board. Most of the officers and men took unto themselves wives, *pro hac vice*— chalked, or rather painted their names upon the doors of their mansions, and made themselves completely at home.

CHAPTER XXI

*Liaisons dangereuses—Ralph diveth into the dilemma of love, and
admireth the fatherly conduct of the parent of his Dulcinea—
Yet rageth and weepeth that she is a slave who hath enslaved him.*

AT this time I had begun to look fierce, if any one did not accede
to me the rights and privileges of a man; and especially since I had
received my bayonet wound: my vanity upon this score became
insupportable. 'Younker' was now a term of bitterness to me; on
the word 'lad' I looked with sovereign contempt; 'boy' I had long
done with. Heartily I prayed for a beard, but it came not; so,
in order to supply the deficiency, I used to practise looking stern
before my dressing-glass. But all my efforts at an outward semblance
of manliness were vain; my face was much too fair and feminine,
though my stature, and the firmness of my frame, were just what
I wished. I was not on board the vessel after the first week that she
lay in the port of Aniana, nor did I rejoin her until she was in the
very act of sailing out of it.

How am I to approach this subject, so romantic, so delicious,
and so delicate! How can I record events, that, in proving to me
that I had a heart, first destroyed its strength by the sweet delirium
of ecstasy, and thus, having enfeebled, almost broke it! Before, the
poetic ardour had often been upon me; but the fire was lighted up
at the shrine of vanity, and I sang for applause. It was to be
rekindled by love; but to burn with a concealed fury, to be whispered
only to my own soul—a feeling too great for utterance, too intense
for song, was to devour me. I experienced ecstasies that were
not happiness; I learnt the bitter truth, that rapture is not bliss.

About a week after we had obtained a quiet settlement in the
town, and very many of us a quiet settlement in the hearts, as well
as in the houses, of the beautiful Creoles and half castes, I also went
on shore, with Modesty walking steadily on my right hand, whilst
Madam Temptation was wickedly ogling me on the left. I looked
in on the establishments of several of my brother officers, and
certainly admired the rapidity with which they had surrounded
themselves with all manner of domestic comforts, including wives,
and, in some instances, large families of children. There was much
more than ready-made love in these arrangements; any one may

buy that for ready money; but a ready-made progeny, a ready-made household, and a ready-made wife, without one stiver of ready money, was the astonishment; but English sailors can do any thing.

Well, at No. 14, Rue Coquine, I accepted the purser's invitation to dinner at four, *en famille*. It seemed quite natural.

'My dove,' said he, 'you'll get us a bit of fish. Mr. Rattlin loves fish.'

'Certainly, my love,' said Mrs. Purser *pro tempore*, looking a battery of amiabilities.

'Allow me to introduce you to my sister-in-law, Ma'amselle D'Avalonge,' said the purser, presenting a very well dressed young lady to me, with all the ease of a family man.

The introduction took place immediately, and the lady and I found each other charming; indeed we said so. After a few more compliments, and a very pretty song, accompanied by the guitar, from mademoiselle, I took my leave, promising to be punctual to my appointment. I was not punctual—I never saw their dear faces again.

I left the town, and strolled up into the interior, keeping, however, our small fleet in sight, and walking seaward. I found the environs well cultivated, and the houses in the various plantations solidly built, and of stone. From every habitation that I passed I had pressing invitations to enter and refresh myself. These I declined. At length I arrived at a beautiful wood, evidently under the care of man; for the different trees were so arranged, as to produce a romantic effect. The shade that the lofty mahogany trees afforded was very grateful, for it was now a little after noon; and in this grove I paced slowly up and down, nursing my pride with all manner of conceits. Now wishing for some adventure, now fancying myself some king, now turning with pitying thoughts upon poor Reud, and then seeing the misery that we, in our honourable vocation, were daily causing, and the vice that we were daily acting, asking myself if there were any thing in life worth living for.

I well remember the crowding, the overbearing thoughts of that solitary and melancholy hour. It seemed to me as if I were compelled into a summing up of all my reflections, before I plunged into some unknown sea of mysterious events. After my mind had exhausted every object of contemplation that the scene around me had suggested, my thoughts travelled home—home! had I a home —had I any thing that loved me—any thing that, in the deep and soul-absorbing sense of the term, any thing that I loved? Should I ever obtain that object in existence, some one on whom to repose in affliction, rejoice with in happiness—a pillow for my head, and a resting-place for my heart? I felt that, whilst I hated none— and there were many to whom I was attached—my heart panted for some one on whom to expend its energies. I panted for an object which I could worship, and by whom I should be worshipped. I may almost say, that I prayed for it—it was granted, and imme- diately.

In the distance, and much below where I stood, I heard voices in violent altercation; among which the '' vast heavings,' 'blow me tights,' 'a stopper over all,' with other such nautical expletives, were predominant. I broke from my cover, and found myself imme- diately on a slope, before a very respectable habitation, nearly sur- rounded by boiling-houses, and other outbuildings necessary to a sugar and coffee plantation. The group before me consisted of a small, energetic, old, and white-haired Frenchman, neatly dressed in a complete suit of nankeen, with his broad-brimmed straw hat submissively in his hand, speaking all manner of fair and unintelligible French words to two Jacks, not of my ship, between which two, now pulled this way, now plucked that, was a timid and beautiful girl, of about fifteen years of age. There were several negroes, grinning and passive spectators of this scene. I understood it in a moment. So did my gentlemen in the tarpaulin hats. They were off to me in a less time than a topgallant breeze takes to travel aft from the flying jib-boom, supposing the ship to be at single anchor.

I took out my pocket-book, wrote down their names (most likely purser's ones), and ordered them on board their vessel directly. They obeyed, or at least appeared to do so, and departed, casting many 'a lingering, longing look behind,' leaving me the triumphant master of the field—the paladin, who had rescued the fair, for which I received much clapping of hands from the dark visages, and an intense look of gratitude from the fair, pale creature, whom I had released from the very equivocal rudeness of her admirers. The thanks from Monsieur Manuel, the father, were neither silent nor few, and, when he found that I could converse in French, he exhausted the vocabulary of that copious language of all its expressions of gratitude. I hardly could perceive that I had rendered any service at all; I had struck no blows and had run no risk; I had merely spoken, and obedience followed. However, as I could not stem the torrent of his gratitude, I determined to divert its course, by yielding to his urgent entreaties to accompany him to his house, and recruit myself, after my perilous and heroic deed.

We were soon seated in the coolest room in his mansion, and every West Indian luxury was quickly produced to tempt my palate. In fifteen minutes he had acquainted me with his parentage, his possessions, and his history. He assured me, with gesticulations, and a few oaths, that he was not at all connected with the brigands that inhabited the town below—that he despised them, knew them all to be pirates, or abettors of pirates, revolutionists, and republicans—that he was at heart, yea, in heart and soul, a royalist, and devotedly attached to the *vieux régime*; that the estate he now cultivated he had inherited from his father, who had been one of the few spared in the revolt of the blacks; that he had been educated at Paris, but, for the last five-and-thirty years, had hardly been off his own grounds—that he had no wife, and, indeed, never married, had no family at all, excepting Josephine, who sate beside him, who was his very dear and only child.

He did not add, 'a slave, and the daughter of a slave.'[1]

I now looked upon her steadfastly for the first time, and with the most intense emotion: but it was pity. I had been sufficiently long in the West Indies to know exactly the relation in which she stood to her father. However, he went on to relate how she had been born to him by a beautiful mulatto, for whom he had given a great sum; yet at this she startled not, moved not, blushed not. But her's was not the calmness of obduracy, but of innocence.

Strongly did I commiserate her, and gently strove to draw her into discourse. I found her ignorant, oh! how profoundly ignorant! She had no ideas beyond the estate in which she lived, and those that she had gathered from the gang of negroes that worked it. Her father had taught her nothing but to play a few tunes by ear upon the guitar, and sing some old French songs. Yet she had been accustomed to all the observances of a lady—had slaves to wait upon her, and was always elaborately, sometimes richly, dressed. Isolated as she had been, I soon discovered that she was a compound of enthusiasm, talent, and melancholy. She was little more than fifteen years old, yet that age, in those tropical climates, answers fully to an European one-and-twenty. In form, she was a perfect woman, light, rounded, and extremely active; all her motions were as graceful, and as undulating, as the gently-swelling billow. If she moved quickly, she bounded; if slowly, she appeared to glide on effortless through space. She had taken her lessons of grace in the woods, and her gymnasium had been among the sportive billows of the ocean. It is but of little use my describing her face; for every one supposes, that in these affairs, the author draws at once, as largely as he can, upon his own imagination, and as he dares, upon the credulity of his readers. Though a slave, she had but little of the black blood in her—in her complexion none. She was not fair, but her skin was very transparent, very pure, and of a dazzling and creamy sort of whiteness. I have seen something like it on the delicate Chinese paintings of the secluded ladies of that very secluded empire, and should imagine it just such a permanent tint as the Roman empress strove to procure by bathing every day in milk. Colour she had none, and thrilling must have been the emotions that could call it into her placid and pensive cheeks. Her features were not *chiselled*, and had any sculptor striven to imitate them on the purest marble, he would have discovered that chiselling would not do. They were at once formed and informed by the Deity. It is of no use talking about her luxurious and night-emulating hair, her lips, and those eyes, that seemed to contain, in their small compass, a whole sea of melancholy, in which love was struggling to support a half-drowned joy.

As I turned to converse with her she looked up to me confidingly. She appeared, as it were, incessantly to draw me to her with her large black eyes; they seemed to say to me, 'Come nearer to me, that I may understand thee. Art thou not something distinct from the beings that I see around me—something that can teach me what I am, and will also give me something to venerate, to idolize, and to love?' As I continued to speak to her, her attention grew into a quiet rapture, yet still a sublime melancholy seemed to hold her feelings in a solemn thraldom.

My name, my rank, and my situation were soon disclosed to the father and daughter; and the former seeing how entranced we were with each other's company, like a prudent parent, left us to ourselves. My French was much purer, and more grammatical than hers, hers much more fluent than mine. Yet, notwithstanding this deficiency on both sides, we understood each other perfectly, and we had not been above two hours together alone, before I told her that I loved her for her very ignorance, and she had confessed to me that she loved me, because—because—the reader will never guess why—because I was so like the good spirit that walked gently through the forest, and gathered up the fever-mists before they reached the dwellings of man.

I very naturally asked her if she had seen this being. She said no, but knew him as well as if she had; for old Jumbila, a negress, had so often talked to her about him, that her idea of him was as familiar to her as the presence of her father.

'You have much to unlearn, my sweet one', thought I, 'and I shall be but too happy in being your preceptor.'

At sunset, Monsieur Manuel returned, led us into another apartment, where a not inelegant dinner was served up to us. Knowing the habits of my countrymen, we sate over some very superior claret, after Josephine had retired. I took this opportunity to reproach him in the gentlest terms that I could use, with the dreadful ignorance in which he had suffered a creature so lovely and so superior to remain.

His reply was a grimace, a hoisting of his shoulders above his head, an opening of his hands and fingers to their utmost extent, and a most pathetic '*Que voulez-vous?*'

'I will tell you, friend Manuel,' I answered, for his wine had warmed me much, his daughter more; 'I would have had her taught, at least, to read and write, that she had an immortal soul, a soul as precious to its Maker as it was to herself. I would have had her taught to despise such superstitious nonsense as obeoism, mist spirits, and all the pernicious jargon of spells and fetishes. I would, my dear Manuel, have made her a fit companion for myself; for with such beauty and such a soul, I am convinced that she would realize female perfection as nearly as poor humanity is permitted to do.'

'*Que voulez-vous?*' again met my ears; but it was attended by some attempt at justification of his very culpable remissness. He assured me, that, according to the laws, social as well as judicial, a person of her class, were she possessed of all the attributes of an angel, could never be received into white society nor wed with any but a person of colour. The light of education, he asserted, would only the more show her her own degradation: he said he felt for her, deeply felt for her, and that he shuddered at the idea of his own death, for in that event he felt assured that she would be sold with the rest of the negroes on the estate, and be treated in all respects as a slave—and she had been so delicately nurtured. She had indeed:—her long white fingers and velvety hand bore sufficient testimony to this.

'But can you not manumit her?' said I.

'Impossible. When the island was more settled and better governed than now, the legal obstructions thrown in the way of the act were almost insuperable: at present it is impossible. I have no doubt that our blood-thirsty enemies, the Spaniards, who are our nearest neighbours, immediately you English leave the town, as you have dismantled our forts, and carried away almost all the male population captive, will come and take possession of this place—not that I care a sous for the brigands whom you have just routed out. I shall have to submit to the Spanish authority, and their slave laws are still more imperative than ours, though they invariably treat their slaves better than any other nation. No, there is no hope for poor Josephine.'

'Could you not send her to France?'

'*Sacré Dieu!* they guillotined all my relations, all my friends—all, all—and, my friend, I never made gold by taking a share in those long low schooners that you have kindly taken under your care. I have some boxes of doubloons stowed away, it is true. But, after all, I am attached to this place; I could not sell the estate for want of a purchaser; and I am surrounded by such an infernal set of rascals, that I never could embark myself with my hard cash without being murdered. No, we must do at Rome as the Romans do.'

'A sweet specimen of a Roman you are,' thought I, and I fell into a short reverie; but it was broken up most agreeably by seeing Josephine trip before the open jalousies with a basket of flowers in her hand. She paused for a moment before us, and looked kindly at her father and smilingly at me. It was the first joyous, really joyous smile that I had seen in her expressive countenance. It went right to my heart, and brought with it a train of the most rapturous feelings.

'God bless her heart; I do love her dearly!' said the old man. 'I'll give you a convincing proof of it, my young friend, Rattlin.

Ah! bah—but you other English have spoiled all—you have taken
him with you.'

'Who?'

'Why, Captain Durand. That large low black schooner was his.
Yes, he would have treated her well, (said Monsieur le Père,
musing,) and he offered to sign an agreement never to put her to
field work or to have her flogged.'

'Put whom to field work?—flog whom?' said I, all amazement.

'Josephine, to be sure; had you not taken him prisoner, I was
going, next month, to sell her to him for two hundred doubloons.'

'Now, may God confound you for an unholy, unnatural villain!'
said I, springing up, and overturning the table and wine into the
fatherly lap of Monsieur Manuel. 'If you did not stand there, my
host, I would, with my hand on your throat, force you on your
knees to swear that—that—that you'll never sell poor, poor
Josephine for a slave. Flog her!' said I, shuddering and the tears
starting into my eyes—'I should as soon have thought of flogging
an empress's eldest daughter.

'Be pacified, my son,' said the old slave-dealer, deliberately
clearing himself of the *débris* of the dessert—'be pacified, my son.'

The words, 'my son,' went with a strange and cheering sound
into my very heart's core. The associations that they brought with
it were blissful—I listened to him with calmness.

'Be pacified, my son,' he continued, 'and I will prove to you that
I am doing everything for the best. The old colonel, our late
governor, would have given three times the money for her. I could
not do better than make her over to a kind-hearted man, who would
use her well, and who, I think, is fond of her. Not to part with her
for a heavy sum would be fixing a stigma upon her;' and wretched
as all this reasoning appeared to be, I was convinced that the man
had really meant to have acted kindly by selling his own daughter.
What a pernicious, d——ble, atrocious social system that must
have been where such a state of things existed! Reader, this same
feature of slavery still exists,—and in free and enlightened America.

END OF VOLUME II

VOLUME III

CHAPTER I

*Ralph deserteth his duty—All for love, or 'the world well lost,'
with his wits into the bargain—Very nice disquisitions on honour.*

THE *soyez tranquille* of Monsieur Manuel had but a transient
effect. It brought no consolation with it. What I had heard seemed
to clog the usual healthy beating of my heart; my respiration
laboured, and I fell into a bitter reverie. The profoundest pity,
the most impassioned admiration, and the most ardent desire to
afford protection—are not these the ingredients that make the all-
potent draught of love? Let universal humanity reply—I loved.
But the feeling, generally so blissful, came upon my young heart,
and steeped it in the bitterness of apprehension. My bosom was
swollen with big resolves, with the deepest affection for one, and
hate for all the rest of my species; and the thought came over me
vividly, of flight with the young and pensive beauty into the in-
accessible seclusion of the woods, and of the unalloyed happiness
and the imaginary glories of a savage life. In this sudden depression of spirits, my mind looked not loathingly on mutual suicide.
It was a black and a desponding hour, and fell upon me with the
suddenness of a total eclipse on a noontide summer's day.

I sat with my clasped hands between my knees, and my head
hanging upon my breast, almost unconscious of the black servitors
around me, who were re-ordering the room that I had so recently
disarranged. I noted all this as something that did not belong to
the world in which I had existence. Every thing around me seemed
the shadows of somebody's dream, in which I had no part, and
could take no interest. I had but two all-absorbing ideas; and these
were—injustice and Josephine. So distraught was I with the vast-
ness of the one and with the loveliness of the other, that, when the
young and splendid reality stole into the apartment softly, and
moved before my eyes in all the fascination of her gracefulness, yet

s

was I scarcely conscious of the actual presence of her whose ideal existence was torturing my brain.

To the cold, the unimpassioned, or the unpoetical, this may seem impossible. I will not go into metaphysical reasonings on the subject. I only know that it was true. Whilst I was conceiving her flying from oppression with me, her protector, into some grim solitude, she came and placed herself, almost unnoticed, by my side, took my unresisting hands between her own, and, seeing how little I appeared to notice the endearment, she gradually sank on her knees before me, and, placing her forehead upon my hands, remained for a space in silence. Feeling her hot tears trickling through my fingers called me back from my dark reverie: and, as I became aware of the present, a sigh so deep and so long burst forth, and it seemed to rend my bosom.

Those dark, lustrous, melancholy eyes, swimming in tears, were then lifted up to mine. Ages of eloquence were contained in that one look. In it I read the whole story of her life, the depth of her love, the fealty of her faith, and the deep, the unspeakable prayer for sympathy, for love, and for protection. The mute appeal was unanswerable. It seemed to be conveyed to me by the voice of destiny; to my mind louder and more awful than thunder. At that moment I pledged myself eternally to her; and, gradually drawing up her yielding, light, and elastic form from my knees to my bosom, I sobbed out, 'Whilst I breathe, dearest, thou shalt never writhe under the lash;' and then, giving way to an uncontrollable passion of weeping, I mingled my tears with her's—and we were happy. Yes, our young love was baptized with tears—an ominous and a fitting rite. We cried in each other's arms like children, as we were; at first, with anguish; then, with hope and affection; and, at length, in all the luxury of a new-born bliss.

When this passion had a little subsided, and smiles, and murmuring ejaculations of happiness, had driven away the symbols of what is not always anguish, old Manuel approached, and appeared much pleased at the tokens of affection that we mutually lavished upon each other. And then, with my arm encircling Josephine's slender waist, and her fair face upon my shoulder, he began his artful discourse. Gradually, he led me to speak of myself, my friends, my views; and, ultimately, my strange and mysterious story was fully unfolded. Even in this prolonged relation, I was amply rewarded by the impassioned looks, at once so tender and so thrilling, of the beauteous listener by my side, and by the ready tear at every passage that told of suffering; the fond creature still creeping more closely to me at every instance of danger; and bright the beam of triumph would flash from her eye, responsive to every incident of my success.

When all was told, and half wondering, and faintly smiling, I finished by the rather silly expression of—'And here I am,' I was immediately imprisoned in the arms of Josephine, as she pathetically exclaimed, 'and for ever!'

'Josephine speaks well,' said Manuel, rising and placing patriarchally a hand on the head of each of us. 'My children, would it were for ever! It appears, by the narrative, that Monsieur has done us the great honour to relate that he is a castaway—an unowned—and, if my young friend makes use of all the wisdom he doubtless possesses in so high a degree, he will join us in blessing Providence, that has given the gallant young homeless one a home; for I need not tell him that all he sees around is his—the land and the house, and, to the hitherto unloved, a young and tender heart that will cherish him, to the fatherless a father.'

And thus the old *emigré* concluded his speech, with a tear glistening in his eye—and an unexceptionable bow. Had he flung himself into my arms, the effect would have been complete. I hate to record scenes of this sort; but, as I have imposed the task upon myself, I will go through it; and, though the temptation is great, seeing what I was then, the disciple as well as the offspring of romance, and what I now am, worldly in the world's most sordid worldliness, to do my penance in self-mockery—for the sake of the young hearts still unseared, I will refrain.

I was exceedingly affected and agitated at this appeal, the purport of which I could not misunderstand. My emotions, at first, prevented me from speaking. I arose from the sofa, Josephine still hanging upon my shoulder, and taking her father's hand, led them both to the window. The sun was near the horizon; and mountain, sea, and green valley, and dark forest, were steeped in a roseate glory. About three miles distant, and beneath us, my gallant frigate sate in the bosom of the gently rippling waters, like a sultana upon her embroidered divan, her ensign and her pennant streaming out fair and free to the evening breeze. I pointed to her, and with a voice scarcely articulate—for, at that period, the sob would rise too readily to my throat, and the tear start too freely to my eye—I exclaimed—

'Behold my home—my country claims the duty of a son!'

'Monsieur knows best,' said Manuel, almost coldly. 'His countrymen have conquered us: you are a gallant race, undoubtedly, but one of them has not shown much mercy to my daughter.'

The passionate girl was at my feet—yes, kneeling at my feet, and her supplicating hands were clasped in that attitude of humility that is due only to God. Who taught her the infinite pathos of that beautiful posture? Taught her! She had no teachers, save Nature and Love.

'Josephine,' said I, lifting her gently up, and kissing her fair brow, 'you are breaking my heart. I cannot stand this—I must rush out of the house. I have never said I loved you.'—(mean subterfuge!)

'But you do, you do—it is my fate—it is your's—for three years I have been expecting you—disbelieve me not—ask the Obeah woman. It is true,'—and then, hurrying out the words like the downpouring of the mountain torrent, she continued, 'Do you love me?—do you love me?—do you love me?'

'I do, Josephine—I do distractedly! But stern honour stands in the way.'

'And what is this honour?' she exclaimed with genuine simplicity; for it was evident that, if she had ever heard the word before, she had not the remotest idea of its meaning: '*Et quelle est cette honneur-là?*' and there was contempt in her tone.

I had no words to reply.

'Will this honour do that for you which my father—which I—will do? What has this honour done for him?—tell me, father. Has it put that gay blue jacket on him, or that small sword by his side? Show him, my dear father, the rich dresses that we have, and the beautiful arms. Will honour watch you in your hours of sickness, take you out in the noon-day heats, and show you the cool shady places and the refreshing rippling springs? What is this honour, that seems to bid you to break my heart, and make me die of very grief?'

'Monsieur Manuel,' said I, extremely confused, 'have the kindness to explain to dear Josephine what honour is.'

'A rule of conduct,' he replied with severity, 'that was never recorded, never understood, and which men construe just as suits their convenience. One honest impulse of the heart is worth all the honour I ever heard of.'

This was a delicate helping of a friend in a dilemma. I turned for relief from the sarcastic father to the beautiful countenance of the daughter, and I there beheld an expression of intense sorrow that agonized me. Her sudden and, to me, totally unexpected animation had disappeared: Melancholy seemed to have drooped her darkest wings over her. I thought that she must soon die under their noxious shadow. For one instant, my eyes caught her's: I could not stand the appeal.

'I will stay,' said I gently, 'until the ship sails.'

I had then, for the first time, to witness the enthusiasm of the melancholy temperament—the eloquence of unschooled nature. The bending figure, that seemed to collapse in weakness upon my supporting arm, suddenly flung herself from me; her rounded and delicate figure swelled at once into sudden dignity; her muscles assumed the rigidity, yet all the softness of a highly-polished Grecian statue; and stood before me, as if by enchantment, half woman, half marble, beautiful inexpressibly. I was sorely tried. There was no action, no waving of the arms, as she spoke. Her voice came forth musically, as if from some sacred oracle, that oracle having life only in words. Monsieur Manuel had very wisely departed.

'Not an hour—not a minute—not an instant, or—*for ever!* Young sir, you have already staid too long, if you stay not always. Leave me to dream of you, and to die. The thorn is in my heart: it may kill me gradually. Go. Why, sir, have you looked upon me as man never before looked? Why, why have you mingled your false tears with mine, that were so true—and, oh, so loving! But what am I, who thus speak so proudly to a being, whom, if I did not know he was treacherous, I should think an angel? (*un des bons esprits*). I, a poor, weak, ignorant girl of colour—born of a slave, to slavery—whose only ambition was to have been loved, loved for a short, short while—for know, that I am to die early—I should not have troubled you long. But you are too good for me—I was a presumptuous fool. Go, and at once, and take with you all that I have to give—the blessing of a young born-bondswoman.'

All this time she had stood firmly and nearly motionless, with her hands folded beneath her heaving bosom, at some distance from me. I approached her with extended arms, and had some such foolish rhapsody on my tongue as 'Beautiful daughter of the sun,' for I had already contemplated her under a new character, when, retreating and waving me from her, she continued—

'Already too much of this—let me die by cruelty rather than by caresses, which are the worst of cruelty. I feel a new spirit living within me. I am a child no more. Yesterday I should have crouched before you, as one degraded, as I ought to do. You have pressed me to your bosom—you have spoken to me as your equal—even your tears have bathed my brow. You have ennobled me. Oh! it is a happiness and a great glory. I, formerly so humble, command you to go—go, dear, dear, Ralph. You will not kill me quite by going *now*, therefore, be generous, and go.'

I was already sufficiently in love, and began to feel ashamed of myself, for not having, as yet, caught a little of her enthusiasm.

'Josephine,' said I, in a quiet, serious tone, 'give me your hand.' I took it—it was deadly cold. At that moment all her best blood was rallying round her young heart. I led her to the open window, and showed her the noble frigate so hateful to her sight, and said, 'Dear Josephine, in that ship there are more than three hundred gallant fellows, all of whom are my countrymen, and some of them my familiar friends. I have often shared with them danger, unto the very jaws of death. I have broken my bread with some of them, constantly, for nearly three years. These are all claims on me: you see that I am speaking to you calmly. I had no idea what a little impassioned orator you were—do not look so dejected and so humble. I love you for it the more. I only made the remark to convince you that what I now say is not the mere prompting of a transient impulse. But, Josephine, in my own far-away land, I have also a few friends; nor am I wholly a castaway; there is a mystery about my origin, which I wish to dissipate, yet that I cherish. If I conduct myself as I have hitherto done, in time I shall have the sole control and government of a vessel, as proud as the one before you, and of all the noble spirits it will contain. The mystery of which I have spoken I am most sanguine will be cleared up; and I may, peradventure, one day take my place among the nobles of my land, as it now is among the nobles of the sea. Weep not thus, my love, or you will infect me with emotions too painful to be borne. Let us be calm for a little space. The reign of passion will commence soon enough. Mark me, Josephine. For you—God forgive me if I commit sin!—for you, I cast off my associates, sever all my ties of friendship, let the mystery of my origin remain

unravelled, renounce the land of my birth—for you, I encounter
the peril of being hung for desertion. Josephine, you will incur
a great debt—a heavy responsibility. My heart, my happiness, is in
your hands. Josephine, I stay.'

'For ever?'

'For ever!' A wild shriek of joy burst from her delighted lips,
as she leaped to my bosom; and, for the first time, our lips sealed
the mysterious compact of love. After a moment, I gently released
myself from the sweet bondage of her embrace, and said, 'Dear
Josephine, this cannot be to me a moment of unalloyed joy. You
see the sun is half below the horizon; give me one moment of
natural grief; for, so surely as I stay here, so surely, like that orb,
are all my hopes of glory setting, and for ever.' And the tears came
into my eyes as I exclaimed, 'Farewell, my country—farewell,
honour—Eos, my gallant frigate, fare thee well!'

As if instinct with life, the beautiful vessel answered my
apostrophe. The majestic thunder of her main-deck gun boomed
awfully, and methought sorrowfully, over the waters, and then
bounded among the echoes of the distant hills around and above
me, slowly dying away in the distant mountains. It was the gun
which, as commodore, was fired at sunset.

'It is all over,' I exclaimed. 'I have made my election—leave me
for a little while alone.'

CHAPTER II

Ralph falleth into the usual delusion of supposing himself happy—
wisheth it may last all his life, making it a reality—As yet no
symptoms of it dispelling; but the brightest sunset may have the
darkest night.

SHE bounded from me in a transport of joy, shouting, 'He stays,
he stays!' and I heard the words repeated among the groups of
Negresses, who loved her; it seemed to be the burthen of a general
song, the glad realization of some prophecy; for, ere the night was
an hour old, the old witch, who had had the tuition of Josephine,
had already made a mongrel sort of hymn of the affair, whilst
a circle of black chins were wagging to a chorus of
'Goramity good, buchra body stays!'

I saw no more of Josephine that night. The old gentleman, her father, joined me after I had been alone nearly two hours—two hours, I assure the reader, of misery.

I contemplated a courtship of some decent duration, and a legal marriage at the altar. I tried to view my position on all sides, and thus to find out that which was the most favourable for my mind's eye to rest upon. It was but a disconsolate survey. Sometimes a dark suspicion, that I repelled from me as if it were a demon whispering murder in my ear, would hint to me the possibility that I was entrapped. However, the lights that came in with Monsieur Manuel dissipated them and darkness together. He behaved extremely well —gave me an exact account of all his possessions, and of his ready money, the latter of which was greatly beyond my expectations, and the former very considerable.

He immediately gave me an undertaking, that he would, if I remained with him, adopt me as his son, allow me during his life a competency fit to support me and his daughter genteelly, and to make me his sole heir at his death. This undertaking bound him also to see the proper documents duly and legally drawn up by a notary, so as to render the conditions of our agreement binding on both parties. We then spoke, as father and son, of our future views. We were determined to leave the island, immediately we could get any thing like its value for the plantation and the large gang of Negroes upon it. But where go to then? England?—my desertion. France?—yes, it was there that we were to spend our lives. And thus we speculated on future events, that the future never owned.

I have said before that, during the whole time that I was in the navy, I never was intoxicated—and never once swallowed spirituous liquors. Both assertions are strictly true. This memorable evening, over our light supper, I drank, perhaps, two glasses of claret more than was my wont at Captain Reud's table. I was excessively wearied, both in mind and body. I became so unaccountably and lethargically drowsy, that, in spite of every effort of mine to the contrary, I fell fast asleep in the midst of a most animated harangue of the good Manuel, upon the various perfections of his lovely daughter—a strange subject for a lover to sleep upon; but so it was. Had Josephine's nurse and the Obeah woman any thing to do with it? Perhaps. They are skilful druggers. If my life, and the lives of all those dearer to me than life itself, had depended upon my getting up and walking across the room, I could not have done it. How I got to bed I know not; but I awoke in the morning in luxuriant health, with a blushing bride upon my bosom.

And then ensued days of dreamy ecstacy; my happiness seemed too great, too full, too overflowing, to be real. Every thing around me started into poetry. I seemed to be under the direction of fairy spirits: all my wants were cared for as if by invisible hands. It appeared to me that I had but to wish, and gratification followed before the wish was half formed. I was passive, and carried away in a trance of happiness. I was beset with illusions; and so intense were my feelings of rapture, mingled with doubt, and my blissful distraction so great, that it was late in the day before I noticed the dress I had on. The light and broad-brimmed planter's hat, the snowy white jean jacket and trowsers, and the infinitely fine linen shirt, with its elaborately laced front, had all been donned without my noticing the change from my usual apparel. It was a dress, from its purity and its elegance, worthy of a bridegroom. I learnt afterwards, that Josephine's old Negress-nurse had, with many and powerful incantations—at least, as powerful as incantations always are—buried under six feet of earth every article of clothing in which I had first entered the mansion.

Well, there we were, a very pretty version of Paul and Virginia[1] —not perhaps quite so innocent, but infinitely more happy, roving hand in hand through orange bowers and aromatic shades. Love is sweet, and a first love very, very delightful; but, when we are not only loved, but almost worshipped, that, that is the incense that warms the heart and intoxicates the brain. Wherever I turned, I found greeting and smiles, and respectful observance hovered along my path. The household adored their young mistress, and me through her.

Old Manuel seemed serenely happy. He encouraged us to be alone with each other. I could write volumes upon the little incidents, and interesting ones too, of this singular honeymoon. I observed no more bursts of passion in Josephine; her soul had folded its wings upon my bosom, and there dreamed itself away in a tender and loving melancholy. How I now smile, and perhaps could weep, when I call to mind all her little artifices of love to prevent my ever casting my eyes upon the hated ship! As I have related before, our little squadron at anchor in this secluded bay departed one by one, leaving only the Eos, with her sorely-wounded captain; yet, though I saw them not, I knew, by Josephine's triumphant looks, when a vessel had sailed. All the *jalousies*[1] in front of the house were nailed up, so that, if by chance I wandered into one of the rooms in that quarter, I saw nothing.

I had been domesticated in this paradise—a fool's, perhaps, but still a paradise—a month; and I was sitting alone in the shade, reading, behind the house, when Josephine flew along the avenue of lemon-trees, and flung herself into my arms, and, sobbing hysterically, exclaimed, 'My dear, dear Ralph, now you are almost wholly mine! there is only one left.'

'And that one, my Josephine?'

'Speak not of it, think not of it, sweet; it is not your's. But, swear, swear to me again, you will never more look upon it; do, dearest, and I will learn a whole column extra of words in two syllables.'

And I repeated the often-iterated oath; and she sate down tranquilly at my feet, like a good little girl, and began murmuring the task she was committing to memory.

And how did the schooling get on? Oh! beautifully; we had such sweet and so many school-rooms, and interruptions still more sweet and numerous. Sometimes, our hall of study was beneath the cool rock, down the sides of which, green with age, the sparkling rill so delightfully trickled; sometimes, in the impervious, quiet, and flower-enamelled bower, amidst all the spicy fragrance of tropical shrubs; and sometimes in the solemn old wood, beneath the boughs of trees that had stood for uncounted ages. And the interruptions! Repeatedly the book and the slate would be cast away, and we would start up, as if actuated by a single spirit, and chase some singularly beautiful humming-bird; sometimes, the genius of frolic would seize us, and we would chase each other round and round the old mahogany trees, with no other object than to rid ourselves of our exuberance of happiness; but the most frequent interruptions were when she would close her book, and, bathing me in the lustre of her melancholy eyes, bid me tell her some tale that would make her weep; or, with a pious awe, request me to unfold some of the mysteries of the universe around her, and commune with her of the attributes of their great and beneficent Creator.

Was not this a state of the supremest happiness? Joy seemed to come down to me from heaven in floods of light; the earth to offer up her incense to me, as I trod upon her beautiful and flower-encumbered bosom; the richly-plumaged birds to hover about me,

as if sent to do me homage; even the boughs of the majestic trees
as I passed them seemed to wave to me a welcome. Joy was in me
and around me; there was no pause in my blissful feelings. I
required no relaxation to enjoy them the more perfectly, for
pleasure seemed to succeed pleasure in infinite variety. It was too
glorious to last. The end was approaching, and that end was
very bitter.

CHAPTER III

A short chapter and a miserable one—the less that is said of it the
better.

I HAD been living in the plantation nearly three months. My little
wife, for such I held her to be, had made much progress in her
education—more in my affection she could not. I had already put
her into joining hand; and I began to be as proud of her dawning
intellect as I was of her person and of her love. I had renounced my
country, and, in good faith, I had intended to have held by her for
ever; and, when I should find myself in a country where marriage
with one born in slavery was looked upon as no opprobrium, I had
determined that the indissoluble ceremony should be legally performed. To do all this I was in earnest; but, events, or destiny, or
by whatever high-sounding term we may call those occurrences
which force us on in a path we wish not to tread, ruled it fearfully
otherwise.

I religiously abstained from looking towards the ship, or even
the sea; yet, I plainly saw, by the alternations of hope, and joy,
and fear, on Josephine's sweet countenance, that something of the
most vital importance was about to take place. They could not
conceal from me that parties of men had been searching for me,
because, for a few days, I had been in actual hiding with Josephine,
three or four miles up in the woody mountain. I must hurry over
all this; for the recollection of it, even at this great lapse of time, is
agonizing. The night before the Eos sailed she would not sleep—
her incessant tears, the tremulous energy with which she clasped
me and held me for hours, all told the secret that I wished not to
know. All that night she watched, as a mother watches a departing

and a first-born child—tearfully—anxiously—but, overcome with fatigue and the fierce contention of emotions as the morning dawned, her face drooped away from mine, her clasping arms gradually relaxed, and, murmuring my name with a blessing, she slept. Did she ever sleep again? May God pardon me, I know not!

I hung over her, and watched her, almost worshipping, until two hours after sunrise. I blessed her as she lay there in all her tranquil beauty, fervently, and, instead of my prayers, I repeated over and over again my oath, that I would never desert her. But some devil, in order to spread the ashes of bitterness through the long path of my after-life, suggested to me that now, as the frigate had sailed for some time, there could be no danger in taking one last look at her; indeed, the thought of doing so took the shape of a duty.

I stole out of bed, and crept softly round to the front of the house. The place where the gallant ship had rode at anchor for so many weeks was vacant—all was still and lonely. I walked on to a higher spot; and, far distant among the sinuosities of the romantic entrance to the harbour, my eye caught for a moment her receding pennant. I, therefore, concluded that every thing was safe—that I was cut off, and for ever, from my country.

A little qualm of remorse passed through my bosom, and then I was exceeding glad. The morning was fresh, and the air invigorating, and I determined to walk down to the beautiful minutely-sanded beach, and enjoy the refreshment of the sea-breeze just sweeping gently over the bay. To do this I had to pass over a shoulder of land to my left. I gained the beach, and stood upon it for some minutes with folded arms. This particular walk had been so long debarred to me, that I now enjoyed it the more. I was upon the point of turning round and seeking the nest where I had left my dove sleeping in conscious security, when, to my horror, I beheld the Eos's pinnace, full-manned and double-banked, the wave foaming up her cutwater, and roaring under her sixteen oars, rapidly round the rocky hummock that formed the eastern horn of the little bay. Her prow soon tore up the sand; and the third lieutenant, a master's mate, and the officer of marines, with four privates, leaped ashore immediately.

For a few moments I was paralysed with terror, and then, suddenly springing forward, I ran at the top of my speed. I need not say that my pursuers gave chase heartily. I had no other choice but to run on straight before me; and that unfortunately was up a rocky, rugged side of a steep hill, that rose directly from the beach, covered with that abominable vegetable, or shrub, the prickly pear. I was in full view; and, being hailed, and told that I should be fired upon if I did not bring-to, in the space of a short three minutes, before I was out of breath, I was in the hands of my captors—a prisoner.

I prayed—I knelt—I wept. It was useless. I have scarcely the courage to write what then took place, it was so fearful—it was so hideous. Bounding down the hill, in her night-dress, her long black hair streaming like a meteor behind her, and her naked feet, usually so exquisitely white, covered with blood, came Josephine, shrieking, 'Ralph! Ralph!' Her voice seemed to stab my bosom like an actual knife. Behind her came running her father, and a number of Negro men and women. Before she could reach me, they had flung me into the stern sheets of the boat.

'Shove off! shove off!' shouted the lieutenant, and the boat was immediately in motion. Like a convicted felon, or a murderer taken in the fact, I buried my craven head in my knees, and shut my eyes. I would not have looked back for kingdoms. But, I could not, or did not, think of preventing myself from hearing. The boat had not pulled ten yards from the beach, when I heard a splash behind us, and simultaneous cries of horror from the boat's crew and those on shore; among which the agonized voice of the heart-broken father rose shrilly, as he exclaimed, 'Josephine, my child!' I looked up for a moment, but dared not look round; and I saw every man in the boat dashing away the tears from his eyes with one hand, as he reluctantly pulled his oar with the other.

'Give way! give way!' roared the lieutenant, stamping violently against the grating at his feet. 'Give way! or, by G—d, she'll over-take us!'

The poor girl was swimming after me.

'Rattlin,' said Selby, stooping down and whispering in my ear, 'Rattlin, I can't stand it; if it was not as much as my life was worth, I would put you on shore directly.' I could answer him only by a long convulsive shudder. The horrible torment of those moments!

Then ascended the loud howling curses of the Negroes behind us. The seamen rose up upon their oars, and, with a few violent jerks, the pinnace shot round the next point of land, and the poor struggler in the waters was seen no more. Tidings never after came to me of her. I left her struggling in the waters of the ocean. My first love, and my last—my only one.

I was taken on board stupified. I was led up the side like a sick man. No one reproached me; no one spoke to me. I became physically, as well as mentally, ill. I went to my hammock with a stern feeling of joy, hoping soon to be lashed up in it, and find my grave in the deep blue sea. At first, my only consolation was enacting over and over again all the happy scenes with Josephine; but, as they invariably terminated in one dreadful point, this occupation became hateful. I then endeavoured to blot the whole transaction from my memory—to persuade myself that the events had not been real—that I had dreamed them—or read them long ago in some old book. But, the mind is not so easily cheated—remorse not so soon blinded.

CHAPTER IV

The Captain taketh to tantrums—and keepeth on board monkeys, bears, and discipline. It is feared, also, that the moon hath too much to do with his observations.

NOTWITHSTANDING my misery, I became convalescent. I went to my duty doggedly. Every body saw and respected my grief; and the affair was never mentioned to me by any, with one only exception, and that was six months after, by a heavy brutal master's mate, named Pigtop, who had been in the pinnace that brought me off.

He came close to me, and, without preparation, he electrified me by drawling out, 'I say, Rattlin, what a mess you made of it at Aniana! That girl of your's, to my thinking, burst a blood-vessel as she was giving you chase. I saw the blood bubble out of her mouth and nose.'

'Liar!' I exclaimed, and, seizing a heavy block that one of the afterguard was fitting, I felled him to the deck.

The base-hearted poltroon went and made his complaint to Captain Reud, who ordered him to leave the ship immediately he came into harbour.

We must now retrograde a little in the narrative, in order to

show what events led to the disastrous catastrophe I have just
related. Captain Reud, having been lying for many, many weeks,
apparently unconscious of objects around him, one morning said,
in a faint, low voice, when Dr. Thompson and Mr. Farmer, the
first lieutenant, were standing near him, 'Send Ralph Rattlin to
read the Bible to me.'

Now, since my absence, some supposed I had been privately
stabbed by one of the few ferocious and angry marauders still left
in the town; but, as no traces of my body could be found, still more
of my shipmates believed that I had deserted. In plain sincerity,
these latter friends of mine were, as our Transatlantic brethren say,
pretty considerably, slap-dashically right. However, as the shock
to the wounded captain would have been the greater to say that
I had been assassinated, they chose the milder alternative, and told
him that 'they feared that I had deserted.'

Captain Reud merely said, 'I don't believe it,' turned his face
to the bulkhead, and remained silent for three or four days more.
Still, as he was proceeding towards convalescence, he began to be
more active, or, rather, ordered more active measures to be taken
to clear up the mystery of my disappearance. Parties were consequently sent to scour the country for miles round; but I was too
well concealed to permit them to be of any utility. The only two
seamen that had seen me near Manuel's premises belonged to the
frigate, which had sailed before my captain had recovered his
faculties.

But I was not to be so easily given up; perhaps he remembered
that what remained of life to him was preserved by me, and, notwithstanding his cruel usage, I well knew that he entertained for
me a sincere affection. As the Eos got under weigh, after remaining
so long at anchor in the port, that the men observed she would
shortly ground upon the beef-bones that their active masticators
had denuded and which were thrown overboard, the wind was
light, and the boats were all out towing, with the exception of the
pinnace, which was ordered to sweep round the bay and look into
all the inlets, in order to seek for some vestige of my important self.
For good or for evil, the heart-rending results ensued.

How short is the real romance of life! A shout of joy—a pulsation
of ecstasy—and it is over! In the course of my eventful life, I have
seen very fair faces and very many beautiful forms. The fascina-
tions of exterior loveliness I have met combined with high intellect,

unswerving principles, and virtuous emotions, awful from their very holiness. The fair possessors of many of these lofty attributes I have sometimes wooed and strove to love; but, though I often sighed and prayed for a return of that heart-whole and absorbing passion, there was no magic, no charm, to call the dead embers into life. That young and beautiful savage swept from my bosom all the tenderer stuff: she collected the fresh flowers of passion, and left —— it is of no consequence—Josephine, farewell.

Let us talk idly. It is a droll world: let us mock each other, and call it mirth. There is my poor half-deranged captain cutting such antics that even authority with the two-edged sword[1] in his hand cannot repress the outbursting of ignoble derision. First of all, he takes a mania for apes and monkeys; disrates all his midshipmen, taking care, however, that they still do their duty; and makes the ship's tailor rig out their successors in uniform. The officers are aghast, for the maniac is so cunning, and the risk of putting a superior officer under an arrest so tremendous, that they know not what to do. Besides, their captain is only mad on one subject at one time. Indeed, insanity seems sometimes to find a vent in monomania, actually improving all the faculties on all other points. Well, the monkey midshipmen did not behave very correctly; so, Captain Reud had them one forenoon all tied up to one of his guns in the cabin, and, one after the other, well flogged with the cat-o'-nine-tails. It was highly ludicrous to see the poor fellows waiting each for his turn, well knowing what was to come; they never, than when under the impression of their fears, looked more human. That night they stole into the cabin, by two and three, in the dead of the night, and nearly murdered their persecutor. This looked very like combination, and a exercise of faculties that may be nearly termed reasoning.

They were all thrown overboard. The next phantasy was the getting up of the forecastle carronades into the tops, thereby straining the ship and nearly carrying away the masts. That folly wore out, and the guns came down to their proper places. Then a huge bear came on board—a very gentlemanly, digni-fied fellow; never in a hurry, and who always moved about with a gracious deliberation. Captain Reud amused himself by endeavouring to teach him to dance; and a worthless black-guard who could play on the pipe and tabor, and who probably had led a bear about the country, was taken into especial grace and was loaded with benefits, in order to assist his captain in his singular avocations.

'Come and see my bear dance, do come and see him dance,' was now the little Creole's continual cry. But the bear did not take his tuition kindly, and grew daily more ferocious; till, at length, seizing his opportunity, he caught up the diminutive skipper and nearly hugged the breath out of his body, and almost rubbed his red nose off his yellow face in endeavouring to bite him through his muzzle. The star of Ursa Major was no longer in the ascendant, and he was bartered away, with the master of the first merchant vessel we met, for a couple of gamecocks; and the bear-leader was turned back into the waist, and flogged the next day for impertinence, whilst, two days before, the vagabond was too proud to say 'sir' to a middy.

But it would be ridiculous to enumerate the long succession of these insane whimsicalities, each later one being more *bizarre* than the preceding.

Whether man be mad or not, Christmas will come round again. Now, Jack, from time immemorial, thinks that he has a right undeniable to get drunk on that auspicious day. In harbour, that right is not discussed by his officers, but is usually exercised *sub silentio* under their eyes, with every thing but silence on the part of the exercisers. Even at sea, without the ship be in sight of the enemy, or it blows hard enough to blow the ship's coppers overboard, our friends think it hard, very hard, to have their cups scored next morning upon their back; and, indeed, to keep all a frigate's crew from intoxication on a Christmas-day would be something like undertaking the labour of Sisyphus,[1] for, as fast as one man could be frightened or flogged into sobriety, another would become glorious.

It was for this very reason that Captain Reud, the Christmas-day after he had received his wound, undertook the task; and, as the weather was fine, he hoped to find it not quite so hard as rolling a stone up a steep hill, and invariably seeing it bound down again before it attains the coveted summit. Immediately after breakfast, he had the word passed fore and aft that no man should be drunk that day, and that six dozen, (not of wine), would be the reward of any who should dare, in the least, to infringe that order. What is drunkenness? What it is we can readily pronounce, when we see a man under its revolting phases. What is not drunkenness

T

is more hard to say. Is it not difficult to ascertain the nice line that separates excitement from incipient delirium? Not at all, to a man like Captain Reud. To understand a disease thoroughly, a physician will tell you that you will be much assisted by the having suffered from it yourself. Upon this self-evident principle, our Æsculapius with the epaulettes was the first man drunk in the ship. After dinner that day, he had heightened his testing powers with an unusual, even to him, share of claret.

Well, at the usual time, we beat to quarters; that is always done just before the hammocks are piped down; and it is then that the sobriety of the crew, as they stand to their guns, is narrowly looked into by the respective officers; for then the grog has been served out for the day, and it is supposed to have been all consumed. The captain, of course, came on the quarter-deck to quarters, making tack and half tack, till he fairly threw out his starboard grappling iron, and moored himself to one of the belaying-pins round the mizen-mast.

'Mister Farmer,' said he to the first luff, 'you see I know how to keep a ship in discipline—not (hiccup) a man drunk on board of her.'

'I doubt it, sir,' was the respectful answer. 'I think, sir, I can see one now,' said he, taking his eyes off his superior, after a searching glance, and looking carelessly around.

'Where is he?'

'Oh, sir, we must not forget that it is Christmas-day: so, if you please, sir, we will not scrutinize very particularly.'

'But we will scru—scrutinize very particularly: remember me of scru—scrutinize, Mister Rattlin—a good word that scru—screws —trenails—tenpenny nails—hammers—iron-clamps, and dog-fastenings—what were we talking about, Mr. Farmer? Oh; sobriety! we will—assuredly (hiccup) find out the drunken man.'

So, with a large *cortège* of officers, the master-at-arms, and the ship's corporals, Captain Reud leaning his right arm heavily upon my left shoulder—for he was cunning enough, just then, to find that the gout was getting into his foot—we proceeded round the ship on our voyage of discovery. Now, it is no joke for a man half drunk to be tried for drunkenness by one wholly so. It was a curious and a comic sight, that examination—for many of the examined were conscious of a cup too much. These invariably endeavoured to look the most sober. As we approached the various groups around each gun, the different artifices of the men to pass muster were most amusing. Some drew themselves stiffly up, and looked as rigid as iron-stanchions; others took the examination with an easy, *debonnair* air, as if to say, 'Who so innocent as I?' Some again, not exactly liking the judge, quietly dodged round, shifting places with their shipmates, so that when the captain peered into the eyes of the last for the symptoms of ebriety, the mercurial rascals had quietly placed themselves first.

To the sharp, startling accusation, 'You are drunk, sir,' the answers were beautifully various. The indignant 'No, sir!'—the well-acted surprise, 'I, sir?'—the conciliatory 'God bless your honour, no, sir!'—the logical 'Bill Bowling was cook to-day, sir,' —and the sarcastic, 'No more than your honour's honour,' to witness, were, as we small wits say, better than a play.

The search was almost unavailing. The only fish that came to the net was a poor idiotic young man, that, to my certain knowledge, had not tasted grog for months; for his messmates gave him a hiding whenever he asked for his allowance. To the sudden 'You're drunk, sir,' of Captain Reud, the simple youth, taken by surprise, and perhaps thinking it against the articles of war to contradict the captain, said, 'Yes, sir; but I haven't tasted grog since——'

'You got drunk, sir; take him aft, master-at-arms, and put him in irons.'

The scrutiny over, our temperate captain went aft himself, glorifying that, in all the ship's company, there was only one instance of intoxication on Christmas-day; and thus he delivered himself, hiccuping, on the gratifying occasion—

'I call that discipline, Mr. Farmer. The only drunken man in his Majesty's vessel under my command, aft on the poop in irons, and that fellow not worth his salt.'

'I quite agree with you,' said the sneering purser, 'that the only fellow who has dared to get disgracefully drunk to-day is not worth his salt, but he is not in irons, aft on the poop.'

'I am sure he is not,' said the first lieutenant.

'That is as—astonishing,' said the mystified extirpator of intemperance, as he staggered into his cabin, to console himself for, and to close his labours with, the two other bottles.

The reader will perceive, from these incidents, that it was time that Captain Reud retired to enjoy his laurels on his *solum natale*,

in *otium cum* as much *dignitate* as would conduce to the happiness
of one of his mischief-loving temperament. The admiral on the
station thought so too, when Reud took the ship into Port Royal.
He superseded the black pilot, and took upon himself to con the
ship; the consequence was, that she hugged the point so closely,
that she went right upon the church steeple of old Port Royal,
which is very quietly lying beside the new one, submerged by an
earthquake, and a hole was knocked in the ship's forefoot,[1] of that
large and ruinous description, which may be aptly compared to
the hole in a patriot's reputation, who has lately taken office with
his quondam opponents. With all the efforts of all the fleet, who
sent relays of hands on board of us to work the pumps, we could
not keep her afloat; so we were obliged, first putting a thrummed
sail under her bottom, to tow her alongside of the dock-yard
wharf, lighten her, and lash her to it.

The same evening, by nine o'clock, she had an empty hull, and
all the ship's company and officers were located in the dock-yard,
and preparations were made, the next day, for heaving the frigate
down. It was the opinion of every body that, had not our skipper
been the nephew of the very high official of the Admiralty,[2] he
would have been tried by a court-martial, for thus attempting to
overturn submarine churches, and cracking the bottom of his
majesty's beautiful frigate. As it was, we were only ordered to be
repaired with all haste, and to go home, very much indeed to the
satisfaction of every body but the captain himself.

As I never intended this to be a mere journal of my life, I have
omitted a multiplicity of occurrences highly interesting in themselves, but which, if they were related, would swell the work to
a small library; as they were not immediately personal to myself,
I have omitted even to enumerate them.

CHAPTER V

A fever case, and a potion of love, if not altogether a love-potion—
What are the doctors about when men die despite of their knowledge,
and are cured without it? Ralph knoweth not.

HOWEVER, I must retrograde. It may seem surprising that I have
made so little mention of my messmates, for it would seem that,
to a midshipman, the affairs and characters of midshipmen would
be paramount. To me they were not so, for reasons that I have
before stated. Besides, our berth was like an eastern caravansary,
or the receiving-room of a pest-house. They all died, were promoted, or went into other ships, excepting two, and myself, who
returned to England. It must not be supposed that we were without young gentlemen; sometimes we had our full complement,
sometimes half. Fresh ones came, and they died, and so on. Before
I had time to form friendships with them, or to study their characters, they took their long sleep beneath the palisades, or were
thrown overboard in their hammocks. This was much the case
with the wardroom officers. The first lieutenant, the doctor, and
the purser, were the only original ones that returned to England
with us. The mortality among the assistant-surgeons was dreadful;
they messed with us. Indeed, I have no recollection of the names,
or even the persons of the majority of those with whom I ate, and
drank, and acted, they being so prone to prove this a transitory
world.

We were tolerably healthy till the capture of St. Domingo;
when, being obliged to convey a regiment of French soldiers to the
prisons at Port Royal, they brought the fever in its worst form on
board, and, notwithstanding every remedial measure that the then
state of science could suggest, we never could eradicate the germs
of it. The men were sent on board of a hulk, the vessel thoroughly
cleansed and fumigated and, finally, we were ordered as far north
as New Providence; but all these means were ineffectual, for, at
intervals, nearly regular, the fever would again appear, and men
and officers die.

Hitherto, I had escaped. The only attack to which I was subjected took place in the capstan-house, for so the place was called
where we were bivouacked during the heaving down of the ship.

I record it, not that my conduct under the disease may be imitated, but on account of the singularity of the access, and the rapidity of the cure.

I had to tow, from Port Royal up to Kingston, a powder-hoy, and, through some misconduct of the cockswain, the boat's awning had been left behind. Six or seven hours under a sun, vertical at noon, through the hottest part of the day, and among the swamps and morasses, so luxuriant in vegetable productions, that separate Port Royal from Kingston, is a good ordeal by which to try a European constitution. For the first time, my stamina seemed inclined to succumb before it.

When I returned to Port Royal, at about four in the afternoon, the first peculiar sensation with which I was attacked was a sort of slipping of the ground from under me as I trod, and a notion that I could skim along the surface of the earth if I chose, without using my legs. Then I was not, as is most natural to a fasting midshipman, excessively hungry, but excessively jocular. So, instead of seeking good things to put into my mouth, I went about dispensing them from out of it. I soon began to be sensible that I was talking much nonsense, and to like it. At length, the little sense that I had still left was good enough to suggest to me that I might be distinguished by my first interview with that king of terrors, Saffron-crowned Jack. 'Shall I go to the doctor?' said I. 'No—I have the greatest opinion of Doctor Thompson—but it is a great pity that he cannot cure the yellow fever. No doubt he'll be offended, and we are the greatest of friends. But, I have always observed, that all those who go to the doctor begin going indeed—for, from the doctor, they invariably go to their hammocks—from their hammocks to the hospital—and from the hospital to the palisades.' So, while there was yet time, I decided to go in quite an opposite direction. I went out of the dock-yard gates, and to a nice, matronly, free mulatto, who was a mother to me—and something more. She was a woman of some property, and had a very strong gang of young Negroes, that she used to hire out to his Majesty, to work in his Majesty's dock-yard, and permit, for certain considerations, to caulk the sides and bottoms of his Majesty's vessels of war.

Notwithstanding this intimate connexion between his Majesty and herself, she did not disdain to wash, or cause to be washed, the shirts and stockings of his Majesty's officers of the navy; that is, if she liked those officers. Now, she was kind enough to like me exceedingly; and, though very pretty, and not yet very old, all in a very proper and platonic manner. She was also a great giver of dignity balls, and, when she was full dressed, Miss Belinda Bellarosa was altogether a very seductive personage. A warrant officer was her abomination. She had refused the hands of many master's mates, and I knew 'for true,' to use her own bewitching idiom, that several lieutenants had made her the most honourable overtures.

Well, to Miss Belinda I made the best of my way. I am choice in my phrases. I could hardly make my way at all, for a strange sort of delirium was supervening. Immediately she saw me, she exclaimed, 'Ah, Goramity! him catched for sure—it break my heart to see him. You know I lub Massa Rattlin, like my own piccaninny. S'elp me God, he very bad!'

'My queen of countless Indians! dear duchess of doubloons! marry me to-night, and then you'll be a jolly widow to-morrow!'

'Hear him! him! how talk of marry me?'

'Oh! Bella, dear, if you will not kill me with kindness, what shall I do? I cannot bear this raging pain in my head. You've been a kind soul to me. Pardon my nonsense, I could not help it. Let one of your servants help me to walk to the doctor.'

'Nebber, nebber, doctor!' and she spat upon the floor with a sovereign contempt. 'Ah, Massa Ralph, me lub you dearly—you sleep here to-night—me lose my reputation—nebber mind you dat. What for you no run, Dorcas, a get me, from Massa Jackson's store, bottle good port? Tell him for me, Missy Bellarosa. You Phœbe, you oder woman of colour dere, why you no take Massa Ralph, and put him in best bed? Him bad, for certainly—make haste, or poor Buckra boy die.'

So, with the assistance of my two dingy hand-maidens, I was popped into bed, and, according to the directions of my kind hostess, a suffocating number of blankets heaped upon me. Shortly afterwards, and when my reeling senses were barely sane enough to enable me to recognise objects, my dear doctress, with two more Negresses, to witness to her reputation, entered, and putting the bottle of port, with a white powder floating at the top of it, into a china bowl, compelled me to drink off the whole of it. Then, with a look of great and truly motherly affection, she took her leave of me, telling the two nurses to put another blanket on me, and to hold me down in the bed if I attempted to get out.

Then began the raging agony of fever. I felt as one mass of sentient fire. I had a foretaste of that state which, I hope, we shall all escape, save one, of ever burning and never consuming; but, though moments of such suffering tell upon the wretch with the duration of ages, this did not last more than half an hour, when they became exchanged for a dream, the most singular, and that never will be forgotten whilst memory can offer me one single idea.

Methought that I was suddenly whisked out of bed, and placed in the centre of an interminable plain of sand. It bounded the horizon like a level sea: nothing was to be seen but this white and glowing sand, the intense blue and cloudless sky, and, directly above me, the eternal sun, like the eye of an angry God, pouring down intolerable fires upon my unprotected head. At length, my skull opened, and, from the interior of my head, a splendid temple seemed to arise. Rows of columns supported rows of columns, order was piled upon order, and, as it rose, Babel-like, to the skies, it extended in width as it increased in height; and there, in this strange edifice, I saw the lofty, the winding, the interminable stair-case, the wide and marble-paved courts; nor was there wanting the majestic and splashing fountain, whose cool waters were mocking my scorched-up lips; and there were also the long range of beautiful statues. The structure continued multiplying itself until all the heavens were full of it, extending nearly to the horizon all around.

Under this superincumbent weight I long struggled to stand. It kept bearing down more and more heavily upon the root of my brain: the anguish became insufferable, but I still nobly essayed to keep my footing, with a defiance and a pride that savoured of impious presumption. At length, I felt completely overcome, and exclaimed, 'God of mercy, relieve me! the burthen is more than I can bear.' Then commenced the havoc in this temple, that was my head, and was not; there were the toppling down of the vast columns, the crashing of the several architraves, the grinding together of the rich entablatures; the breaking up, with noise louder than ever thunder was heard by man, of the marble pavements, the ruins crushed together in one awful confusion above me;—nature could do no more, and my dream slept.

The sun was at its meridian height when I awoke the next day in health, with every sensation renewed, and that, too, in the so sweet a feeling that makes the mere act of living delightful. I found nothing remarkable, but that I had been subjected to a profuse perspiration.

Miss Bellarosa met me at breakfast all triumph, and I was all gratitude. I was very hungry, and as playful as a schoolboy who had just procured a holiday.

'Eh! Massa Ralph, suppose no marry me to-day—what for you say yes to dat?'

'Because, dear Bella, you wouldn't have me.'

'Try—you ask me,' said she, looking at me with a fondness not quite so maternal as I could wish.

'Bella, dearest, will you marry me?'

'For true?'

'For true.'

'Tanky, Massa Rattlin, dear, tanky; you make me very happy; but, for true, no. Were you older more fifteen year, or me more fifteen year younger, perhaps—but tank ye much for de comblement. Now, go, and tell buckra doctor.'

So, as I could not reward my kind physician with my hand, which, by the by, I should not have offered had I not been certain of refusal, I was obliged to force upon her as splendid a trinket as I could purchase for a keepsake, and gave my sable nurses a handful of bits each. Bits of what? say the uninitiated.

I don't know whether I have described this fever case very nosologically,[1] but, very truly I know I have.

CHAPTER VI

A new character introduced, who claimeth old acquaintanceship—Not very honest by his own account, which giveth him more the appearance of honesty than he deserveth—He proveth to be a steward not inclined to hide his talent in a napkin.

DURING all the time that these West Indian events had been occurring, that is, nearly three years, I had no other communication with England than regularly and repeatedly sending there various pieces of paper, thus headed, 'This, my first of exchange, my second and third not paid;' or, for variety's sake, 'This, my second of exchange, my first and third,' &c.; or, to be more various

still, 'This, my third, my first and second,'—all of which received
more attention than their strange phraseology seemed to entitle
them to.

But I must now introduce a new character; one that attended me
for years, like an evil shadow, nor left me until the 'beginning of
the end.'[1]

The ship had been hove down, the wound in her forefoot healed,
that is to say, the huge rent stopped up; and we were beginning to
get water and stores on board, and I was walking on the quay of
the dock-yard, when I was civilly accosted by a man having the
appearance of a captain's steward. He was pale and handsome, with
small white hands: and, if not actually genteel in his deportment,
had that metropolitan refinement of look that indicated contact with
genteel society. Though dressed in the blue jacket and white duck
trowsers of the sailor's Sunday best, at a glance, you would pronounce him to be no seaman. Before he spoke to me, he had looked
attentively at several other midshipmen, some belonging to my
own ship, others, young gentlemen who were on shore on dock-
yard duty. At length, after a scrutiny sufficient to make me rather
angry, he took off his hat very respectfully, and said—

'Have I the honour of speaking to Mr. Ralph Rattlin?'

'You have: well, my man?'

'Ah, sir, you forget me, and no wonder. My name, sir, is Daunton
—Joshua Daunton.'

'Never heard the name before in my life.'

'Oh, yes, you have, sir, begging your pardon, very often indeed.
Why, you used to call me Jossey; little Jossey, come here you little
vagabond, and let me ride you pick-a-back.'

'The devil I did!'

'Why, Mr. Rattlin, I was your fag at Mr. Root's school.'

Now, I knew this to be a lie; for, under that very respectable
pedagogue, and in that very respectable seminary, as the reader
well knows, I was the *fagged*, and not the fagger.

'Now, really, Joshua Daunton,' said I, 'I am inclined to think
that you may be Joshua the little vagabond still; for, upon my
honour, I remember nothing about you. Seeing there were so
many hundred boys under Mr. Root, my schoolfellow you
might have been; but may I be vexed if ever I fagged you or
any one else! Now, my good man, prove to me that you have
been my schoolfellow first, and then let me know what I can do

for you afterwards, for I suppose that you have some favour to ask, or some motive in seeking me.'

'I have, indeed,' he replied, with a peculiar intonation of voice, that might have been construed in many ways. He then proceeded to give me many details of the school at Islington, which convinced me, if there he had never been, he had conversed with some one who had. Still, he evaded all my attempts at cross-examination with a skill which gave me a much higher opinion of his intellect than of his honesty. With the utmost efforts of my recollection, I could not recall him to mind, and I bluntly told him so. I then bade him tell me who he was and what he wanted.

'I am the only son of an honest pawnbroker of Shoreditch. He was tolerably rich, and determined to give me a good education. He sent me to Mr. Root's school. It was there that I had the happiness of being honoured by your friendship. Now, sir, you perceive that, though I am not so tall as you by some inches, I am at least seven or eight years older. Shortly after you left school, to go to another at Stickenham. I also left, with my education, as my father fondly supposed, finished. Sir, I turned out bad. I confess it with shame—I was a rascal. My father turned me out of doors. I have had several ups and downs in the world since, and I am now steward on board of the London, the West Indiaman that arrived here the day before yesterday.'

'Very well, Joshua: but how came you to know that I went to school at Stickenham?'

'Because, in my tramping about the country, I saw you, with the other young gentlemen, in the play-ground on the common.'

'Hum! but how, in the name of all that is curious, came you to know that I was here at Port Royal dock-yard, and a young gentleman belonging to the Eos?'

'Oh! very naturally, sir. About two years ago, I passed again over the same common with my associates. I could not resist the wish to see if you were still in the play-ground. I did not see you among the rest, and I made bold to inquire of one of the elder boys where you were. He told me the name of the ship and of your captain. The first thing on coming into the harbour that struck my eye, was your very frigate alongside the dock-yard. I got leave to come on shore, and I knew you directly that I saw you.'

'But why examine so many before you spoke to me? However,

I have no reason to be suspicious, for time makes great changes. Now, what shall I do for you?'

'Give me your protection, and as much of your friendliness as is compatible with our different stations.'

'But, Daunton, according to your own words, you have been a sad fellow. Before I extend to you what you require, I ought to know what you really have done. You spoke of tramping—have you been a tramper—a gipsy?'

'I have.'

'Have you ever committed theft?'

'Only in a small way.'

'Ah! and swindled—only in a small way, of course?'

'The temptations were great.'

'Where will this fellow stop?' thought I: 'let us see, however, how far he will go;' and then, giving utterance to my thoughts, I continued, 'The step between swindling and forgery is but very short,' and I paused—for even I had not the confidence to ask him, 'are you a forger?'

'Very,' was the short, dry answer. I was astonished. Perhaps he will confess to the commission of murder.

'Oh! as you were just saying to yourself, we are the mere passive tools of fate—we are drawn on, in spite of ourselves. If a man comes in our way, why, you know, in self-defence—hey?'

'What do you mean, sir?'

'A little prick under the ribs in a quiet way. The wanderings and jerkings of the angry hand will happen. You understand me?'

'Too well, I am afraid, sir. I have never yet shed man's blood—I never will. Perhaps, sir, you would not depend upon my virtue for this—you may upon my cowardice. I tremble—I sicken—at the sight of blood. I have endeavoured to win your confidence by candour—I have not succeeded. May I be permitted to bid you a good day?'

'Stop, Daunton, this is a singular encounter, and a still more singular conference. As an old schoolfellow, you ask me to give you my protection. The protection of a reefer is, in itself, something laughable: and then, as an inducement, you confess to me that you are a villain, only just in guilt short of murder. Perhaps, by this bravado sort of confession, you have endeavoured to give me a worse impression of your character than it really deserves, that you might give me the better opinion of your sincerity. Is it not so?'

'In a great measure, it is.'

'I thought so. Now, let me tell you, Daunton, that that very circumstance makes me afraid of you. But, still, I will not cast aside the appeal of an old schoolfellow. What can I do for you?'

'Give me the protection afforded me by a man-of-war, by taking me as your servant.'

'Utterly impossible! I can press you directly, or give the hint to any of the many men-of-war here to do so. But the rules of the service do not permit a midshipman to have a separate servant. Do you wish to enter?'

'Only on board of your ship, and with the privilege of waiting upon you, and being constantly near your person.'

'Thank you; but what prevents my impressing you, even as you stand there?'

'These very ample protections.' And he produced them.

'Yes! I see that you are well provided. But why give up your good berth on board the London?'

'Mr. Rattlin, I have my reasons. Permit them, as yet, to remain secret. There is no guilt attached to them. May I sail with you in the capacity of your servant?'

'I have told you before, that you cannot be my servant solely. You must be the servant of the midshipmen's berth.'

'Yes, with all my heart, provided you pledge me your honour that I shall never be put to any other duty.'

I was astonished at this perseverance, and very honestly told him all the miseries of the situation for which he seemed so ambitious. They did not shake his resolution. I then left him, and spoke to Mr. Farmer. 'Let the fool enter,' was the laconic reply.

'But he will not enter but on the conditions I have mentioned, and his protections are too good to be violated.'

'Then I authorize you to make them. We are short of men.'

But Joshua would not enter: he required to be pressed; so I went on board his own merchant ship, according to previous arrangement, and pressed him. He made no resistance, and produced no documents: he only called the master of the ship and the first and second officer to witness that he was a pressed man, and then, taking his kit with him, he even cheerfully tripped down the side into the boat; and thus, for nearly an eventful year, I was the instrument of placing my evil genius near me.

CHAPTER VII

The Art of Mischief made easy—rather hard upon the experimented—'Heaven preserve me from my friends! I'll take care of my enemies myself,' say the honest Spaniards, and so says honest Ralph.

AND SO, filling our cabins with invalided officers, we sailed for England. We took home with us a convoy: and a miserable voyage we made of it. I had none of those exhilarating feelings so usual to every one who is about, after a long period of absence, to revisit his native land. I grew dull and irritable, a mixture of qualities as unpleasant as they are contradictory. I began to cast up accounts with that stern old reckoner, Time, and I found the balance dreadfully in my disfavour. What had I, in exchange, for the loss of the three most sunshiny years of life, comprised between the ages of sixteen and nineteen! To look back upon that period, it seemed a dreary waste, with only one small bright spot blooming upon it. Indeed, the contemplation of that oasis was so dazzling, that, when my mental eye was no longer riveted upon it, like a gaze upon the sun, it made all else seem dark and indistinct.

The indomitable pride natural to every bosom, and perhaps too plentiful in mine, had also its share in filling my mind with an unceasing and cankering disgust. I began to feel the bitterness of being unowned. What was country to me? The chain that binds a man to it is formed of innumerable small, yet precious, links, almost all of which were wanting in my case. Father, mother, family, a heritage, a holding, something to claim as one's own— these are what bind a man's affections to a particular spot of earth, and these were not mine: the fact was, I wanted, just at that time, excitement of good or of evil, and I was soon supplied with that aliment of life, *ad nauseam*.

In taking my *soi-disant* schoolfellow on board the Eos, I had shipped with me my Mephistopheles. The former servant to the midshipmen's berth was promoted to the mizen-top, and Joshua Daunton inducted, with due solemnities, to all the honours of waiting upon about half a dozen fierce, unruly midshipmen, and as many sick supernumeraries; and he formally took charge of all the mess-plate and munitions *de bouche* of this submarine establishment.

There was no temptation to embezzlement. Our little society was a commonwealth of the most democratic description—and, as usually happens in these sort of experiments, there was a community of goods that were good for nothing to the community.

I will give an inventory of all the moveables of this republic, for the edification of the curious. Among these, it being continually in motion, I must first of all enumerate the *salle à manger* itself, a hot, little hole in the cock-pit, of about eight feet by six, which was never clean. This dining-parlour and breakfast-room also contained our cellars, which contained nothing, and on which cellars we lay down when there was room—your true midshipman is a recumbent animal—and sat when we could not lie. For the same reason that the Romans called a grove *lucus*, these cellerets were called lockers, because there was nothing to lock in them, and no locks to lock in that nothing withall. In the midst stood an oak table, carved with more names than ever Rosalind accused Orlando of spoiling good trees with, besides the outline of a ship, and a number of squares, which served for an immoveable draught-board. One battered, spoutless, handless, japanned-tin jug, that did not contain water, for it leaked; some tin mugs; seven, or perhaps eight, pewter plates; an excellent old iron tureen, the best friend we had, and which had stood by us, through storm and calm, and the spiteful kick of Reefer, and the contemptuous 'slings and arrows of outrageous fortune,'[1] in the galley, which contained our cocoa in the morning, our pea-soup at noon, and, after these multiplied duties, performed the character of wash-hand basin, whenever the midshipman's fag condescended to cleanse his hands. It is a fact that, when we sailed for England, of crockeryware we had not a single article. There were a calabash[2] or so, and two or three sections of cocoa-nut shells.

We had no other provisions than barely the ship's allowance, and even these were of the worst description. Bread, it is well remarked, is the staff of life; but it is not quite pleasant to find it life itself, and to have the power of locomotion. Every other description of food was in the same state of transition into vivification. There is no exaggeration in all this. From the continual coming and going, and the state of constant disunion in which we lived, it was every man for himself, and God, I am sorry to say, seemed to have very little to do with any of us. So complete was our disorganization, and so great our destitution as a mess, that, after the first week, the supernumerary sick young gentlemen were relieved from this candle-light den of starvation and of dirt, and distributed among the warrant officers.

It was to wait upon our persons, to administer to our wants, and to take care of our culinary comforts, that Joshua Daunton was duly installed. It was very ludicrous to see our late servant giving up his charge to our present one—the solemnity with which the iron tureen, and the one knife, and the three forks, that were not furcated, seeing that they had but one prong each, were surrendered! Joshua's contempt at the sordid poverty of the republic to which he was to administer was quite as undisguised as his surprise. I again and again requested him to do his duty in some capacity in the ship, but he steadily refused.

The silky, soft spoken, cockney-dialected Josh got me into continual hot water. At first he seemed to consider himself as my servant only; consequently, he was continually thrashed, and I, on his appeal, taking his part, had to endeavour to thrash the thrasher. Now, this could not always conveniently be done. The more I suffered for this Daunton, the more ardently he seemed to attach himself to me. But there appeared to be much more malice than affection in this fidelity. Nothing prospered either with me or my messmates. He contrived, in the most plausible manner possible, to spoil our almost unspoilable meals. He always managed to draw for us the very worst rations, and to lay the blame on the purser's steward. In bringing aft our miserable dinners, his foot would slip, or a man would run against him—or somebody had taken it off the galley-fire, and thrown it in the manger. Salt water would miraculously intrude into my messmates' rum-bottle, and my daily pint of wine was either sour, or muddy, or sandy, or afflicted with something that made it undrinkable. In one word, under the care of the good Joshua, Messieurs the midshipmen ran a most imminent risk of being actually starved.

Many a time, after we had gone through the motions of dining, without eating, and as we sate in our dark, hot hole, over our undrinkable potations and our inedible eatables, each of us resting his hungry head upon his aching elbows, watching the progress of some animated piece of biscuit, would Master Daunton, the slave of our lamp, which, by-the-by, was a bottle bearing a miserably consumptive purser's dip, beside which a farthing rushlight would look quite aldermanic—I say, this slave of our lamp would perch himself down on the combings of the cable-tier hatchway, in the midst of the flood of Heaven's blessed daylight, that came pouring from aloft into this abyss, and very deliberately take out his private store of viands, and there insultingly wag his jaws, with the most complacent satisfaction, in the faces of his masters. The contrast was too bad—the malice of it too tormenting. Whilst he was masticating his beautifully white American crackers, and smacking his lips over his savoury German sausage, we were grumbling over putrid bones and weavilly biscuit, that we could not swallow, and yet hunger would not permit us to desert. It was a floating repetition of the horrors of Tantalus.

Well, to myself, this rascal was most submissive—most eager in forcing upon me his services. He relieved my hammock-man of his duty; but, somehow, nothing prospered to which he put his hand. The third night, the nails of the cleet that fastened my head-clews up to the deck above me, drew, and I came down by the run, head foremost; and immediately where my head ought to have alighted on the deck, was found the carpenter's pitch kettle, with the blade of an axe in the centre of it, and the edge uppermost. No one knew how it came there, and, had I shot out as young gentlemen usually do on such occasions, I should, if I had not been quite decapitated, at least have died by the axe. Not being asleep when the descent took place, I grappled with my neighbour, the old fat assistant surgeon, and he with the next, and the three came down on deck with a lunge that actually started the marine officer—who, every body knows, is the best sleeper on board. Happily for myself, I fell from my hammock sideways. Next, the accommodating Joshua got the sole charge of my chest, and, though nothing was missed, in a short time every thing was ruined. The cockroaches ate the most unaccountable holes in my best uniforms, my shoes burst in putting them on, my boots cracked all across the upper leathers, and the feet of my stockings came off when I attempted to draw them on.

The obsequious Joshua was equally assiduous with his other six masters, and even more successful; so that, in addition to being starved, there was every possibility of our being reduced to nakedness. This was no pleasant prospect, running out of tropical latitudes towards England, in the month of January. In the course of six weeks, such a ragged, woe-begone, gaunt, and famished gang of reefers was never before huddled together in one of his Majesty's

U

vessels of war. The shifts we were obliged to have recourse to were quite amusing, to all but the shiftmakers. The only good hat, and wearable uniform coat, went round and round; it was a happy thing for this disconsolate seven that we were all nearly of a size. To aggravate our misfortunes, we could no longer get an occasional dinner, either in the captain's cabin or the ward-room, for our clothes were all in rags.

In the meanwhile, Joshua Daunton grew more and more sleek, and pale, and fat. He throve upon our miseries. He played his part at length so well, as to avoid thrashings. He possessed, in perfection, that which, in classic cockpit, is called 'the gift of the gab.' He was never in the wrong. Indeed he began to get a favourite with each of the individuals over whom he was so mercilessly tyrannizing, while each thought himself the tyrant. All this may seem improbable to well-nurtured, shore-bred, young gentlemen and ladies; but midshipmen were always reckless and idle—that is, personally. On actual service, they have ever been equally reckless, but commensurably active. This kindness of Joshua, in taking all trouble off our hands, soon left us almost nothing wherewith to trouble ourselves.

CHAPTER VIII

An anticipated dinner—All the enjoyment spoiled by the first cut— A suit of clothes ill suited for wearing—and Joshua Daunton trying on a pair of iron leggings—more easily put on than shaken off.

THIS imp, this Flibbertygibbet, was killing us by inches. At length, one of the master's mates, no longer being able to starve quietly and philosophically, as became a man of courage, was again determined, by one last effort, to dine, and breakfast, and sup, in the captain's cabin and ward-room as often as he could. So, finding that there was enough new blue cloth on board, with buttons, &c., to make him a complete suit, he purchased them, at an enormous price, *on credit;* and set the ship's tailors to work incontinently. By this time, we were, with our homeward-bound convoy, on the banks of Newfoundland. It was misty and cold— and we were chilly and ragged. In such a conjuncture of circumstances, even the well clothed may understand what a blessing a new suit of warm blue must be—that suit bearing in its suite a long line of substantial breakfasts, dinners, and suppers. All this was about to be Mr. Pigtop's, our kind messmate, and respectable mate of the orlop deck. He had already begun to protest upon the unreasonableness of rotatory coats, or of having a quarter-deck pair of trowsers, like the wives of the ancient Britons, common to the sept. The ungrateful rogue! He had on, at the very time, the only quarter-deck-going coat among us, which was mine, and which he had just borrowed to enable him to go on deck, and report every thing right below.

'Captain Reud's compliments to Mr. Pigtop, and would be glad of his company to dinner.'

Angelic words, when the invited reefer has a clean shirt, or collar, and a decent uniform.

'"Mr. Pigtop's compliments to Captain Reud, and will be most happy to wait on him." There, you dogs,' said the elated Pigtop, 'I say, no more lending of clothes. Here, you Josh, jump forward, and tell the tailor I must have my uniform by four bells.'

Josh jumped forward with a very intelligent grin upon his tallow-complexioned but handsome countenance.

Now, the captain and the ward-room officers all knew very well of the unaccountable destruction of our clothes, which, they affected to believe, was not unaccountable to them. They said it arose from very natural causes; a little of which was to be ascribed to dampness, a little to the cockroaches, and a great, a very great deal to our proverbial carelessness. Well. A midshipman careless! But some people *may* libel with impunity. Whatever they thought, they enjoyed our dilemmas, both of food and of clothing.

An hour before the captain's dinner was ready, the much-envied suit was brought aft, and duly displayed on Mr. Pigtop's chest. The ward-room officers, or at least those of them with whom he could take that liberty, were invited out to view it. It was pronounced, for ship-tailoring, excellent.

Pigtop's elation was great. So was Josh Daunton's; but all in a quiet, submissive way. Our envy was proportionate. Josh was an excellent barber, and he volunteered to shave the happy diner-out —the offer was accepted. Then came the turn of fate—then commenced the long series of the poor mate's miseries. It was no fault of Daunton's, certainly—but all the razors were like saws. The blood came out over the black visage of Mr. Pigtop; but the hair stayed most pertinaceously on. The sufferer swore—how horribly he swore! The time was fast elapsing. After a most tremendous oath from the sufferer, which would have almost split an oak plank, Joshua said in his lowly and insinuating voice, 'Mr. Pigtop, pray do—do, do, sir, try the razors yourself. My heart bleeds, sir, more than your face—do try, sir, for I think the captain's servant is now coming down the hatchway to tell you dinner is ready.'

In despair, the hungry depilator seized the razors; and, being exasperated with hurry, he made a worse job of it than Joshua. Where Josh had made notches, Pigtop made gashes. The ship's barber was then sent for, and he positively refused to go over the bloody surface.

But Joshua Daunton was the true friend, the friend in need. With Mr. Pigtop's permission, he would go and borrow one of Dr. Thomson's razors. The offer was gratefully accepted. In the mean time, dinner was actually announced. It is just about as wise to attempt to keep the hungry tiger from his newly-slaughtered prey, as for a mid to make the captain of a man-of-war wait dinner. Reud did not wait.

However, the fresh razor did its work admirably, in the adroit hand of Joshua. The hitherto intractable beard flew off rapidly, and Joshua's tongue moved more glibly even than his razor. Barbers in the act of office have, like the House of Commons, the privilege of speech. They are not amenable afterwards for what they say. In the act they are omnipotent, for, who would quarrel with a man who is slipping a razor over your carotid artery? Not certainly Mr. Pigtop. Thus spoke Joshua, amid the eloquent flourishes of his instrument:

'Mr. Pigtop, I've a great respect for you—a very great respect indeed, sir. If you have not been a good friend to me yet, you will—I know it, sir; you are not like the other flighty young gentlemen. I have a respect for years, sir—a great respect for years, and honour a middle-aged gentleman. Indeed, sir, it must be a great condescension in you to permit yourself to be only a master's-mate of a frigate, seeing that you are quite an elderly gentleman——.'

'Da——!'

'There!—that was very imprudent indeed, sir, of you to open your mouth. It was not my fault, you know, that the brush went into it: indeed, some people like the taste of soapsuds—wholesome,

I assure you—very. A stubble of your growth, sir, always requires a double lathering—don't speak. Oh, sir, you are a happy man—exceeding. Your face will be as smooth as a man's borrowing money. You, boy, just run up the after-hatchway, and tell the captain's steward that Mr. Pigtop will be in the cabin in the flourish of a razor, or before a white horse can turn grey. Permit me to take you by the nose; the true handle of the face, sir: it gives the man, as it were, a sort of a command, sir, of the whole head; he can box the compass with it. Happy indeed you are, sir, and much to be envied. There was one of the captain's turtles killed yesterday—Jumbo is a cook, a most excellent cook—a spoonful of the soup to-day will be worth a king's ransom—a peck of March dust! pooh!—I wouldn't give a spoonful of that soup for a hundred bushels of it. Take my advice, sir, and have soup twice, sir. As it was carried along the main-deck, I'm dishonest, if the young gentlemen didn't follow it with the water running down in streams from the corners of their mouths, and their tongues intreatingly lolling out like a parcel of hungry dogs in Cripplegate, following the catsmeat-man's barrow. One more rasp over your upper lip, and you are as smooth as the new-born babe—talking of lips, as the first spoonful of that turtle-soup glides over them—the devil! I'll take God to witness, it was an accident—the roll of the ship!'

Joshua Daunton was on his knees before Mr. Pigtop, who was in an agony of pain, holding on his upper lip, which was nearly severed from his face, whilst the blood was streaming through his fingers.

Doctor Thompson with diachylon[1] and black sticking-plaister was soon on the spot to the assistance of the almost dislipped master's mate. After the best was done for it, the poor fellow cut but a sorry appearance; still his extreme hunger, made almost furious by the vision of the turtle-soup, so artfully conjured up by the malicious Joshua, got the better of his sense of pain; and, with a great band of black plaister reaching transversely from the right nostril to the left corner of his mouth, the grim-looking Mr. Pigtop made haste to don the new uniform.

In the meantime, the protestations and tears of Joshua had convinced every body that the horrible gash was merely the effect of accident, for the ship was rolling a great deal at the moment. What the captain and his guests were doing in the cabin above with the turtle-soup it is needless for me to state, for that same soup was never fated to gladden the wounded lip of Mr. Pigtop.

The hasty and famishing gentleman, in his very first attempt to draw on his new trowsers, to the astonishment of all his mess-mates, who had now gathered round him, found them separate in the middle of each of his legs. He might as well have attempted to clothe himself with cobweb continuations; they came to pieces almost with a shake. The waistcoat and coat were in the same pre-dicament: they had not the principle of continuity in them. Every body was lost in amazement, except Mr. Pigtop, whose amaze-ment, quite as great as our's, was lost in his still greater rage. It was extremely unfortunate for Joshua Daunton that he had cut the lip that day. The kind doctor was still by during the apparelling, or the attempt at it. He examined the rotten clothes, and he soon discovered that they had been saturated in different parts by some corrosive liquid, that, instead of impairing, really improved the brilliancy of the cloth.

During these proceedings, Captain Reud and his guests had eaten up the dinner; but the captain, not being pleased to be pleasantly humoured that day, sent word for Mr. Pigtop to go to the mast-head till midnight, for disrespect in not attending to the invitation that he had accepted. There was no appeal, and aloft went the wounded, ragged, famished hoper of devouring turtle-soup. Joshua looked very demure and very unhappy; but Dr. Thompson set on foot an inquiry, and the truth of the destruction of the clothes was soon ascertained. The lob-lolly boy, that is, the young man who had charge of the laboratory where all the medicines were kept, confessed, after a little hesitation, that for certain glasses of grog he had given this pernicious liquid to Daunton. So, while one of his masters was contemplating the stars from the mast-head, the destroyer of reefers' kits had nothing else to do but to con-template the beauty of his own feet, placed, with a judicious exactitude, in a very handsome pair of Bilboes[1] under the half deck.

CHAPTER IX

The cat-of-nine-tails begets a tale the most annoying to Ralph—
The story of the three crows beaten hollow—Seven's the main and
a losing cast—A promised treatise on ornithology put an end to
rather abruptly by the biplumal resolving themselves into the
mere bipedal.

WHEN fully secured, the poor wretch sent for me. He was in
a paroxysm of fear: he protested his innocence over and over again:
he declared that he should die under the first lash: that it was for
love of me only that he had come on board of a man-of-war; he
conjured me, by the fellowship of our boyish days, by all that I
loved and that was sacred to us, to save him from the gangway.
The easiness of my nature was worked upon, and I promised to
use my influence to procure for him a pardon. I went to Mr.
Farmer, but all my efforts were unavailing. The culprit passed
a sleepless night in the intolerable agony of fear. Before he was
brought up to be flogged, Mr. Pigtop had been fully avenged.

The gratings are rigged, the hands are turned up, and Joshua
Daunton is supported by two ship's corporals, in a nearly fainting
state, and stripped by another—he is too much paralyzed to do it
himself. The officers are mustered on the break of the quarter-
deck, and the marines are drawn up, under arms, on the gangway.
Captain Reud looks fierce and forbidding, and Mr. Farmer, for
his generally impassible features, really quite savage. I come forward shudderingly and look down. The wandering and restless
eyes of the frightened young man meet, in an instant, what, most
probably, they are seeking—my own.

'Ralph Rattlin, speak for me to the captain.' The words were in
themselves simple, but they were uttered in a tone of the most
touching pathos. They made me start: I thought that I knew the
voice, not as the voice of Joshua Daunton, the mischievous imp
that had tormented us all so scientifically, but of some dear and
long-forgotten friend. 'Ralph Rattlin, speak for me to the Captain
—this must not be.'

'But it shall be, by G—!' said the irascible Creole.

'Captain Reud,' said I, 'let me intreat you for this once only—'

'Boatswain's mate—'

'Oh, Captain Reud, if you knew what a strange sympathy—'

'The thief's cat.'

'Indeed, sir, since he has been on board he has never stolen—'

'Mr. Rattlin, another word, and the mast-head. Stand back, Stebbings!—let Douglas give him the first dozen.'

Now, this Douglas was a huge raw-boned boatswain's mate, that flogged left-handed, and had also a peculiar jerk in his manner of laying on the cat-o'-nine-tails, that always brought away with it little knobs of flesh wherever the knobs fell, and so neatly, that blood would, at every blow, spout from the wounds as from the puncture of a lancet. Besides, the torture was also doubled by first scoring over the back in one direction, and the right-handed floggers coming after in another, they cut out the skin in lozenges.

I looked in the captain's face, and there was no mercy; I looked below, and there appeared almost as little life. After the left-handed Scotchman had bared his brawny arm and measured his distance, and just as he was about to uplift it and strike, Daunton murmured out, 'Ralph Rattlin, I knew your father! beware, or your own blood will be dishonoured in me!'

'That voice!—they shall flog you through me!' I exclaimed, and was about to leap into the waist and cover him with my arms, when I was forcibly withheld by the officers around me, whilst the captain roared out, 'He shall have another dozen for his impudent false-hood—boatswain's mate, do your duty.'

The terrific lash, like angry scorpions, fell upon the white and quivering flesh, and the blood spurted out freely. It was a vengeful stroke, and loud, and long, and shrill, was the scream that followed it. But, ere the second stroke fell, the head of the tortured one suddenly collapsed upon the right shoulder, and a livid hue spread rapidly over the face and breast.

'He is dead!' said those around, in a half-hushed tone.

The surgeon felt his pulse, and placed his hand upon his breast to seek for the beating of the heart, and, shaking his head, requested him to be cast loose. He was immediately taken to the sick bay, but, with all the skill of the doctor, his resuscitation was, at first, despaired of, and only brought about, at length, with great diffi-culty. The fact was, not that he had been flogged, but very nearly frightened, to death.

And I was utterly miserable. The words that Daunton had spoken at the gangway, and the strange interest that I had taken in his behalf, gave rise to supicions that I felt to be degrading. He had declared himself to be of my blood; the officers and crew construed the expression as meaning my brother. I was now, for the first time, looked coldly upon: I felt myself avoided. Such conduct is chilling—too often fatal to the young and proud heart: it will rise indignant at an insult, but guarded and polite contumely, and long and civil neglect, wither it. I was fast sinking into an habitual despondency. This confounded Joshua had previously completely ruined my outward man: the inward man was in great danger from his conduct, perhaps his machinations. I was shunned with a studied contempt; the more particularly as my messmates were the subjects of the constant jibes of the captain and the other officers, which messmates were of an unanimous opinion that Master Joshua ought to have been hung, inasmuch as it is now apparent that their ruined apparel was all derivable from his malice and his 'Practice of Chemistry made easy.' They all panted with impatience for his convalescence, in order that they might see Mr. Rattlin's *elder brother* receive the remainder of his six dozen.

I verily believe that, as I approached my native shores, I should have fallen into a settled depression of spirits, which would have terminated in melancholy madness, had I not been roused to exert my moral energies and awaken my half entombed pride by a stinging and a very wholesome insult.

As soon as we were ordered home, Captain Reud's mental aberrations became less frequent, but, when they supervened, they were more extravagant in their nature. He grew aguish, fretful, and cruel. Though he never spoke to me harshly, he addressed me more rarely. I had not dined with him for a long while: he had taken the mysterious destruction of my wardrobe as a valid excuse; and had gone so far, on one occasion, in a very delicate manner, as to present me with a complete change of linen, which perished like the rest, under the provident care of Joshua. But, after the claim of relationship by that very timid personage, there was no consideration in Reud's look; and, whenever he did speak to me, there was a contemptuous harshness in his tone that would have very much wounded my feelings at any other time. But, just then, I took but little notice of and interest in any thing.

When I say that we were reduced to rags in our habiliments, the reader is not to take the words *au pied de lettre*. By taking up slops from the purser, and by aid of the ship's tailor, we had been enabled to walk the quarter-deck without actual holes in our dress; but, the dresses themselves were grotesque, for the imitation of our spruce uniform was villainous, and our hats were deplorable; they were greased with oil, and broken, and sewed, and formless, or rather multiform: bad as were our fittings out, we had not enough of them.

One morning, as we were, with our convoy, approaching the chops of the channel, we fell in with a frigate, one of his majesty's cruisers. I was walking sulkily up and down the gangway, that is, that portion of the deck that divides the quarter-deck from the forecastle. Captain Reud was on deck with most of his officers, all very anxious to hear news of England, and get the sight of an English newspaper. The ships ranged up within hail of each other; and, after the usual queries, and three or four newspapers, made heavy with musket-balls, had been thrown on board, the following dialogue between the two frigates took place in the persons of their respective captains, Reud saying:

'I wish you'd lower your gig, and come on board and lunch.'

'If you command it, of course.'

'Oh, no, no!—I am not going to hoist the commodore's broad pennant, but I really wish you'd come. We can jog on under easy sail.'

'Why, really, Captain Reud, the sea is rather high—and don't you see the Mother Carey's chicken[1] astern of you?'

By a particular hitch of his gait, and a peculiar twisting up of his nose, I perceived the fit of mischief or insanity was coming on poor Reud. *The frayed chord had been struck.* He grinned, he fenced with his speaking trumpet, he shoved the mouth of it in the first lieutenant's ribs, begged his pardon with a very gentlemanly air, and then, giving it a whirling flourish, that met and fetched blood from the tip of the marine officer's nose, he placed it in his mouth, and continued—

'Talking about Mother Carey's chickens, Captain Reeves, I think I'll tempt you on board. I have got seven of the most curious ornithological specimens in my ship that a naturalist ever beheld.'

'Have you, indeed?' said Captain Reeves, who fancied himself a great naturalist. 'Pipe the gigs away—be with you in a moment, Captain Reud. Pray, may I inquire of what genus?'

'The genus Corvus,' said Reud, jumping down from the

hammock nettings. 'Send for all the young gentlemen, just as they are, into my cabin:—bring them up immediately—the mate of the lower deck also—there's Mr. Rattlin on the gangway.'

Obedience always treads upon the heels of command on board of a man-of-war. Long before Captain Reeves was alongside, our gang of seven miserably-looking famished reefers was ranged up side by side in the fore-cabin, whilst the steward and servants were heaping the table with all the appurtenances of a glorious luncheon.

'What does the captain want with us?' said one.

'Ask us to lunch.'

'Pooh!—how could you, Pigtop, come up such a figure?'

'Come, Staines, let the kettle keep a clean tongue in its mouth, and not call——.'

'I'll tell you what it is,' said another, 'the captain is going to change the whole batch of us as a bad bargain. I want to get to England—I won't go.'

'Nor I.'

'Yes,' said I, 'my loving friends, as sure as we stand here, a ragged regiment of reefers, that the swabwasher's assistant would be ashamed to march through the Point or Common Hard with, he is going to introduce us and all our perfections to Captain Reeves.'

'If I thought so, I'd bolt.'

'Bolt,' said Pigtop, 'I should like to bolt that fowl.'

'No sooner said than done,' said another, advancing to the tempting delicacy. The steward and servants had left the cabin, having completed their arrangements.

'Stop—let us have no pilfering. This is one of Reud's pranks—I *think* that *I* was invited to lunch with the captain. Mr. Pigtop, will you take the chair?—that is to say, if you think that you were invited, also—you know it is a matter of conscience.'

'I *think* I was.'

'I am sure of it.'

'Well, we have no time to lose—to your chairs, gentlemen. Heavens! they are—that is to say, the rest of the guests—are coming. Permit me to propose, in his absence, the health of our gallant commander, with three times three—hip, hip, hip, hurrah!'

Captains Reud, Reeves, and our first lieutenant, entered at the moment that we were all standing with inverted glasses. The positions of the three gentlemen as they entered were quite theatrical. Mr. Farmer had smothered his laughter by clapping his hand over his mouth; Captain Reeves looked very droll and very much puzzled; Captain Reud, our own inestimable commander, looked really frightful. The impudence was utterly beyond his comprehension. His wild looks so much alarmed my messmates, that they slunk away like a parcel of cravens from the table; as for myself, just then, I neither feared nor cared for anything. The explosion took place thus, a rather hard substitution for 'Gentlemen, for the honour that you have done me in my absence—'

'You, Rattlin'—Mr. Rattlin, over the glass he had just emptied, bowed, standing in his place—'you rascals!—how dare—dare you to steal my wine?'

'Sir, I stand here as your guest—waiting to be requested to be seated. The impression upon my mind was, that I was asked into the cabin to luncheon. It is seldom that so many midshipmen find themselves collected together at their captain's table, no other officer being present. The situation was novel. I hope, Captain Reud, that you will not make it unpleasant. We seized the golden opportunity, very fervently, to drink your health, with due honours, in your absence. *I* am conscious of no offence, without too much devotion to my commander may be construed into one. What my messmates may think of their conduct, by their desertion from your table, it is not for me to say. As yet, I do not feel unworthy of a place at it. If there has been any little mistake in the invitation, I shall be most anxious to retire.'

During this impertinent speech of mine, the offspring of utter recklessness as to consequences, I had, without moving from my place at the table, fixed my eyes composedly on Captain Reud. I did not mean the expression of them to be insulting, nor did I wish it to be supplicatory. Whatever it might have been, it had the effect of gradually dispersing the angry scowl from his brow, though a certain degree of sternness still remained. When I had finished, expecting of course to be under an arrest, or sent to the mast-head, I was surprised, and a good deal gratified, by hearing him say distinctly, though not very cordially—

'Mr. Rattlin, you know your place—your messmates know their's. Captain Reeves, Mr. Farmer, Rattlin, pray be seated.'

The half dozen of poltroons all stood huddled together, like a small flock of intimidated sheep, between the two guns in the cabin, right opposite me. I was tolerably hungry, and yet I enjoyed the tantalized expression of the countenances of the renegades, quite as much as the good viands with which I so plentifully supplied myself.

The wine circulated. Captain Reud grew gracious, and Captain Reeves impatient to view the seven curious ornithological specimens of the genus Corvus, that his host had brought with him from the West. I guessed what was coming, which prevented my warming towards my captain, with his returning kindness.

Captain Reeves could talk of nothing else but birds, and of these particular seven birds. 'Where were they?'

'Oh! close at hand.'

'Large?'

'Stand from five to six feet high.'

'Good God! they must eat enormously.'

'Voraciously,' and here the wicked Creole gave me a right jovial look. 'They are a great expense to me, as well as annoyance.'

'But birds of this size must be very heavy on the wing. In their natural state do they fly?'

'Sluggishly enough; but I have seen them very often aloft.'

The naturalist was completely mystified; but our host would not produce them, as he said, that, when his curiosity was gratified, he should no longer have the pleasure of his company, and the happiness of passing the decanters to him. It was in vain that Captain Reud endeavoured to lead him to speak of subjects interesting to persons about to visit England, after the space of more than three years. He could speak of nothing but the genus Corvus.

'Upon my word, Captain Reud,' said he, 'I don't wish to seem impatient, but the wind is freshening. I long to be on board. I wish I could take one of these huge specimens with me.'

'You are heartily welcome to the whole batch.'

'Thank you, Captain Reud,' said I, rising and making him my best bow.

'Sharp lad, upon my soul!' said Reud.

'Thank you heartily, and very kindly, too. I will write a treatise upon them,' said Reeves.

'I should like to read it,' said I, turning to the naturalist.

'You shall, my good boy, you shall,' said he, patting me very kindly on the head. 'He *is* a sharp lad, indeed, Captain Reud; he wishes to read my treatise. After this treatise is finished, I shall send all the specimens to the Linnæan Society, of which I am an *unworthy* member,' (with a great emphasis on the word unworthy). 'I will first send them to Pidcock's menagerie,' (there were no Zoological Gardens then), 'with a perfect understanding, that, when they are dead, they shall be well stuffed.'

'They would much rather be stuffed alive,' said Reud, all glee, for he was now in his element. Our first lieutenant was totally in the dark, and looked silly in trying to look sapient. Pigtop and company, between the guns, were staring like those white, delicate-looking monsters with four feet, that own so many pettitoes, so general in poulterer's shops about Christmas, with remarkably protuberant eyes. Who could mention a stuck pig, in these days of refinement, under a less redundant paraphrase?

'A joke, of course—a very good joke,' said the learned in ornithology. 'A very good joke in a goose's mouth. I've seen it before somewhere—but never mind. However, seeing whence it came, it will do.'

'But I rather think,' said Reud, 'that these birds would not like to be stuffed when they are dead.'

'Nonsense—but what do they care about it? By-the-by, now you have got them on board, and in a state of confinement, do they still carry on the process of incubation?'

'Continually. They are all day and all night long hatching—'

'Gracious heavens! what?'

'Mischief.'

'You are laughing at me—pray let me see them at once.'

'In the first place, permit me to retract my offer of the whole—you are welcome to six of them heartily; and I wish that I may induce you to take them away,—filthy creatures! The seventh I shall retain for the sake of past good feelings; though I begin to suspect that he is not quite of so *good a breed* as I once thought him.'

This was wormwood to me. With a flushed brow I rose from my chair, and I cursed, in my heart, Joshua Daunton and his plausible tongue.

'I shall not even thank you, Captain Reud, for the preference,' said I, 'but request that I may be caged off with the lot.'

Reud, seeing that the equivoque could be carried no farther, explained, 'Don't be a fool, Rattlin, but sit down. Captain Reeves, these seven ornithological curiosities are of the generic description

Corvus, or crow, their specific term, scare—there is one beside you, and the other six are between the guns. If you have seen finer specimens of *scarecrows*, I'll eat them, when you have roasted them as well as I have roasted you.'

And then he indulged for a minute in his low, venomous giggle, that seemed to be the most perfect enjoyment of which his malicious bosom was capable.

'Captain Reud,' said I, 'tell me, sir, when, not seven months ago, I stood between you and death, did I show any white feather?'

'On my soul, you did not.'

'Then, sir, let me tell you—as far as I am concerned—I find your joke as deficient in wit as it is bad in taste.'

'Stop—beware—'

'I am quite of the same opinion with the young scarecrow that has just cawed,' said Captain Reeves, who was a grave man, and who never could see any point in a joke against himself. 'With your permission I will return on board, and look after my own poultry.'

So, after a formal exchange of bows, the strange commander left the cabin, Reud hallooing out to him as he left, 'You won't forget the treatise, Reeves.'

CHAPTER X

A dissertation on naval glory—Ralph falleth into disgrace, and findeth the march of his miseries arrested, by being himself put under an arrest—A fine ship run down, and nobody to blame but 'the Reefer.'

THE incident recorded in the last chapter will be read as a fiction —but it is fact, unexaggerated fact, as to the circumstances, though a little fined down in the relation; for the broad coarseness of the scene, as it was really acted, would be deemed too improbable, even for farce. It was events like these, and the previous overstraining of the mind, that fully determined me to take the first opportunity of quitting the service—not in disgust at it, for it was even then, in its unimproved state, a beautiful one—but it had, and still hath, its anomalies: they are but few, and I had stumbled upon the worst of them. It was very singular, but no less true, since the self-introduction of Joshua Daunton, I had never been happy, and never fortunate.

Through the rude and the cold flying mists of winter, after we had struck soundings, we again saw England. It was in the inclement month of January. I was starved and half clad. A beggar of any decent pretension, had he met me in the streets of London, would have taken the wall of me, though I had, at the time, more than three hundred dollars in cash, Spanish doubloons and silver, a power for drawing bills for a hundred a year, more than three years' pay due, and prize-money to a very considerable amount.

Under these circumstances, my eyes once more greeted my native land. Where were my glow of patriotism and my passion of poetry? They were not. I saw nothing before me but a black, a barren, and a forbidding coast. I endeavoured to fix my mind upon the fields over which I had bounded in my boyhood—I measured them in my mind's eye, hedge by hedge—they were distinct enough, but there was no sunshine upon them. Alas! I had seen a brighter sun elsewhere. And the friends that had been kind to the unowned one at Stickenham—yes, I would see them. But I had no longer the frank heart to offer. Yes, I would seek them, and be cold and studiously polite. I felt that I had not succeeded in my profession, with what *they* would call success. I had done my duty, and perhaps done it with high promise. Good, easy souls! I am sure they fancied that I should have returned something—perhaps a little—short of an admiral, but not very much.

I should like to know how a midshipman is to distinguish himself, otherwise than by doing his duty honourably and strictly, and that is no distinction at all, for they almost all do it. 'I wish we may have some brilliant action,' says one of the uninitiated, 'for I wish to distinguish myself.' 'Very well, my young aspirant'—which used, by-the-by, to be the corresponding term for midshipman in the French language—'very well, my young sir; here you are, in your frigate, alongside a heavier vessel than your own. Nay, it shall be a seventy-four, if you please, all for your particular honour and glory. There you are, stationed at the four after-guns on the main-deck. Blaze away, and distinguish yourself now.' 'O dear! I can't, for the smoke, and the smother, and the noise. I can't perform any heroical act here.' 'Well, but what *can you* do for your country and his majesty?' 'I can only see that the men train their guns well, and that they are properly supplied with powder and shot—this will never get my name in the gazette.' 'Only do that well, sir, and you will distinguish yourself. Never mind the gazette; your turn will come when you are a skipper, even, perhaps, when a lieutenant.'

The same applies to the young gentlemen, station them where you will. Gouty old gentlemen, who have sons at sea, and are prone to read the lives of Nelson and of our many other noble naval heroes, must rid themselves of the illusion of seeing the darlings of their hopes start away from their obscure yet important quarters, jump up in the faces of the enemy, flourish valorously their little dirks, lead the boarders over a handspike from ship to ship, put the French captain, surrounded by his officers, to the sword, haul down the tricolor with his own hands, and finally exclaim—'Hurrah for glory and Old England!' I say, elderly ladies, and gentlemen as elderly, must not expect this, notwithstanding their own folly, and some very funny naval novels that have been published. People must not desert their stations in action, even to do little bits of glorious heroism. The whole fraternity of reefers ought to thank me for this digression.

Thus, in the naval-novel sense of the word, I had not distinguished myself. My name had certainly appeared some few times in the captain's despatches, to the effect that 'Mr. Rattlin, in the cutter, had gallantly supported Lieutenant Selby, in cutting out a schooner,' &c. Glory! what did the world at large care about the paltry schooner, or the unknown lieutenant, who really did a prodigy of valour?—or the infinitely more insignificant 'Mr. Rattlin, who gallantly supported the said lieutenant in the cutter?' But of all this I do not complain. It is just as it should be—only—only I wish that our discriminating countrymen should comprehend what a vast amount of unrecorded heroism goes to make up even a single victory—heroism which is not, but ought to be, glory.

I got into disgrace. I record it frankly, as my boast is, throughout this biography, to have spoken the truth of all the different variations of my life. Since the captain's incipient insanity, the Eos had gradually become an ill-regulated ship. The gallant first lieutenant, formerly so smart and so active, had not escaped the general demoralization. He was a disappointed man. He had not distinguished himself. God knows, it was neither for want of daring nor expense of life. He had cut out every thing that could be

X

carried, and had attempted almost every thing that could not. I am compelled to say that these bloody onslaughts were as often failures as successes. He was no nearer his next step on the ladder of promotion than before. His temper became soured, and he was now often lax, sometimes unjust, and always irritable. The other officers shared in the general falling off, and too often made the quarter-deck a display for temper.

The third lieutenant—yes, I think it was the third—had mast-headed me, about the middle of the first dog-watch; most likely deservedly, for I had lately affected to give the proud and sullen answer. Before I went aloft to my miserable station, I represented to him that I had the first watch; that there were now about three of the young gentlemen doing their duty, the others having very wisely fallen ill, and taken the protection of the sick-list. I told him, respectfully enough, 'that, if he kept me up in that disagreeable station from half-past five till eight, I could not possibly do my duty, for very weariness, from eight till midnight. It was a physical impossibility.' But he was inexorable. Up I went, the demon of all evil passions gnawing at my heart.

It was almost dark when I went aloft. It was a gusty, dreary night, bitterly, very bitterly, cold. I was ill clad. At intervals, the fierce and frozen drifts, like the stings of so many wasps, drove fiercely into my face; and I believe that I must confess that I cried over my crooked and aching fingers, as the circulation went on with agony, or stopped with numbness. It is true, I was called down within the hour; but that hour of suffering had done me much constitutional mischief. I was stupified as much as if I had committed a debauch upon fat ale. However, I was too angry to complain, or to seek relief from the surgeon. I went on deck at half-past eight, with obtuse faculties and a reckless heart.

The frigate was, with a deeply-laden convoy, attempting to hold her course in the chops of the channel. It blew very hard. The waves were bounding about us with that short and angry leap peculiar, in tempestuous weather, to the narrow seas between England and France. It was excessively dark; and, not carrying sufficient sail to tack, we were wearing the ship every half hour, showing, of course, the proper signal lights to the convoy. We carried also the customary poop-light of the commodore.

Such was the state of affairs at a little after nine. The captain, the first lieutenant, the master, the officer of the watch, and the channel pilot, that we had taken on board off the Scilly Islands, with myself, were all on deck. Both the signal midshipmen were enjoying the comforts of sickness in their warm hammocks below. Now, I will endeavour to give a faithful account of what happened; and let the unprejudiced determine, in the horrible calamity that ensued, how much blame was fairly attributable to me. I must premise that, owing to shortness of number, even when all were well, there was no forecastle midshipman.

A dreadful gust of icy wind, accompanied by the arrowy sleet, rushes aft, rather heading us.

'The wind is getting more round to the east. We'd better wear at once,' said the pilot to the master.

'The pilot advises us to wear,' said the master to the captain.

'Mr. Farmer,' said the captain to the first lieutenant, 'watch and idlers,[1] wear ship.'

'Mr. Pond,' said Mr. Farmer to the lieutenant of the watch, (a diminutive and peppery little man, with a squeaking voice, and remarkable for nothing else excepting having a large wife and a large family, whom he was impatient to see), 'wear.'

'Mr. Rattlin,' squeaked Mr. Pond through his trumpet, 'order the boatswain's mate to turn the watch and idlers up—wear ship.'

'Boatswain's mate,' bawled out the sleepy and sulky Mr. Rattlin, 'watch and idlers, wear ship.'

'Ay, ay, sir—whew, whew, whittle whew—watch and idlers, wear ship! Tumble up there, tumble up. Master-at-arms, brush up the bone-polishers.'[2]

'What an infarnal nonsensical ceremony!' growled the pilot, *sotto voce:* 'all bawl and no haul—lucky we've plenty of sea-room.'

'Jump aft, Mr. Rattlin,' said the captain, 'and see that the convoy signal to wear is all right.'

Mr. Rattlin makes one step aft.

'Is the fore-topmast staysail halliards well manned, Mr. Rattlin? —Jump forward and see,' said the officer of the watch.

Mr. Rattlin makes one step forward.

'Is the deep sea-lead ready?' said the master. 'Mr. Rattlin, jump into the chains and see.'

Mr. Rattlin makes one step to the right—*starboard*, the wise call it.

'Mr. Rattlin, what the devil are you about?—where's the hand stationed to the foresheet?' said the first lieutenant. 'Jump there and see.'

Mr. Rattlin makes one step to the left hand,—*port*, the wise call it.

'Where's the midshipman o' th' watch—where's the midshipman o' th' watch?' roars out the captain. 'By Heavens, there's no light to show over the bows! Mr. Rattlin, be smart, sir,—jump forward, and see to it.'

The chilled, the torpid, and half-stupified Mr. Rattlin finally went forward on the forecastle, where he ought to have been from the first, the more especially as the boatswain was also on the sick list.

The consequence of all these multitudinous and almost simultaneous orders—to jump and see, when, by-the-by, it was too dark to see anything a yard off properly—was, that one of the signal lanterns was blown out, and the signal consequently imperfect—that the fore-topmast staysail halliards were so badly manned, that those upon them could scarcely start that then necessary sail from its netting—that the people were not ready with the deep sea-lead —that little Mr. Pond was obliged to put down his trumpet, and ease off the foresheet himself till relieved by the quarter-master; but, still, there actually *was* a lantern over the bows, and that in good time.

Well, the noble ship was no longer buffeted on her bows by the furious wind: as the haughty Essex turned on his heel from the blow of his termagant mistress queen, so did the Eos turn her back to the insulting blast, and flew rapidly before it. Owing to the darkness of the night, assisted by the weak voice of Mr. Pond, whose orders could not be very distinctly heard, perhaps a little to his lubberly manner of working the ship, the bounding frigate was much longer before the wind than necessary. I was straining my sight near the cathead[1] on one side, and the captain of the forecastle on the other, but we could discover nothing in the nearly palpable obscure.

It is an awful thing, this rushing through the darkness of a large floating world. The planets urge for ever their sublime course, but not as does a ship when the veil of night is on the ocean. The glorious luminaries travel through regions of light, directed by unerring wisdom, but the ark of man stumbles and reels through mists and folly, and rashness too often stands at the helm. And yet, I seldom viewed our frigate careering at night through the waters, with nothing to be seen but these the gorgeous stars above her, but I was apt to fancy she was as one of the heavenly brotherhood, humble certainly in her imitation, and lowly in her sphere.

On she dashed, and our anxious eyes saw nothing, whilst our minds feared greatly;—she is at her utmost speed. In her reckless course she seems sufficiently powerful to break up the stedfast rock, or tear the shoal from its roots at the bottom of the ocean. On she rushes! I think I hear faintly the merchant cry of 'Yeo —yo—yeo!' but the roar of the vexed waters beneath our bows, and the eternal singing of the winds through the frost-stiffened shrouds, prevent my being certain of the fact. But, I tremble excessively—when, behold, a huge long black mass is lying lazily before us, and so close that we can almost touch it!

'Hard a-port,' I roared out at the very top of my voice.

'Hard a-starboard,' sang out the captain of the forecastle, equally loudly.

Vain, vain were the contradictory orders. The frigate seemed to leap at the object before her as at a prey; and dire was the crash that ensued. As we may suppose the wrathful lioness springs upon the buffalo, and, meeting more resistance from its horny bulk than she had suspected, recoils and makes another spring, so did the Eos strike, rebound, then strike again.—I felt two distinct percussions.

The second stroke divided the obstacle; she passed through it or over it, and the eye looked in vain for the vast West Indiaman, the bearer of wealth, and gay hopes, and youth, and infancy, manly strength, and female beauty. There was a smothered feminine shriek, hushed by the whirling and down-absorbing waves, almost as soon as made. It was not loud, but it was fearfully distinct, and painfully human. One poor wretch only was saved, to tell her name and speak of the perished.

As usual, they had kept but a bad look-out. Her officers and her passengers were making merry in the cabin—the wine-cup was at their lips, and the song was floating joyously from the mouths of the fair ones returning to the land of their nativity. The blooming daughters, the newly-married wife, and two matrons with their innocent ones beside them, were all in the happiness of their hopes, when the Destroyer was upon them suddenly, truly like a strong man in the darkness of night; and they were all hurled, in the midst of their uncensurable revelry, to a deep grave, over which no tombstone shall ever tell 'of their whereabout.'

Our own jib-boom was snapped off short, and as quickly as is a twig in frosty weather. Supposing the ship had struck, every soul rushed on deck. They thanked God it was *only* the drowning of some forty fellow-creatures, and the destruction of a fine merchant-ship. We hauled the single poor fellow that was saved on board. The consternation among the officers was very great. It blew too hard to lower the boats: no effort was or could be made to rescue any chance struggler not carried down in the vortex of the parted and sunken ship—all was blank horror.

Besides the consternation and dismay natural to the appalling accident, there was the fear of the underwriters, and of the owners, and of damages, before the eyes of the captain. I was sent for aft.

'I had not charge of the deck,' said Captain Reud, looking fiercely at the first lieutenant. '*I* am not responsible for this lubberly calamity.'

'I had not the charge of the watch or the deck either,' said Mr. Farmer, in his turn looking at small Mr. Pond, who was looking aghast; 'surely, I cannot be held to be responsible.'

'But you gave orders, sir—I heard you myself give the word to raise the fore-tack—that looks very like taking charge of the deck —no, no, *I* am not responsible.'

'Not so fast, not so fast, Mr. Pond. I only assisted you for the good of the service, and to save the foresail.'

Mr. Pond looked very blank indeed, until he thought of the master, and then he recovered a great portion of his usual vivacity. Small men are always vivacious.

'No, no, I am not responsible—I was only working the ship under the directions of the master. Read the night orders, Mr. Farmer.'

'The night orders be d——d!' said the gruff old master.

'I will not have my night orders d——d,' said Reud. 'You and the officer of the watch must share the responsibility between you.'

'No offence at all, sir, to you or the night orders either. I am heartily sorry I d——d them—heartily; but, in the matter of wearing this here ship precisely at that there time, I only acted under the pilot, who has charge till we are securely anchored. Sure*lye*, I can't be 'sponsible.'

'Well,' said the pilot, 'here's a knot of tangled rope yarn—but that yarn won't do for old Weatherbrace, for, d'ye see, I'm a Sea

William (civilian), and not in no ways under martial law—and I'm only aboard this here craft as respects shoals and that like—I'm clearly not 'sponsible!—nothing to do in the varsal world with working her—'sponsible! pooh!—why did ye not keep a better look-out for'ard?'

'Why, Mr. Rattlin, why?' said the captain, the first lieutenant, the lieutenant of the watch, and the master.

'I kept as good a one as I could—the lanterns were over the bows.'

'You may depend upon it,' said the captain, 'that the matter will not be permitted to rest as it is. The owners and underwriters will demand a court of inquiry. Mr. Rattlin had charge of the fore-castle at the time. Mr. Rattlin, come here, sir. You sang out, just before this calamity happened, to port the helm.'

'I did, sir.'

'Quarter-master,' continued Reud, 'did you port the helm? Now, mind what you say; did you, sir? because if you *did not*, six dozen.'

'We did, sir—hard a-port.'

'And the ship immediately after struck?'

'Yes, sir.'

'Pooh! the case is clear—we need not talk about it any longer. A clear case, Mr. Farmer. Mr. Rattlin has charge of the forecastle—he descries a vessel a-head—he takes upon himself to order the helm a-port, and we run over and sink her accordingly. He is responsible, clearly.'

'Clearly,' was the answering echo from all the rejectors of responsibility.

'Mr. Rattlin, I am sorry for you. I once thought you a promising young man; but, since your desertion at Aniana—we must not mince matters now—you have become quite an altered character. You seem to have lost all zeal for the service. Zeal for the service is a thing that ought not to be lost; for a young gentleman without zeal for the service is a young gentleman, surely—you understand me—who is not zealous in the performance of his duty. I think I have made myself tolerably clear. Do you think, sir, that I should hold now the responsible commission I do hold under his majesty, if I had been without zeal for the service? I am sorry that I have a painful duty to perform. I must place you under an arrest, till I know what may be the port admiral's pleasure concerning this

unpleasant business; for—for the loss of the Mary Anne of
London you are clearly responsible.'

'Clearly,' (*omnes rursus*).

'Had you sung out hard a-starboard, instead of hard a-port, the
case might have been different.'

'Clearly.'

'Go down below to your berth, and consider yourself a prisoner.
The young gentlemen in his majesty's service are not permitted to
run down West Indiamen with impunity.'

'Clearly.'

In these kind of capstan-head court-martials, at which captains
will sometimes administer reefers' law, 'Woe to the weakest!'
a defence was quite a work of superfluity; so, consoling myself
with the vast responsibility with which, all at once, I found myself
invested, I went and turned in, anathematizing every created
thing above an inch high and a foot below the same dimensions.
However, in a very sound sleep I soon forgot every thing—even
the horrible scene I had just witnessed.

CHAPTER XI

*Distressing disclosures, and some very pretty symptoms of brotherly
love—with much excellent indignation utterly thrown away—
Joshua Daunton either a very great man, or a very great rogue—
perhaps both, as the terms are often synonymous.*

I HOPE the reader has not forgotten Joshua Daunton, for I did not.
Having a very especial regard to the health of his body, he took
care to keep himself ill. The seventy-one lashes due to him he
would most generously have remitted altogether. His eagerness to
cancel the debt was only equal to Captain Reud's eagerness to
pay, and to that of his six midshipmen masters to see it paid. Old
Pigtop was positively devout in this wish; for, after the gash had
healed, it left a very singular scar, that traversed his lip obliquely,
and gave a most ludicrous expression to a face that was before
remarkably ill-favoured. One side of his visage seemed to have
a continual ghastly smirk, like what you might suppose to
decorate the countenance of a half-drunken Succubus; the other,

a continual whimper, that reminded you of a lately whipped baboon.

I concluded that Daunton was really ill, for he kept to his hammock in the sick bay; and Dr. Thompson was much too clever, and too old a man-of-war's man, to be deceived by a simulated sickness.

The day after, when I was enjoying my arrest in the dignified idleness of a snooze in a pea-jacket, on one of the lockers, the loblolly-boy came to me, saying that Daunton was much worse, and that he humbly and earnestly requested to see me. I went, though with much reluctance. He appeared to be dreadfully ill, yet an ambiguous smile lighted up his countenance when he saw me moodily standing near him.

He was seated on one corner of the bench in the bay, apparently under the influence of ague, for he trembled excessively, and he was well wrapped up in blankets. Altogether, notwithstanding the regularity of his features, he was a revolting spectacle. The following curious dialogue ensued.

'Daunton, I am ready to hear you.'

'Thank you, Ralph.'

'Fellow! you may have heard that I am a prisoner—in disgrace —but not in dishonour; but know, scoundrel, that, if I were to swing the next minute at the yard-arm, I would not tolerate or answer to such familiarity. Speak respectfully, or I leave you.'

'Mr. Rattlin, pray do not speak so loudly, or the other invalids will hear us.'

'Hear us, sirrah! they may, and welcome. Scoundrel! can *we* have any secrets?'

The fiery hate that flashed from the eye of venomous impotence played upon me, at the very moment that the tone of his voice became more bland, and his deportment more submissive.

'Mr. Rattlin, your honour, will you condescend to hear me? It is for your own good, sir. Pray be no longer angry. I think I am dying; will you forgive me?—will you shake hands with me?' And he extended to me his thin and delicate hand.

'Oh, no, no!' I exclaimed, accompanying my sneer with all the scorn that I could put in my countenance. 'Such things as you don't die—reptiles are tenacious of life. For the malicious and ape-like mischiefs that you have done to me and to my messmates— though in positive guilt I hold them to be worse than actual felony

—I forgive you—but, interchange the token of friendship with such as you—never!'

'Ralph Rattlin, I know you!'

'Insolent rascal! know yourself; dare to send for me no more. I leave you.'

I turned upon my heel, and was about leaving this floating hospital, when again that familiar tone of the voice that had struck the inmost chord of my heart in his shrieking appeal at the gangway, arrested me, and the astounding words which he uttered quickly brought me to his side. In that strange tone, that seemed to have been born with my existence, he exclaimed, distinctly, yet not loudly, 'Brother Ralph, listen to me!'

'Liar, cheat, swindler!' I hissed forth in an impassioned whisper, close to his inclined ear, 'my heart disowns you—my soul abhors you—my gorge rises at you. I abominate—I loathe you—most contemptible, yet most ineffable liar!'

'Oh, brother!' and a hectic flush came over his chalky countenance, whilst a sardonic smile played over his features. 'You can speak low enough now. 'Tis a pity that primogeniture is so little regarded in his majesty's vessels of war; but methinks that you are but little dutiful, seeing that I am some ten years your senior, and that I do not scorn to own *you*, though you are the son of my father's paramour.'

The horrible words shot ice into my heart. I could no longer retain my stooping position over him, but, feeling faint, and very sick, I sat down involuntarily beside him. But the agony of apprehension was but for a moment. A mirth, stern and wild, brought its relief to my paralysed bosom, and, laughing loudly, I jumped up and exclaimed, 'Josh, you little vagabond, come, carry me a-pick-a-back—son of a respectable pawnbroker of Whitechapel—how many paramours was the worthy old gentleman in the habit of keeping? Respectable scion of such a respectable parent, who finished his studies by a little tramping, a little thieving, a little swindling, a little forging—I heartily thank you for the amusement you have afforded me.'

'Oh, my good brother, deceive not yourself! I repeat that I have tramped, thieved, swindled, ay, and forged. And to whom do I owe all this ignominy? To you—to you—to you. Yet I do not hate you very, very much. You showed some fraternal feeling when they seared my back with the indelible

scar of disgrace. I have lied to you, but it suited my purpose.'

'And I have given you the confidence due to a liar.'

'What! still incredulous, brother of mine! Do you know these
—and these?'

The handwriting was singular, and very elegant. I knew the
letters at once. They were the somewhat affected amatory effusions
of that superb woman, Mrs. Causand, whom I have described in
the early part of this life. They spoke of Ralph—of Ralph Rattlin—
and described, with tolerable accuracy, my singular birth at the
Crown Inn at Reading.

There were three letters. The two first that I read contained
merely passionate protestations of affection; the third, that had
reference to myself, spoke darkly. After much that is usual in the
ardent style of unhallowed love, it went on, as nearly as I can recollect, in these words—'I have suffered greatly—suffered with you,
and for you. The child is, however, now safe, and well provided
for. It is placed with a decent woman of the name of Brandon, Rose
Brandon. A discovery now is impossible. We have managed the
thing admirably. The child is fair,' &c., &c.

In the midst of my agitation, I remarked that the writer did not
speak of the infant as 'my child,' nor with the affection of a mother
—and yet, without a great stretch of credulity, the inference
seemed plain that she was the parent of it, though not a fond one.

'Mysterious man! who are you, and who am I?'

'Your disgraced, your discarded, yet your legitimate, brother.
More it suits me not now that you should know. I am weak in
frame, but I am steel in purpose. You, you have been the bane of
my life. Since your clandestine birth, our father loved me no more.
I will have my broad acres back—I will—they are mine—and you
only stand between me and them.'

'Desperate and degraded man!—I believe, even after this pretended confession, that you are an impostor to me, as much as you
are to the rest of the world. I now understand some things that
were before dark to me. My life seems to stand in your way—and
your cowardice only prevents you from taking it. You tell me you
are a forger—these letters are forgeries. Mrs. Causand is not my
mother, nor are you my brother. Pray, where did you get them?'

'I stole them from our father's escritoire.'

'Amiable son! But I weary myself no more with your tissue of falsehoods. To-morrow we shall cast anchor. I will leave the service, and devote the rest of my life to the discovery of my origin. I will learn your real name, I will trace out your crimes—and the hands of justice shall at once terminate my doubts, and your life of infamy —we are enemies to the death!'

'A fair challenge and fairly spoken. I accept it, from my soul. You refused my hand in brotherly love; for, by the grey hairs of our common parent, in brotherly love it was offered to you—will you now take it as a pledge of a burning, a never-dying, enmity between us—it is at present emaciated and withered. It has been seized up at your detested gangway—it has been held up at the bar of justice; but it will gain strength, my brother—there, take it, sir—and despise it not.'

I shuddered as I received the pledge of hate; and his grasp, though I was in the plenitude of youthful vigour, was stronger than my own.

This dreadful conference had been carried on principally in whispers; but, owing to several bursts of emotion on my part, enough had transpired among those present to give them to understand that I had been claimed as a brother, and that I had very hard-heartedly rejected the claim. The sick murmured among themselves, and looked upon me displeasingly.

After we had passed our mutual defiance, there was silence between us for several minutes; he coiling himself up like an adder in his corner, and I pacing the deck, my bosom swelling with contending emotions. 'If he should really be my brother,' thought I. The idea was horrible to me. I again paused in my walk, and looked upon him stedfastly; but I found no sympathy with him. His style of thin and pallid beauty was hateful to me—there was no expression in his countenance upon which I could hang the remotest feeling of love. He bore my scrutiny, in his weakness, proudly.

'Daunton,' said I, at length, 'you have failed: in endeavouring to make a tool, you have created an enemy and an avenger of the outraged laws. I shall be in London in the course of eight-and-forty hours—you cannot escape me—if it cost me a hundred pounds, I will loose the bloodhounds of justice after you—you shall be made in chains to give up your hateful secret. I am no longer a boy, nor you, nor the lawyer that administers my affairs, shall no longer make a plaything of me. I will know who I am. Thank God, I can always ask Mrs. Cherfeuil.'

At that name, a smile, no longer bitter, but deeply melancholy, and almost sweet, came over his effeminate features. But it lasted not long. That smile, like a few tones of his voice, seemed so familiar to me. Was I one of two existences, the consciousness of the one nearly, but not quite, blotting out the other? I looked upon him again, and the smile was gone; but a look of grief, solemn and heart-rending, had supplied its place—and then the big and involuntary tear stood in his eye. I know not whether it fell, for he held down his arm to the concealment of his face, and spoke not.

Had the wretch a heart, after all?

As I turned to depart, he lifted up his face, and all that was amiable in its expression had fled. With a calm sneer he said, 'May I trouble you, Mr. Rattlin, for those letters which I handed over to you for your perusal?'

'I shall keep them.'

'Is your code of equity as low as mine? They are my property; I paid dearly enough for them. And what says your code of honour to such conduct?'

'There, take your detested forgeries! We shall meet in London.'

'Mr. Rattlin forgets that he is a prisoner.'

'Absurd! The charge cannot be sustained for a moment.'

'Be it so. Peradventure, I shall be in London before you.'

CHAPTER XII

*Listeners seldom hear good things of themselves—Ralph at a
dreadful discount with his messmates, but contrives to settle his
accounts with his principal debtor.*

I LEFT him, with a strong foreboding that he would work me some direful mischief. Wretched, unutterably wretched, were the ensuing day and night that I passed. I retired to the gloom of the midshipmen's den, and battened on my terrible reflections to a fulness of misery that none but youth can feel, or feeling bear up against. I could not disbelieve, and I would not believe, him. The sweet creations of my dreams by night, of my visions and my imaginings by day, were that I was of honourable, if not of distinguished, birth. Over these the base enchanter had waved his wand; and they stood before me now in hideous shapes. Contumely had overtaken me, even where I was; and scorn and contempt, succeeded by its pitiful train of followers, seemed to be collecting their venom, in order to hoot me through the world.

For the long day, I sate, with my head buried in my hands on the sordid table of our berth. I ate not, I spoke not. The ribaldry of my coarse associates moved me not; their boisterous and vulgar mirth aroused me not. They thought me, owing to my arrest, and my anticipations of its consequences, torpid with fear. They were deceived. I was never more alive. My existence was—if I may so speak—glowing and fiery hot; my sense of being was intense with various misery. My brain was at once clear and scorching. With all this excitement, there came not the least taint of mental aberration. My intellects were never more unclouded. I was never more capable of girding up my loins, and doing battle with the world, like a strong man.

Towards evening, another piece of intelligence reached me, that alarmed and astounded me. Since the laying on of the one lash on the back of Joshua Daunton, our old servant had descended from the mizen-top, again to wait upon us. He was, in his way, an insatiate news-gatherer; but he was as liberal in dispensing it as he was eager in acquiring it.

The midshipmen were drinking, out of the still unbroken cups and two or three tin panikins, their grog at eight o'clock in the evening, when our unshod and dirty attendant spoke thus:

'Oh, Mr. Pigtop!—such news!—such strange news! You'll be so very sorry to hear it, sir, and so will all the young gentlemen.'

'What, has the ship tumbled overboard, or the pig ballast mutinied for arrears of pay?'

'Oh, sir, ten thousand times worse than that! That thief of the world, sir, Joshua Daunton, is not to have his six dozen, after all, sir, though he did corrupt all the midshipmen's clothes, sir. Dr. Thompson has taken him into his own cabin, and nothing is now too good for him.'

'But hanging,' said the indignant and scarred master's-mate. 'If he's not flogged, I'll have the life out of him yet, though he should turn out to be the only son of my Lord Dun-know-who.' Pigtop was a wit, in a small midshipman-like way. 'He's turned out to be some great man, they say, however—in clog or so, I think they call it; though, for my part, I remembers him in irons well

enough not more than a fortnight aback—and he's had a taste of
the girl with nine tails, however—that's one comfort to me, whatever he may turn out.'

The vulgar have strange sources from which to derive comfort.

'But, are you sure of all this, Bill?' said Mr. Staines. 'Because,
if he should turn out to be somebody, I'll make him pay me for
my traps; that's as certain now as that he'll be sent to Old Davy.'

'Certain sure. He showed the Doctor papers enough to set up
a lawyer's shop. But that's not the best of it—hum—ha! Do you
think, Mr. Pigtop, that Mr. Rattlin's caulking?' (i.e., asleep).

'He has not moved this three hours. I owe Rattlin one for bringing this blackguard on board. There may be something in this,
after all. He claimed Rattlin as his brother at the gangway, or something of that sort. Now, that makes me comfortable. It will take our
proud messmate down a peg or two, I'm calculating—with his
smooth face, and his little bits of Latin and Greek, and his parley-
vooing. Oh ho! but it's as good as a bottle of rum to me. With all
his dollars, and his bills, and his airs, I never had a brother seized
up at the gangway. And the captain and the officers once made such
a fuss about him! D——n his smooth face!—I've a great mind to
wake him, and hit him a wipe across the chaps. He knocked me
down with the davit-block, for twitting him about that girl of his,
that was drowned swimming after him. I'll have satisfaction for
that. The captain ordered me to leave the ship for being knocked
down. Well—we shall see who'll be ordered to leave the ship now.
I never caused a girl's death by desarting her. Upon my soul, I've
a great mind to rouse him, and hit him a slap of the chaps. I hate
smooth faces.'

'Well,' said Staines, 'you may depend upon it, Rattlin *is* asleep,
or he would have wopped you, Pigtop, for your compliments.'

'He! I should very much like to see it—the spooney!'

'If Mr. Rattlin is caulking,' said our *valet de chambre*, 'there
can't be no harm done whatsomever. But they do say, in the sick
bay, as how Mr. Rattlin isn't himself, but that Joshua Daunton is
he, and that he is nobody at all whatsomever; though Gibbons says,
and he's a cute one, that if Mr. Rattlin is not Mr. Rattlin, seeing as
how Joshua Daunton is Mr. Rattlin, Mr. Rattlin must be somebody else—and, as a secret, he told me, as like as not, he must be
Joshua Daunton.'

'Well, here's comfort again. If Mr. Rattlin—*Mr.* indeed!—

turns out to be a swindler, as I'm sure he will, it wouldn't be law-ful, nor right, nor proper, in me to pay him the money I owe him,' said the conscientious Mr. Pigtop, 'D—n his smooth face!—I should like to have the spoiling of it.'

Here was important information for me to ruminate upon. I was determined to remain still so long as I could gain any intel-ligence. But the conversation—if conversation we must term the gibberish of my associates—having taken another turn, I slowly lifted up my smooth face, and, confronting Mr. Pigtop's rough one, I said to him very coolly, 'Mr. Pigtop, I am going to do what you would very much like to see—I am going to wop you.'

'Wop me!—no, no, it's not come to that yet. I have heard some-thing—I've a character to support—I must not demean myself.'

'There is my smooth face right before you—I dare you to strike it—you dare not! Then, thus, base rascal, I beat you to the earth!' And Pigtop toppled down.

Now, all this was very wrong on my part, and very imprudent; for I must confess that he had before beaten me in a regular fistic encounter. But it was really a great relief to me. I longed for some vent to my angry and exasperated feelings. We were soon out in the steerage. Oh! the woolfishness of human nature! That low and brutal fight was a great luxury to me. Positively, at the time, I did not feel his blows. At every murderous lunge that I made at him, I shouted, 'Take that, Daunton;' or, 'Was that well planted, brother?'

Had we fought either with sword or pistol, the enjoyment would have been infinitely less to me. There was a stern rapture in pound-ing him beneath me—in dashing my hands in his blood—in dis-figuring his face piecemeal. In our evil passions, we are sad brutes. Pigtop had the pluck natural to Englishmen—he would rather not have fought just then; but, having once begun, he seemed resolved to see it out manfully. The consequence was—to use a common and expressive phrase—I beat him to within an inch of his life, and then cried with vexation, because he could no longer stand up to be beaten out of the little that my fury had left him.

When the fray was over, my sturdy opponent had no reason to be envious of my smooth face.

Rather inflamed than satiated with the result of my encounter, whilst my opponent turned in his hammock, and there lay moan-ing, I, with both my eyes dreadfully blackened, and my countenance puffed up, threw myself upon the lockers, and there sleeplessly passed the whole night, devouring my own heart. If, for a moment, I happened to doze, I was tearing, in my imagination, Joshua Daunton piecemeal, hurling him down precipices, or crushing him beneath the jagged fragments of stupendous rocks. It was a night of agony.

Twenty-five years ago, a set-to in a midshipman's berth was the general way of settling a dispute, or of avenging an insult. It was thought to be neither ungentlemanly nor degrading. Then we held our pistols and swords for enemies only; our fists were at the service of our friends.

We have altered all that now. I do but describe things as they were: let the christian, and the moralist, and the gentleman, settle the matter between them, as to the manner in which these things ought to be arranged.

CHAPTER XIII

Soft tack, one of the best tacks, after all—Legs of mutton sometimes produce friendships of long standing completely proved, as well as the value of good grain best ascertained, after it has been well thrashed.

The next day we anchored in the Downs. Weak, stiff, and ill, I surveyed myself in my dressing-glass. My battered features presented a hideous spectacle. But I cared not. I was a prisoner— I should have no occasion to emerge from the gloom of the steerage. This was truly a happy return to my native shores.

But I was not altogether left without commiseration—not altogether without sympathy. Both Dr. Thompson and the purser looked in to see me. The Doctor, especially, seemed to feel deeply for my situation. He told me that he had heard a strange story; but that, as yet, he was not at liberty to mention any particulars. He assured me that he entirely acquitted me of any participation in a series of base deceptions that had been practised upon an ancient, a distinguished, and wealthy family. He bade me hope for the best, and always consider him as my friend. The purser spoke to the same effect. I told them that my conviction was that

Y

it was they, and not I, who were the victims of deception. I stated that I had never pretended to rank or parentage of any sort; I acknowledged that every thing connected with my family was a perfect mystery; but I asked them how they could place any faith in the assertions of a man who was in a mean capacity when I met with him—who had confessed to me a multiplicity of villainies —and who had corroborated the truth of his own confessions by his uniformly wicked conduct whilst on board.

To all this they both smiled very sapiently, and told me they had their reasons.

'Well,' said I, 'you are wise, and, compared to me, old men. You cannot think this Daunton a moral character—you cannot think him honest. Still, telling me you are my friends, you champion him against me. And yet I know not how or in what manner. If he should prove my brother, the world is wide enough for us both: let him keep out of my way, if he can. Depend upon it, doctor, he is acting upon an after-thought. He has been forced into a desperate course. You marked his abject cowardice at the gangway. During the many hours that he was in irons, before that punishment he so much dreaded was inflicted, why did he not then send for you, and, to save himself, make to you these important disclosures?—Merely because he did not then think of it. By heavens!—a light rushes on me—he is a house-breaker!—he has committed some burglary, and stolen papers relating to me; and no doubt he has followed me, first, with the intention of selling to me the purloined secret at some unconscionable price, and he has since thought fit to change his plan for something more considerable, more wicked.'

'My poor boy,' said the doctor kindly, 'you are under a delusion. Let me change the subject, and puncture you with my lancet under the eyes—they are dreadfully contused. Well, Rattlin, we are to go to Sheerness directly, and be paid off. You may depend upon it, the captain will think better about this arrest of your's, particularly as the two men at the wheel positively contradict the quarter-master, and affirm that the helm was put hard a-starboard, and not hard a-port. It appears to us that it was of little consequence, when the ship was first discovered, how the helm was put. The fault was evidently on the part of those who so awfully suffered for it. By-the-by, there has been a change among the lords of the Admiralty—there are two new junior ones.'

'Begging your pardon, doctor, what the devil is a change among the junior lords of the Admiralty to a half starved, imprisoned, blackened-eyed, ragged reefer?'

Much more than I was aware of.

'Now,' said I to the purser, 'if you wish to do me a real kindness, change me some of my Spanish for English money, and let the first bumboat that comes alongside be ready to go ashore in ballast, for I shall certainly clear it.'

My request was immediately complied with; and my friends, for the present, took their leave.

Those blessed bearers of the good things of this life, the bumboats, were not yet permitted alongside. Every five minutes, I sent Master Bill up to see. Great are the miseries of a midshipman's berth, when the crockery is all broken, and the grog all drunk, and the salt junk all eaten. But great, exceedingly great, are the pleasures of the same berth, when, after a long cruise, on coming into port, the first loaf of soft tack is on the table, the first leg of mutton is in the boiler, and the first pound of fresh butter is before the watering mouths of the expectants. Aldermen of London, you feed much—epicures of the West end, you feed delicately; but neither of you know what real luxuries are. Go to sea for six months upon midshipman allowance, eked out by midshipmen's improvidence; and, on your return, the greasy bumboat, first beating against the ship's sides, will afford you a practical lesson upon the art of papillary[1] enjoyment.

It is, I must confess, very unromantic, and not at all like the hero of three volumes, to confess that, for a time, my impulses of anger had given way to the gnawings of hunger; and I thought, for a time, less of Joshua Daunton than of the first succulent cut into a leg of Southdown mutton.

The blessed *avatar*[2] at length took place. The bumboat and the frigate lovingly rubbed sides, and, like an angel descending from heaven, I saw Bill coming down the after-hatchway, his face radiant with the glory of expectant repletion, a leg of mutton in each hand, two quartern loaves under each arm, and between each pair of loaves was jammed a pound of fresh butter. I had the legs of mutton in the berth, and laid on the table that I might contemplate them, whilst I sent my messenger up for as many bottles of porter as I could buy. But I was not permitted to enjoy the divine contemplation all to myself. My five messmates came to partake of this access of happiness. As the legs of mutton lay on the table, how devoutly we ogled their delicate fat, and speculated upon the rich and gravy-charged lean! We apostrophized them—we patted them endearingly with our hands—and, when Bill again made his appearance laden with sundry bottles of porter, our ecstacy was running at the rate of fourteen knots an hour.

My messmates settled themselves on the lockers smiling amiably. How sorry they were that my eyes were so blackened, and my face so swollen! With what urbanity they smiled upon me! I was of the right sort—the good fellow—d—n him, who would hurt a hair of my head. They were all ready to go a step farther than purgatory for me.

'Gentlemen,' said I, making a semicircular barricade round me of my four quartern loaves, my two pounds of fresh butter, and eleven of my bottles of porter, for I was just about to knock the head off the twelfth, (who under such circumstances could have waited for corkscrews?) 'Gentlemen,' said I, 'get your knives ready, we will have lunch.' Shylock never flourished his more eagerly than did my companions their's, each eyeing a loaf.

'Gentlemen, we will have lunch—but, as I don't think that lately you have used me quite well, (countenances all round serious), and as I have, as you all well know, laid out much money, with little thanks, upon this mess, (faces quite dejected), permit me to remind you, that there is still some biscuit in the bread-bag, and that this before me is private property.'

The lower jaws of my messmates dropped, as if conscious that there would be no occupation for them. I cut a fine slice off the new bread, spread it thickly with the butter, tossed over a foaming mug of porter, and, eating the first mouthful of the delicious preparation, with a superfluity of emphatic smacks, I burst into laughter at the woe-begone looks around me.

'What,' said I, 'could you think so meanly of me? You have treated me according to your natures, I treat you according to mine. Fall to, dogs, and devour!—peck up the crumbs, scarecrows, as the Creole calls you, and be filled. But, pause and be just, even to your own appetites. Notwithstanding our lunch, let us dine. Let us divide the four loaves into eight equal portions. There are six of us here, and Bill must have his share. We will have more for our dinner, when the legs of mutton make their appearance.'

We drank each of us a bottle of porter, and finished our half-quartern loaves with wonderful alacrity, Bill keeping us gladsome company. My messmates then left the berth, pronouncing me a good fellow. The eighth portion of soft tommy[1] and butter, with a bottle of porter, I made the servant leave on the table; and then sent him again to the bumboat, to procure other necessaries, to make the accompaniments to our mutton perfect.

In the mean time, Pigtop, who lay in his hammock, directly across the window of our berth, had been a tantalized observer of all that had passed. I crouched myself up in one corner of the hole, and was gradually falling into disagreeable ruminations, when Mr. Pigtop crept out of his hammock and into the berth, and sate himself down as far from me as possible.

'Rattlin,' said he at length dolefully, 'you have beaten me dreadfully.'

'It was your own seeking—I am sorry for your sufferings.'

'Well—I thank ye for that same—I don't mean the beating—you know that I stood up to you like a man. Is there malice between us?'

'On my part, none. Why did you provoke me?'

'I was wrong—infarnally wrong—and, may be, I would have owned it before—but for your quick temper, and that hard punch in the chaps. I have had the worst of it. It goes to my heart, Rattlin, that I, an old sailor, and a man nearly forty, should be knocked about by a mere boy—it is not decent—it is not becoming—it is not natural—I shall never get over it. I wish I could undo the done things of yesterday.'

'And so do I, heartily—fervently.'

'Well—that is kindly said—and I old enough to be your father—and twenty-five years at sea—beaten to a stand still. Sorry I ever entered the cursed ship.'

'How much of all this,' thought I, 'is genuine feeling, how much genuine appetite?' I was sorry for the poor fellow, however.

'Rattlin, owing to one crooked thing and another, we have lately fared miserably. The ship has been a hell upon the waters. I am faint for the want of something to support me. Is that prog and that bottle of porter private property?'

'They are my property. I do not offer them to you, because I would not that you thought that I was aping magnanimity. For the respect that I shall always owe to an old sailor, I say to you frankly, that, if your feelings are sufficiently amicable towards me to take it, take it, and with it a welcome and a wish that it may do you much good—but, if your blood is still evil towards me, for the sake of your own integrity you would reject it, though you starved.'

'Rattlin, I break bread with you as a friend. I am confoundedly sorry that I have been prejudiced against you—and there's my hand upon it.'

I shook hands with him heartily, and said—'Pigtop, I cannot regret that I did my best to repel your insult, but I sincerely regret its consequences. Henceforward, you shall insult me twice before I lift my hand against you once.'

'I will never insult you again. I will be your fast friend, and perhaps I may have the means of proving it.'

It now became my turn to be astonished. Instead of seeing the hungry oldster fall to, like a ravenous dog, he broke off a small corner from the bread, ate it, and was in the act of retiring, when I hailed him.

'Halloa!—Pigtop—what's in the wind now? My friend, you do but little honour to my cheer, and I am sure that you must want it.'

'No, no,' said Pigtop, with much feeling—'you shall never suppose that the old sailor sold the birthright of his honour for a mess of pottage.'

'Well felt and well said, by all that's upright! But, nevertheless, you shall drink this bottle of porter, and eat this bread and butter—and so I'll e'en cut it up into very excellent rounds. D—n it, you shan't accept my friendship without accepting my fare. I like your spirit so well, Pigtop, that, for your sake, I will never judge of a man again, until I have thrashed him soundly.'

To the surprise of my messmates, when they assembled punctually to the feast of mutton, they discovered me and old Pigtop, hand in hand across the table, discussing another bottle of porter.

CHAPTER XIV

Ralph is placed in an awkward predicament, being put upon his trial to prove his identity, and having no witnesses to call but himself—All voices against him but his own.

At this period, every day, nay, almost every hour, seemed to bring its startling event. Ere good digestion had followed our very good appetites, bustle and agitation pervaded the whole ship. It had been telegraphed from on shore that one of the junior lords of the Admiralty was coming on board immediately. There was blank dismay in our berth. How could my messmates possibly go on the quarter-deck, and assist to receive the dignified personage? Much did I enjoy the immunity that, I supposed, being a prisoner gave to me.

The portentous message came down that 'the young gentlemen, in full uniform, are expected to be on the quarter-deck to receive the lord of the Admiralty.' All the consolation that I could give was quoting to them the speech of Lady Macbeth to her guests—'Go, nor stand upon the order of your going.' The firing of the salute from the main-deck guns announced the approach, and the clanking of the muskets of the marines on the deck, after they had presented arms, the arrival of the lord plainly to me, in my darksome habitation. Ten minutes had not elapsed, during which I was hugging myself with the thought that all this pomp and circumstance could not annoy me, when, breathless with haste, there rushed one, two, three, four messengers, each treading on the heels of the other, telling me the lord of the Admiralty wished to see me immediately in the captain's cabin.

'Me! see me! What, in the name of all that is disastrous, can he want with me?' I would come when I had made a little alteration in my dress. Trusting that he was as impatient as all great men usually are when dealing with little ones, I hoped by dilatoriness to weary him out, and thus remain unseen. Vain speculation! A minute had scarcely elapsed, when one of the lieutenants came down in a half friendly, half imperative manner, to acquaint me that I *must* come up immediately.

The scene that ensued—how can I sufficiently describe it! Had I not been sustained by the impudence of desperation, I should have jumped overboard directly I had got on deck. I found myself, not well knowing by what kind of locomotion I got there, in the fore-cabin, where was spread a very handsome collation, round which were assembled some fifteen officers, all in their full-dress uniforms, in the midst of which, a feeble, delicate-looking, and excessively neatly dressed old gentleman stood, in plain clothes. His years must have been far beyond seventy. He was fidgetty, indeed, to that degree that would induce you to think that he was a little palsied.

I cannot answer for the silent operations that take place in other men's minds, but, in my own, even under the greatest misfortunes, a droll conceit will more rally my crushed spirits than all the moral consolations that Blair ever penned.

'If this be the *junior* lord of the Admiralty,' thought I, 'how venerably patriarchal must be his four seniors!' I smiled at the idea as I bowed.

Let us describe the person that smiled and bowed to this august assembly.

Figure to yourself a tall youth, attired in a blue cotton jacket, with the uniform button, a once white kerseymere waistcoat, and duck trowsers, on which were mapped, in cloudy colours—produced by stains of black-strap, peasoup, and the other etceteras that may be found in that receptacle of abominations, an ill-regulated midshipman's berth—more oceans, seas, bays, and promontories, than nature ever gave to this unhappy globe. Beneath these were discovered a pair of dark blue worsted stockings, terminated by a pair of purser's shoes—things of a hybrid breed, between a pair of cast off slippers and the ploughman's clodhoppers, fitting as well as the former, and nearly as heavy as the latter. Now, this costume, in the depth of winter, was sufficiently light and *bizarre*; but the manner in which I had contrived to decorate my countenance soon riveted all attention to that specimen of the 'human face divine,' marred by the hand of man. Thanks to the expertness of Mr. Pigtop, my eyes were singularly well blackened, and the swelling of my face, particularly about the upper lip, had not yet subsided. Owing to my remaining so much, since my arrest, in the obscurity of the between-decks, and perhaps to some inflammation in my eyes, from my recent beating, I blinked upon those before me like an owl.

'As—ton—ish—ing!' said my Lord Whiffledale. 'Is that Mr. Ralph Rattlin?'

'The same, my lord,' said Captain Reud. 'Shall I introduce him to your lordship?'

'By no manner of means—yet—for his father's sake—really—ridiculous!—Henry, the fifth baron of Whiffledale—ah!—black eyes, filthy costume, very particularly filthy, upon my honour. How is this, Captain Reud? Of course, my present visit is not official; but, merely to satisfy my curiosity as a gentleman, how is it that your first lieutenant permits the young gentlemen to so far disgrace—I must use the word—the service—as you see—in—in my young friend, there, with the worsted stockings, and swelled lip, and—black eyes—'

When I first made my appearance, all the captains, then and there collected, had looked upon me with any thing but flattering regards; some turned up their noses, some grinned, all appeared astonished, and all disgusted. At the conclusion of this speech, I was surprised at the benignity which beamed upon me from under their variously shaped and coloured eyebrows. There was magic in the words 'for his father's sake,' and 'my young friend.'

Captain Reud replied, 'It is not, my lord, so much the fault of Mr. Rattlin as it would at the first blush appear to be. He himself pressed a wicked, mischievous young blackguard, who was appointed the young gentleman's servant. Incredible as the fact may appear, my lord, he contrived, in a manner that Dr. Thompson can best explain to you, to destroy all the clothes of his young masters, merely in the wantonness of his malice. I know that Mr. Rattlin is well provided with money, and that he will take the first opportunity again to assume the garb of a gentleman; and I do assure your lordship that no man becomes it better.'

'Sir, if this youth be Mr. Rattlin—I believe it—the very oldest blood in the country flows in his veins—but, it does seem a sort of a kind of a species of miracle how a scion of that noble house should stand before me, his father's friend, with two black eyes and a ragged jacket—there may be some mistake after all. I was going, Mr. Rattlin, to take you with me to my hotel, having matters of the utmost importance to communicate to you; but, oh no!—I am not fastidious, so we had better first have a little private conference in the after—gentlemen, will you excuse us?' bowing round—'Captain Reud will perhaps do me the favour to be of the party?'

So, into the after-cabin we three went, I burning with impatience, and speechless with agitation, supposing that the much-coveted secret of my parentage would be at length unfolded to me.

Lord Whiffledale and Captain Reud being seated with their backs to the cabin-windows, and I standing before them with the light full upon my disfigured face, I must have had a great deal more the look of a battered blackguard, being tried for petty larceny, than a young gentleman on the eve of being acknowledged the heir to greatness by a very noble lord.

There was a pause for some minutes, during which Lord Whiffledale was preparing to be imposing, and the light of mischief began to beam with incipient insanity in Reud's eye. 'Certainly,' I said to myself, 'he will not dare to practise one of his mad pranks upon a lord of the Admiralty!' What will not madness dare?

His lordship, having taken snuff very solemnly, and looked round him with a calm circumspection, fixing his dull eye upon me, and wagging his head, with an equable motion, slowly up and down, spoke as follows:

'There is a Providence above us all. It is seen, Mr. Rattlin, in the fall of a sparrow—it has protected our glorious constitution—it has sanctified the pillars of the state. Providence is, Mr. Rattlin—do you really know what Providence is?—I ask you the question advisedly—I always speak advisedly—I ask you, do you know what Providence is?—Do not speak—interruptions are unseemly—there are few who interrupt me. Providence, young man, has brought me on board this frigate to-day—the wind is north-easterly, what there is of it, may increase my catarrh—there is the hand of Providence in every thing. I promised my most honourable friend, that I would see you as you are—how equipped, how lodged, "how cabined, cribbed, confined."[1] Apt quotation!—you are cabined—you are cribbed—you are confined—*cribbed*—look at your countenance—as I said before, 'tis the hand of Providence—'

'Begging your lordship's pardon,' said Reud submissively, with the dubious twinkle in his eye, 'for interrupting a nobleman who is so seldom interrupted—I rather think that it was the fist of Pigtop.'

'Pigtop!—Providence—my quotation. Captain Reud, I have not really the pleasure of understanding you. This young gentleman, who has been so lately under the chastising hand of Providence—'

'Pigtop's.'

'Is now about to receive from that bountiful hand some of the choicest gifts it is the happiness of man to receive; rank, wealth, a father's blessing. Oh! 'tis too much—I am affected—what can I possibly do with him with those black eyes? Mr. Ralph Rattlin, you have not yet spoken to me—indeed, how can you? What words would be sufficiently expressive of—of—what you ought to express! Captain Reud, don't you find this scene rather affecting? Young gentleman, I am here to verify you—are you fully prepared, sir, to be, as it were, verified?'

'My lord, my lord, I am bursting with impatience!'

'Bursting with impatience! The scene is affecting, certainly—touching—complete, with the exception of the black eyes. What would not Miss Burney make of it in one of her admirable novels! But you might have made use of a better word than bursting—I am ready to dissolve with emotion at this tender scene—the discovery of his parentage to a tall ingenuous youth—bursting—you might have used, firstly, burning—secondly, glowing—thirdly, consuming—fourthly, raging—fifthly, dying—sixthly, there is perishing; but I will not much insist upon the last, though it is certainly better than bursting. You mean to say that you are burning, not bursting, with impatience—it is a natural feeling, it is commendable, it is worthy of a son of your most honourable father—I will faithfully report to him this filial impatience, and how eager I was to remove it. I do not say, satisfy it—a person less careful of the varieties of language would have said satisfy—an impatience satisfied is what?—a contradiction of terms; but, an impatience removed, is—is—the removal of an impatience. This interview will grow very touching. Those blackened eyes—I would that there were a green shade over them. Are you prepared to be verified?'

I bowed, fearing that any other expression of my wishes would lead to farther digression. His lordship, then putting on his spectacles, and reading from a paper, commenced thus, I, all the while, trembling with agitation:

'Are you the person who was nursed by one Rose Brandon, the wife of Joseph Brandon, by trade a sawyer?'

'I am.'

'What name did you go by, when under the care of those persons?'

'Ralph Rattlin Brandon.'

'Right, very good. I shall embrace him shortly—my heart yearns towards him. Were you removed to a school, by a gentleman in a plain carriage, from those Brandons?'

'I was.'

'To where?'

'To Mr. Root's academy.'

'Right—a good boy, an amiable boy, he was removed to Mr. Roots; and, having there imbibed the rudiments of a classical education, you were removed to where?'

'To a boarding-school, kept by a French gentleman at Stickenham, where, in his wife, I thought I had found a mother—'

'Stop, we are not come to that yet, that is too affecting—of that anon—as somebody says in some play. Have you, Captain Reud, a glass of water ready, should this amiable youth or myself feel faint during this exciting investigation?'

'Perfectly ready,' said the Creole, decidedly in one of his insane fits, for he immediately skipped behind his lordship, and, jumping upon the locker, stood ready to invert a glass of water upon his nicely powdered-head, containing at least three gallons, this glass being a large globe containing several curious fish, which swung, attached to the beam, directly over my interrogator.

Here was a critical situation for me! A mad captain about to blow the grampus, (*i.e.* souse), a lord of the Admiralty, that same lord, I firmly believed, about to declare himself my father. I was, in a manner, spell-bound. Afraid to interrupt the conference, I bethought me that my Lord Whiffledale would be no less my father wet or dry, and so I determined to let things take their course. So I permitted his lordship to go on with his questions, at every one of which Captain Reud, looking more like a baboon than a human being, canted the globe more and more.

'All very satisfactory, all very satisfactory, indeed! And now, Ralph, on whom have you been in the habit of drawing for your allowance while you were in the West Indies?'

'Mr. ———, of King's Bench Walk, in the Temple.'

'Perfectly correct—perfectly'—(still reading.)

'Are you a well grown youth for your age?'

'I am.'

'Of an interesting physiognomy?'

Here the malicious madman grinned at me in the most laughable manner, over the devoted head of the ancient lord.

'I hope you will think so, my lord, when I have recovered my usual looks.'

'Ugh—hum—ha—of dark brown hair, approaching to black?'

'*No.*'

'With intensely black eyes?'

'No.'—'YES.' Mine was the negative, Captain Reud's the affirmative, spoken simultaneously.

At this crisis, his lordship had made a very proper and theatrical start. Captain Reud grasped the glass with both hands; and, the severe bright eye of Doctor Thompson fell upon the prank-playing captain. The effect was instantaneous: he slank away from his intended mischief, completely subdued. The fire left his eye, the grin his countenance; and he stood beside his lordship, in a moment, the quiet and gentlemanly post-captain, deferentially polite in the presence of his superior. I understood the thing in a moment—it was the keeper and his patient.

'I am particularly sorry, my lord,' said the doctor—'I am very particularly sorry, Captain Reud, to break in upon you un-announced; the fact is, I did knock several times, but I suppose I was not heard. This letter, my lord, I hope will be a sufficient apology.'

His lordship took the letter with a proud condescension. Captain Reud said, 'Dr. Thompson's presence is always acceptable to me.'

Lord Whiffledale read this letter over three times distinctly; then, from his usual white he turned a palish purple, then again became white. In no other manner did he seem to lose his self-possession.

'Dr. Thompson,' said he, at length, very calmly, 'let me see some of these documents immediately.'

'Anticipating the request, my lord, I have them with me.' The doctor then placed in his hands several letters and papers. At length, his lordship exclaimed:

'I am confounded. It is wholly beyond my comprehension— I know not how to act. It is excessively distressing. I wish, on my soul, I had never meddled in the business. Can I see the young man?'

'Certainly, my lord; I will bring him to you immediately.'

During Dr. Thompson's short absence, his lordship walked up and down with a contracted brow, and much more than his usual fidgetty movements. Not wholly to my surprise, but

completely to my dismay, the doctor re-appeared with my arch
and only enemy in his hand—Joshua Daunton.

The contrast between him and me was not at all in my favour.
Not in uniform certainly, but scrupulously clean, with a super-
fine blue cloth jacket and trousers, white neckerchief, and clean
linen shirt; he looked not only respectable, but even gentlemanly.
I have before described my appearance. I may be spared the hateful repetition.

'And, so,' said his lordship, turning to Joshua, 'you are the true
and veritable Ralph Rattlin?'

'I am, my lord,' said the unblushing liar. 'The young gentleman
near you is my illegitimate brother; his mother is a beautiful lady
of the name of Causand, a most artful woman. She first contrived
to poison Sir Reginald's mind with insinuations to my disfavour;
and, at last, so well carried on her machinations as to drive me first
from the paternal roof, and, lastly, I confess it with horror and
remorse, into a course so evil as to compel me to change my name,
fly from my country, and subject me to the lash at the gangway.
If these documents, that I confide to your hands, and to your's
only, will not remove every doubt as to the truth of my assertions,
afford me but a little time, till I can send to London, and every
point shall be satisfactorily cleared up.'

He then placed in Lord Whiffledale's hands the papers that had
been so convincing to Dr. Thompson. Captain Reud, now reduced
by the presence of the good doctor to the most correct deportment,
stepped forward, and assured his lordship that I, at least, was no
impostor, and that, if imposition had been practised, I had been
made an unconscious instrument.

'Perhaps,' said his lordship, after scrutinizing the papers, and
returning them to Joshua, 'the young gentleman with the blackened
eyes will do us the favour, in a few words, to give us his own version
of the story—for, may I die consumptive, if I can tell which is the
real Simon Pure!'[1]

Placed thus in the embarrassing situation of pleading for my
own identity, I found that I had very little to say for myself. I could
only affirm that, although always unowned, I had been continuously cared for—and, that the bills I had drawn upon Mr. ——,
the lawyer in the King's Bench Walk in the Temple, had always
been honoured. My lord shook his head when I had finished,
diplomatically. He took snuff. He then eyed me and my adversary

carefully. He now waved his head upwards and downwards, and at length opened his mouth and spoke:

'Captain Reud, I wash my hands of this business. I cannot decide. I was going to take on shore with me the legitimate and too-long neglected son of my good old friend, Sir Reginald. Where is that son? I come on board the Eos, and I ask him at your hands, Captain Reud. Is that person with the discoloured countenance my friend's son? Certainly not. Is that other person his son—a disgraced man? Knowing the noble race of my friend, I should say, certainly not. Where is Sir Ralph's son? He is not here—or, if he be here, I cannot distinguish him. I wash my hands of it—I hate mysteries. I will take neither of them to London. I am under some *slight* obligations to Sir Reginald—and yet—I cannot decide. The weight of evidence certainly preponderates in favour of the new claimant. Captain Reud perhaps will permit him to land, and he may go up to town immediately, and have an interview with Mr. —— the lawyer; and, if he can satisfy that person, he will receive from him further instructions as to his future proceedings.'

CHAPTER XV

The confessions of a madman, which, nevertheless, embrace a very wise caution—Ralph gets his liberty-ticket—very needless, as he is determined henceforward to preserve his liberty—and, being treated so uncivilly as a sailor, determines to turn civilian himself.

HERE Captain Reud interrupted the speaker, and told him that Joshua was a prisoner under punishment, and waiting only for convalescence to receive the remainder of his six dozen lashes. At hearing this, his lordship appeared truly shocked; and, drawing Reud aside, they conversed, for some minutes, in whispers.

At the conclusion of this conference, Captain Reud stepped forward; and, regarding Joshua with a look of much severity, he said: 'Young man, for the sake of other parties, and of other interests, your errors are overlooked. Your discharge from this ship shall be made out immediately. If you are the person you claim to be, your three or four months' pay can be of no consequence to you. Have you sufficient money to proceed to London immediately?'

'Much more than sufficient, sir.'

'I thought so. Proceed to London to the lawyer's. If you are no impostor, I believe that a father's forgiveness awaits you. Forget that you were ever in this ship. My clerk will make out your discharge immediately. Take care of yourself. You are watched. There is a wakeful eye upon you: if you swerve from the course laid down for you, and go not immediately to Mr. ——'s office, be assured that you will be again in irons under the half-deck. Have I, my lord, correctly expressed your intentions?'

'Correctly, Captain Reud.'

'Joshua Daunton, get your bag ready; and, in the mean time, I will give the necessary orders to the clerk. You may go.'

With an ill-concealed triumph on his countenance, Joshua Daunton bowed submissively to all but myself. To me he advanced with an insulting smile and an extended hand. I shrank back loathingly.

'Farewell, brother Ralph. I told you that I should be in London before you. Will you favour me with any commands? Well—your pride is not unbecoming—I will not resent it for your father's sake: and, for his and for your sake, I will forgive the juggle that has hitherto placed the natural son—that is, I believe, the delicate paraphrase—in the station of the rightful heir. Farewell.'

I made no reply: he left the cabin, and, in an hour after, the ship. I shall not advantage myself of that expression, so fully naturalized in novels, that 'my feelings might be conceived, but cannot be expressed:' for they *can* be expressed easily enough—in two words, stupified indignation. After Joshua had departed, the other persons remaining in the after-cabin followed shortly after—with the exception of myself; for Reud told me to stay where I then was, until he should see me again.

In the course of an hour, Lord Whiffledale went on shore with his *cortège*; and Captain Reud returned into the after-cabin, which I had been, during his absence, disconsolately pacing. He was a little flushed with the wine he had taken, but perfectly sane. He came up to me kindly, and, placing his hands upon my shoulders, looked me fully and sorrowfully in the face. There was no wild speculation in his eyes; they looked mild and motherly. The large tear gathered in each gradually, and, at length, overflowing the sockets, slowly trickled down his thin and sallow cheeks. He then pressed his right hand heavily on the top part of his forehead, exclaiming, in a voice so low, so mournful, and so touching, that my bosom swelled at its tones, 'It is here!—it is here!'

'Ralph, my good Ralph,' said he, after he had seated himself, weeping all the while bitterly, 'we will take leave of each other now. We are true brothers in sorrow—our afflictions are the same—you have lost your identity, and I mine. Ever since that cursed night at Aniana, John Reud's soul was loosened from his body; I have the greatest trouble to keep it fixed to my corporeal frame: it goes away, in spite of me, at times, and some other soul gets into this withered carcase, and plays me sad tricks—sad tricks, Rattlin— sad tricks. My identity is gone, and so, poor youth, is your's. We will part friends. These tears are not all for you—they are for my- self, too. I do not mind crying before you now, for it is not the true John Reud that is now weeping. You think that I have been a tyrant to you—but, I tell you, Rattlin, there is a tyrant in the ship greater than I—it is that horrible Dr. Thompson. He is plotting to take away my commission, and to get me into a madhouse—a mad- house!—oh, my God!—my God! remove from me this agony. Hath Thine awful storm no thunderbolt—Thy wave no tomb! Must I die on the straw, like a beast of burden worn to death by loathsome toil?—and so many swords to have flashed harmlessly over my head, so many balls to have whistled idly past my body! But, God's will be done! Bear yourself, my dear boy, carefully in the presence of all medical men. They have the eye of the fanged adder. You know that your identity also has been questioned; but your fate is happier than mine, for you can hear, see, touch, your double; but mine always eludes me, when I come home, after an excursion, to my own temple. But, if I were you, when I got hold of the thing that says it is, and is *not*, yourself, I would grind it, I would crush it, I would destroy it!'

'I will, so may Heaven help me at my utmost need!'

'Well said, my boy, well said—because he has no right to get himself flogged, and thus give a wretched world an opportunity of saying that Ralph Rattlin had been brought to the gangway. But do not let this cast you down. You will do well yet—while I—Oh that I had a son!—I might then escape. God bless you!—I must pray for strength of mind—strength of mind—mark me, strength of mind. Go, my good boy; if misfortunes should overtake you, and they leave me any thing better than a dark cell and clanking chains, come and share it with me. Now go, (and he wrung my

Z

hands bitterly), and tell Doctor Thompson I wish to speak with him, and just hint to him how rationally and pleasantly we have been discoursing together—and remember my parting words—deport yourself warily before the doctors, carefully preserve your identity, and sometimes think on your poor captain.'

This last interview with Captain Reud, for it was my last, would have made me wretched, had it not been swallowed up by a deeper wretchedness of my own.

Early next morning, we weighed, and made sail for Sheerness. On anchoring in the Medway, Captain Reud went on shore; and, as I shall have no more occasion to refer to him, I shall state at once, that the very fate he so feared awaited him. Six months after he left the Eos, he died raving mad,[1] in a private receptacle for the insane.

At Sheerness we were paid off. Those of the ship's company who, by the length of their service, were entitled to that grace, received a month's leave of absence, with only half their pay; in order to ensure their return, the other half being kept back. They had their passes signed—I call them passes instead of liberty-tickets—because they were overhauled by the sentries at the out-posts of Sheerness, as if, in landing, they had found themselves in a town in an enemy's country. My leave was also for one month. Instead of drawing my pay at Sheerness, I took the pay-ticket with me, in order to present it at Somerset House, when I should arrive in London.

As I went over the side of the Eos for the last time, I was tempted to shake the dust from off my feet, for, of a surety, it had lately been an accursed abode to me. I parted from all my shipmates and mess-mates without a greeting. I was indignant at some, dissatisfied with all. They had, in my opinion, too easily listened to the varnished tale of a common cheat. They went east, and west, and north, and south; and few of them I ever again met—and those few, with one single exception, I either shunned or repelled.

In order entirely to elude all observation from my late com-panions, I abandoned every thing I had on board, not much worth, truly, with the exception of my sextant and telescope; and took on shore with me only the clothes (miserable they were), in which I stood. I went to no hotel or inn; but, seeing a plain and humble house in which there were lodgings to let for single men, I went and hired a little apartment that contained a press-bedstead. I took things leisurely and quietly. I was now fully determined to discover my parentage; and, after that event, entirely to be governed by circumstances, as to my future course of life, and the resuming of the naval profession. The old couple, in whose house I was for the present located, were as orderly and uninquisitive as I could wish. The man was a superannuated and pensioned dockyard mate.

My first operations were sending for a tailor, hatter, and those other architects so essential in building up the outward man. The costume I now chose was as remote from official as could be made. I provided myself with one complete suit only, leaving the rest of my wardrobe to be completed in London.

Knowing that I had an active and intelligent enemy who had two days the start of me, I was determined to act with what I thought caution. I had more than a half-year's stipend due to me. I accordingly drew for it upon the lawyer, nearly £75, intimating to him, at the same time, by letter, my arrival in England, and asking if he had any instructions as to my future disposal. This letter was answered by return of post, written with all the brevity of business, stating that no such instructions had been received, and enclosing an order on the Sheerness Bank for the money.

So far, all was highly satisfactory. It proved two things; first, that Joshua Daunton had not yet carried his machinations in the quarter from which arose the supplies; and, secondly, that I should now have considerable funds wherewith to prosecute my researches.

In the space of three days, behold me dressed in the fashionable costume of the period—blue coat, broad yellow buttons, yellow waistcoat with ditto, white corduroy continuations, tied with several strings at the knees, and topped boots. It was in the reign of the 'bloods' and the 'ruffians,' more ferocious species of coxcombs than our dandies, and much more annoying. They wore a number of white kerchiefs round the neck, so as generally to bury the chin in them almost to the upper lip; and a knotted and crooked stick was usually carried in the hand, or knowingly twisted round the right arm. The hat was high and conical, like that of the present French republican. As to their manners, their walk was a swagger, their look an impudence, and their conversation a tissue of oaths. They were rude to the men upon principle, and careless of the ladies in practice, drunkards by profession, and, being sworn enemies to lavender, they drew their perfumes from the storehouse of Bacchus, and despised the laboratory of Flora. Like one of these it was my ambition to make myself look. I conclude that I was tolerably successful; for, as I occasionally walked about the streets of Sheerness, I continually met some of the late crew of the Eos, but never, on their part, with any signs of recognition.

Poor fellows!—more than half of them never got beyond the precincts of Sheerness. For a week after their discharge, numbers of them were to be found at all hours, rolling, or lying, about the streets, in all phases of drunkenness, and, in all degrees, approaching to actual nudity. He who took a week to squander his three years' earnings was dilatory—three days was the average period; whilst one, more than usually blessed with the genius of despatch, contrived to get ruined in three hours, and was snugly on board the guard-ship in the fourth. The first hour found him beastly drunk; the second, robbed and stripped to his banyan; the third, turned out in this state into the snow-covered streets; and the fourth, in mere pity taken on board the guard-ship in a state of insensibility.

By all this demoralization and this great expenditure, nobody ever benefits, but the Jews and the keepers of public-houses. The ladies who first rob the seamen are always wretchedly poor.

The pawnbroker, the publican, and the Jew, share the spoils between them. During the late war, many a vast fortune has been picked up in this shabby manner. It is a pity some means cannot be devised to make Jack almost as prudent as he is brave. More liberty on shore would, perhaps, teach him to make better use of it.

Drunk or sober, my late shipmates knew me not, at which I was extremely well pleased. But, notwithstanding my excellent management—excellent, at least, in my own opinion—there was one eye continually upon me, though, at the time, I knew it not.

CHAPTER XVI

Ralph finds every where great changes—Gives way to his feelings, and makes a fool of himself—This Chapter will be found either the worst or the best of Ralph's confessions, according to the feelings of the reader.

HAVING stayed one week at Sheerness, and laid down my plan of future action, I started in the passage-boat for Chatham. I don't know whether any Margate-hoys are now in existence. Probably not, being all puffed away by steam. This passage-boat was a similar vessel in construction; but the company were like what we consider will be the case in the kingdom of Heaven, a mixture of all classes. The cabin was very full—sailors and their wives, marines, soldiers, dock-yard artificers, Jews, fishermen, peripatetic vendors of mussels—all upon an equality. Indeed, the only method to be exclusive, consisted in wrapping one's self up in silence and a large cloak. This method I adopted. Silence on my part, and the continued hubbub on the part of my shipmates, produced sleep—but my sleep was unsound and continually broken. There was not much room for recumbency. I found it, however; and placed the only luggage that I had, a small parcel, covered with brown paper, under my head as a pillow. The parcel contained my logs, and my certificates, and a single change of linen. Very providentially, I had placed my pay-ticket, with my bank notes, in my pocket-book.

Once, as I opened my eyes at the explosion of an oath more loud than usual, methought I saw the sodden and white-complexioned face of Joshua Daunton hanging closely over mine. I started up, and rubbed my eyes, but the vision had fled. I was determined to be watchful; and, with this determination in full activity, I again fell asleep: nor was I once more properly awakened until we had arrived at Chatham, alongside of the landing-place. When I had roused myself up, to my consternation, I discovered that my pillow was no where to be found. Many of the passengers had already gone their ways, and those that remained knew nothing about either me or my packet. Indeed, I only drew suspicions on myself, as my paucity of baggage and the pretensions of my dress were decidedly at variance. The gentleman in top-boots and with the brown paper parcel seemed ridiculous enough. Seeing how

ineffectual noise was, I held my peace, now that I had nothing else
to hold; got on the outside of the first coach for London; and, by
ten at night, found myself in the coffee-room of the White Horse,
in Fetter Lane.

I ordered supper—I ordered wine—and, after I had discussed
these, I ordered a bed. But the waiters were suspicious of the
solvency of 'the gentleman with no luggage.' So, instead of the
attendant bringing me the bootjack, the fellow, placing one hand
on my cloak that hung over the partition of the coffee-box, placed
the bill before me with the other, saying that it was invariably the
custom, at the White Horse, for gentlemen to pay for every thing
as they had it. To this invariable custom, I replied that I could have
no objection, but that I did a little object to pay for what I had had
twice over; so, pulling out a handful of gold, I asked to speak to the
master.

The man was exceedingly civil, and acknowledged, at once, that
the charges were exorbitant; so, whilst he was reducing them with
the pen in his hand, he reminded me that he ought to consider risk,
especially as I had arrived with no luggage.

'But my appearance?' said I, a little nettled.

'Is,' said he, 'or rather was, put down in the bill.'

Now, as I perceived, by my landlord's manner, that he had no
wish to be offensive, I declined any farther discussion on appearances: but I did not fail to make some salutary reflections upon
them, upon which I was determined to act next morning.

I must necessarily be minute in detailing the circumstances that
were now leading me on so rapidly to the grand catastrophe of my
life; and, if I dwell less upon my feelings and more upon my
actions, it must be remembered that events are of more consequence than reflections, if the former be properly studied. The
next morning, when I arose, it was my birthday, the 14th of
February; and I stood at mine inn, a being perfectly isolated. But
I was not idle; on descending into the coffee-room, I procured the
Court Guide; but my most anxious scrutiny could discover no such
person among the baronets as Sir Reginald Rattlin. Paying my bill,
I next went to Somerset House, and drew my pay; I then repaired
to the aristocratic mansion of Lord Whiffledale, in Grosvenor
Square. 'Not at home,' and 'in the country for some time,' were
the surly answers of the indolent porter.

It was a day of disappointments. The lawyer who cashed my

bills was civil and constrained. To all my intreaties first, and to my leading questions afterwards, he gave me cold and evasive answers. He told me that he had received no farther instructions concerning me; reiterated his injunctions that I should not endanger the present protection that I enjoyed, by endeavouring to explore what it was the intention of those on whom I depended to keep concealed; and he finally wished me a good morning, and was almost on the point of handing me out of his office.

But I would not be so repelled. I became impassioned and loud; nor would I depart until he assured me, on his honour, that he knew almost as little of the secret as myself, and that he was only the agent of an agent, never having yet had any communication with the principal, whose name, even, he assured me, he did not know.

I had now nearly exhausted the day. The intermingling mists of the season and the heavy smoke of the town were now shrouding the streets in a dense obscurity. Then the nights of gas[1] were not. Profoundly ignorant of the intricacy of the streets of the metropolis, I was completely at the mercy of the hackney-coachmen, and they made me buy it extremely dear. Merely from habit, I again repaired to the White Horse, and concluded my nineteenth natal day in incertitude, solitude, and misery. During the ensuing night, I scarcely slept. The depression of my spirits was horrible. I sighed for the breaking of the day, and it seemed to be an event that was never again to happen.

To Stickenham—yes, I would go there immediately. But the resolve gave no exulting throb to my bosom. I doubted every thing—I dreaded every thing. For more than three years, I had heard no tidings of its once-beloved inhabitants. Besides, my heart sickened when I remembered the insinuations of Daunton, that my beautiful schoolmistress was not the person who had any claim to call me son.

As it did not actually rain, and the place was but seven miles from London, I determined to walk thither immediately after breakfast. As I was the 'gentleman without luggage,' my motions were sufficiently unconstrained. I procured the necessary directions to enable me to free myself from London, and, when over Blackfriars Bridge, my memory supplied the rest of the road. I had often traversed it when a happy schoolboy.

As I walked rapidly along, my feelings assumed a different hue every hundred yards. Now, I would figure to myself the rapturous embrace, the tearful eye, the hearty welcome, and all the holy joy of the Prodigal's return; and then, the surmise would come over me that my life had been a mistake, that hearts had grown cold, and that studied civility would be the mask under which estrangement would strive to hide its cruelty. But, as I left the town behind me, the atmosphere cleared up, the sun shone out brightly; even a few hardy birds, by their chirping, seemed to understand that the day before had been blessed by St. Valentine. So, with a lighter heart, I struggled vigorously up the steep hill, at the brow of which I should be able to discover my own dear play-ground, the romantic heath that lay before it, and the elegant white and rough-cast front of the school, in which happiness had first been mine, where I had been loved by all, and idolized by one.

One bound, and I was on the brow of the hill, and the vast scene lay extended before me. A sharp cry of anguish broke from my lips. Where was the heathery and wild common, so beautiful in the wantonness of nature? Alas! where was it? The spirit of Mammon had breathed balefully over the expanse. It was broken up into miserable pittances. The plough had gone over the pleasant walks; the bituminous and oppressive stench of the brick-field had displaced the living fragrance of the wild thyme; the weary foot was confined to one gravelled road. Mud cabins were profusely spread over the surface; and, with cultivation, had come sordid poverty, and dirt, and toil, and squalor. I could have wept at this change— why need I be ashamed of my feelings?—I did weep. I received this alteration as a sorrowful presage. I asked my labouring heart, if three short years were sufficient thus to alter the lovely face of Nature so hideously, what I might expect in man. My heart answered, Change. But the cup of my misery was not yet full. The first arrow only, as yet, had pierced.

I came to that spot, so consecrated to my memory by bright skies and brighter faces; the spot where I had so often urged the flying ball and marshalled the mimic army—it was there that I stood; and I asked of a miserable, half-starved woman, 'where was the play-ground of my youth?' and she showed me a 'brick-field.'

I thought of the Egyptian bondage, and the sons and daughters of Judah, and my heart was exceeding sad.

I walked a few steps farther, and asked for the school-house of my happiest days—and one pointed out to me a brawling ale-house. I saw the depraved reeling out, and the beggarly and the hungry standing round the doors. It was a bitter change. It was to me as if hope after hope was dying beneath my gaze. My step tottered, my voice faltered. It was nearly choked with emotion, when I asked of another where was now my old light-hearted, deeply-learned, French schoolmaster, Monsieur Cherfeuil. He had gone back to France. The *emigrés* had been recalled by Napoleon; he had taken with him the fortune that he had made in England—and the man cursed him. I was too dejected to avenge the insult, and I turned away from the wretch loathingly.

I looked to the right and to the left, and truly may I say that I saw my rural and my household gods shattered around me. At length, my eye rested upon a bench, that had been placed for years between the two tall elms, the only two trees on this gentle hill; and I hastened to seat myself upon it. The spoilers had left that. My anguish was intense; I cursed in my heart the speculators that had destroyed the pleasantest oasis in my thoughts. Each succeeding reflection came upon me more despondingly than the last. All was disappointment and gloom around and within me. I gazed and gazed on the desecration before me, until my very eye-balls seemed to participate in the agony of my heart. At length, unable longer to bear the hateful view, I placed my handkerchief before my eyes for a space—and then, and there, on my old play-ground, and amidst my old and violated associations, I prayed to God for strength to bear up against the many griefs that were devouring me. I had not prayed for years before—and, yet—depraved and cast away as I had been—I was strengthened.

There was one other question that I dreaded, yet burned to ask —I need not state how fearful it was to me, since it was to learn the fate of her whom I had honoured, and loved, and hailed, as my mother—the beautiful and the kind Mrs. Cherfeuil. I conjectured that she, too, had gone to France with her husband, and the idea was painful to me. When I lifted up my head after my silent prayer, I found that a little girl, of perhaps twelve years of age, had nestled herself close to my side. She was evidently in very humble circumstances, yet particularly clean, and very good looking. She was innocently endeavouring to attract my notice. Upon looking at her with more attention, I believed that I recollected her features. I resolved to speak to her, and, if she were the person whom I supposed her to be, to draw from her all the information that I was so anxious to acquire.

'There have been great alterations here, my good girl.'

'Very great, indeed, sir—they have ruined father and mother.'

'Who are your father and mother—and where are they?'

'Father is gone to sea, and mother is in the workhouse. Before they enclosed the common, father cut furze and dug gravel, and kept us all with a good bellyful and a warm back. They said that they enclosed it for the good of the poor—but the gentry have got it all, and nobody knows where the poor men's lots are. At first, the poor of the parish wouldn't stand it, so they went a-rioting, and broke down the fences, and turned in their cows, and their sheep, and their geese, as they did before. But the law was too strong for them. Old Edgely, the leader, was transported for life; my father got off by being allowed to go on board of a man-of-war; my brothers are all gone this way and that; and mother, being oldish, is now settled in the workhouse. It has never been happy Stickenham since.'

'Your name, my dear, is Susan Archer.'

'Bless me, so it is, sir!'

'And you seem a very intelligent little girl, indeed.'

'Yes, I have had a good deal of book-learning, but all that is past and gone now. When Mrs. Cherfeuil lived in that house, she took care that we should always have a home of our own, fire in the grate, and a loaf in the cupboard—she had me sent to school—but now she is gone?'

'Gone!—where?—with her husband?'

'Don't you know, sir?' said she, rising from her seat with a quiet solemnity, that made me shudder with dreadful anticipations. 'If you will come with me, I will show you.'

I dared not ask the awful question, 'Is she dead?' I took my gentle guide by the hand, and suffered her to lead me slowly through the village. Neither of us spoke. I obstinately refused to swallow the cup that was offered to my lips. I cheated my heart as long as I was able. She is going, I said to myself, to lead me where I shall find her in comparative poverty—sheltered perhaps by some humble friend. She may be even sick, bed-ridden, dying—but cold, dead, that form that I left in the radiance of matronly beauty, the prey of loathsome corruption—it is unnatural, impossible!—and, consoling myself thus, we slowly passed through the village.

I recognized several of my old friends, but they knew me not. I had left the place a boy, and I returned, at least in appearance, a man. In my habiliments I had nothing of the sailor about me. They looked upon me, and knew me not, and I was exceedingly content. I was in no humour to satisfy idle inquiry—I wished for no companion but my own thoughts, no adviser but my own impetuous feelings.

We passed through the village, I keeping up obstinately my forced delusion that I was about to be soon in the presence of one who could solve the mystery that was crushing my young energies, and fast destroying all that was good and healthy in my mind. I planned how I should act, what I should say; and I even began to revel in the thoughts of the maternal endearments she would bestow upon me. But, the thunder-cloud of misery broke upon me suddenly, and enveloped me at once in its despairing blackness. We had almost attained to the end of the hamlet, when my sad guide gently plucked me by the arm to turn down to the right.

'No,' said I, tremulously, 'that is not the way; we must go forward. That lane leads to the churchyard.'

'And to Mrs. Cherfeuil.'

'Go on, and regard me not.'

In another minute we were both sitting on a newly-made grave, the little girl weeping in the innocent excess of that sorrow that brings so soon its own sweet relief.

My at first low and almost inaudible murmurs gradually grew more loud and more impassioned. At last they aroused the attention of my weeping companion, and she said to me artlessly, 'It is of no use taking on in this way, sir; she can never speak up from the grave. She is in heaven now; and God does not permit any of His blessed saints to speak to us sinners below.'

'You are quite right, my good girl,' said I, ashamed of this betrayal of my emotion. 'It is very foolish indeed to be talking to the dead over their damp graves, and not at all proper. But, I have a great fancy to stay here a little while by myself. Pray go and wait for me at the end of the lane. I will not keep you long, and I have something to say to you.'

'I will do as you tell me, sir, most certainly. I will tell you all about her death, for I was a sort of help to the nurse. I know you now, sir, and thought I knew you from the first. May the God that my good friend first taught me to revere make this stroke light to you!'

I shall not repeat the extravagances that I uttered when alone.

I was angry with myself and with all the world; and I fear that I exasperated myself with the thought that I did not sufficiently feel the grief with which I strove to consecrate my loss. I remember, I concluded my rhapsody thus:

'Again I call upon you by the sacred name of mother—for such you were—and no other will my heart ever acknowledge. I adjure you to hear me swear that I will have all the justice done to your memory that man can do; and may we never meet in those realms where only the injured find redress, if I fail to scatter this sacred earth in token of dishonour upon the head of him who has dishonoured you—were he even my own father! It is an oath. May it be recorded, should that record be used as my sentence of death!'

Having made this harsh and impious vow, the effect of over-excitement, I tore a considerable portion of the earth from the grave, and, folding it in my handkerchief, I knotted it securely, and placed it round my heart next to my skin, like those belts that are worn by Roman Catholics as instruments of penance.

Now, in my maturer years, I see the folly and am ashamed of my extravagance; but, at the time, I actually thought it a virtue. I had no friendly counsellor near me—none who could acquaint me that, in this rash oath, I was binding myself to violate the laws of man, whilst I was outraging the ordinance of the Deity. Notwithstanding all this folly, my love, my grief, and my anger, were all sincere. I had even a strong superstitious feeling about me, that, whilst I was girded by this sacred dust, I should bear a charmed life. Such are the wildness and folly of an ill-regulated imagination.

With a wish for something very like the shedding of blood in my heart, and with a fervent prayer in my imagination and on my lips, I left Mrs. Cherfeuil's humble grave, and joined my companion.

CHAPTER XVII

Ralph meets with old friends and old enemies, and nearly has his grog stopped, whilst listening to a very pleasant discussion, to which he is an unwilling party—He has a something to thank romance for.

I SHALL here be very rapid in my narrative. I wish to hurry over all these distressing points of my biography. I feel now, and I even felt then, that there was something ridiculous, as well as excruciating, in them. I suspected that I was not acting naturally—that I was endeavouring to model myself too much upon the character of a hero of romance: and—must I confess it?—in one little half hour, I found my belt of vengeance so cold and so inconvenient, that I heartily wished I was well rid of it: it is a miserable confession, a sad falling off in my heroics; but the oath that I had voluntarily and so solemnly taken prevented me from ridding myself of the disgusting incumbrance.

Although my history has been most romantic, I was never formed for the hero of a romance. Pushed aside as I have been from the well-trodden paths of common-place life, I have been always most eager to regain them. I am capable of great exertions upon great emergencies; but I detest a repetition of them; I abhor trouble; and have a very horror of any thing approaching to bodily pain. Why did I then subject myself to such an annoyance? Because I was a fool, and a watchful Providence was so gracious as to work out safety for me from my very folly.

Il faut manger. In a young and healthy subject, the more vigorous the sorrow, alas! it too often happens the more unconquerable the appetite. Full as I was of high resolve of vengeance, and of a just indignation against oppression, it was upon an empty stomach. The mortifications of the mind I could endure; those of the body I could never long sustain. Contrition, the most sincere and the most intense, would never have induced me to become a monk of La Trappe. So, with a bursting heart, the little girl by my side, and a keen idea of the necessity of digestion, I entered the first inn, and ordered an ample provision of beef-steaks. These were grovelling aspirations most certainly, but, who shall say that they were not natural?

Really, just at that time, I had so little taste for any thing but my

approaching repast, that I missed the opportunity of an effect that
might have been produced, by the bereaved son weeping in unison
with the child who had lost her friend: it would have been pretty
and pathetic—but I was too hungry, so I only gave her a shilling
as an earnest of my future bounty, and told her to call again in
a couple of hours, in order that she might unfold all that she knew
of a subject so deeply interesting to myself.

I sorrowed and I dined heartily. The girl came, and I prepared
to return to town. Let it not be supposed, notwithstanding my sins
of appetite, that I did not feel acutely when I heard her simple
relation. It appeared that all was smiles, and happiness, and sunshine, around Mrs. Cherfeuil, when a person made his appearance,
by the description of whom I at once recognized that fiend,
Daunton. All domestic happiness then ceased for the poor lady;
rumours of the worst nature got abroad; her little French husband,
instead of being, as for twelve years before he had been, her
shadow, her slave, and her admirer, became outrageous and cruel,
and after the horrid word bigamy had been launched against her,
she never after held up her head.

She sickened and died. Nor did Daunton succeed in his plans
of extorting money—but his scheme was infinitely more deep and
more hellish. He had, *but not till after her death*, declared himself
to be her son. This, instead of having any effect upon the outraged
widower, only made him more eager to drive the impostor from
his presence; and, the opportunity offering itself to leave the spot
now so hateful to him, and the country that had sheltered him, and
in which he had grown so rich, for ever, he availed himself of it
eagerly. This account did not aggravate my implacable feelings
against this Daunton; for my hate was beyond the capability of
increase. I detested him with all my heart, and all my strength, and
all my soul. The feeling next powerful to this was to unravel my
mystery and his; for now I felt assured in some subtle manner that
they were intimately connected.

Those who look upon this as a novel, as a tissue of well or ill-
devised fictions, are mistaken. Were it so, characters would not
rise, make a few unimportant speeches, and perform a few unimportant acts, and then disappear from the stage for ever. The
writer would not so exhaust his materials, so multiply his characters. He would have brought only those persons before the eye of
the public who would answer some end toward the development

of the whole—they would be all concentrated on the boards in the last scene. Poetical justice, the only justice existing in perfection at present, would be done to all parties, and the curtain drop upon the reader, the hero married to the constant and beautiful heroine, and nothing to be imagined for them both but a long period of mundane happiness. But, as this is nothing less or more than an actual biography, in which nought is changed but names, and nothing falsified excepting a few localities, the reader must expect nothing of the concordance, and the satisfactory results, of Romance—no sustained course of grand action, but all the vicissitudes of every-day life, in which the lofty is continually tripped up by the ridiculous, and the marvellous may seem exaggerated, merely because it is strictly true.

It is your actual facts that puzzle your critics with the idea of the impossible. How absurd, they will say, to suppose that a mere youth could, in these matter-of-fact days, go and utter imprecations over the grave of his supposed mother, belt round his body a portion of the cold earth of her grave, and the mad act be afterwards the means of preserving his life, when it ought to have killed him by an attack of pleurisy—they would repeat, it is, altogether, out of the course of nature, and utterly impossible: to all which I have only calmly to reply that it is positively true, and it is related because it is as strange as true.

After hearing all that the little wench had to discover, and rewarding her, I proceeded alone to wander over the spots that were once so dear to me. In this melancholy occupation, when the cold mists of the early evening fell, I continued heaping regret upon regret, until a more miserable being, short of being impelled to suicide, could not have trod the earth. About five, it began to grow dark; and, weary both in mind and body, I commenced climbing the long hill that was the boundary of the common, on my return to London.

On the Surrey side of the hill, for its apex separated it from another county, the descent was more precipitous—so much so, that it is now wholly disused as a road for carriages; and not only was it precipitous, but excessively contorted, the bends sometimes running at right angles with each other. High banks, clothed with impervious hedges, and shadowed by tall trees, made the road both dank and dark; and, at the time that I was passing, or, rather, turning round one of the elbows of this descent, a sturdy fellow, with a heavy cudgel, followed at some distance by a much smaller man, accosted me in a rude tone of voice, by bawling out—

'I say, you sir, what's o'clock?'

'Go about your business, and let me pass.'

'Take that for your civility!'—and, with a severe blow with his stick, he laid me prostrate. I was not stunned, but felt very sick, and altogether incapable of rising. In this state, I determined to feign stupefaction, so I nearly closed my eyes, and lay perfectly still. The huge vagabond then placed his knee upon my chest, and called out to his companion—

'I say, Mister, come and see if this here chap's the right un.'

The person called to came up; and, immediately after, through my eyelashes, I beheld the diabolical white face of Daunton. It was so dark, that, to recognize me, he was obliged to place his countenance so close to mine that his hot breath burned against my cheek. He was in a passion of terror, and trembled as if in an access of ague.

'It is,' said he, whilst his teeth chattered. 'Is he stunned?'

'Mister, now I take that as an insult. D'ye think that John Gowles need strike such a strip of a thing as that ere twice?'

'Hush!—how very, very cold it is! Where is your knife? Will you do it?'

'Most sartain*ly* not. There—he's at your mercy—I never committed murder yet—no, no, must think of my precious soul. A bargain's a bargain—my part on't is done.'

'Gowles, don't talk so loud. I can't bear the sight of blood—and, oh God!—of this blood—it would spirt upon my hand. Strike him again over the head—he breathes heavily—strike him!'

'No,' said the confederate, sullenly. 'Tell ye—u'll have neither art nor part in this ere murder.'

During this very interesting conference, I was rallying all my energies for one desperate effort, intending, however, to wait for the uplifted knife, to grasp it, in order that I might turn the weapon against the breast of one assassin, and then use it as a defence against the other.

'Would to God,' said the villain, adding blasphemy to concerted murder—'would to God that my hand was spared this task! Give me the knife now. Where shall I strike him?—I have no strength to drive it into him far.'

'Tell ye, Mister, u'll have nought to do with the murder—but u'd advise thee to bare his neck, and thrust in the point just under his right ear.'

'Hush! Will it bleed much?'

'Damnably!'

'Horrible!—horrible! Do you think the story about Cain and Abel is true?'

'As God is in heaven!'

'Then, my brother's blood will turn every thing to scarlet as long as I live. Can't it be done without blood?'

'I'll have nothing to do with the murder. But, Mister, if so be as you are so craven-hearted, take your small popper, and send a ball right into his heart. It is a gentleman's death, and will make the prettiest small hole imaginable, and bleed none to signify. But, mind ye, this ere murder's all your own.'

At this critical moment, as I was inhaling a strong breath, in order to invigorate my frame for instant exertion, I heard two or three voices in the distance carolling out, in a sort of disjointed chorus—

> 'Many droll sights I've seen,
> But I wish the wars were over.'

'Now or never,' said Joshua, producing and cocking his pistol. I leaped up on my legs in an instant, and, seizing the weapon, which was a small tool, manufactured for a gentleman's pocket, by the barrel with my left hand, and this amiable specimen of fraternity by the right, the struggle of an instant ensued. The muzzle of the pistol was close against my breast when my adversary discharged it. I felt the sharp hard knock of the ball upon my chest, and the percussion, for the moment, took away my breath, but my hold upon the villain's throat was unrelaxed. The gurgling of suffocation became audible to his brutal companion.

'Ods sneckens!' said the brute, 'but this ere murdered man is throttling my Mister in his death-throe.'

Down at once came his tremendous cudgel upon my arm. I released my grip, and again fell to the earth.

'He's a dead man,' said Gowles; 'run for your life! Mind, Mister, I had neither art nor part in this ere—'

And they were almost immediately out of sight and out of hearing.

At the report of the pistol, the jolly choristers struck up prestissimo

A a

with their feet. They were standing round me just as the retreating feet of my assassins had ceased to resound in the stillness of the darkness.

A voice, which I immediately knew to be that of my old adversary, the master's mate, Pigtop, accosted me.

'Holloa, shipmate!—fallen foul of a pirate, mayhap—haven't slipped your wind, ha' ye, messmate?'

'No; but I believe my arm's broken, and I have a pistol-ball between my ribs.'

'Which way did the lubbers sheer off' Shall we clap on sail, and give chase?'

'It is of no use. I know one of them well. They shall not escape me.'

'Why, I know that voice. Yes—no—damn me—It must be Ralph Rattlin—it bean't, sure—and here on his beam-ends, a shot in his hull, and one of his spars shattered. I'd sooner have had my grog watered all my life than this should have fallen out.'

'You have not had your grog watered this evening, Pigtop,' said I rising, assisted by himself and his comrades. 'I don't feel much hurt, after all.'

'True, true, shipmate. But we must clap a stopper over all. Small shot in the chest are bad messmates. We must make a tourniquet of my skysail here.'

So, without heeding my cries of pain, he passed his handkerchief round my breast; and, by the means of twisting his walking-stick in the knot, he hove it so tight, that he not only stopped all effusion of blood, but almost all my efforts at breathing. My left hand still held the discharged pistol, which I gave into the custody of Pigtop. Upon farther examination, I found that there was no fracture of the bone of my arm; and that, all things considered, I could walk tolerably well. However, I still felt a violent pain in my chest, attended with difficulty of breathing, at the least accelerated pace.

CHAPTER XVIII

Ralph appears before a magistrate, and proves to be more frightened than hurt, though frightened as little as a veritable hero should be—A great deal of fuss about a little dust, not kicked up, but finally laid down.

WE got on, nevertheless, Pigtop shaking his head very dolefully, whenever I paused to recover breath.

We entered the first house that we came to; that of an agricultural labourer. We told our adventure, and the good man immediately proceeded to acquaint the patrole and the constable. I was anxious to examine the nature of my wound, to which my old messmate would not listen for a moment. He was particularly sorry that he saw no blood, from which symptom he argued the worst—looking upon me as a dead man, being certain that I was bleeding inwardly.

I decided for a post-chaise, that I might hasten to town and make my depositions; for I was determined to let loose the hounds of the law after my dastardly enemies, without the loss of a moment. The chaise was soon procured; and, much to the satisfaction of Pigtop, we drove directly to Bow Street—the good fellow having a firm persuasion that the moment his make-shift tourniquet was withdrawn, I should breathe my last. I had no such direful apprehensions.

When we arrived at the office, the worthy magistrate was on the point of retiring. The clatter of the chaise driving rapidly up to the door, and the exaggerated report of the post-boy, heralded us in with some *éclat*. The magistrate, when he had heard that it was a case of murder, very well disguised his regret at the postponement of his dinner.

Mr. Pigtop insisted upon supporting me, although I could walk very well—quite as well as himself, considering his potations: and insisted also upon speaking, although, without self-flattery, I could speak much better than himself. He was one of the old school of seamen, and could not talk out of his profession. Accordingly, he was first sworn. We will give the commencement of his deposition verbatim, as he is one of a class that is fast disappearing from the face of the waters.

'If you please, your worship, I and my two consorts that are lying-to in my wake, after having taken in our wood and water at Woolwich, we braced up sharp, bound for London.'

'What do you mean by your wood and water?' said the magistrate.

'Our bub and grub—here's a magistrate for you! (aside to me). Your worship down to our bearings. So, as Bill here said, as how we were working Tom Coxe's traverse[1]—your worship knows what that means, well enough.'

'Indeed, sir, I don't.'

'It's the course the lawyers will take when they make sail for heaven. I can see, in the twinkling of a purser's dip,[2] that your worship is no lawyer.'

'This, sir, is the first time that any one has had the impertinence to tell me so.'

'Well, well, no offence, I hope, your worship?—there is no accounting for taste, as the monkey said when he saw the cat pitch into the tar barrel', and then the worthy witness embarked into a very irrelevant digression about land-sharks. The magistrate, however, was patient and sensible, and at length overcame the great difficulty arising from his never having been to sea, and Pigtop never having been to law.

His deposition, having been translated into the vulgar tongue, out of nautical mysticisms, was duly sworn to; yet not without an interruption when the magistrate heard that it was supposed that I had the pistol-ball still somewhere in my body—he wishing me to be examined by a surgeon immediately. Mr. Pigtop was opposed to this, lest I should die upon the spot; but I gave the magistrate more satisfaction by telling him I had good reason to suppose that the ball had not penetrated deeply.

I was the last examined; and I almost electrified Pigtop when I deposed that I knew well the person of my murderous assaulter, and that it was Joshua Daunton.

At this announcement, my quondam messmate slapped his hand upon his knee with a violence that echoed through the court—grinned—then looked profoundly serious; but made me very thankful by holding his peace, and shaking his head most awfully. When I proceeded to give a very accurate description of this wretch's person, looks of understanding passed between three or four of the principal runners, who were attentively listening to the proceedings. When this business was concluded, the magistrate said to me, 'The young man who has committed this outrage upon your person, we have strong reason to believe, is amenable to the laws for other crimes. He has eluded our most active officers; and, it was supposed, that he had left the kingdom. It appears now that he has returned. You have had a most providential escape. This pistol will give us a good clue. There is no doubt but that shortly we shall be able to give a good account of him. Let me now advise you, Mr. Rattlin, to have your hurt examined. Come into my private room; a surgeon will be here in an instant.'

Pigtop and I were then ushered into a room on one side of the office. I looked extremely foolish—almost, in fact, as confused as if I had been charged with an offence. The surgeon soon made his appearance; but, in the short interval, the magistrate had begun to thrust home with his questions as to who I was, what were my intentions, and the probable motives of Daunton's attempt on my life. All these I parried as well as I could, without letting him know any thing of the supposed consanguinity between myself and the culprit—his motive I accounted for, as revenge for some real or imaginary insult inflicted by me when we were on board the Eos.

Upon my persisting to refuse, for some time, to strip, that the wound might be examined, the magistrate began to look grave, and the surgeon hinted that it was, perhaps, as well not to seek for what was not to be found. The dread of being looked upon as an impostor overcame my shame at the *exposé* of my romantic weakness. Poor Pigtop had alarms upon totally other grounds. He watched with painful anxiety the unwinding of his tourniquet, ready to receive me dying into his arms. His surprise was greater, I fear me, than his joy, when he discovered no signs of bleeding when his handkerchief was removed.

'What, in the name of pharmacy, is this?' said the surgeon, detaching my belt of earth; 'but here is the ball, however,—it has more than broken the skin; and there has been a good deal of blood extravasated, but it has been absorbed by the mould in this handkerchief. By whatever means this singular bandage was placed where I found it, you may depend upon it, young gentleman, that it has saved your life.'

'I presume, Mr. Rattlin, that you are a Catholic?' said the magistrate, 'and that you have been a very naughty boy—if so,

the penance that your confessor has enjoined you has been miraculously providential, and I shall think better of penances for the
rest of my life.'

The lie so temptingly offered for my adoption I was about to
make use of. But, when I reflected from whence I had collected
that sacred earth, I dared not profane it by a falsehood. So, with
a faltering voice, and my eyes filling with tears, I thus addressed
the magistrate.

'Do not laugh at me, sir, do not despise me. I will tell you the
exact truth. I am a silly, romantic boy, that am too apt to give way
unduly to sudden emotions, and, perhaps, false feelings. I returned,
sir, after being three years away, to a home which I left a mere child,
and where I had also left a dear, sweet, good mother, in beauty, in
happiness, and in health. When I asked for my home, they showed
me the house of a stranger—for my mother—and they led me to
a newly-made grave. In a fit of enthusiasm, I gathered up the earth
from over her body and bound it round my bosom. I did it, and
may God pardon me! with wicked thoughts in my head. But I am
not sorry for this insane act, for, methinks, the honoured lady has
stretched forth her hand from the grave, and placed it before the
heart of her son that she so loved when living.'

'I think so too,' said the magistrate, much moved. 'But, my
young friend, these superstitious fancies and acts are best omitted.
I am sure that you do not need this earth to remember your mother.
Besides, it must be prejudicial to your health to carry it about your
person, to say nothing of the singularity of the deed—take my
advice, and convey it carefully to the nearest consecrated ground,
and there reverently deposit it. We will preserve this ball with the
pistol, and now let Mr. Ankins dress your slight wound. We must
see you well through this affair, and the Admiralty must prolong
your leave of absence, if it be necessary. I should wish to know
more of you as a private individual—there is my card. You are a
very good lad for honouring your mother. Fare ye well.'

With many compliments from the surgeon also, and a roller or
two of cotton round my chest, we mutually took leave of each
other—the gentleman, very considerately, refusing the guinea that
I tendered him.

Having discharged the post-chaise, Mr. Pigtop, his two companions, and myself, left the office, I bearing in my hand the
handkerchief nearly filled with mould. What did I do with it—

saturated as it was with my blood, and owing as I did my life to it?
Perhaps, sweet and gentle lady, you think that I preserved it in
a costly vase, over which I might weep, or had it made up by some
fair hands systematically in a silken belt, and still wore it next my
heart, or, at least, that I placed it in a china flower-vase, and planted
a rose tree therein, which I watered daily by my tears. Alas! for the
lovers of the romantic, I did none of these. I told you before, all
my incidents turn out mere matter-of-fact affairs. Like a good boy,
I did as the magistrate bade me. As I passed by St. Paul's, Covent
Garden, I turned into the churchyard; and with a silent prayer for
the departed, and asking pardon of God for the profanation of
which I had been guilty, I poured out the whole of the dust, with
reverence, on a secluded spot, and then returned and joined my
companions.

Taking leave of them shortly after, I repaired to the White
Horse, in Fetter Lane; and, eating a light supper, retired to bed
early, and thus finished this very memorable day.

CHAPTER XIX

*Ralph begins to form his establishment, and engages a travelling
tutor—travelling in the widest sense of the word—Prepares for
a journey, and timorously knocks at the door of an old friend—
gets repulsed; and, finally, gains his ends by showing his credentials,
which means something very like showing fight.*

ON the day succeeding, I found my arm so much swollen and
myself altogether so ill, that I kept my bed. Mr. Pigtop called, and
was very friendly in his behaviour. He seemed to have something
weighing upon his mind; but, either from innate modesty, or his
natural deficiency of elocution, he was unable to relieve the pressure by words. I suspected that he was in want of money, and came
to solicit a loan. I was deceived. He wished to make *me* a tender,
and no less a one than of himself. I need not mention that the same
surgeon attended me. I took this opportunity of furnishing myself
with a few necessaries and a carpet-bag. I employed the chamber-
maid on this momentous occasion. She was very moderate. She
made only cent per cent profit on the purchases, which was paying

remarkably cheaply for respectability, in her eyes, and those of the waiters; for I was now no longer the gentleman without any luggage.

On the third day of my confinement to the house, sitting alone in the deserted coffee-room, chewing the cud of my bitter fancies, Mr. Pigtop made his appearance. Though I knew the man to be thoroughly selfish, I believed him to have that dogged sort of honesty not uncommon to very vulgar minds. As, just then, any society was welcome, I received his condolements very graciously, and requested his company to dinner. My invitation was gladly accepted; and he occupied the time previously to that repast in giving me a history of his life. It was a very common one. He was the son of a warrant-officer. He was all but born on board a man-of-war. At the age of fifteen, he got his rating as a midshipman, and thence rose to be a master's-mate. There his promotion ceased, and, to all appearances, for ever. He had been already twenty-three years in the service, and was turned forty.

Never having had any thing beyond his pay, his life had been one of ceaseless privation and discontent. He had now nearly spent all his money, and had omitted to make those reparations in his wardrobe, rendered so necessary by the malignity of Joshua Daunton. He wished to leave the service, and be any thing rather than what he had been. He had no relations living, and positively no friends. His prospects were most disconsolate, and his wretchedness seemed very great. However, he found considerable relief in unburthening himself to me.

After our frugal dinner of rump-steaks and our one bottle of port, he returned to the subject of the morning by asking my advice as to his future conduct.

'Nay, Pigtop,' I replied, 'you should not ask me. You are much more capable of judging for yourself; you, who have been so much longer in the world than I.'

'There you are out of your reckoning. I have lived more than twice your years, and have never been in the world at all. On shore, I'm like a pig afloat in a washing-tub. What would you advise me to do?'

'You have no relations or friends to assist you?'

The mournful shake of his head was eloquently negative.

'And yet you will not resume that life for which alone you were educated?'

'I will not, and I cannot.'

'Well, you must either go on the highway, or marry a fortune.'

'Look at this figure-head—look at this scar. No—no one will ever splice with such an old ravelled-out rope-yarn as Andrew Pigtop. The road is no longer a gentlemanly profession. I intend to be a servant.'

'You, Pigtop!—begging your pardon, who the devil would be encumbered with you?'

'You, I hope—no, don't laugh; I know you to be a gentleman born, and that you have a hundred a year. By hints that I have picked up, I believe, when you come of age, and that all is done right by you, that you'll have thousands. We have one view in common—to hang that rogue, Daunton. I certainly do not wish to put on your livery, without you insist upon it. Call me your secretary, or any thing you like—only let me be near you—your servant and your friend.'

I saw the poor fellow's eye glisten, and his weather-worn features quiver. I looked upon his worn and shabby uniform, and reflected upon his long and unrequited services. Venerate him I knew that I never could; but I already pitied him exceedingly. I resolved, at least, to assist him, and to keep him near me for some time.

'Well, Pigtop,' I at length said, 'if you would be faithful—'

'To the back-bone—to the shedding of my blood. Stand by me now in my distress; and, while I have either soul or body, I will peril them for your safety.'

'Pigtop, I believe you. Say no more about it. I engage you as my travelling tutor; and I will pay you your salary when I come of age—that is, if I am able. Now, what money have you?'

'Three pounds, fifteen shillings, and seven pence half-penny. Not enough to take me down to the guard-ship when I have paid my bill at the tavern.'

'Then, my good fellow, go and pay it immediately, and come back with all possible speed.' The prompt obedience that he gave to my first order argued well for his attention.

On his return, I addressed him seriously to this effect: 'My friend, you shall share with me to the last shilling; but, believe me, my position is as dangerous as it is unnatural. It is full of difficulty, and requires not only conduct, but courage. I have a parent that either dares not, or, from some sinister motive, will not, own me—and I fear me much that I have a half-brother that I know is pursuing me with the assassin's knife, whilst I am pursuing him with the vengeance of the law. It is either the death of the hunted dog for me, or of the felon's scaffold for him. The event is in the hand of God. We must be vigilant, for my peril is great. My implacable enemy is leagued with some of the worst miscreants of this vast resort of villainy; he knows all the labyrinths of this Babel of iniquity; and the fraternal steel may be in my bosom even amidst the hum of multitudes. That man has a strong motive for my death, and to personify me afterwards. Already has he stolen my vouchers and my certificates. The mystery to me appears almost inscrutable; but his inducements to destroy me are obvious enough. I think that I am tolerably safe here, though I am equally sure that I am watched. Here is money. Go now, and purchase two brace of serviceable pistols and a couple of stout sword-canes. We will be prepared for the worst. Of course, you will sleep here, and hereafter always take up your abode in whatever place I may be. As you return, you must find, in some quiet street, an unobtrusive tailor—he must not have a shop—bring him here with you. I must put you in livery, after all.'

'Why, if so be you must, I suppose you must—I'm off.'

Pigtop did his commissions well. He returned with the arms and the tailor. 'I hope,' said he, 'you won't want me to wear this livery long?'

'Not long, I hope. My friend,' said I, addressing the man of measures, 'this gentleman, lately in the navy, has had recently a very serious turn. He is profoundly repentant of the wickedness of the past life—he has had a call—he has listened to it. It is not unlikely that he may shortly take out a license to preach. Make him a suit of sad-coloured clothes, not cut out after the vanities of the world. Your own would not serve for a bad model. You go to meeting, I presume?'

'I have received grace—I eschew the steeple house—I receive the blessed crumbs of the word that fall from the lips of that light of salvation, the Reverend Mr. Obadiah Longspinner.'

'A holy and a good man, doubtless; would that we were all like him! But, our time will come—yes, our time will come. As is the outward man of the Reverend Mr. Obadiah Longspinner, so would my friend have his outward man—verily, and his inward also—improved unto sanctity.'

The devout tailor snuffled out 'Amen,' and did his office. Whilst

Pigtop's clothes were preparing, he was not idle. He procured all the requisites for travelling, and I sent him on a fruitless mission to discover the residence of the Brandons. He was told by the neighbours that, a year back, they had all emigrated to Canada. Every thing seemed to favour the machinations of my enemy, and to prevent my gaining any clue by which to trace him out, or the object of my search. However, I had one chance left—an interview with the superb Mrs. Causand, that lady that Joshua had so kindly bestowed upon me for a mother.

In three days, behold us in private lodgings, the Reverend Mr. Pigtop looking as sour as any canting Methodist in Barebones' parliament, and quite reconciled to the singularly starched figure that he presented. There was certainly a sad discrepancy between his dress and his discourse. However, it was a good travelling disguise, and very serviceable to a petty officer breaking his leave of absence.

With my health perfectly recovered, dressed with the greatest precision, and, with a beating heart, I went to call upon Mrs. Causand. On her all my hopes rested. I knew that, as a schoolboy, she was extremely fond of me, and I really loved her as much as I admired her. As I advanced towards her house, my heart beat with strange emotions.

I had never before visited her, and was, consequently, totally ignorant of the style in which she lived. From the expense in which she habitually indulged, and from the costliness of her dress when she used to visit Mrs. Cherfeuil, at Stickenham, I augured that it must be something above mediocrity. I found the house which she inhabited, for I had always carefully preserved her address, to be one of those which faced Hyde Park. I was rather chilled as I observed its quiet aristocratic appearance. The dubious position that I held in society, and the continual rebuffs that I apprehended, made me, at that time, very nervous upon the point of intruding myself any where.

I was obliged to recall to my mind her white and jewelled hand running through my hair, and her prolonged caresses when I was a schoolboy, to give me courage to lift the knocker. I acquitted myself, however, of this task, creditably enough. It was opened, not by a porter, but by a very smart footman.

'Is Mrs. Causand at home?' said I, with amiable meekness.

The man surveyed me leisurely from top to toe; I even felt

myself blushing under his scrutiny. After he had satisfied himself by his examination, he answered so rapidly, 'No, sir,' that the two words sounded exactly like 'Noser.'

As I was turning away slowly, and overcome with disappointment, a smart carriage stopped with a plunge at the doorway, the steps rattled, and out sprang a dapper, well-dressed, middle-aged gentleman. Taking three of the stone steps at a time, he was beside me in the hall, the impudent lacquey at the same time endeavouring to pass me on one side with his extended arm, in order to make room for the new comer.

'Mrs. C?' said he.

'Front drawing-room, sir.'

And away sprang up the visitor with almost mounteback activity. Now, from my youth upwards, I have always been a mild creature —very milk—a flagon of sweet oil and gunpowder, the oil, of course, at the top. But, the gunpowder will sometimes ignite, and away goes all the oil in the face of the imprudent igniter.

'You lying scoundrel!' said I, seizing the fellow by his worsted lace collar, and shaking the powder out of his crisped locks, ''tis not a minute ago that you told me Mrs. Causand was not at home!'

'Sir, she is only at home to her particular friends.'

'Know this, sirrah, that I am her most particular friend, and that I have come three thousand miles to see her.'

My violence produced for me much more respect than my civility. The fellow became humble: and told me that if I would walk into the adjoining parlour, and favour him with my name, he would go up immediately she was alone and announce me. Being shown into the room, which I found to be furnished with a most refined taste, though evidently only used for repasts, I began very naturally to make several reflections, neither very pleasing to myself, nor very honourable to the lady whom I was so anxious to see.

CHAPTER XX

The miseries of suspense are sometimes pleasingly prolonged.
Ralph, finding himself in pleasant places, prepareth a love-speech,
which is not uttered in this Chapter—Ralph describeth only.

MANY were the contending emotions, that, each of them struggling
for mastery in my bosom, almost seemed to rend it; and, strange as
it may be thought, jealousy was one of the most dominant. Yet was
it not the sensual jealousy of passion, though passion was undoubtedly mixed up with it—for, despite the differences of age
between this matured beauty and myself, I could not prevent my
memory rioting in contemplation of her stately and perfect figure,
her clear and brilliant complexion, and the liquid or the scorching fires of her full black eyes, equally beautiful, either in anger or
in tenderness.

I was displeased, I was mortified, at the alacrity and freedom
with which I saw the middle-aged and dapper gentleman skip up
the well-carpeted stairs; and I was compelled to ask myself the
revolting question, Is this, the goddess of my boyish idolatry,
a wanton? This meeting, I felt, would be a momentous one. On it
depended every thing that could interest or direct me—the resolving the mystery of my birth. My whole course of life hung upon the
conversation of the next half hour, perhaps upon the caprice of—
a what?—I grew sick with apprehension—the fifteen minutes of
my expectancy seemed so many long and sorrow-laden years.

My senses preternaturally excited, I distinctly heard the bounding step of the visitor who had forestalled me spring from stair to
stair; the door opened, and the plunge and the rattle of the wheels
of the carriage, common-place as they were, seemed to me to have
something in them ominous. The servant opened the door, and
entered the apartment. I trembled excessively, and must have
appeared deadly pale.

'Shall I get you a glass of water, sir?' said the footman, respectfully.

'I thank you, no. Can I see the lady?'

He retired for about five minutes, then returned, bowed, and led
the way. He stepped up quietly and slowly. There was an awe in
his deportment that chilled me. He opened the door of the

drawing-room with extreme caution and gentleness, bowed, and closed it upon me. As I stood near the threshold, the last low tones of some plaintive and soothing melody, sung in a tone much more subdued than that of common conversation, died faintly away to the vibrating of a chord of the harp; and a youthful figure, bathed in a misty light from the window recess, rose, and, moving silently across the room, without once casting her eyes upon myself, disappeared through a door parallel to the one by which I had entered.

I saw, in her quiet transit, that she was very lovely, and her presence gave my heart a sudden gush of joy—for it proved to me that Mrs. Causand had not been alone when she had received her former visiter—and I felt my felicity depended upon her character; for, putting aside every other consideration, had not Daunton told me that she was my mother? I believed it not—but the mere doubt of it was dreadful.

Whilst I remain in the darker portion of this saloon, it is necessary for me to describe it. I could not have imagined such a combination of taste and luxury. At first, I was almost over-powered by the too genial warmth of the apartment, and the aromatic and rose-imbued odours that filled it. I trod on, and my step sank into, a yielding carpet, that seemed to be elastic under my feet, and which glowed with a thousand never-fading though mimic flowers. The apartment was not crowded, though I saw candelabra, vases, and side-tables of the purest marble, supported upon massive gilt pedestals. In all this there was nothing singular—it was the work of the upholsterer; but the beautiful arrangement was the work of a presiding taste.

At the farther end of this superb room, stood two fluted and gilded pilasters, and two pillars of the Corinthian order, the capitals of which reached the ceiling; but they were not equi-distant from each other, the space from the pilaster to the pillar, on either side, being much less than that between the two pillars. Between the two former, there were placed statues of the purest marble; what fabled god or goddess they were sculptured to represent I know not; I only felt that they personified male and female beauty. I was too agitated to permit myself to notice them accurately. Between this screen of pillars and statues, hung two distinct sets of drapery, the one of massive and crimson silk curtains, entirely opaque by their richness and their weight of texture, that drew up and aside with golden cords; the other of a muslin, almost transparent, how managed I had no time to examine.

When the draperies fell in their gorgeous and graceful folds to the ground, they made of the saloon two parts, and the division that embraced the windows had then all the privacy of a secluded apartment. When the curtains were let fall, thus intercepting the light from the bayed windows, there was still sufficient from the three sash-windows on the left of this large apartment to give splendour to what would then become the inner room.

The heavy draperies that hung between the pillars were drawn up, but the light muslin was dropped even with the rich Turkey carpet, through which I caught but a dim and glowing view of the recess. It was, as nearly as I can recollect, about three o'clock in the afternoon; and the sun, just dallying with the tops of the trees in the distant Kensington Gardens, sent his level beams directly through the large windows, and the orange-trees and exotics that were placed about them.

I advanced to the screen; and, when close upon it, I perceived the figure, though but faintly, of Mrs. Causand, reclining upon a couch. I paused—I do not think, on account of the distribution of the light, that she could have seen me through the veil that intervened between us. I dared not break through it without a summons; and there I stood, for two unpleasant minutes, endeavouring to imagine of what nature my reception would be; and, whether a lady surrounded by so much magnificence would listen to the appeal of her former pet-playfellow.

At this time, it was the fashion, in full dress, to show the whole of the arm bare to the shoulder. At length, from out of the mass of rich shawls, there was lifted the white, rounded, exquisitively-shaped, though somewhat large, arm of the lady, beckoning me to enter; but sound there was none. 'She is delighted to play the empress,' said I, as I pushed aside the curtain, and stood before her in her odoriferous sanctum.

Verily, in the pride of her beauty, she never looked more beautiful. She was in full dress—and, as I surveyed her in mute admiration, and my mind was busy at once with the past and the present, I pronounced her improved since I had last seen her; for I could perceive no difference in her countenance, except that her rounded and classic cheek glowed with a ruddier hue, and her eye sparkled with a more restless fire.

I stood before her at the foot of the couch, and my heart confessed that the perfection of womanly beauty lay beneath my wondering eyes, but a beauty which, if in smiles, would rather madden with voluptuousness, than subdue with tenderness, and, if in repose, seemed to command worship, more than solicit affection.

As I stood mutely there, I looked into her regal countenance for some encouragement to speak—I saw none. I then strove to read there the sentiment then passing in her mind, and to my confusion, to my dismay, it seemed to me that she was endeavouring to conquer in her countenance the expression of pain. I watched intently—I was not deceived—a sudden convulsion passed over her features, succeeded by the paleness of an instant, and then a gush of tears—I was moved, almost to weeping, yet dared not advance. Her tears were hurried off instantly; and then again her dear smile of former days sunned up her countenance into something heavenly.

CHAPTER XXI

Ralph beginneth a conversation totally beyond his comprehension, and yet comprehendeth more than the conversation is meant to convey—He feeleth some inclination towards love-making, but checketh himself valiantly.

'My own brave Ralph,' said she, extending to me both her hands.

'Your schoolboy lover,' said I; an immense weight of anxiety removed from my mind, as I kissed her jewelled fingers.

'Hush, Ralph! such words are vanities—but ask me not why. Oh, my dear boy, make the most of this visit—'

'I will, I will—how beautiful you are! how very, very beautiful!'

'Am I?—I rejoice to hear you say so! Ralph, speak to me as my own devoted, my more than loved friend—by all the affection that I have lavished on you, speak to me truly; do you, dearest Ralph, see no alteration in me?'

'A little,' said I, smiling triumphantly, 'a very little, for there was never room for much—you are a little more beautiful than when I last beheld you.'

'Thank you—you have given me more happiness by the fervent honesty of that speech than I have experienced for days and weeks, nay, months before. Stand from me, and let me look at you—you, Ralph, are also much, very much improved—perhaps there is a little too much cast of thought upon your brow—that thought is a sad wrinkle-maker—but, Ralph, you are not well dressed. But come and sit by me now there, on that low footstool. I always loved to play thus with your pretty curls—I wish that they were a shade darker; as you have grown so manly, it would have been as well. Truly, as I look into the ingenuous brightness of your countenance, the joys of past happy hours seem to wing themselves back, and whisper to me that word so little understood—Happiness. But, Ralph, we will be alone together for this day at least—you shall dine with me here—we will have no interruption—you shall tell me all your deeds of arms—and, you naughty boy, of love also. Reach that bell, and ring it—but gently.'

I obeyed, and the same handsome young lady whom I had before seen answered the silver summons. She glided in, and stooped over to Mrs. Causand, as she lay on the couch, and their short conference was in whispers. As she retired, I was rather puzzled by the deep sorrow on her countenance, and the unfeigned look of pity with which she regarded her mistress or her friend. When we were again alone, I resumed my low seat, and was growing rather passionate over one of her beautiful hands, when, looking down, apparently much pleased with these silly endearments, she said, 'Yes, Ralph, make the most of it; hand and heart, all, all are your's, for the little space that they will be mine.'

Strange and disloyal thoughts began their turmoil in my bosom; and speculation was busy, and prospects of vanity began to dance before my eyes. Old enough to be my mother! What then? Mother! the thought brought with it the black train of ideas of which Daunton was the demoniac leader. He had asserted that the superb woman before me might claim from me the affection of a son. I then felt most strongly that I was not there to play any ridiculous part.

The protestations that I was about to utter died on my lips—I spake not, but pressed the hand that I held to my heart.

'Now, Ralph,' said Mrs. Causand, 'relate to me all the wonders that you have encountered—speak lowly'—and she threw a white and very thin handkerchief over her face.

B b

'But, my dear madam, why may I not gaze upon a countenance that you know is very dear to me? And this setting sun—how glorious! Do you know that, at his rising and his setting, I have often thought of you? Pray come to the window, and look upon it before it is quite hid among the trees.'

'Ralph, by all the love that I bore your mother, by the affection that I bear to you, do not talk to me of setting suns! I dread to look upon them. You ask me to rise—oh, son of my best friend—know, that I cannot—without assistance—without danger—I am on my sick couch—on my dying bed—they tell me—me—me, whom you just now so praised for improved beauty, that my days are numbered —but, I believe them not—no—no—no—but hush, softly!— I may not agitate myself—you, my sweet boy, have surely come to me the blessed messenger of health—your finger shall turn back the hand upon the dial, and years, whole years of happiness, shall be your's and mine.'

'Inscrutable ruler of heaven!' I exclaimed, 'it is impossible! You are but trying my affection—you do but wish to witness the depth of my agony—you would prove me—but this is with a torture too cruel. Say—oh say—my dear Mrs. Causand, that you are trifling with me—you—you are now the only friend that I have upon earth.'

'These emotions, my dear boy, will slay me outright—the monster is now, even now, grappling with me—give me your hand.' She took it, and placed it over the region of her heart. The shock it gave me was electric—that heart trembled beneath her bosom rapidly as flutter the wings of the dying bird—then paused —then went on. I looked into her face, and saw again the instant and momentary pallor, that had surprised me so much on my first entrance. The paroxysm was as short as it was violent, and her features again returned to their usual placidity of majestic beauty.

'You know it all now, Ralph—the least motion sets my heart in this unaccountable fury—and—alas, alas! every attack is more acute than the last. They tell me that I am dying—I cannot believe it. I cannot even comprehend it. I have none of the symptoms of death upon me. Every thing around me breathes of health and happiness —you alone were wanting to complete the scene—you are here—no —no, I will not die. Had my hair whitened, my form bowed, my complexion withered—why then—I might have been reconciled— but, no—it is impossible—no—no—Ralph, I am *not* dying.'

'Fervently do I pray God that you are not. It also seems to me impossible—but still, the youngest of us cannot always escape— hoping, trusting, relying on the best, we should be prepared for the worst.'

'But I am not prepared,' she exclaimed with a fierce energy that breathed defiance; and then, relapsing into a profound melancholy, she mournfully continued—'and I cannot prepare myself.'

'Have you spoken to a clergyman?' said I, not knowing exactly what else to say. 'Is not this some book of divine consolation?'

I took it up; it was the popular novel of the day, entitled, 'The Rising Sun.' What a profound mockery for a death-bed!

'I tell you, my dear Ralph, that you must not agitate me. Talk of any thing but my approaching death—for know, that I am resolved *not* to die. To-morrow, there will be a consultation over my case of the very first of the medical faculty in the world. Ralph, do you not league together with the rest of the world, and con- demn me to an untimely death.'

'Untimely, indeed.'

She had now evidently talked too much; she closed her eyes, and seemed to enjoy a peaceful and refreshing slumber. I sat by and watched her. Was I then in a sick chamber?—was that personi- fication of beauty doomed? I looked round, and pronounced it incredible. I gazed upon the recumbent figure before me, so still, so living, and yet so death-like—and moralized upon the utter deception of appearances.

At length she awoke, apparently much reanimated.

'My dear Ralph,' said she, 'why are you not in mourning?'

'I understand you—and I perceive now that you are in black. But I must not disturb you—yet, if I dared, I would ask you one question—oh, in pity answer it—was she my mother?'

'Does death absolve us from our oaths?'

'I am not, my dear lady, casuist enough to answer you that question. But, do you know that I have become a desperate charac- ter lately? I write myself man, and will prove the authenticity of the signature with my life. I have renounced my profession—every pursuit, every calling, every thought—that may stand between me and the development of the mystery of my birth. It is the sole pur- pose of my life—the whole devotion of my existence.'

'Ralph—a foolish one—just now. Bide the course of events.'

'I will not—if I can control them. Through this detestable

mystery, I have been insulted, reviled—a wretch has had the hardi-
hood, the turpitude, to brand both you and me—me as the base-
born child, and you as the ignominious parent.'

'Who, who, who?'

'A pale-faced, handsome, short, smooth-worded villain, with
a voice that I now recognise, for the first time—a coward—
a swindler, that calls himself, undoubtedly among other aliases—'

'Stop, Ralph, in misery!' and, for the first time, she sat upright on her couch. 'The crisis of a whole life is at hand—I
must go through it, if I die on the spot—ring again for Miss
Tremayne.'

The gentle and quiet lady was soon at Mrs. Causand's side.
There was a little whispering passed between them, some medicines put on the small work-table near the head of the couch, and
finally, a tolerably large packet of papers. She then cautioned Mrs.
Causand most emphatically to keep herself tranquil, and, bowing
to me slightly, glided out of the room.

CHAPTER XXII

The veil is fast dropping from before Ralph's mysterious parentage—
Strange disclosures, and much good evidence that this is a very bad
world—Ralph's love-symptoms are fast subsiding.

'RALPH,' said the lady, when we were again alone, 'I have, through
the whole of my life, always detested scenes, and, to the utmost of
my power, ever repelled all violent emotions. I am not now going
to give you a history of my life—to make my confessions, and ask
pardon of you and God, and then die—nonsense; but I must say
that your fate has been somewhat strangely connected with my own.
I acknowledge to you, at once, that I am a fallen woman—but, as I
never had the beauty, so I never had the repentance of a Magdalen.
I fell to one of the greatest upon the earth. I still think it was
a glorious fate. I know that you are going to wound me deeply.
I will take it meekly; may it be, in some measure, looked upon as
a small expiation for my one great error! But, spare me, as long as
you are able, the name of this person you have described with such
bitterness—it may not, after all, be he who has been almost the only

bitterness that has yet poisoned my cup of a too pleasurable existence—'tis pleasurable, alas! until, even in this, my eleventh hour. Tell me all, and then I shall be able to judge how much it may be my duty to reveal to you.'

It was a fine study, that of observing the gradual emotion of this worldly and magnificent woman, as I proceeded with my eventful tale. I took it up only at that period when Joshua Daunton first made his application to me to be allowed to enter the Eos. The beginning of my narrative fell coldly upon her, and her features were strung up to that tension which I had often before observed in persons who were bracing up their nerves to undergo a dangerous surgical operation. They were certainly not impassive, for, in the fixed eyes that glared upon me, there was a strange restlessness, though not of motion.

The first symptoms of emotion that I could perceive took place when I described the lash descending upon the shrinking shoulders of Daunton. She clasped her hands firmly together, and upturned her eyes, as if imploring Heaven for mercy, or entreating it for vengeance. I perceived, as I proceeded, that I was gradually losing ground in her affections—that she was, in spite of herself, espousing the cause of my pledged enemy; and when I told her of the defiance that I had received in the sick bay, she murmured forth, 'Well done! Well done!' followed by a name that was not mine.

When I related to her the documents that he had shown me to convince me that he was no impostor, she said 'Ralph, it is enough —it is of little consequence now what name you may give him. *He is my son!*'

'And my half-brother?'

'Oh no, no, young sir! Disgraced as he has been, a nobler blood than that of Rattlin flows in his veins. Degraded, disgraced as he is, neither on the side of the father nor of the mother need he blush for his parentage. But, you are his sworn enemy—I can now listen more calmly to what you have to say. But, graceless as he is, he should not have denied his own mother.'

'Mrs. Causand,' said I, in a tone of voice more cold than any with which I had yet addressed her, 'it seems that you have, and that most unreasonably too, taken part against me. In no point have I sinned against you or your's. I have all along been the attacked, the aggrieved party. I will no longer offend your ears, or wring your heart, by a recapitulation of your son's delinquencies.

He has done me much wrong; he is contemplating more—only place me in a situation of doing myself justice, and silence on the past shall seal my lips for ever; but know that he has stolen all my documents, and intends passing himself off to whomever may be my father, as his legitimate son, as myself.'

'This must not be—foolish, mad, wicked boy! That I, his mother, must stand up his accuser! must act against him as his enemy; but I have long ago discarded him—almost cursed him. Oh, Ralph, Ralph! had he been like you—but, from his youth upwards, he has been inclined to wickedness—no fortune could have supplied his extravagance—he has exhausted even a mother's love. I refused him money, and he stole my papers—I never dreamt of the vile use that he intended to put them to. Spare me for a little while, and I will let you know all; but, should you once get his neck under your heel, oh! tread lightly on my poor William!'

She had evidently another and a most severe attack of her complaint, which passed rapidly over like the rest; but she now had, for the first time within my observation, recourse to her medicines. When sufficiently recovered, she continued:—

'Ralph, neither you nor any one shall know my private history. It is enough for you to understand that I was, almost from infancy, destined to associate with the greatest of the sterner sex. Early was I involved in this splendid—degradation, the austere would call it, though degradation I never held it to be. Even appearances were preserved; for, before my wretched son was born, I was married to one of the pages of a German court, who was sixty years of age, and properly submissive and distant. To the English ear, this sounds like a confession of infamy. Let me not, Ralph, endeavour to justify it to you—I was taught otherwise—now, if I could, I would not regret it. Your father, then an only son, sometimes visited at the house of the person over whose establishment I presided, and—and, mark me, Ralph, injuriously as you must now think of me, I presided over but one. Deride me not when I tell that to that distinguished personage I was chaste.'

She paused, and I thought that her voice faltered strangely, and that the assertion died upon her lips, and I made no reply. I was by no means astonished at this detail. I could only look upon her most anxiously, and await her future disclosures.

'I have,' she continued, 'lived for the world, and found it a glorious one. The husband of my heart, and the husband of

ceremony, have long both been dead. I enjoy a competency—nay,
much more—and yet, they talk to me of dying. To-morrow will
decide upon my fate. I have lived a good life, according to my
capabilities—it is no delusion—but, should the sentence of
to-morrow's consultation be fatal, then the lawyer and the clergyman—'

'And why not to-day?'

'Because it is our's, Ralph, or rather your's. Well, your mother
was of good, though not of exalted, family, the daughter of a considerable freeholder in our neighbourhood. She was the eldest of
many children, and the most beautiful born of all in the county.
Her father sent her to London; and she became thus, for her
station and the period, over-educated. She foolishly preferred
the fashionable, and refined, and luxurious, service in a nobleman's
family to a noble independence in her honest father's spacious
house. It was her mistake and her ruin.

'Ralph! I loved your mother—you know it—but, as a governess
in the Duke of E's family, I hated and feared her. I don't think
that she was more beautiful than I, but he—he whom I will never
mention—began to be of that opinion—at least, I trembled.
Reginald Rathelin loved her—wooed her—I entered with eagerness into his schemes—his success was my security. Miss Daventry
at first repulsed me; but, at length, I overcame her repugnance—
many ladies, notwithstanding my ambiguous position, awed by
the rank of my protector, received me—we became friends. The
beautiful governess eloped—I managed every thing—they were
married. I was myself a witness to the ceremony.'

'Thank God!' I exclaimed fervently.

'Reginald was wild and dissipated, poor and unprincipled—he
cajoled his wife, and suffered her again to return to her menial
station in the duke's family. In due time there was another journey
necessary. It was when you were born at Reading. "A little while,
and yet a little while," was the constant plea of the now solicited
husband, "and I will own you, my dear Elizabeth, and boast of
you before all the world."'

'My poor mother!'

'About two years after this marriage, Sir Luke, the father of
Reginald, fell ill, and the neglect of the husband became only
something a little short of actual desertion. Your mother had
a proud as well as a loving spirit. She wrote to the father of Reginald

—she interested the duke in her favour—she was now as anxious for publicity as concealment; but the expectant heir defied us all. He confessed himself a villain, and avowed that he had entrapped your mother by a fictitious marriage.'

'And *he* my father!—but you, *you*, *her friend?*'

'He deceived me also. He declared the man who pretended to perform the marriage ceremony was not in holy orders. He dared us to prove it. His father, bred up in prejudice of birth and family, did not urge the son to do justice to your mother, but satisfied his conscience by providing very amply for yourself: he first took credit to himself for thus having done his duty, then the sacrament, and died.

'Your father, now Sir Reginald, in due time proposed for the richest heiress in the three adjacent counties, and was rejected with scorn. We made a strong party against him—the seat of his ancestors became hateful to him—he went abroad. His princely mansion was locked up—his estates left to the management of a grinding steward; and the world utterly forgot the self-created alien from his country.'

'Then, alas! after all, I am illegitimate.'

'And if you were?—but, methinks, that you are now feeling more for yourself than for your mother.'

'Oh no, no! tell me of her!'

'After this *exposé*, she lived some few years respected in the duke's family; but she changed her name—home to her father's she would never go—no tidings ever reached her of the man she looked upon as her seducer. It must be confessed, however, that he took great care of his child—he appointed agents to watch over your welfare, though I firmly believe that he never saw you in his life.'

'I think that he once made the attempt when I was at Root's school; but, before I was brought to him, his conscience smote him, and he fled like a craven from his only and injured son.'

'Most probably. Rumour said that he had made several visits to England under a strict incognito. But I must pause—the evening is fast waning—let me repose a little, and then we will have lights and dinner.' She fell back upon her couch, and appeared again to slumber.

CHAPTER XXIII

Ralph thinks seriously about changing his name—Gets a little unwilling justice done to himself, and gains much information— The whole wound up suddenly and sorrowfully.

IT was nearly dark, as I sat for more than half an hour by the side of the impenitent beauty—I could not conceive that she was in any danger. Whilst she discoursed with me so fully, her voice was firm, though not loud, and, were it not for a short and sudden check, sometimes in the middle of a word, I should say that I never before heard her converse more fluently or more musically.

Whilst she yet reclined, the servants brought in lights, and made preparations for our little dinner, a small table being laid close to Mrs. Causand's couch. When this exquisite repast was ready, and Miss Tremayne made her appearance, Mrs. Causand rose, apparently much renovated. She looked almost happy: without assistance, she walked from her sofa, and took her place at the table.

'There, Fanny,' said she, quite triumphantly—'and not a single attack! This dear Ralph has surely brought health with him. Yesterday, this exertion would have killed me.'

'Do not, however,' said the lady, 'try your self too much.'

We dined cheerfully: she seemed to have forgotten her son, and I my much injured mother. After the dinner was concluded, and Miss Tremayne had retired, and my hostess had returned to her sofa, she sent for her writing-desk, and then proceeded with her narrative.

'Your mother, my dear Ralph, yearned for your society. She had saved a considerable sum of money—she wished for a home, to procure which, she married that little ugly, learned Frenchman, Cherfeuil—but even that she did not do, until it was currently reported, and generally believed, that your father was dead.'

'I admire the delicacy of the scruple—I honour her for it.'

'Sip your wine, Ralph—you'll find it excellent—I will indulge in one glass, let Dr. Hewings say what he will—to your health, my little lover, and may I soon hail you as Sir Ralph Rathelin!'

'How is it possible?'

'You shall hear. We were talking about your good mother. When she had married this Cherfeuil, who was the French assistant at a large school, she found out the agents to whom you were entrusted, and soon arranged with them that you should be domesticated under her own roof—you were removed to Stickenham, and she and you were happy.'

'Oh, how happy!'

'Well, you know it was in those happy days that I had first the pleasure of forming an acquaintance with the inimitable Ralph Rattlin.'

'But why Rattlin?—my name must be either Daventry or Rathelin.'

'Rathelin, of a surety—it was first of all corrupted to Rattlin, by that topmost of all top-sawyers, Joe Brandon—it having ever been so established, for many reasons, concealment among the rest, your mother thought it best for you to retain it. Now, Ralph, mark this—about eight, or rather seven, months ago, I took a short trip to my native country in Germany. Never was my health more redundant. I left your mother prosperous and happy, and beautiful as ever—she had heard of you, and heard much in your favour, though you never once condescended to write to any one of us. Whilst I was in——your father returned, a changed man—changed in every thing, even in religion: he had turned penitent and a Catholic, and so had his travelling companion, the very man who had married him to your sweet mother.'

'Then he was in holy orders?'

'He was.'

'God of infinite justice, I thank you!'

'The Reverend Mr. Thomas came here to my very house, when I was away, with a long and repentant letter from his patron—full of inquiries for yourself, and for your mother, Lady Rathelin.'

'Where is that inestimable letter?'

'Oh, where?' said the again agonised Mrs. Causand. 'Ralph, much mischief was done in that absence—my boy, my lost William! he, whom you know as Joshua Daunton, broke into his mother's house, rifled my escritoire, and carried off some of my most important documents, that unread letter among the number.'

'But how know you its contents?' said I, breathless with agitation.

'By the tenor of these succeeding ones from Sir Reginald and his priest.'

She opened her desk, and gave me two letters from my father to

her. They were, as she described them, repentant, and spoke most
honourably and most fondly of my deceased mother—praying
Mrs. Causand most earnestly to tell him of the happiness and the
whereabout of his wife.

'And you did, of course.'

'No, Ralph, I did not—look at the dates. It was a fortnight after
these arrived before I returned home. I weep even now when
I think of it—three days before I returned, your mother had died,
almost suddenly.'

'Ah, true, true!' said I mournfully. But, a sudden pang of agony
seizing my inmost heart, I suddenly started up, and, seizing her
roughly by the hand, I said sternly—

'Look me in the face, madam—do you see any resemblance there
to my poor, poor mother?'

'Oh, very, very great—but why this violence?'

'Because I now understand the villainy that caused her death.
Your son murdered her—see in me her reproachful countenance—
oh, Mrs. Causand, you and your's have been the bane, the ruin of
me and mine.'

'What do you mean by those horrible words? Ralph, beware,
or you will yourself commit a dastardly murder upon me, even as
you stand there.'

'Mrs. Causand, I will be calm. I see it all. With the first letter
of Sir Reginald's in his hand, he went to Stickenham; and, with
the murderous intent strong in his black bosom, he branded my
mother with bigamy, incensed the weak Frenchman against her,
and, in twenty-four hours, did the mortal work that years of
injustice and injury could not effect.'

'Good God, it must be so!—Ralph, I do not ask you to forgive
him—but pity his poor suffering mother—he has broken my
heart—not Ralph, in the mystical, but in the actual, the physical,
sense. In the very hour in which I returned home, I found a warrant had been issued for his apprehension as a housebreaker; and
the stony-hearted reprobate had the cruelty to insult his mother by
a letter glorying in the fact, at the same time demanding a thousand
pounds for his secrecy and the papers that he had stolen. The shock
was too much for me. I had an attack, a fit—I know not what—I fell
senseless to the earth—my heart has never since beaten healthfully.
Oh, perhaps, after all, it would be a happiness for me to die!—Poor
Elizabeth—my more than sister, my friend!'

'But why do I waste my time here?' said I, starting up, and seizing my hat. 'The reptile is at work. Where lives Sir Reginald? —my demon-like double may be there before me. He may personate me long enough to kill my father and rifle his hoards. I must away—but, ere I go, know that, with these abstracted papers, he sought me in the West Indies, cheated me out of my name on my return to England, and, finally, waylaid and attempted, with a low accomplice, to assassinate me on my return from Stickenham.'

'God of Heaven, let me die!—he could never have been son of mine—let me know the horrid particulars.'

'No—no—no—I must away—or more murders will be perpetrated.'

'Stop, Ralph, a little moment—do not go unprovided. Take these and these—he stole not all the documents—let me also give my testimony under my own hand of your identity. It may be of infinite service to you.'

She then wrote a short letter to Sir Reginald, describing accurately my present appearance, and vouching that I, and none other, was the identical Ralph Rattlin, who was nursed by the Brandons, and born at Reading.

'Take this, Ralph, and show it to Sir Reginald. I only ask one thing: spare the life—only the life—of that unfortunate boy!— and in his, spare mine—for I am unprepared to die!'

'The mercy that he showed my mother—'

I had proceeded no farther in my cruel speech, when a great noise was heard at the door, and two rough-looking Bow Street officers, attended by the whole household, rushed into the room. They advanced towards the upper end of this elegant sanctum. Mrs. Causand sprang up from her sofa, and, standing in all the majesty of her beauty, sternly demanded, 'What means this indignity?'

'Beg your ladyship's pardon, sorry to intrude—duty—never shy, that you know, ma'am—only a search-warrant for one Joshua Daunton, alias Sneaking Willie, alias Whitefaced——.'

'Stop, no more of this ribaldry—you see he is not here—I know nothing concerning him—of what is he accused?'

'Of forgery, housebreaking, and, with an accomplice, of an attempt to murder a young gentleman, a naval officer, of the name of Ralph Rattlin.'

Mrs. Causand turned to me sorrowfully, and exclaimed, 'Oh,

Ralph! was this well done of you?' Her fortitude, her sudden accession of physical strength, seemed to desert her at once; and she, who just before stood forth the undaunted heroine, now sank on her couch, the crushed invalid. At length, she murmured forth, feebly, 'Ralph, rid me of these fellows.'

I soon effected this. I told them that I was the culprit's principal accuser; that I was assured he was not only not within the house, but I verily believed many miles distant. They believed me, and respectfully enough retired.

Miss Tremayne, the companion and nurse of the invalid, now with myself stood over her. She had another attack upon the region of her heart; and it was so long before she rallied, that we thought the fatal moment had arrived. When she could again breathe freely, her colour did not, as formerly, return to her cheeks. They wore an intense and transparent whiteness, at once awful and beautiful. Yet she spoke calmly and collectedly. I entreated to be permitted to depart—my intercessions were seconded by the young lady. But the now cold hand of Mrs. Causand clasped mine so tightly, and the expression of her eyes was so imploring, that I could not rudely break away from her.

'But a few short minutes,' she exclaimed, 'and then fare you well. I feel worse than I ever yet remember—and very cold. It is not now the complaint that has cast me down upon a sick bed that seems invading the very principle of life—a chilly faintness is coming over me—yet I dare not lay my head upon my pillow, lest I never from thence lift it again. Ralph, there is warmth in your young blood—support me!'

I cradled her head upon my shoulder, and whispered to Miss Tremayne, who immediately retired, to procure the speedy attendance of the physician.

'Are we alone, Ralph?' said the shuddering lady, with her eyes firmly closed. 'I have a horrid presentiment that my hour is approaching—every thing is so still around and within me. Every sensation seems deserting me rapidly, but one—and that is a mother's feelings! You will leave me here to die, amongst menials and strangers!'

'Miss Tremayne?' said I, soothingly.

'Is but a hired companion; engaged only since the occurrence of these attacks. Yes, you will desert me to these—and for what, God of retribution!—to hunt down the life of my only son! Will you, will you, Ralph, do this over-cruel thing?'

'He has attempted mine—he still seeks it. Let us talk, let us think of other matters. Compose your mind with religious thoughts. Your strength will rally during the night; to-morrow comes hope, the consultation of physicians, and, with God's good blessings, life and health.'

'To hear, to know, that he is to die the death of the felon! Promise me to forego your purpose, or let me die first!'

'I have sworn, over the grave of my mother, that the laws shall decide this matter between us. If he escape, I forgive him, and may God forgive him, too!'

'And must it come to this?' she sobbed forth in the bitterness of her anguish, whilst the tears streamed down her cheeks from her closed eye-lids. 'Will this cruel youth at length extort the horrible confession!—it must be so—one pang—and it will be over. Let me forego your support—lay me gently on the pillow, for you will loathe me. A little while ago, and I told you I had been faithful to *him*—it was a bitter falsehood—know, that my son, my abandoned William, is also the son of your father—say, will his blood now be upon your hands?'

'Tell me, beautiful cause of all our miseries, does your miserable offspring know this?'

'Yes,' said she, very faintly.

'Yet *he* could seek my life—basely—but, no matter. His blood shall never stain my hand—I will not seek him—if he crosses my path, I will avoid him—I will even assist him to escape to some country, where unknown, he may, by a regenerated life, wipe out the dark catalogue of his crimes, make his peace with man here, and with his God hereafter.'

'Will you do all this, my generous, my good, my godlike Ralph?'

'You and God be my witnesses!'

She sprang up wildly from her apparent state of lethargy, clasped me fervently in her arms, blessed me repeatedly, and then, in the midst of her raptures, she cried out, 'Oh, Ralph, you have renewed my being, you have given me long years of life, and health, and happiness. You—' and here she uttered a loud shriek, that reverberated through the mansion—but it was cut short in the very midst—a thrilling, a horrible silence ensued—she fell dead upon the couch.

I stood awe-struck over the beautiful corpse, as it lay placidly extended, disfigured by no contortion, but, on the contrary, a heavenly repose in the features—a sad mockery of worldly vanity. Death had arrayed himself in the last imported Parisian mode.

At that dying shriek in rushed the household, headed by the physician, and closely followed by the companion, with the hired nurses. Methought that the doctor looked on this wreck of mortality with grim satisfaction. 'I knew it,' said he, slowly; 'and Doctor Phillimore is nothing more than a solemn dunce. I told him that she would not survive to be subjected to the consultation of the morrow.—And how happens it,' said he, turning fiercely to the companion and the nurses, 'that my patient was thus left alone with this stripling?'

'Stripling, sir!' said I.

'Young man, let us not make the chamber of death a hall of contention. Tell me, Miss Tremayne, how comes my patient thus unattended, or rather thus ill attended?'

'It was her own positive command,' said the young lady, in a faltering voice.

'Ah, she was always imperious, always obstinate. There must have been some exciting conversation between you, sir, (turning to me) and the lady; did you say any thing to vex or grieve her?'

'On the contrary; she was expressing the most unbounded hope and happiness when she died.'

'And the name of God was not on her lips, the prayer for pardon not in her heart, when she was snatched away.'

I shook my head. 'Well,' said he, 'it is a solemn end, and she was a wilful lady. Do you know, Miss Tremayne, if she have any relations living?—they should be sent for.'

'I know of none. A person of distinction, whose name I am not at liberty to mention, sometimes visited her. We had better send for her solicitor.'

Some other conversation took place, which I hardly noticed. The body was adjusted on the couch, we left the room, and the door was locked. As I walked quietly, almost stealthily, home, I felt stunned. Health and mortality, death and life, seemed so fearfully jumbled together, that I almost doubted whether I was not traversing a city of spirits.

No sorrow then hung about my heart—I was rather inclined to

deride earth and all that it contained. The reckless and hard mirth, more expressive of pain than the bitterest tears, was fast seizing upon me; and, when I broke into the room of our humble lodgings, it was with a ribald jest and a sneer at the scene that I had just witnessed with which I accosted my newly-endowed travelling tutor, Pigtop.

My Achates[1] stared at me when I had described to him the late occurrences, and shook his head. 'I don't see much cause for sniggering,' said he.

'Why, has not John Bull one pension less to pay—and a glorious one, too?—don't we love our country, Pigtop? But, we must be off to-morrow. There's my double, depend upon it, doing the filial with my honoured and most Catholic father.'

'And have you at length discovered him?' said he.

'I have—a voice almost from the grave has imparted to me all that I wished to know—and something more. I have sprung from a beautiful race—but, we must not speak ill of kith and kin, must we, Pigtop?'

'For certain not. And, so your father actually did send that old lord to look after you at your return from the West Indies. Well, that shows some affection for you, at all events.'

'The fruits of which affection Daunton is, no doubt, now reaping.'

'Well, let us go and cut his throat, or rather turn him over to the hangman.'

'No, Pigtop; I have promised his mother that I will not attempt his life.'

'But, I have not.'

'Humph—let us to roost. To-morrow, at break of day, we will be off for Rathelin Hall. See that our arms are in order. And now to what rest nature and good consciences will afford us.'

CHAPTER XXIV

Mr. Pigtop believeth in Ghosts, and hath some trust in Witches, but none at all in Lawyers—A Consultation after supper, and, after supper, action.

EARLY next morning, Mr. Pigtop and myself were seated in a post-chaise, making the best of our way towards the western extremity of England. Notwithstanding the speed of our conveyance, the journey was necessarily long, and our debate was frequent and full upon the plan of our operations. When we had arrived at Exeter, where we found it necessary to stop in order to gain some little restoration from the fatigues of our incessant travelling, we made up our minds to hire three horses and a groom, and, having very accurately ascertained the exact site of Rathelin Hall, which was situated a few miles to the north-eastward of Barnstaple, we arrived there towards the close of the day, and put up at a very decent inn in an adjoining village.

The old and large house was distinctly visible, notwithstanding the well wooded park in which it was situated, from the windows of our inn. A conference with our host fully realized our worst fears. He informed us that Sir Reginald was not expected to live many days; that his whole deportment was very edifying; and, moreover, that his dying hours were solaced and sweetened by the presence and the assiduities of his only and long-disowned, but now acknowledged, son, Ralph. We, moreover, learned that this Ralph came attended by a London attorney, and that they, with the priest Thomas, in the intervals between rest, refection, and prayer, were actively employed in settling his sublunary affairs, very much to the dissatisfaction of a Mr. Seabright, the family solicitor, and the land-steward of the estate.

'Where does Mr. Seabright reside?' was my question, instantly.

'Why, here, sir, to be sure, in our town of Antwick, and mortally in dudgeon he has taken all this.'

'Undoubtedly, and with justice,' was my reply. 'So faithful a servant, who has for so many years had the sole management of the Rathelin affairs, should not be cast off so lightly. Give us as good a supper, landlord, as your skill and Antwick can produce, and let us have covers for three. Send your porter down to Mr.

Seabright—but, I had better write him a note.' So I sent to him a polite invitation to sup with us, telling him that two strangers wished to see him on important business.

To all these proceedings Pigtop demurred. He was for the summary process of going before a magistrate next morning, and taking out a warrant to apprehend Joshua Daunton on the capital charge for which he was pursued in London, and thus, at one blow, wind up the affair.

But, I held my promise to Mrs. Causand to be sacred, and determined to give him, my fraternal enemy, one chance of escaping. Pigtop's repugnance, however, to the employment of a lawyer could not be overcome; so, not being able to obtain his consent, I determined to try and do without it, which my friend averred to be impossible.

At nine o'clock precisely, as the smoking dishes appeared, so did the lawyer. A sudden emotion was perceptible on his iron-bound visage when his eyes first fell upon me, of the nature of which I could form no idea. Mr. Pigtop bowed to him very stiffly; and it was some time before the genuine cordiality of my manner could put Mr. Seabright at his ease.

While we were at table, I begged to decline giving him our names, as I was fearful that the intelligence might travel to the Hall, and thus give some scope for further machinations on the part of Joshua. But, as is too often the case, we were prudent only by halves.

The groom that we had hired, not being enjoined to secrecy, had unhesitatingly told every one belonging to the establishment our appellations. The landlord and his household were much struck by the similarity of the name by which I still went, Rattlin, and that of Rathelin: and, thus, whilst I was playing the cautious before Mr. Seabright, the news had already reached the Hall, and those most concerned to know it, that two gentlemen, a Mr. Rattlin and a Mr. Pigtop, with their groom, had put up at the Three Bells in the village, and had sent for the lawyer.

Had I been inclined for amusement, I should have found it to satiety, in the humorous scene between the stiff lawyer and the dissatisfied old sailor—the lawyer always speaking of Pigtop as the reverend gentleman, and addressing him as reverend sir. When, after supper, we had carefully secured the privacy of our apartment, amidst many nudges and objurgations from my former shipmate, I proceeded to relate to the astonished solicitor who I was, and what were my motives for appearing at that juncture in the neighbourhood. I also told him of the personation of myself that I understood was then going on at the Hall, at the same time totally suppressing every other guilty circumstance of Daunton's life.

When I had finished my recital, I produced my documents; and, notwithstanding that he was almost breathless with wonder, he confessed that he believed implicitly all my assertions, and would assist me to recover my rights, and disabuse my father, to the utmost of his abilities.

'You have lost much valuable time,' said he. 'This impostor has now been domesticated some days with Sir Reginald. I think, with you, that he has no ulterior views upon the title and the estates. His object is present plunder, and the inducing your father, through the agency of that scoundrel London lawyer, to make him sign such documents, that every thing that can be willed away will be made over to him. We must, to-morrow, proceed in a body to the Hall, and take the villains by surprise. I will now return home, and prepare some necessary documents. As this is a criminal matter, I will also take care to have the attendance of an upright and clear-seeing magistrate, who will proceed with us—not certainly later than ten o'clock to-morrow.'

He then took his leave with an air of much importance, and more alacrity than I could have expected from a man of his years.

When Pigtop and myself were left alone, neither the first nor second nor-wester of brandy and water could arouse him from his sullen mood. He told me frankly, and in his own sea-slang, that he could not disintegrate the idea of a lawyer from that of the devil, and that he was assured that neither I nor my cause would prosper if I permitted the interference of a land-shark. I was even obliged to assume a little the authority of a master in order to subdue his murmurings—to convince his judgment I did not try—in which forbearance I displayed much wisdom. We each retired to our respective room, with less of cordiality than we had ever displayed since our unexpected re-union.

I had no sooner got to bed, than I determined, by a violent effort, to sleep. I had always a ready soporific at hand. It was a repeating and re-repeating of a pious little ode by a late fashionable poet. It seldom failed to produce somnolency at about the twelfth or

thirteenth repetition. I would recommend a similar prescription
to the sleepless; and I can assure them that there is much verse
lately printed, and by people who plume themselves no little upon
it, that need not be gone over more than twice at farthest; excepting the person may have the St. Vitus's dance, and then a third
time may be necessary. I would specify some of these works were
it at all necessary—but the afflicted have only to ask, at random,
for the last published volume of poems, or take up an annual, either
old or new, and they may be *dosed* without the perpetration of
a pun.

Three times had I slept by the means of my ode, and three times
had I awaked by some horrible dream, that fled my memory with
my slumbers. I could draw no omen from it, for my mind could
not bring it out sufficiently distinct to fix a single idea upon it.
However, as I found my sleep so much more miserable than my
watchfulness, I got up, and, putting on a portion of my clothes,
began to promenade my room with a slow step and a very anxious
mind.

I had made but few turns, when my door was abruptly thrust
open, and Pigtop stalked in fully dressed.

'I can't sleep, Rattlin,' said he, 'and tarnation glad am I to see
that you can't caulk[1] either. A dutiful son you would be to be
snoozing here, and very likely, at this very moment, the rascal's
knife is hacking at your father's weasand.[2] It is not yet twelve
o'clock; and I saw from my window, from whence I can see the
Hall plainly, a strange dancing of lights about the windows, and
you may take an old sailor's word that something uncommon's in
the wind. Let us go and reconnoitre.'

'With all my heart; any action is better than this wretched
inactivity of suspense. I will complete my dress, and you, in the
mean time, look to the pistols.'

We were soon ready, and sallied forth unperceived from the inn.
We had no purpose, no ultimate views; yet, both Pigtop and myself
seemed fully to understand that we should be compelled into some
desperate adventure. I was going armed, and by night, like an
assassin, to seek the presence, or, at least, to watch over the safety,
of a father whom I have never seen, never loved, and never respected.

I cannot elevate the moral feelings of my readers by any display
of filial affections. My impulses were utterly selfish, and decidedly
revengeful and unchristian.

The space that separated the abode of my father from the inn was soon passed; and, a little after midnight, I stood within the gloomy and park-like enclosure that circumscribed the front of the large old mansion. The lodge was a ruin, the gates had been long thrown down, and we stumbled over some of their remnants, imbedded in the soil, and matted to it with long and tangled grass. I observed that there was a scaffolding over the front of the lodge; but whether it were for the purpose of repairing or taking down, I could not then discover.

As my companion and myself advanced to the front of the building, we also observed that, lofty as were its walls, it was scaffolded to the very attics, and some part of the roof of the right wing was already removed. Altogether, a more comfortless, a more dispiriting view could hardly have been presented; and its disconsolateness was much increased by the dim and fitful light that a young moon gave, at intervals, upon gables, casement, and clumps of funereal yews.

'And this,' as we stood before the portals, said I, to Pigtop, 'is my inheritance—mine. Is it not a princely residence?'

'It looms like a county jail, that's being turned into a private madhouse. If so be as how witches weren't against the law of the land, this seems the very place for them. Do you believe in ghosts?'

'Verily, yes, and—no.'

'Because, I think that I see the ghosts of a hearse and four horses among those tall trees in that corner.'

'Then, Pig, we must be on the alert—for I see it, too—but, the vision has assumed the every-day deception of a post-chaise and four.'

'Jeer as you will, it is a hearse: somebody's just losing the number of his mess;[1] it will take away a corpse to-night, depend upon it. That a post-chaise! pooh!—I can see the black plumes waving upon the horses' heads—and—hark at the low, deep moanings that seem to sweep by it—that is not at all natural—let us go back.'

'I was never more resolved to go forward. There is villainy hatching—completing. Wrap your cloak closely about your countenance; don't mistake the wind for groans, nor the waving branches of cedar-trees for hearse-plumes—but follow me.'

'Who's afraid?' said Pigtop.

His chattering teeth answered the question.

As I was prepared for every thing, I was not surprised to find the principal door open, and the hall filled with iron-bound cases, and several plate-chests. As we stepped into the midst of these, completely muffled in our cloaks, a fellow came and whispered us, 'Is all ready?'

'Hush!' said I.

'Oh, no fear—they are at prayers in Sir Reginald's bed-room—he is going fast—he is restless—he cannot sleep.'

'Where are the servants?'

'Snoring in their nests.'

'And who is with Sir Reginald?'

'Nobody but the priest and his son, Master Ralph—without the lawyer has gone up since; he saw all right about the chaise. But am I on the right lay?'

'Surely. Joshua Daunton and I—'

'Enough—you're up to trap—so lend us a hand, and let us take the swag to the shay—though swag it aint, for it's all Joshe's by deed of law. Sir Reginald signs and seals to-night, as they say he can't live over to-morrow.'

'No, there is no occasion to stir yet—which is the way to Sir Reginald's room? I must speak one word to Joshua before we start. I know the countersign—it will bring him out to me in a moment. I would advise you, in the meantime, just to step to the chaise and see all right, and bring it up nearer the door quietly, mind—quietly—for these boxes are d—d heavy.'

'You're right there,' said the accomplice, and departed on his errand, after previously showing me the staircase that led to the apartment of my sick father.

When the rascal's steps were no longer heard, 'Now, Pigtop,' said I, 'show your pluck—help me to lock and bar the hall-door—good—so one bloodhound is disposed of; he dare not make a noise, lest he should rouse the establishment. Now follow me—but, hark ye—no murder—the reptile's life must be spared.'

Pigtop made no answer; but pointed to his scarred and disfigured lip, with a truly ferocious grin.

It is necessary, for the fully understanding of the catastrophe that ensued, that I describe the site of the old building in which such startling events were passing. The front approach was level from the road; but, on the back, there was a precipitous, and rugged, and rocky descent, up to the very buttresses that supported the old walls—not certainly so great or so dangerous as to be called a precipice; for, on the extreme right wing of the rear of the house, it was no more than a gentle inclination of the soil, deepening rapidly towards the left, and there, directly under the extremity of that wing, assuming the appearance of a vast chasm, through the bottom of which a brawling stream chafed the pointed stones, on its way to the adjacent sea.

Sir Reginald's sleeping-room was a large tapestried apartment on the first floor; the windows of which occupied the extreme of the left wing of the house, and was directly over the deepest part of the chasm which I have described.

All this part of the mansion was scaffolded also; the ends of the poles having what appeared to be but a very precarious insertion on the projections of the rocks below. It had been the intention of Sir Reginald thoroughly to repair his mansion; but, falling sick, and in low spirits, he had ordered the preparations to be delayed. The scaffolding had been standing through the whole of the previous winter; and the poles, and more especially the ropes that bound them to the cross-piece, had already gone through several stages of decay.

CHAPTER XXV

The concluding Chapter, in which at least one subject is dropped— At length get into my inheritance according to law—that is, I am heir to three law-suits—discover a new Method of putting down Poaching—and come to London to enact the character of 'Cælebs in Search of a Wife.'

MY associate and myself advanced stealthily and noiselessly up the staircase. We met no one. The profoundest security seemed to reign every where. Favoured by the dark shadows that hung around us, we advanced to the door that was nearly wide open, and we then had a full view of every thing within. The picture was solemn. Seated in a very high-backed, elaborately-carved, and gothic chair, supported on all sides by pillows, sat the attenuated figure of my father. I gazed upon him with an eager curiosity, mingled with awe. His countenance was long and ghastly—there was no beauty in it. Its principal expression was terror. It was evident that his days were numbered. I looked upon him intently. I challenged my heart for affection, and it made no answer.

Directly before my father was placed a table, covered with a rich and gold embroidered cloth, bordered with heavy gold fringe, upon which stood four tall wax candles, surrounding a mimic altar surmounted by an ebony crucifix. His chaplain, dressed in popish canonicals, was mumbling forth some form of prayer, and a splendidly-illuminated missal lay open before him. There was also on the table a small marble basin of water, and a curiously inlaid box filled with bones—relics, no doubt—imbued with the spirit of miracle-working. The priest was perhaps performing a private midnight mass.

The fitful attention that Sir Reginald gave to this office was painful to contemplate. His mind was evidently wandering, and he could bring himself to attend only at intervals. At another table, a little removed from the one I have described, sate the person of the London attorney; he had also two lights, and he was most busily employed in turning over and indexing various folios of parchment. But I have yet to describe the other figure—the, to me, loathsome person of my illegitimate half-brother. He was on his knees, mumbling forth the responses and joining in the prayers of the priest. He was paler and thinner than usual; he looked, however, perfectly gentlemanly, and was scrupulously well dressed.

As yet, I had not heard the voice of Sir Reginald; his lips moved at some of the responses that the two made audibly, but sound there was none. At length, when there was a total cessation of the voices of the other, and a silence so great in that vast apartment that the rustling of the lawyer's parchments was distinctly heard, even where I stood—even this hardened wretch seemed to feel the general awe of the moment, and ceased to disturb the tomb-like silence.

In the midst of this, the prematurely-old Sir Reginald suddenly lifted up his voice and exclaimed loudly, in a tone of the most bitterest anguish, 'Lord Jesu, have mercy upon me!'

The vast and ancient room echoed dolorously with the heart-broken supplication. It was the first time that my father's voice fell upon my ear—it was so plaintive, so imbued with wretchedness, that the feeling of resentment which, I take shame to myself, I had long suffered in my bosom melted away at once, and a strange tenderness came over me. I could have flung myself upon his bosom and wept. I felt that my mother's wrongs had been avenged. Even as it was, with all the secrecy that I had then thought it my interest to preserve, I could not refrain, in a subdued, yet earnest tone, from responding to his broken ejaculation, from the very bottom of my heart, 'Amen.'

A start of surprise and terror, as my hollow response reached the ears of all then and there assembled, followed my filial indiscretion. Each looked at the other with a glance that plainly asked, 'Was the voice thine?' and each in reply shook his head.

'A miracle!' exclaimed the priest. 'The sinner's supplication has been heard. Let us pray.'

During this solemn scene, events of a very different description were taking place at the inn which we had just clandestinely left. Our exit had been noticed. The landlord was called up; he became seriously alarmed, the more especially when the direction that we had taken had been ascertained. He immediately concluded that we had gone to Rathelin Hall to commit a burglary, or perhaps a robbery. He summoned to his aid the constables of the village—called up the magistrate, and the lawyer, Mr. Seabright; and, with a whole posse of attendants, proceeded to the rescue. We will conduct them to the door that Pigtop and myself had secured when we barred out Daunton's accomplice, and, there leaving them, return to the sick chamber.

After the reverend gentlemen had concluded his extempore prayer, but few of the sentences of which reached our place of concealment, Sir Reginald said, 'My friends, the little business that we have to do to-night had better be done speedily. I feel unusually depressed. I hope that it is not the hand of death that is pressing so heavily upon me. I would live a little while longer—but the will of God, the Redeemer of our sins, be done! Bring the papers here—I will sign them. My friend Brown, and you, my poor and too long neglected Ralph, (addressing Joshua) I trust to your integrity in all this matter; for not only am I averse to, but just now incapable of, business. But, my dear Ralph, before we do this irrevocable deed, kneel down and receive a repentant father's blessing, and hear that father ask, with a contrite heart, pardon of his son and of his God.'

The parchments were brought and placed before the baronet by the assiduous lawyer, and the son—for son to Sir Reginald he really was—with looks of the most devout humility, and his eyes streaming with hypocritical tears, knelt reverently down at the feet of the trembling and disease-stricken parent. His feeble hands are outstretched over the inclined head of the impostor, his lips part —this—this—I cannot bear—so, before a single word falls from our common father, I rush forward, and, kneeling down beside my assassin-brother, exclaim, in all the agony of wretchedness, and the spirit of a newly-born affection, 'Bless me, even me also, O my father!—he has taken away my birthright, and, behold, he would take away my blessing also. Bless even me!'

'Ralph Rattlin, by all that's damnable!' screamed forth the self-convicted impostor.

Thus, this apparently imprudent and rash step was productive to me of more service than could have been hoped from the deepest-laid plan. In a moment we were on our feet, and our hands on each other's throats. This sudden act seemed miraculously to invigorate our father—he rose from his seat, and, standing to the full height of his tall and gaunt figure, placing his bony hand heavily on my shoulder, and looking me fixedly in the face, said, 'If thou art Ralph Rathelin, who then is this?'

'The base-born of your paramour!'—and with a sudden energy I hurled him from me, and he lay bruised and crouching beneath the large oriel window, at the extremity of the room.

'It was unseemly said, and cruelly done,' said the baronet sorrow-fully. 'Oh, but now my sins are remembered upon me! I cast my sons loose upon the face of the earth, and, in my dying hour, they come and struggle together for their lives before my eyes—verily am I punished; my crime is visited heavily upon me.'

The other parties in the room were little less affected with various emotions. The London attorney was making rapidly for the door, when he was met by the advancing Pigtop, who thrust him again into the apartment, and then boldly faced the priest—the latter still in his canonicals, the former dressed as a sectarian preacher.

Their antipathy was mutual and instantaneous. But, ere the really reverend gentleman could begin some pious objurgation at this apparent interference with his communicant, Pigtop indulged in one of the heaviest oaths that vulgarity and anger together ever concocted, and straightway went and seized the crouching Joshua, and lugged him before the agonized father, exclaiming, 'Warrants out against him, Sir Reginald, for burglary, forgery, and assassination—he is my prisoner.'

The craven had not a word to say—his knees knocked together —he was a pitiable object of a terror-stricken wretch. Sir Reginald already began to look down upon him with contempt; and my heart bounded within me, when I already found him leaning parentally on my shoulder. 'Speak, trembler!—is this person the veritable Ralph Rathelin?'

'Pity me, pardon me, and I will confess all.'

'Splits!' said the attorney, and vanished through the now unguarded room.

'Speak.'

'This gentleman is your lawful son—but I also—'

'No more—escape—there is gold—escape—hide yourself from the eye of man for ever!'

'No,' said Pigtop, giving him a remorseless shake—'Do you see this scar?'

'Let him go instantly, Pigtop!—obey me—I have promised his mother—it is sacred.'

'For my sake!' said Sir Reginald.

At this instant, the steward rushed in, partly dressed, crying out, 'Sir Reginald, Sir Reginald, the constables and the magistrates have broken down the hall-door, and are now coming up stairs, to arrest the housebreakers—they have packed up all the plate, and it lies in the hall, ready to be carried off!'

'My God! It is too late,' said Sir Reginald, wringing his hands.

'No,' said I; 'let him escape by the window. Be so good, sir,' said I to the priest, 'to secure the door—we shall gain time. Hold it as long as you can against all intruders. The scaffolding will enable the culprit to reach the ground with comparatively little danger.'

The priest obeyed; and not only fastened the door, but also barricaded it with furniture.

'Now, Pigtop,' said I, 'if you wish to preserve my friendship, assist this poor wretch to escape—he is paralyzed with his abject fears. Come, sir,' addressing Joshua, 'you will certainly be hung if you don't exert yourself.'

'He'll be hung yet,' said Pigtop sulkily. 'But I am an old sailor, and will obey orders—nevertheless, I know that I shall live to see him hung. Come along, sirrah!'

Between us we led him to the window. We then thrust him out, and he stood shivering upon the cross boarding of the scaffolding level with the window-sills.

'Slide down the poles, and run,' said I and Pigtop together.

'I can't,' said he shuddering; 'the chasm is awfully deep.'

'You must, or die the death of the felon.'

'Oh, what shall I do?'

'Cast off the lashing just above you,' said Pigtop; 'pass it over the cross-piece over your head, make a running noose, put it under your arms, and keep the other end of the rope in your hand. You may either cling to the pole with your legs as you like, or not—for then you can lower yourself down at your ease, as comfortably as if you were taking a nap.'

'Come away, Pigtop—shut the window, close the shutters—the constables are upon us!' I exclaimed. This was done immediately, and thus was the immaculate Joshua shut out from all view. As the attacks on the door of the apartment became more energetic, and we concluded that Joshua was now safe, we were going to give the authorities entrance, when we heard a dreadful crash on the outside of the window.

'The lubber's gone by the run, by G—d!' said Pigtop; 'he'll escape hanging, after all!'

'Let us hope in mercy not,' said Sir Reginald, shuddering. 'I trust it is not so. I hear no scream, no shriek. I am sure, by the sound, that it was the toppling down of the boards—he has most likely displaced some of them in his descent.'

'Shall we admit, Sir Reginald, the people who are thundering at the door?'

'Not yet: let there be no appearance of disorder—remove these;' pointing to the small altar and the crucifix; 'and would it not be as well, my friend, to divest yourself of those holy vestments?—they are irritating to heretical eyes. Assist me, sir, to my chair.'

I placed him respectfully nearly in the position in which I first discovered him. All vestiges of the Catholic Religion were carefully removed, and the door, at last, thrown open. The crowd entered.

Hurried explanations ensued; but we could not conceal from the magistrate that a robbery had been planned and nearly effected, and that the real culprits, for whom, at first, Pigtop and I had been mistaken, had escaped.

At length, the master of the inn suggested that perhaps they had passed out of the window, and might be still upon the boarding of the scaffolding. The shutters were hastily thrown open—and, sight of horrors, Joshua Daunton was discovered hanging by the neck— dead! Sir Reginald gazed for some moments in speechless terror on the horrible spectacle, and then fell back in a death-like swoon.

The body was brought in, and every attempt at resuscitation was useless. He had died, and was judged; may he have found pardon! Some thought that he had hung himself intentionally, so completely had the noose clasped his neck; others, among whom were Pigtop, thought differently. The old sailor was of opinion, from the broken boards that had given way beneath his feet, that, when he had got the noose below his chin, and no lower, that his footing or the scaffolding had failed him; and that, letting go the other end of the rope, it had taken a half hitch, and thus jammed upon the cross pole. However the operation was brought about, he was exceedingly well hung, and the drop represented to perfection. As Pigtop had prophesied, the post-chaise in the shrubbery was turned into a hearse, in order to convey his body to the inn for the coroner's inquest.

'I knew I should live to see him hung,' said Pigtop, doggedly, as he bade me good night, when we both turned into our respective rooms for the night, in the house of my father.

Contrary to all expectations, the shock, instead of destroying, seemed to have had the effect of causing Sir Ralph to rally. He lived for six months after, became fully satisfied of my identity; and, just as he was beginning to taste of happiness in the duty and affection of his son, he died, having first taken every legal pre- caution to secure me the quiet possession of my large inheritance.

My grief at his decease was neither violent nor prolonged. After his burial, I was on the point of repairing the old mansion, when I found myself involved in three law-suits, which challenged my right to it all. I soon came to a determination as to my plan of action. I paid off all the establishment; and, having got hold again of my foster-father and mother, Mr. and Mrs. Brandon, I rebuilt the lodge for them comfortably, and there I located them. I shut up the whole of the Hall, excepting a small sitting-room, and two bed-rooms, for Pigtop and myself; and thus we led the lives of recluses, having no other attendants than the Brandons.

By these means I was enabled to reserve all my rents for carry- ing on my law-suits, without at all impairing the estate. In eighteen years, I thank God, I ruined my three opponents, and they all died in beggary. The year after I came into undisputed possession of my estates, the next heir got a writ issued against me of '*de inquirendo lunatico*,' on the ground of the strange and unworthy manner that I, as a baronet with an immense estate, had lived for those last eighteen years. I told my reasons most candidly to the jury, and they found me to be the most sensible man that they had ever heard of, placed in a similar position.

After having thus speedily settled these little matters, as I was fast approaching my fortieth year, I began to alter my style, and live in a manner more befitting my rank and revenues; yet I still held much aloof from all intimacy with my neighbours.

I am now in my forty-first year, and grown corpulent. It is now twenty-one years since I saw my unfortunate parent interred, and I walk about my domains Sir Ralphed to my heart's content— or, more properly speaking, discontent. Old Pigtop is a fixture, for he has now really become old. I cannot call him my friend, for I must venerate him to whom I give that title, and veneration, or even esteem, Pig was never born to inspire. My humble companion he is not, for no person in his deportment towards me can be less humble than he. He is as quarrelsome as a lady's lap-dog, and seems never so happy as when he has effectually thwarted my intentions. Prince Hal said of the jolly wine-bibber Jack, that 'he could have better spared a better man.' Of Pigtop I am compelled to say more—'I could not spare him at all.' He has become necessary to me. He was never very handsome; but now, in his sixty-second year, he is a perfect fright; so, at least, every body tells me, for I don't see it myself.

His duties about my person seem to be continually healthily irritant; the most important one of which is, to keep me a bachelor, and scare away all womankind from Rathelin Hall. He controls my servants, and helps me to spoil them. Such a set of heavy, bloated, good-for-nothing, impudent, and happy dogs, never before fed upon a baronet's substance, contradicted him to his very face, and fought for him behind his back. The females in my establishment bear but a most niggardly proportion to the males—in the ratio of Falstaff, one pennyworth of bread to his many gallons of sack: and these few are the most hideous, pox-marked, blear-eyed damsels that the county could produce—all Pigtop's doing.

Never shall I forget the consternation, the blank dismay, of his countenance, when, one fine, sunshiny morning, I announced to him my intention of installing in the mansion some respectable middle-aged gentlewoman as my housekeeper. It was some time before he could find his speech.

'Blood and thunder! bombs and fury! what have I done, that you should turn me out of your house in my grey hairs? Now, I'm dismantled, as it were, and laid up in ordinary.'[1]

'Turn you out, Piggy! what could put that in your foolish noddle?'

'If madam comes in, I cut my cable, and pay off Rathelin Hall right abaft[2]—even if I die in a ditch, and am buried by parish. Take a housekeeper!—oh Lord! oh Lord! oh Lord! I would just as soon see you married, or in your coffin.'

'But some such a person is absolutely necessary in an establishment of this extent, so a housekeeper I'll have, of some sort.'

'Why the devil need it be a woman, then? why won't a man do— why won't I do?'

'You?'

'Yes, me—Andrew Pigtop. I ask the appointment—do, there's a good Sir Ralph, make it out directly. Clap your signature to it, and let it run as much like a commission as possible. I ask it as a favour. You know the great sacrifices that I have made for you.'

'The first time I ever heard of them, upon my honour. Pray, enlighten me.'

'Why, you must be convinced, Sir Ralph, if I had not left the navy to attend you all the world over, as the pilot-fish sticks to the shark, I should, by this time, have been an old post-captain, and very likely C. B. into the bargain.'

'You, who remained one quarter of a century a master's-mate during an active war, should rush up through the grades of lieutenant and commander to be posted, during another quarter of profound peace! But, perhaps, you would have depended upon your great family interest. Well, if I make out your commission as my housekeeper, will you do the duties of the office?'

'On course.'

'And wear the uniform?'

'On course, if so be it be such as a man might wear. I bar petticoats and mob-caps, and female thingamies.'

'Will you carry the keys?'

'On course.'

'And see that the rooms and the passages are well swept, and that the maids are up betimes in the morning?'

'D—n them!—on course—certainly.'

'And, when Lady Aurelia Cosway, and her five beautiful daughters, drive up to the door, will you go and receive them in the hall; and, making them a profound curtsey, beg to conduct them into a dressing-room?'

'No—because, d'ye see, no ladies ever come farther than your door.'

'And whom may I thank for that?'

'Me, assuredly,' said Pigtop, very proudly.

'I do.'

However, neither Pigtop nor myself carried our points. I did not make out his commission, which vexed him; but, on the other hand, I did not get me a housekeeper, which, at first, a little vexed me; but, really, my friend, in an ex-officio manner, does most of the duties of the office to which he aspired extremely well.

Without vanity, I still preserve my good looks, though I must confess to a little unbecoming obesity of figure; yet, through my indolence, and the perseverance of Pigtop, and perhaps certain recollections of a green and bright bay in one of the summer islands, I do fear that I am a confirmed bachelor. However, I am not altogether one of those *nati fruges consumere*, for, I can safely say, there is not a pauper on my estate, and that I have considerably added to my paternal acres.

I have always been honest; and, I shall, acting up to my principles, confess that I am in somewhat bad odour with the neighbouring gentry. The word neighbouring must be understood quite in a rural sense. The nearest resident to myself who can legally write 'Squire to his name is remote from the Hall about five miles. My neighbours at that distance lie thickly around my estate, among whom I may enumerate a couple of newly-made lords, two magistrates, and several decently-estated gentlemen. My retired habits gave them their first unfavourable impression of my character; and, having no female presiding over my establishment, the ladies were necessarily kept aloof from my celibate abode.

It is true, that, after my return from a long tour I made with Pigtop, immediately that I had worsted my legal adversaries, at first I received all the dinner invitations that were sent to me, and returned them, by giving gentlemen's parties.

These invitations, however, soon grew less numerous and less frequent, till at length they altogether ceased.

'My Lord Sparrowclose, be known to Mr. Pigtop, my friend; Mr. Pigtop, be known to Lord Sparrowclose.' This kind of speech, wherever we went, was received with a grim courtesy.

'Why does he always bring that sea-ruffian about with him?' it was my misfortune often to hear from Lady Mammas and honourable Misses; but, when I ever chanced to hear similar speeches, I always replied, with all manner of deprecating humility, 'Because, my dear Madam, or Miss, he is my friend.'

It must be confessed that Pigtop had not the talent of becoming popular. Not that he was deficient in knowledge of the usages of society, or the courtesies of the *salle-à-manger*, or the drawing-room. But he was obstinate and brusque to the men, and sneering and universally ill-natured to the ladies. He would tell his story after dinner, which, in his technical jargon, was bad enough; but, what was infinitely worse, he always insisted upon explaining it, and, then if he were thwarted, of explaining that explanation. Moreover, he had a decided contempt for all who had not had a nautical education, and no unlimited affection for all manner of alcoholized fluids.

In the presence of the ladies, when he was dragged there, and nothing had that power but his anxiety to take care of me, he was always in my way. No sooner was the white hand of some fascinating young lady, with auburn ringlets shaking from them ambrosial odours, laid with encouraging familiarity upon my arm, than this Pigtop would thrust himself between us, and commence some horrid calumnious tale, dishonourable to the fair sex. But, why, it may be asked, did I endure all this? The answer is very obvious. The mongrel rough-coated cur, that is so surly to all but its master, is cherished by him the more fondly on account of the general hate. Besides, Pigtop had certainly saved my life once, if not twice; and I was accustomed to him from the habit of years.

I at length became as unpopular as my fidus Achates among the men. Among the women I was only pitied. But, the finishing stroke to my complete isolation from the surrounding society arose from the following circumstances. Our part of the county abounded in game, and, consequently, in poachers. I enrolled myself, soon after I felt myself secure of my estate, in the association to extirpate poaching.

D d

I employed two gamekeepers and four helpers, upon high wages. It would not do. Crack, crack! all night—my plantations ravaged, and my fences broken down. The expence was enormous, and so was my exasperation. Pigtop sided with my angry feelings. So, night after night, he and I went out watching, in order to apprehend the rascals.

The whole eight of us, at last, after many a weary and a wet night, at length fell in with a party of seven. Instead of surrendering upon being summoned, they commenced a regular and very pretty bush-fighting sort of skirmish. Guns were fired on both sides. I, myself, got well stung with several small shot, buried in my person. I confess it with some shame, we were beaten, owing to the cowardice of my servants, and our guns taken from us and broken.

Pigtop, who had been unnecessarily violent, even when he saw that violence was no longer of service, was thrashed with the stock of his piece almost to a mummy, and then flung into a muddy pool, where he had well nigh been suffocated. The poachers, having, at length, satisfied their vengeance, withdrew, carrying off their one wounded man.

The next morning I began to reflect seriously upon what I had gained. There was my friend nearly killed, and in bed with a raging fever; myself scarified and insulted, and defied, and well blooded. The outrage made a great noise; but everyone was astonished and offended at the cool and quiet method of my proceedings.

The wounded poacher, the son of a tenant of my own, a most respectable man, had received his mortal summons. I was reviled for interfering to prevent his removal to the county jail. He died some days after, in my presence.

He never betrayed his accomplices. I was much affected by the scene, and was as kind as I could be to his wretched and bereaved parents. Upon which, I received a polite letter from the committee of my neighbours, acquainting me that I was expelled by a unanimous vote from the Society for Eradicating Poaching in the County of ——. To which I returned thanks for the honour done me.

So, when Pigtop was convalescent, I ordered him to take pen and ink, and calculate the yearly expence for the preservation of my game—when it appeared that, what with the salaries of the worthless cowards called keepers, damages, &c., it exceeded four hundred pounds!

'And we never, Pigtop, get game when we want it in sufficient quantities.'

'Never.'

'Then, what do we get? what have we got for it?'

'Devilishly well beaten!'

'We must alter our plan.—A brilliant thought strikes me. I'll have more game at command than any man in England!'

So, that day I discharged all my gamekeepers.

'What do you intend to do?' said Pigtop.

'To poach on my own manors.'

After a little negociation, the man relying implicitly on my honour, I obtained an interview with the leader of the gang, now reduced to six.

'Giles Grimjaw,' said I, 'I am going to give you unlimited license, both by day and by night, to poach over all my manors'—the fellow would not believe me—'upon these conditions, that you supply me with whatever game I want'—he grinned forth his rapture—'that you shall not hurt my fences.' He and his party that very morning would set about repairing them, and in repair they would keep them. 'Very well; but, mark—you must allow no other gang to poach upon my estate but your own.' He should like to see any attempt it. I had bound them to me body and soul. Their lives were at my service.

'I ask nothing of you, Giles, but an honourable fulfilment of your contract. My larder is very empty just now.'

The fellow departed, I really believe, as happy as if I had bestowed upon him an estate.

Now, I call this extirpating poaching effectually. I had, by this manœuvre, changed six desperate rascals into as many active and unsalaried gamekeepers. My grounds and my kitchen are the best stocked with game, and I am the man most hated by my neighbours in the county. I am very sorry for the latter predicament, the more especially as they say, that my gamekeepers levy on the surrounding preserves, instead of my own. However, as I must shortly come to town to superintend this biography through the press, I shall thus give time for their angry feelings to subside.

When I live in the metropolis, which I have not visited for so many years, I shall go into society; and, should I find a lady as beautiful and loving as ——, I may marry after all, let Pigtop say what he will.

THE END

D d 2

TEXTUAL NOTES

THE first fifty-eight chapters of the book appeared in monthly instalments in the *Metropolitan Magazine* from September 1834 to February 1836 without the chapter divisions and synopses, which may not be Howard's. Some of the changes made in the version published in July 1836 were syntactical, others apparently intended to deepen the anonymity of the author. Passages were omitted at the behest of Marryat, who wrote to Howard on 5 February: '. . . I have received your MS.: as far as it goes it is very well but, as I observed before, there is alteration and omission required in the first part of the work and if that is not made I will not put my name to it—I mention this as you say Bentley has commenced printing.'

The names 'Ralph' and 'Rattlin' were 'Edward (Edderd, Ned)' and 'Percy' respectively in the magazine version throughout. The other main changes are noted below.

The following preamble to the magazine version was replaced in July 1836 by the Advertisement which purported to explain the book's origin.

'A Sub-Editor. I wonder what the word implies with the generality of readers. The humiliating first syllable that seems to fraternize so readily with those pariahs among words, *sub*mission, *sub*jection—and all the slavish family connected with them, would naturally lead one to suppose that the thing called a sub-editor was an animal made to be snubbed, a sort of lackey in the courts of literature, an errand-boy well stricken in years, to the slipshod muse of a magazine, an humble official to stand behind the back of genius, with a paste-pot suspended round his neck, and a pair of scissars in his right hand—in fact, a piece of literal prostration, that any man who has got as far as his *as in praesenti*, would honour by 'voiding his rheum on'; in short, an inky personification sometimes tolerated among booksellers, of consideration only among printer's devils, and great only in his own estimation. It is good to undeceive the world. If every writer were to disabuse mankind, each of only one "vulgar error", so many books would not be written in vain, and the state of society would be more improved than if Sir Andrew Agnew had passed his bill, or the Bishop of London had prevented two pair of oars from plying on the Sabbath-day.

'I freely grant that there *is* a difference between an editor and a sub-editor; the latter generally has had his pap administered with a wooden spoon; or, if he has been very fortunate, a horn one may have been the dignified instrument; whilst the former, almost invariably, is born with a silver ladle in his mouth; the editor always keeps a cab, the sub has been known, on an emergency, to call one for his superior; the editor resides in a large house in a large square—even attics now are above the reach of his slave, and the sub-editor is usually *sub*terraqueously lodged. There is certainly a very equal division of operations between the two, the one doing almost all the work, the other taking almost all the money. I do not treat my readers like simpletons, by explaining everything. They will be able with a little study, to assign to each of us his proper portion.

'In the sub-editor, the fable of Atlas is verified. His unlucky shoulders bear the weight of all errors, all mistakes and all accidents; whilst the editor himself is actually the mountain upon those over-burthened shoulders, his head thrust into the skies, catching every ray of glory, and revelling in the eternal sunshine of reputation.

'There is such a thing as truth in the world: indeed there is, let the bishops say what they will about our moral depravity. It is a very unwhole-some practice, that of judging from what we find at home. I do not mean the naked truth. We are now too decent, too much refined to allow such an abomination as that to walk about in our civilized times. To suffer that, would be almost as shocking as tolerating the naked lie. Yes, there is such a thing as truth permitted still among us, provided it be decently clothed.

'I have not done with the editor yet, and, in order that he may not have done with me, if he should see it, I am going to offer another truth to my falsehood-abhorring readers, but very decently clothed in a simile. Look at the church clock, view its broad and burnished face, mark the golden indices. In all this accumulation of display you see the editor, the observed of man, the praised of women; but the delicate little wheels, where are they? and the powerful and ever elastic mainspring:—obscured, concealed, unnoted, like the unvalued, invaluable sub-editor.

'But it may be thought that my truth, apparelled as it is, will, by its want of a mask, still give offence to the object of my comparison; but let not the pitying public expend its valuable sympathy upon the risk I run. The editor peruses only his own articles, (by which means he secures at least one, attentive, enthusiastic admirer), and counts the advertisements on the covers and the spare leaves, which is, to him, really a profitable kind of reading. So secure am I on this point, that I boldly, and at once say, d——n the editor.

'I think now, that I have sufficiently explained what the editor is not, and what I am—and, I trust, that this explanation has given me that degree of importance that will excite some curiosity, as to the manner in which I came into the world, the manner in which I got on in the world,—and, as to the manner in which I may go out of the world, I would willingly postpone that chapter, *sine die*.'

Other substantive and significant changes from the magazine version are as follows (references are to page and line):

5. 4 the volumes] what *M*   5. 20 float down it.!] float down it! What a turmoil! *M*   6. 4 17—] 1794 *M*   7. 16 at a certain spot] at a certain hour at a certain spot *M*   8. 23 embryo reefer] embryo sub-editor, spotless and unstained *M*   10. 32 half an eternity] half an eternity! the said saws being the instruments with which Satan shall set his subordinate devils to work to saw in twain the flinty hearts that turn little children out of doors—for that is the manner in which I—not four hours old—was treated *M*   10. 33 swore that I should be turned from his inhospitable roof immediately] swore *M*   10. 36 was compelled to carry me back] was I carried back *M*   12. 4 omniscient justice] Omniscient justice. Then, as I would have done here, had it been in my power, may I be permitted to hold her hand, to vindicate her conduct, to participate in her feelings, and to share her fate. O how I loved that woman, all the more intensely, as I knew that her love for me was a love that she cherished, though she concealed—a love which I dared not challenge, but which she made me conscious was wholly and enthusiastically mine *M*   12. 23 on them, gratis, some blithe rides] in them, gratis-like, some rides *M*   12. 32 libel] libel on their neighbour *M* 13. 17 only it so happened that when he was settled] however, when he was settled *M*   27. 21 on the afternoon of his election] on that day *M* 29. 27 undertaking of greengroceries and sawpits] undertaking *M*   36. 24 old Isaac's (my soldier schoolmaster)] old Isaac's *M*   38. 4 nine years] eight years *M*   39. 17 three years] four years *M*   44. 21 Very, both in a breath] Very *M*   46. 1 ten years old] nine years old *M*   46. 23 tenderness] timidity *M*   47. 5 love you] like you *M*   48. 27 ten years old] nine years old *M*   54. 22 twelve years of age] between eleven and twelve years of age *M*   59. 30 which will serve anyone that was engaged in it, as long as he lives, to talk of with honest enthusiasm, even if he has been happy enough to have been engaged in real warfare—it is necessary to describe] which will serve as long as he lives, anyone engaged in it to talk of, even if he has been happy enough to have been engaged in real warfare; with honest enthusiasm, it is necessary to describe *M*   62. 2 Whig] Tory *M*   70. 22 18—] 1799 *M*   73. 28 1837] 1836 *M*   74. 7 thirteenth year] twelfth year *M*   81. 16 at thirteen years of age] at twelve years of age *M* 81. 25 at thirteen] at twelve *M*   97. 1 forgotten, enclosed them to me very lately] Forgotten, having recognised scenes and events that I have described, enclosed them to me but very lately *M*   107. 25 now ranting, now conversing] now rhyming, now ranting, now conversing *M*   108. 30 sixteen] fifteen *M*   112. 13 Thirty five years] Forty years *M*   114. 1 but the lady of the house and myself, when

Mrs. Causand herself gave it me at the eve of my departing for the ship] but the lady of the house *M*   114. 13 thirty five] forty *M*   114. 14 of fifteen] a lad not yet fifteen *M*   124. 33 gratuity for fear of giving him offence] gratuity *M*   128. 11 explanation] explanation, Farmer nodded to the captain *M*   148. 23 in silent admiration at] in admiring disorder at *M*   166. 36 reefers] sub-editors *M*   171. 5 say, as every novelist has a right to do once in his three volumes—'I was lapped in Elysium'] say that my dream went to sleep too *M*   235. 26 nineteenth] eighteenth *M*   237. 33 conned] carried *M*   266. 22 master's mate, named Pigtop] master's mate *M*   269. 15 ridiculous] impertinent *M*   281. 38 nearly an eventful year] three eventful years *M*   282. 14 sixteen and nineteen] fifteen and eighteen *M*   283. 9 clean] still *M*   283. 34 life itself and] so replete with life as *M*   290. 3 famishing] verlote *M*   297. 2 tolerably] intolerably *M*   311. 11 Crown Inn at Reading. This concludes the final (February 1836) instalment of the novel in the *Metropolitan Magazine*.

EXPLANATORY NOTES

Page 6. About seven o'clock . . . 17—: the magazine version gave 1794 as the birth date, but the true one is almost certainly October 1793 when Lord Peters wrote, of a rumoured miscarriage of Lady Elizabeth Howard within months of her elopement with Bingham, 'it would have been more agreeable if the lady had really miscarried as that would have made everything quite easy. Now the delay and uncertainty of the law renders it more precarious' (Lucan Papers, 26 Dec. 1793). It was vital for Bingham to conceal the birth of a son before the *crim. con.* trial of February 1794 and the Lords' debates of the following months in order to defeat Bernard Howard's excessive claims based on the possibility of a bastard succession. October 1793 is the latest date compatible with the birth of Elizabeth's daughter in July 1794.

Page 11. in a northerly direction: towards Oswestry where Elizabeth and Bingham went into hiding to elude Howard's spies.

Page 12. all this building . . . property: the reference is to the building schemes of successive Archbishops of Canterbury. At the turn of the century the Dean and Chapter leased or sold land to speculative builders like Penton. Charles Manners-Sutton (d. 1828), although during his twenty-three years as Archbishop 'he never issued a single charge to his clergy', had given thought to the amenities of Lambeth Palace and in 1827 was having a new private road made for his convenience 'from Stangate, at the back of the Mitre, to the back of the Jolly Sawyers' (Allen, *History of Lambeth* (1827), pp. 324–5). The work was completed during the episcopate of his successor, Howley, a High Churchman, opposed to all liberal measures, who tried to put down jollity in Lambeth and elsewhere by supporting Sir Andrew Agnew's puritanical Sabbath Observance Bills. Popular feeling against the Anglican hierarchy ran high in the thirties on account of their opposition to the Reform Bill.

Page 16. (1) the mistake of the Omniscient: this lay in providing that population should increase in a geometrical, while the means of subsistence increased only in an arithmetical progression. Malthus was about to point this out in his *Essay on Population* (published anonymously in 1798, and revised in 1803 and 1806) in which the solution proposed was 'moral restraint' by the individual.

(2) *the preventive check*: in her story 'Weal and woe in Glen Varlock' (from *Illustrations of Political Economy*) she applied Malthus's views and advocated celibacy and later marriages as a check on over-population—not, like Francis Place, birth control. Her views provoked ribald comments from Croker and Lockhart in the *Quarterly* and *Fraser's*.

Page 17. *prayer-meetings at our house*: cf. also ch. VII. Stiggins, a notable performer in this line, made his appearance at the end of 1836, a few months after the publication of *Rattlin* in July.

Page 25. (1) *the elected could never again fall*: the doctrine dramatized by Hogg in his *Memoirs of a Justified Sinner* (1824).

(2) *would have pleased Sir Andrew Agnew*: who tried from 1832 to 1836 to have bills passed to close public houses and in effect prevent the lower classes from taking any recreation on Sunday. Dickens attacked him in *Sunday under three heads* (May 1836).

Page 35. (1) *Mr. Root, the pedagogue . . . formerly . . . a subordinate where he now commanded . . . had a shrill girlish voice*: a real-life Squeers, with a touch of Creakle. In fact, he was Edward Flower, a former writing master at the Islington school, who married the widow of his predecessor, John Price, succeeded him in 1793, and ran the school for forty years (S. Lewis, *History of Islington* (1842), p. 163).

(2) *speculation in his eye*: *Macbeth*, III. iv. 95.

Page 41. *Chesterfieldian power to look amiable*: Howard's readers were no doubt familiar with the letters of advice from the fourth earl to his natural son, which were often published under such titles as 'The Art of Pleasing' or 'The Principles of Politeness'.

Page 45. *affected as much by her manner as her gift*: the evidence in the *crim. con.* trial of 1794 had shown that Elizabeth was always very popular with her servants.

Page 47. (1) *I cannot have you home. By-and-by, perhaps*: the date of this visit must have been around 1803 by which time Elizabeth's second marriage was heading for the rocks. Either she was still hoping to persuade Bingham to acknowledge the boy or (more likely) she was already contemplating the separation of 1804.

(2) *had formerly been one of the suburban palaces of Queen Elizabeth*: Lewis described Flower's schoolhouse as 'of about the time of Elizabeth, with ceilings of stucco in crocket work, with medallions, etc., similar to other Elizabethan houses in the district. One chimney piece represented Adam and Eve, while in 1812 another old chimney piece was discovered, during demolition, bearing the arms of England' (*History of Islington*, p. 162). Islington was a district much favoured by the court of Queen Elizabeth.

Page 48. a strongly painted altar piece: almost certainly the painting of the Annunciation which Nathaniel Clarkson had presented to the church at Islington twenty years before, the 'sleeping Jesus' being attributable to poetic licence.

Page 49. Wordsworth hath said or sung: in his poem 'My heart leaps up'.

Page 52. (1) the nether millstone: Job 41 : 24.

(2) *the stricken hart*: *Hamlet*, III. ii. 282.

Page 53. (1) a pampered menial drove him from the door: in T. Moss's *Beggar's Petition*, 15, 'a pampered menial forc'd me from the door'.

(2) *Trim's hat all to ribbons*: *Tristram Shandy*, V. vii.

Page 55. (1) Joe Mantons: Joseph Manton (?1766–1835), a noted gunmaker.

(2) *his custom at the hour of noon*: Hamlet's father (I. v. 60) was 'Sleeping within mine orchard, / My custom always in the afternoon' when killed by his brother.

Page 57. Mr. Scales: Michael Scales, Esq., butcher and vehement radical reformer, was, between 1831 and 1833, thrice elected Alderman for the Portsoken Ward of the City of London, but thrice rejected by the Court of Aldermen on the ground of personal unfitness, viz. having (*inter alia*) been concerned in the distribution of forged tickets of admission to the Guildhall. Litigation continued briskly until 1839 when the House of Lords finally ruled in favour of the Court of Aldermen.

Page 61. a barring out: such schoolboy insurrections were common in the seventeenth, eighteenth, and early nineteenth centuries. The principle was that of the stay-in strike.

Page 62. the whole year of the comet: Halley's comet had been seen in 1835.

Page 67. like Niobe, all in tears: *Hamlet*, I. ii. 149—'like Niobe, all tears'.

Page 73. (1) tempering the wind to the shorn lamb: Sterne's translation of the French *Dieu mesure le froid à la brebis tondue* (*A Sentimental Journey*, O.E.N., ed. Jack (1968), p. 115 and note).

(2) *a very Bobadil . . . a juvenile Bavius*: Bobadil was the cowardly bully of Jonson's *Every man in his humour*; Bavius, the vile poet of Virgil's *Eclogues*, iii. 90, was mentioned also in Pope's *Prologue to the Satires*.

Page 86. Mr. Cherfeuil: in fact, Charles George Kerval (a Breton name). His school at Peak Hill on the edge of Sydenham Common was approved by Campbell, who sent his own son there. He speaks of 'Mr K. the schoolmaster crossing the Common on the bitterest day with nankeen pantaloons' (Beattie's *Life* (1849), ii. 140, 199).

Page 99. the family of which I have just made mention: that of Joseph Marryat, M.P. for Sandwich, Chairman of Lloyd's and colonial agent for the island of Grenada, whose second son, Frank (i.e. Frederick), was the future captain and novelist. Although he was Howard's boyhood hero they seem to have been out of touch after Howard left Sydenham until 1832, when he renewed the acquaintanceship by sending Marryat the draft of a novel. Marryat at first advised revision and later suggested instead 'an autobiography of your own life in one or two volumes' which was the genesis of *Rattlin*.

Page 103. (1) *fields of Hope*: Thomas Campbell, who made his name in 1799 by publishing *The Pleasures of Hope*, of which there were four editions within the year.

(2) *wore a wig*: this is corroborated by Cyrus Redding in his *Fifty Years' Recollections* (1858), ii. 206. Campbell's French lessons are not otherwise recorded.

Page 104. *Dr.* ——, *a retired head-master of one of our principal public schools*: Dr. William Langford, lower master at Eton, was once honoured by the interest of George III and in 1804 was 'resident at and does church duty at Lewisham in Kent' (Farington's *Diary* (1926), v. 6).

Page 105. *Mr. R*——: since he had (p. 107) 'amiable daughters', he was probably the father of the Misses Redman whose school at Sydenham Campbell mentioned in 1808 (Beattie's *Life*, ii. 14).

Page 106. *Mrs. Barbauld's Ode*: the 'Ode to Spring', no doubt. Mrs. Barbauld (1743–1825) was schoolmistress, poetess, and editor of the *British Novelists*. Fox was a warm admirer of her songs.

Page 114. *as Ophelia said*: *Hamlet*, II. i. 91.

Page 117. *Harpocrates*: the god of silence (Ovid, *Meta.* ix. 691).

Page 122. (1) *with the grace of a Chesterfield*: see note to p. 41.
(2) *Petruchio's orders*: *The Taming of the Shrew*, IV. iii. 98.

Page 123. (1) *Hamilton Moore*: author of the accepted manual of navigation, *The New Practical Navigator* (1793), constantly revised and enlarged down to 1814.

(2) *relieving the Danes from the onerous care of their navy*: this action was taken on 2 September 1807 to prevent the Danish fleet falling into French or Russian hands.

Page 124. *weekly account*: properly a return of the whole ship's complement, but often a sobriquet for the white patch on the midshipman's collar.

Page 125. (1) *purser's name*: i.e. an assumed one. Pressed men often gave false names with a view to deserting at the earliest opportunity and avoiding recovery.

(2) *slops*: ready-made clothing supplied from ship's stores.

Page 126. (1) *Captain Reud of H.M.S. Eos*: as we are told later (p. 159) 'a West Indian creole' with 'large patrimonial estates in Antigua' and

(p. 272) 'nephew of the very high official of the Admiralty'. His ship was, in fact, the *Aurora* (Greek, *Eos*) and his name John Duer, grandson of the prosperous Devonshire merchant of the same name who acquired estates in Antigua and Dominica in the eighteenth century (*Dict. American Biography*) and married one of his daughters to George Rose, Treasurer of the Navy from 1807 until his death in 1818.

(2) *casimere*: i.e. cashmere, cloth made from the wool of the Cashmere goat. By false association with the Suffolk wool village, the variant Kerseymere was used by Marryat (*Japhet*, ch. XI) and in Courtney's version of this passage.

Page 127. (1) *the curse of God*: slang for cockade.

(2) *those poodles*: i.e. the lions mentioned in the first sentence of this chapter.

(3) *the foul anchor*: or rather, fouled or entangled.

VOLUME II

Page 133. (1) *à me tirer les vers du nez*: to worm secrets out of me.

(2) *my Lord A——*: very likely Charles George Perceval, Baron Arden, Registrar of the Court of Admiralty from 1790 to 1840, brother of Spencer Perceval.

(3) *Mr. Rose*: see note 1 to p. 126.

Page 134. *podagre*: a sufferer from gout.

Page 136. (1) *like a snail unwillingly*: Jaques's schoolboy (*As You Like It*, II. vii. 146).

(2) *I found the Eos*: Howard joined on 18 March 1808.

Page 138. *soft tommy*: soft tack, loaves of bread served out instead of biscuit.

Page 141. *sea lawyer*: a seaman with an awkward knowledge of service regulations.

Page 145. *Mr. Croker himself*: the powerful Secretary to the Navy and redoubtable contributor to the *Quarterly Review*.

Page 146. *Mr. Lushby, the respectable boatswain*: the boatswain of the *Aurora* was Daniel Sosbe, who was court-martialled for drunkenness, disrespect, and neglect of duty at Port Royal in 1810.

Page 151. *began to pale its effectual fire*: the magazine version read more correctly *ineffectual*. 'The glow-worm shows the matin to be near, / And 'gins to pale his uneffectual fire' (*Hamlet*, I. v. 89-90).

Page 154. *C.P.*: convicted prisoner.

Page 155. *bring his grey hairs with sorrow to the grave*: Gen. 42: 38.

Page 159. (1) *near and dear relations*: i.e. George Rose (see note 1 to p. 126).

(2) *not loud but deep*: Macbeth's phrase (v. iii. 22).

(3) *Yellow Jack*: the yellow fever.

(4) *palisades*: 'those graves of sand, turned into a rich compost by the ever-recurring burial'; see p. 219.

Page 162. (1) *Dr. Kitchener*: William Kitchener (d. 1827), an epicure and writer on gastronomic and other topics.

(2) *anasarca*: a dropsical affection.

(3) *luff*: lieutenant.

Page 164. (1) *walked the waters like a thing of life*: Byron's *Corsair*, i. 93.

(2) *sick of Irish affairs*: which had been dominated in the twenties and thirties by O'Connell's agitations.

Page 165. *drogher*: coasting vessel employed in carrying stores.

Page 166. *the Marine Society*: established in 1756 for the reform and training of young criminals, it sent a number of boys to sea each year.

Page 175. *a world too big*: the old man's hose is, in Jaques's phrase, 'a world too wide / For his shrunk shank' (*As You Like It*, II. vii. 159).

Page 177. *the active operations of Dr. Sangrado*: Gil Blas's master. A lawyer, hearing that his client was in Sangrado's hands, exclaimed 'Vive dieu! partons donc en diligence, car ce docteur est si expéditif qu'il ne donne pas le temps à ses malades d'appeler des notaires. Cet homme-là m'a bien soufflé des testaments' (*Gil Blas*, ii. 2).

Page 179. (1) *Captain Reud had determined he should not be invalided*: Dr. Thompson's counterpart on the *Aurora*, Thomas Johnston, was in fact invalided after an outbreak of yellow fever in the West Indies. The novel most probably gives us the irreverent, schoolboy fabrications of the midshipmen's mess and shows Howard yielding to the established farcical tradition of the naval novel.

(2) *Amphitryon*: in the modern sense of a generous host; cf. Molière's comedy of that name.

Page 182. *macerating*: an old medical term, mortifying or 'reducing' drastically.

Page 189. *catachrestical*: inappropriate.

Page 191. (1) *blushing rosy-red*: Blake, 'The Angel', l. 10 (*Songs of Experience*).

(2) *damnation round the land*: Pope, 'Universal Prayer', l. 27.

(3) *Fretted with golden fires*: *Hamlet*, II. ii. 316.

Page 193. *Shake off dull sloth, and early rise*: more properly 'joyful rise' (Bishop Ken's 'Morning Hymn').

Page 194. *driven from the ship*: the second lieutenant, Walter Wade, fell foul of Captain Duer, was confined for contempt and disobedience of orders, and left the ship about the time Silva does in the novel. The laconic entries in the ship's log and Howard's elaborate farce may have a common basis in fact.

Page 195. *John Hamilton Moore*: see note 1 to p. 123.

Page 202. (1) *Jean Bart*: the celebrated French naval hero of humble origins, who rose to the rank of admiral in the service of Louis XIV.

(2) *Crapaud's*: crapaud, literally, toad; colloquially, an ugly person.

Page 203. *that doth become a man*: *Macbeth*, I. vii. 46.

Page 205. *as noble as your namesake's*: probably Captain George Farmer (1732-79), lieutenant of the *Aurora* frigate, who gained a posthumous baronetcy for his gallant death in action against the French.

Page 206. *Lord Camelford*: Thomas Pitt, second and last baron Camelford, a notoriously pugnacious naval commander who was killed in a duel in 1804.

Page 207. (1) *whipper-in*: later, *whip*. Dickens uses this form in *Sketches by Boz* ('Parliamentary Sketches') but the later form in *Bleak House*, ch. 58.

(2) *light bobs*: soldiers in the light infantry or artillery.

Page 215. *Lord Ogleby*: probably James Ogilvie (1760-1820), a native of Aberdeen who became a leading lecturer on oratory in America. He is said to have been a claimant to the earldom of Findlater. Of his *Philosophical Essays* (Philadelphia, 1816) *Blackwood*'s commented 'mere talk— nothing more. We have not seen them for years and hope never to see them again. He was a man of genius destroyed by opium eating' (xvii (1825), 198).

Page 217. *put under arrest*: see note to p. 194.

Page 220. (1) *à l'ecrevisse*: crab-like.

(2) *à reculons*: backwards.

(3) *even tenor of their way*: Gray's *Elegy*, l. 76.

Page 229. *to have always lacked gall*: *Hamlet*—'I am pigeon-livered and lack gall to make oppression bitter' (II. ii. 605).

Page 231. *no statement was ever more true*: the fact that the log of Duer's first ship, *La Dedaigneuse*, records his having in 1804 taken the exceptional step of flogging a midshipman for disobedience and neglect of orders supports Howard's assertion here, but there is no record of it in the *Aurora*'s logs. Such punishments as this, and the later mastheading on a very cold night, wrought, Howard declared, 'much constitutional mischief', and were a probable cause of his later deafness and the tendency to internal haemorrhage from the bursting of small blood vessels which shortened his life.

Page 237. *deeply, beautifully blue*: Don *Juan*, iv. 873.

Page 239. Aniana: in fact, Samana on St. Domingo, held by a small, isolated French force which offered little resistance when attacked by the *Aurora* and four other British ships (Guillermin de Montpinay, *Journal de la Révolution de l'Est de St. Domingue*, p. 57, and *Naval Chronicle*, XXI. 163).

Page 242. the whole crown of Captain Reud's skull completely blown away: the action against Samana was clearly a useful and well-timed operation, but hardly the exciting one which the novel describes. So, too, Reud's hand-to-hand combat is apocryphal. Ten days after the action, the captain of one of the accompanying ships noted in his log: 'At 11 a Boat passing the ship and not answering altho repeatedly hailed, it was fired upon, in consequence of which Captain Duer of H.M. Ship Aurora was wounded in the head by a Musquet Ball.'

Page 243. never afterwards perfectly sane: this, too, is certainly exaggerated. The *Aurora* stayed in port for a fortnight after the other ships sailed, but next year Duer, after taking part in the blockade of St. Domingo, was sent ashore to treat for the surrender of the city.

Page 248. a slave, and the daughter of a slave: Howard was writing just after Wilberforce's Anti-Slavery Society had (in 1833) got legislation through Parliament establishing a period of apprenticeship for negroes which was to end in complete emancipation in 1838. The emancipation decrees during the revolutionary and Empire period in France were ineffective and France finally decreed emancipation only in 1848.

VOLUME III

Page 261. Paul and Virginia: Bernardin de St. Pierre's love story (1788) of a boy and girl who grow up isolated from society. Virginia dies in a shipwreck through the selfishness of 'civilized' men.

Page 262. jalousies: shutters.

Page 268. authority with the two-edged sword: such a sword is used as a symbol of divine authority in Heb. 4: 12 and Rev. 1: 16.

Page 269. Sisyphus: the legendary king of Corinth set to roll uphill a huge stone which forever ran down again.

Page 272. (1) *a hole was knocked in the ship's forefoot*: the master shipwright found 'the lower piece of the Stern gone, the Gripe, False Keel and wooding ends much injured, & Copper off'. Rowley, the admiral in charge of the station, forwarded this to the Admiralty without comment. The master of the *Elk* met with less consideration when he ran the ship aground in 1810, being immediately called to account by court martial.

(2) *nephew of the very high official of the Admiralty*: see note 1 to p. 126.

Page 277. nosologically: according to the science of classification of diseases.

Page 278. beginning of the end: 'le commencement de la fin', Talleyrand's comment after Napoleon's defeat at Borodino (1812) or, according to some authorities, after Leipzig (1813).

Page 283. (1) *slings and arrows of outrageous fortune*: Hamlet, III. i. 58.

(2) *calabash*: gourd or pumpkin, the shell of which can be used for cooking.

Page 289. diachylon: ointment.

Page 290. Bilboes: iron bars with sliding shackles to secure prisoners by the feet. Supposedly so called because originating in Bilboa.

Page 294. Mother Carey's chicken: Mother Carey is sometimes held to be an irreverent anglicization of *Mater Cara* (French *Notre Dame*) and her chicken is the stormy petrel, called by the French *l'oiseau de Notre Dame*.

Page 303. (1) *idlers*: tradesmen and others (cooks, barbers, painters, tailors, etc.) who, having constant day duties, did not normally stand a night watch, but turned out in an emergency.

(2) *bone-polishers*: slang, cat o' nine tails.

Page 304. cathead: machinery housed in the bow of the ship for raising the anchor.

Page 319. (1) *papillary*: refers presumably to the gustatory papillae of the tongue.

(2) *avatar*: strictly, the manifestation of a deity in human form; loosely, as here, a longed-for appearance.

Page 321. soft tommy: see note to p. 138.

Page 326. cabined, cribbed, confined: Macbeth, III. iv. 24.

Page 330. the real Simon Pure: Fainswell, the hero of Mrs. Centlivre's *A bold stroke for a wife*, impersonates Simon Pure, an American quaker, in order to have access to his mistress, until the real Simon Pure arrives.

Page 334. Six months after . . . he died raving mad: the date of his will shows that Duer survived four years after leaving the service, and the codicil which he made a year before his death was not invalidated.

Page 339. nights of gas: Howard is speaking of 1810/11. Gas was used as illuminant before 1810 only on private premises. Westminster Bridge was lighted by gas in 1813 and from 1814 onwards the Gas, Light, and Coke Company was actively installing gas lighting.

Page 352. (1) *Tom Coxe's traverse*: up one hatchway and down another, the course followed by an artful dodger.

(2) *purser's dip*: the smallest variety of dip-candle.

Page 380. Achates: the hero's faithful companion in Virgil's *Aeneid*.

Page 384. (1) *caulk*: to sleep on deck (i.e. (?) in the position of the trades-man who caulks the seams of the deck).

(2) *weasand*: windpipe.

Page 385. *losing the number of his mess*: i.e. die suddenly. The seaman's number on the ship's book was used to mark his belongings in the mess.

Page 395. (1) *ordinary*: as opposed to active service.

(2) *pay off . . . right abaft*: cast loose, fall back, and let the ship continue without him.

PRINTED IN GREAT BRITAIN
AT THE UNIVERSITY PRESS, OXFORD
BY VIVIAN RIDLER
PRINTER TO THE UNIVERSITY